MAR   2014

GLASS
HOUSES

A Birdie Keane Novel

GLASS HOUSES

TERRI NOLAN

MIDNIGHT INK
WOODBURY, MINNESOTA

FIRST EDITION
First Printing, 2014

Book design and format by Donna Burch-Brown
Cover art: iStockphoto.com/8620414/budazhok
iStockphoto.com/14588871/Chris Pritchard
iStockphoto.com/5809157/theproshoppe
iStockphoto.com/22754112/cuiphoto
iStockphoto.com/3332698/Chad Purser
Cover design by Kevin R. Brown
Editing by Connie Hill

Midnight Ink, an imprint of Llewellyn Worldwide Ltd.

Library of Congress Cataloging-in-Publication Data (Pending)

ISBN: 978-0-7387-3635-8

Midnight Ink
Llewellyn Worldwide Ltd.
2143 Wooddale Drive
Woodbury, MN 55125-2989
www.midnightinkbooks.com

Printed in the United States of America

ALSO BY TERRI NOLAN

Burden of Truth

For Kathleen,
workout buddy, therapist

ONE

Sunday, May 13

THE KILLER BROUGHT THE requisite murder tools: never-before-worn leather gloves that slid over a latex pair, surgical booties over new, smooth-soled shoes (two sizes too large), safety glasses, paper mask, hooded Tyvek coverall, WD-40, a foam craft brush, and a .22 revolver. The gun, a weapon of convenience, was especially pleasing, .22-caliber rounds pinball in the brain. Devastatingly perfect for executions.

The best and most important murder tool? The house key.

Once the killer unlocked the front door's deadbolt, there were no tentative steps. Someone had recently plugged night lights into the wall sockets. The soft yellow glow wasn't necessary. The killer knew how to zigzag the maze of chairs and couches; knew the squeaky portions of the floor to avoid; knew how many stairs led to the twin's room; knew how to push down slightly on the knob because the door sticks. Afterward, eleven steps to the master bedroom; the knob turned left because the door doesn't open when turned right.

The deed was quick and snappy.

There was one brief moment of compulsion to peel off the gloves and experience the slick of fresh blood on the fingertips. Or would it be sticky? The scent was metal and musk. Would it taste the way it smelled?

No time for temptation.

There was much to accomplish.

The killer checked the time.

Three minutes.

Four lives gone.

Five shots.

Three-four-five.

Good numbers.

TWO

Birdie Keane stepped into the shower. She braced against the cold water and pushed down an expletive. Her body shivered with the quick warming response fired up by nerve endings. She turned her back to the flow. Tiny pinpricks of icy pain sluiced her backside, waterfalled between buttocks, swirled around thighs before streaming down slender legs. How could tap water be so friggin' cold?

She had stoppered the drain. Her toes seemed to shrink away like a turtle's head pulling into the safety of its shell. She checked the water level. Three inches before the shower overflowed.

Her teeth chattered. A vice constricted her lungs. Her spine felt stiff. Birdie's heart labored to increase the blood flow to frigid extremities. Her brain argued for her to step away.

"What about heart failure?"

"Ever heard of hypothermia?"

She resisted the temptation. Bore down against the numbing pain.

She spread her arms and turned, gasped for breath when it hit her face and accidentally swallowed. The cold seemed to flash freeze her throat. She could almost feel her metabolism shutting down to save vital blood necessary to operate the heart.

Birdie fisted two objects on the chain around her neck. One was a sterling silver medallion of Saint Francis de Sales, the patron saint of journalists and writers; the other, a brass handcuff key that once belonged to Matt Whelan. He'd worn it on his boot. For him, it was part talisman, part "just in case." After his death she took it for her own. She had only taken the chain off once. On that day she was kidnapped. She hadn't removed it since.

She stood in the freezing shower long enough for her toes to turn blue. Only then did she kick away the stopper. As the water drained, she sank to the travertine and curled herself into a ball. She cried as she muttered, "Please give me strength," for the uncertainty of what she'd done. "Please give me strength," to get through another day of sobriety. "Please give me strength," for another day of survival. "Please give me wisdom," to deal with another day of questions.

THREE

Thom Keane woke up hating himself. He was cocooned in unfamiliar sheets. His clothes stank of gardenias and cigarettes. Sugary smoke roiled his stomach as he tried to suppress the nausea. Stale scotch muck thickened his tongue and lined his cheeks. He smacked his mouth in search of moisture. Found none. Weepy eyelids fluttered, afraid to open fully, afraid of whom he might find. Maybe the blonde with the Russian accent.

Thom wiped his hand across his eyes and rolled his aching body toward the center of the bed. The cool sheets relieved him of guilt. He flopped onto his back and praised the Lord for small miracles. He didn't need more trouble.

His life had become a cliché. The not-yet middle-aged, slightly overweight, gray-haired, old beyond his years, hard-drinking ass-chaser was a bad character in a bad pulp novel. He hated it. But not enough. Exercise more, lose ten pounds, eat right, improve his attitude? Too much work.

In the twilight of the still morning he retraced yesterday and remembered he was in the guestroom of his cousin's house—a safe harbor from the storm of home.

His pants vibrated. He wrestled with pockets to recover the cell. "What?"

"Hey, partner, we got called out to play," said George Silva, much too peppy for this time of morning. "I'll pick you up at home."

"I'm at the Bird House."

"Better still. Birdie's house isn't as far west. Don't want the division dicks to wait longer than they have to."

"Aren't you considerate. What day is it?"

"Sunday."

"Our names aren't on the callout board. What's up?"

"Multiple DBs."

"Oh, goodie, a long-ass day and a long-ass investigation."

"Shit happens. Get your butt out of bed and in the shower. I'll give you a wail from the street."

The cold jolt of the bathroom tile floor on Thom's bare feet was the equivalent of a splash of water. An empty bladder, a shower, and a shave turned him into a sub-human. He leaned on the counter and pinched his temples. Looked at his eyes. His best feature—so he'd been told. Pale blue like a baby blanket, they were disarming, sexy in a way that suggested he was always ready for a roll. This morning they were bloodshot. He rummaged through the medicine cabinet for drops. Found none.

Thom entered the massive built-in closet; empty except for a yard's length of hanging garments. He picked a suit at random and yanked off the dry cleaning plastic. Shirt, tie, belt, holster, firearm, personal cell, business cell, BUG, badge. Good to go.

He followed the mahogany hallway toward the stained glass window at the end of the hall. Backlit with a recently installed security light, he studied the scene as if seeing it for the first time. An iconic figure stood in a garden under a canopy of olive trees and flowering plants. He saw small details never before realized: bees buzzing the flowers, an orange butterfly in flight, a perched bird with a branch in its beak. Thom reflected briefly on the beauty of stained glass, of which this house had plenty.

Wood became marble and Thom descended the service stairs. The moment he reached the landing and made a sharp turn, he smelled the coffee from the kitchen. It was just as refreshing as the shower. And it'd knock back the pounding headache.

His cousin, Birdie, sat at the bar, palms flat on the paper, enveloped in a man-sized, silk kimono robe, hair shower damp. Her legs dangled off the barstool, feet encased in ratty fuzzy slippers. Only she could make them look cool.

An antiquated transistor radio tuned to a classic rock station sat on the windowsill over the sink. Birdie had to be the only Hancock Park millionaire who listened to great music betrayed by mono. She hummed along to the rhythm of Led Zeppelin's *Kashmir*.

"Oh, God," he said, "you're a morning person like George."

Cocoa bean colored hair fluttered as she turned and flashed him a smile. At once unsentimental and easily imperiled by reality and yet exquisite as it stretched from her chin to the corners of her sky blue eyes.

"This is my favorite time of day," she said. "It offers the promise of forgetfulness."

Forgetfulness. A concept worth embracing. She'd had more than a fair share of grief lately. The scars on her face daily proof. She started an investigation and became part of the story when she was kidnapped and remade into a crime victim. Her illusions of safety lost forever. The violence done to her … well, Thom didn't like to dwell on it. He still felt guilty for the way he mistreated her afterward, but hell, he did what he had to and she forgave him. Besides, everybody has scars.

He gave her a good morning peck on the lips.

"Christ," she said, wiping her mouth with the back of her hand. "You're still waxed. Johnnie Walker was it?"

"Damn, you're good. Know a hangover cure?"

"Aspirin and lots of water."

"Boring. I'll take coffee instead."

"Put some milk in your eyes."

"No shit?"

"Good word. Describes how you look."

"Thanks." Thom opened his arms and twirled. "I work hard at this image." He opened the mostly empty fridge and removed a bottle of milk. "Where'd you get bottled?"

"An organic dairy. They deliver."

"Of course." Thom wouldn't ask how much it cost.

"Working today?"

"Yeah." He poured milk into a cup, dipped a finger, flicked the liquid at his eyes and blinked it in. "I hate missing Mass," he deadpanned.

"I'm sure you do," she echoed. "How was the first night in your temporary digs?"

"I didn't have a night. I had a few early morning hours."

"Do I want to know?"

"Not if you believe your eldest cousin has any dignity."

She crossed her arms schoolmarm fashion, but said nothing.

He downed the leftover milk. "That's good stuff." He poured another cupful, shot it back then filled the cup with coffee.

"Who's the dude on the window in the hall?"

Birdie rolled her eyes. "It's Jesus in the Garden of Gethsemane."

"Considering this manse was once owned by the Church, I should've known."

"You should've known regardless. Eat something."

"No thanks. I'll take the sports section though."

Birdie slid the front page instead. His eye went straight to the headline:

FORMER LAPD COMMANDER SUSPECTED OF RUNNING A RING OF ROBBERS

By Elizabeth Keane
Special to The Times
Part 1 of 2

So there it was. He knew it was coming. He'd even read a confidential draft like the rest of the family. But actually seeing it in print made his heart jump, his breath catch. From here forward nothing would ever be the same.

Thom scanned the front page then flipped to the continuation inside. His eye lingered on the department portrait of his uncle—Birdie's father—Gerard Keane. He folded it closed; not having the heart to continue. He pushed the paper away just as a truncated siren blew. "My ride's here. Gotta go."

"Today's my first birthday," said Birdie. "Ron's coming to town. He's making dinner. Join us. George, too."

"And eat the healthy shit your boyfriend makes? No thanks. I prefer trans fat."

He was already around the corner when she said, "Yeah, you look like it, too."

"I heard that."

"Dinner's at seven. I expect you here!"

———

Thom noted that George had already been to Motor Transport Division to pick up his designated city car. On the first day of any new investigation they always arrived together. Partners. Teammates. A practical construct considering they both lived in the city for which they served.

George was dressed in his usual triumph of fine tailoring. Today it was a black suit with a lilac shirt woven with shiny vertical threads. A paisley tie in a palate of pinks, dark browns, and a smattering of black anchored the ensemble. George was a flash dresser, *GQ* style, but he wore his wardrobe in a non-fussy way, never seeming to make a show of his appearance. On his feet he wore sturdy, rubber-soled wingtips that he owned in four colors. Despite their high-end appearance, he could climb a mountain and give them a brand-new shine afterward. Good police shoes.

Compared to George, Thom felt like a rumpled slacker in an off-the-rack suit he bought on sale at a department store. His ties were devoid of patterns and matched the hue of his shirts. An adult version of Garanimals.

George tossed him a foil-wrapped burrito. "Eggs, potato, bacon, rice, salsa, pinto beans, extra peppers."

"Hosannas for Betty in her rolling coach of cuisine." Thom ripped the foil and waxed paper from one end and dug his teeth into a thick layer of folded tortilla.

"Why did I pick you up at Birdie's?" said George.

"Anne kicked me out."

"It's about time your wife threw your cheating ass out of the house."

Thom swallowed a mouthful of food, picked up the Styrofoam cup and took a burning sip of French roast to wash it down.

"Women aren't the problem," said Thom. "Anne wants to save face with her woman's group. She'll moan about my sullied reputation and pretend we're in therapy. Before you know it, I'll be a man reformed and move back in."

"Don't get cocky. She might make it permanent this time."

"Not my wife." Thom took another bite. "Where're we going?"

"Hollywood Hills, baby."

"Fancy. I hope we won't miss Bird's birthday dinner."

"What?"

"Yeah, you're invited. Ron's gonna make one of those meals he's famous for. Dinner bell rings at seven."

"I'll pass."

"Why, Georgie boy? Still pining for your ex-girlfriend? Is that why you wailed from the street? Can't bear to look at her?"

"Screw off."

Thom chortled and spit eggs onto the dash.

"You're a pig," said George, throwing napkins.

"Come on, it's an important day. She's one year sober. Did you ever think she'd get this far?"

"Still not going."

11

Thom's cell rang. He unclipped it from his belt and palmed it so George could hear as well. "L.A.'s finest detectives," he said.

"I just love the tinny sound of the speaker," said Lance Craig, their Lieutenant at Robbery/Homicide Division. "Suppose you can't multitask, Keane?"

"G-man is driving, but you know it's illegal, don't you, LT?"

"Whatever. Where are you monkeys? SID is already here. If you want a look before they mess up the scene with powder and chemicals you better get your asses here pronto."

George flipped an auxiliary switch and stomped the accelerator. The blue and red LEDs on the windshield pulsed.

"What we looking at?" said Thom.

"Four bodies. Looks professional. One of the dead is a city attorney. Dominic Lawrence. High profile, boys. You're point."

"Roger that," said Thom. "We're bat speed." He disconnected the call and continued scarfing his breakfast not knowing when he'd get another meal.

"We're maxed on overtime," said George.

"He's a city guy. We'll get paid."

"That means media."

"Damn straight. It's gonna be double bad. Birdie's article launched this morning. The second part comes out Tuesday."

George's face blanched.

"Gerard is the only family member guilty of anything," said Thom.

"Still on message."

Thom ignored the dig. "Gerard confessed to Bird in person. He mailed her letters and affidavits. He gave her more than he gave Eubanks"—Deputy District Attorney Daniel Eubanks—"that last bit is between you and me."

"She still shouldn't have done it."

"She's a journalist, George. That's what she does. It's her obligation to get in front of the shit storm."

Thom glared out the window. Side streets passed in a blur as George ran one red light after another.

"No doubt it's going to hurt. But it could be worse." It was the most artful lie Thom could present under the circumstances.

FOUR

<small>LET ME INTRODUCE MYSELF.</small>

My name is Mayo.

I borrowed the name from the big jar of mayonnaise in Jerry Deats' refrigerator. He ate it by the spoonful. That kind of gross does not deserve to live. Also, he was a pain in the ass.

I did not kill Jerry Deats.

He was not my mistake.

Why should I have to open the curtains so the busybody across the alley would see his body and call the police?

I did not like going. Jerry was a slob. The worst kind of trash-collecting, crusty-dishes-piled-in-the-sink, toilets-black-with-filth kind of slob. His apartment was stinky. He was stinky. After two weeks of dead, he was leaky.

Trust me, leaky stink is the worst kind of stink.

FIVE

The residence of Dominic Lawrence was a decrepit '60s tri level sandwiched between a massive glass and steel job and an impeccably maintained Spanish villa.

Warped garage doors, rusty wrought iron, cracked windows repaired with duct tape, and twisted rain gutters were a few flaws that added detail to the random patches of missing stucco. A broad concrete stairway, edges chipped with hard use, hugged the house with nothing but a rickety wood rail offering protection from a slope of ivy and bougainvillea.

The stairs led to a narrow side yard overlooking the villa's red roof tiles and a smattering of satellite dishes. A small concrete entry lined with broken brick planters contained anemic green things attempting to survive. Beyond a lawn of crab grass and dandelions was the only good thing the property offered: canyon and city views. A real estate bifecta worth millions.

Thom wondered how Lawrence got along with the neighbors, considering his house was the dog on the street.

Spenser Hobart from Scientific Investigation Division greeted them from the other side of the yellow tape. He had the spit-shine of a '50s television personality. He gave George an earnest smile and said, "It's about time you showed up, Silva. I was beginning to worry."

"I had to pull Thom out of church," said George.

"No doubt from the confessional," said Spenser. Then to Thom, "Did the priest thank you for freeing up his morning?" He chuckled at his own joke.

Thom scratched his nose with his middle finger and turned his attention to the uniform with the sign-in log. He printed his name, badge number, and arrival time on the sheet. George did the same.

"Who called you out, Spenser?" said Thom, ducking under the tape.

"S&M."

"James Seymour and Mortimer Morgan. Conceited blowhards of RHD." Thom hated being second string to S&M. But he got some satisfaction knowing they screwed up by pinning Birdie's abduction on Emmett Whelan despite her protestations.

"*Sweet*," added George, his voice rimmed with astringent.

There was a rivalry between the two pairs of partners that stemmed from a long-ago tiff between Morgan and George. That was back when George was undercover vice working the southside of prostitution. They had an altercation that neither man would talk about, allowing idle speculation and gossip.

"I hear they have the highest clearance rate," said Spenser.

"Because they've been there the longest," said Thom. "It's called attrition."

Near the front door a second yellow tape marked a smaller, more important perimeter. A patrol officer at the tape held a clipboard with a second sign-in log. His nametag read S. Cross. He nodded in greeting as Thom flashed the badge.

"RHD Detectives Keane and Silva," said Thom. "Where do I know you from?"

"I was in rotation at Birdie's hospital door."

Birdie's abductors had dumped her naked body on a city street. She spent the next week in the hospital with a twenty-four-seven police guard.

Thom wagged his finger in recognition. "That's right. You worked for Gerard at Hollywood Station." The implication being he was one of Gerard's dirty guys.

"I play softball with Patrick Whelan," said Cross. "He asked me to volunteer for the duty."

The Whelan clan was close family friends with the Keane clan. Thom made a mental note to ask Patrick for the lowdown on Cross because he didn't trust anybody these days. "What do we have?"

"Four dead. Two Asian minors in the front bedroom. Two Caucasian adults in the back bedroom. All shot with a small caliber weapon. Killer wrote a message in blood on a bathroom mirror. No sign of forced entry. Other than that, it's a peaceful crime scene."

"Really?" said Thom. "I didn't know murder can be peaceful."

"You'll see what I mean," said Cross.

"IDs?"

"The adults are Dominic and Rachel Lawrence. The minors appear to be foster kids."

"Give me entry details."

"The person reporting said she touched the front door handle, a magazine, and the door knob of the master bedroom," Cross said. "I was the first responder. All the doors were shut so I gloved and two-fingered the knobs. I left them open so that the paramedics wouldn't have to touch anything."

George took notes.

"You certain that every door was shut?" said Thom.

"Yes, sir."

"You create a path?"

"Preserved the center." He gave Thom a map drawn on graph paper. "I recognized Lawrence from court and directed the watch commander to call RHD right away, but the Hollywood suits and Sergeant Anselmo rolled out anyway. There was the usual discussion and it got kicked. S&M arrived and then Lieutenant Craig came and changed it up."

"Craig still in there?"

"Never went in." Cross angled the clipboard toward Thom.

Thom studied the log. "You locked it down and restricted access," he said.

Admiration replaced Thom's trepidation of Cross. Thom had seen too many crime scenes wrecked by adrenaline-jacked patrol cops or overzealous detectives. Investigations are a methodical process and Cross had a keen awareness to protect and maintain. Not only did his thorough actions make the detective's job easier, there'd be little to question by a savvy defense attorney. And Thom was always thinking of the endgame.

"You've got a pair," said Thom.

"Lawrence is a big fish," said Cross.

"Who's the PR?"—"Person reporting."

"Speaking of whom," interjected Spenser. "Seymour got her to agree to a field process."

"Oh?"

"Yeah. I checked her hands and clothing for GSR, took an index card and a hair sample. She even gave signed consent." He passed the form to George.

"What's the name of this helpful PR?" said Thom.

Cross held up a driver's license. "Jelena Shkatova. She's in a car waiting for you guys."

Thom plucked the license from Cross' hand and stared at the tiny photo of the blond-haired, green-eyed beauty. The odoriferous memory of cigarettes, sickly-sweet gardenias, and latex smacked him hard across the face. He felt disconnected. Woozy.

He had sex with Jelena last night.

Thom coughed to mask emote. "What connection does she have with the victims?"

"They were her foster parents," said Cross.

Thom rocked slightly, felt sick, tried to stay focused. He had followed the rules of catch and release. No last name. No occupation. Nothing personal about family. The rules burned him.

"Talk to the residents next door?" he said, unsteady on his feet.

"We've got FI cards." Field Interview. "No one heard or saw anything."

"Security cameras?"

"One resident up the street has a partial view of the street. Spenser has the disc."

Thom turned too suddenly and faltered.

George grasped Thom's elbow and led him away from the yellow tape. "What's up? You look like you're about to faint."

"The girl, Jelena," whispered Thom. "I met her in a bar last night. We were together."

George raked his fingers through his hair—an obvious tell that presented when he was upset or nervous. There was nothing to say. The panic on Thom's face said it all.

Thom's hands shook as he pulled free his business phone from the holder and punched Craig's number. Despite the shock of learning he had an intimate encounter with the PR he had the presence of mind and temerity to call it. They walked to the far edge of the crab grass. George leaned toward the phone to listen.

"Keane. You better have a good reason for calling," answered Craig. "Last I saw, you have four homicides to solve."

"I can't work the case."

"What?" said Craig. "It sounds like you're talking shit."

"I had a sexual encounter with the PR last night."

"Aren't you married?"

"That doesn't change the fact that I'm compromised. My involvement will jeopardize the integrity of the case."

"Be professional and figure it out," said Craig, killing the call.

"Damnit," said Thom.

"What the hell?" said George. "He's the one always quoting the manual and spouting off about procedure."

Thom swept his eyes over the corps of uniforms and SID who stared back, confused. Thom's gaze landed on an abandoned coffee cup resting on a planter. Next to it was a folded newspaper. He turned back to George.

"When was the last time Craig came to a crime scene?" said Thom.

"One of ours?" said George. "Never."

"Exactly. And why were S&M dispatched?"

"They were on the callout board."

"Then Craig arrived and changed it up?" Thom took a step aside so that George had eyes on the front door. "Over my shoulder. Two-o'clock."

George flicked his eyes and hissed. "Birdie's article?"

"The department has clear written policies about conflict of interest," said Thom.

"The rules are up for interpretation when lawyers get involved at the trial stage."

"But when an officer *needs* to be excused because of the potential, the department usually errs on the safe side. Craig knows this more than anyone."

"Which is why it doesn't make sense. What's his game?"

Thom shook his head. "I don't know."

He looked out on the city of his birth. The city where he worked. The city where he lived. The city he loved. He knew he was in mud and had a sick feeling he might be on the verge of losing something he'd always taken for granted.

"Well," he said, in a self-aware way, "we work it squeaky clean. You take the girl. I'll take the house." And with that he turned away and then—almost as an aside—he whispered, "I think I'm being screwed."

"And me along with you," said George.

SIX

Detective George Silva leaned into the backseat of the black-and-white and said, "It's cramped in there. Come out and get some fresh air."

Keen green eyes looked up at him. Other than pink gloss on her lips, her skin was makeup free. She offered her hand for assistance. When George didn't oblige, she shrugged and wiggled out on her own.

"I'm Detective Silva," he said.

"Lena Shkatova."

"Russian?"

"On my father's side. Can I sit?"

"Of course." George gestured toward the hood of the car. Lena tried several leaning positions before settling on one she liked. She smoothed the crown of her long, blond hair.

"Can I smoke?" she said.

"If you wish."

Slender fingers reached into her back pocket and pulled out a slim cloisonné case. She popped it open and George glanced inside: six cigarettes, a book of matches, and a lip gloss. She stuck a cigarette between her lips and struck a match. She met George's eyes through the flame and took a single seductive pull.

George felt it as a tickle in his stomach. If only this were another time, another place, another circumstance.

"How long have you been in the United States?" he said. All business.

"Since I am eight," she said, exhaling. "My parents die when I am ten. I go to house for girls with no family. I am naughty and get trouble, but they let me stay. This is where Dom found me when I am thirteen. He brought me here. It is not improvement."

"What kind of trouble?"

"Curfew, smoking, stealing. *Boys.*"

"What was the name of the home?"

"Compass. It is orphanage in Rosemead."

"So the Lawrence's are ...?"

"Foster parents."

George gave Jelena's license one last look before handing it to her. She was twenty-two. Much younger than Thom's usual. "Lena is your nickname?"

"Yes."

"It states this as your address."

"I move two months ago, but have not changed license. Now I live at apartment. Downtown with other girls. It is near library. Close to work at courthouse."

"Address."

"Six-twelve Flower. Between Wilshire and Sixth. Pegasus apartments."

George wrote it down and check-marked **courthouse**.

"Can you tell me what happened?"

"No, but I can tell you what I see."

He liked that she was literal. Most people weren't.

"I come here at seven. I do this every Sunday morning. Rachel makes big breakfast. Today, we take twins to Exposition Park to see exhibit at museum."

"Twins?"

"Girls. They are new foster kids. They are ten."

Oh, shit, thought George. Thom had five children. His youngest were 10-year-old twins. Females. He needed to get Thom's head ready for what he was about to see. He quickly tapped a text message to Thom's cell.

HEDZ UP POS TWIN 10YO XX

He snapped the phone shut, clipped it to his belt.

"What door did you use when you arrived at seven?" said George.

"Front door."

"Was it unlocked?"

"Dom and Rachel are strict about locking doors. I use key."

"Are you certain it was locked and not just closed?"

"It was locked."

"What kind of lock is on the door?"

"The dead kind. And there is button you push on handle."

"What did you see when you entered the house?"

Lena shrugged and puffed on the cigarette. "Nothing. Usually everybody is up and Rachel is in kitchen making cinnamon rolls.

They are my favorite. But today … I think everyone sleep late. I wait with magazine. Then I hear beeping of Dom's alarm and knock on door, but they do not answer. I open door and see blood. I close door and run away." Her eyes welled.

"What then?"

"I call nine-one-one and all these people come," she said as she dabbed her eyes on her shoulder. "I sit in police car, and get inked and I wait for you."

George thought Lena's use of the word inked was an odd usage, but he knew what she meant. As a city employee, she would've been fingerprinted.

"What phone did you use to dial nine-one-one?"

She slid a hand into the other back pocket and produced a cell phone.

"May I?" said George.

She pressed it into his waiting palm and he scrolled through the most recent calls. Her last was indeed to 9-1-1 at 7:07 a.m. No calls since. The last call prior was at 10:30 p.m.

Though Lena's accent wasn't yet Americanized, her fashion was. She wore expensive designer jeans, a pearl and gold chain belt, a white, formfitting t-shirt, a short denim jacket, and wedge sandals. The trendy color of her toenails matched the short fingernails. She looked like every other young, party-girl-wannabe, yet her phone log showed few calls and no text messages, unlike other girls her age. This bothered George.

He passed the phone back. "What was your relationship like with the Lawrence's?"

"They are hard people. Dom is very discipline man and Rachel does not hug. Living here is very strict. If I behave, I get reward. The twins get lots of rewards. But they are tricky and fool Dom and Rachel. I am glad I no longer live here. But Dom help me learn English and become citizen and he teach me how to make good work. Now I live on my own, can stay out late, sleep late, do what I want. I am sad they are dead." She took a deep drag.

"How do you know they're dead?"

"I saw blood."

"Did you see the twins?"

"NO," said Lena, blowing smoke out her nose. "They are dead because no one is up. Rachel would be in kitchen. Every Sunday. Cinnamon rolls."

She spread her hands like George didn't get what she was saying, but he understood perfectly.

"If your relationship wasn't good, then why come and visit?"

"Cinnamon rolls!" She flicked an ash. "But also, Dom wants me to help twins, so I come because he is my boss."

"You work for him?"

"Yes. In his office. Me and Claudia both."

"Who's Claudia?"

"Claudia Stepanova. One of my roommates."

"You've been sitting here for a couple of hours with your phone and it didn't occur to you to call Claudia and tell her that her boss, your foster dad, was dead?"

Lena shrugged.

"What did you do last night and when did you do it?" said George. "And be specific about the times." He didn't really want to hear the exploits of Lena and Thom, but it was necessary to establish a timeline.

Lena eyed him suspiciously through the smoke. It gave her a sinister aura. When the smoke dissipated, so did the mysterious movie still. "You think I do this?"

"It's standard procedure, Miss Shkatova. We'll find evidence of you in the house. It needs to be placed into context."

She sighed. "I understand now. Last night I go to Hank's with Claudia. It is downtown bar on Grand. I like it. I can talk to nice man. Claudia does not like it. So she leave."

"What time did your friend leave?"

She thought a moment. "I think midnight. I have two drinks with nice man and we leave before one-thirty."

George braced. "What is the name of the man you left with?"

"Thomas. He is old gentleman. Very nice kisser."

"Last name?"

"I do not know."

"How are you sure of the time?"

"I want to have sex with Thomas. When we get to my car, the clock say one-thirty."

George was momentarily dumbfounded by Thom's ability to attract women. How did he consistently pull it off? He must have that *thing* that less attractive men learn at a young age—how to be charming and work women. It couldn't be the way he dressed off duty; khakis, deck shoes, and a polo shirt—typical yuppie clothing for men with no style. Thom did have great conversational skills, but still, the whole package didn't add up. Then he wondered if Lena saw Thom as a potential rich husband.

"Were you drunk?" said George.

"No."

"Did this man—" he had a hard time saying his partner's proper name, "—Thomas, take advantage of you?"

"No. I ask him for sex. He say okay. We go to my car and have good sex."

"Not your apartment?"

"I ask, but Thomas say no."

"Then what?"

"Thomas leave at two-thirty. I go to apartment for sleep."

"Were your roommates home?"

"Not Claudia. Her door is open when I go home, but it is closed when I leave in morning. I share room with Dona. She is sleeping when I go home and sleeping when I leave."

"Can anyone verify your whereabouts from two-thirty until seven this morning?"

Lena shook her head. "I not think so unless Dona wake up during night."

"I'll need to verify with Thomas. How can I reach him?"

"I did not get his number. But bartender knows him so I can see him again."

"You had sex with a man you don't know?" It was irrelevant. George's curiosity compelled the question.

"Is it necessary? I talk with him. I like him. He call me 'little Jelena.'" She smiled. "I like having sex with him so I will see him again."

Why some women used sex as a barometer for a potential relationship confused George. He suspected Birdie did it with him. On their first date Birdie asked him for sex. Hell, he didn't complain. It wasn't until later that he realized she was testing the water. If the sex was good, she'd give it a go. If not, why bother putting in the time?

He was pretty certain that Birdie did it with her current boyfriend, Ron Hughes, as well. Only this time, she fell in love. So she said.

"Does Dona also work for Mr. Lawrence?"

"No." She dropped the cigarette butt on the street, stepped on it.

"May I have that?" said George.

"I do not care."

He plucked a small envelope from the inside pocket of his jacket and scooped up the butt with the flap. He placed it in the breast pocket, right next to the micro recorder.

"Is there anybody you know who would like to see Mr. Lawrence dead? From work or home?"

"I can not say."

"What about you?"

She took a long-winded breath. "I already said that I am sad Dom and Rachel are dead. But not twins. I do not like them."

Lena's frankness surprised George the detective, not the man, and he could see why Thom was attracted to her. He probably felt liberated by her forwardness.

George's phone chirped. He read Thom's text.

TWINS DONE 1ST

"Are we finished?" said Lena, exasperated.

"Not by a long shot."

SEVEN

"I've been thinking about kids lately," said Birdie.

Father Frank spit tea all over his devotional notes.

"Not as in, I want to have them, but as in, about them. In general. More specifically, I've been thinking about childhood."

"What brought this on?" said Frank, dabbing the paper with his handkerchief.

"Louise."

"Ron's dog?"

"Exactly. Last time I stayed at his house Louise had torn up a new accent pillow. They weren't cheap and Ron was pissed. He collected all the stuffing and bits of torn fabric and piled the mess on the floor. Ron commanded Louise to sit and then he sat just behind the destroyed pile so that Louise could see him and the pillow parts. So Louise is sitting there, eyes tracking between the pillow and Ron. He's mad, but not showing it. A sort of stare down went on for minutes. After a while Louise began to shake. Ron ignored her. Then she began to whine. Poor thing, after a few more minutes she's beside herself. Shaking and whining, but not moving her butt from that spot of floor. After a few more minutes, I'm really feeling sorry for Louise. I'm about to plead her case when Ron moved the pillow stuff out of sight. Meanwhile, Louise is practically spastic and crying, but still not daring to move from the floor. Finally, Ron releases her and she jumps into his lap. He gives her all his attention and love. Kisses. Belly rubs. The works. Later that day, we were on the couch and Ron threw the other pillow near her. She completely ignored it. She had learned her lesson."

Frank leaned back in his desk chair. "That can't be all to this child genesis."

"Louise is prone to eye infections and Ron has to put this gel-like medicine in her eyes. She hates it and always cries and fusses. He shushes her and talks all sweet while he's doing it. Afterward, he cradles her like a baby and distracts her from wiping her eyes with her paw. I've seen him do this before, but this time I think back and realize that he's never hit her. He's trained her, disciplined, loved, but never hit. Not even a swat on the flank. While he's got Louise in his arms, an image pops into my mind and I see him holding a baby. And I think he'd make a great father."

"Training animals isn't on the same scale as raising babies," said Frank.

"Of course not. But that doesn't diminish the import of my thought. It was random, but not random at all. You've said that we, as mere humans, self-actualize. I wonder if this is God's way of making us look at ourselves in a new light. Like the proverbial light bulb going on. Anyway, this not-so-random thought leads to another and another until I'm thinking about childhood. My childhood."

Frank clapped his hands together. "Finally! We're getting somewhere."

"Frank, I'm serious."

"Me, too. I have the asperges rite to deliver soon."

"Okay, I'll hurry. So I remembered one thing about myself that I had never given any thought to. Something I took for granted. Only... I never knew I had taken it for granted because I knew no alternative. It was my normal. At some point in time all children go through a phase where this one thing rules their lives. It becomes a scourge of parents worldwide who lose sleep. This one thing is also a bonding opportunity between parents and offspring. Thing is, I never had nighttime soothing sessions. Mom and Dad never had to come to my room in the middle of the night because their daughter was screaming and afraid of the boogeyman under the bed, or ghosts in the closets. I've been dwelling on this one thing. Really thinking about it."

"You're talking about being afraid of the dark."

"Exactly," said Birdie. "I've never been afraid of the dark. For me, even as a child, the night brought safety. Night swallowed the fear. That's why I've always had blackout shades on my windows."

"But that changed. You're afraid of the dark now."

"Yes," she said quietly. "It drives Ron crazy that the hallway remains lit and there're night lights in my bedroom."

"It's a symptom of post-traumatic stress."

"That's what Ron keeps saying, too. And I know that. But the whole point is that I came to this thought on my own. Frank, it may seem trivial to you, but I'm proud about this realization. You always say to me that I have to own what happened to me because it is a permanent part of me now. And I'll try. I promise. But for now, I've learned something. And maybe that something will help me become less afraid of the dark or lead to another something and eventually my comfort level and actions."

Birdie plopped into an overstuffed chair and a puff of dust floated upward and caught the window light of Frank's rectory office. "You think me silly," she said.

"No. I'm glad. Even if it's a black pug that gets you there. You're making progress. Slow and steady and forward."

"Yes. That's what I want."

A soft knock on the door announced its opening. A young boy with a mop of blond peeked in. "Father?"

"I'm coming," said Frank. "Go on, I'll be right there."

The door closed with a soft click.

Frank kissed Birdie's head. "This is good. Thank you for sharing."

"You know me, Frank. I always share."

"A little too much sometimes," he said smiling. "Do you have a confession?"

"Not this week."

His eyes shot to the cross hanging next to the window. "Miracles do happen," he whispered. He made the sign of the cross over Birdie. "*In Nomine Patris, et Filii, et Spiritus Sancti, Dominus vobiscum.*"

"*Et cum spiritu tuo.*"

"Amen," they said together.

"By the way," he said, "how did Ron command Louise to sit?"

"He said in a firm voice, 'sit' then 'stay.'"

"How did he release her?"

"He said, 'come.'"

"Only three words," he mused. Frank then excused himself. He had a Mass to celebrate. A congregation to attend. Birdie was not his only customer today.

After he left the room Birdie was struck by the feeling that her vulnerability was not a weakness. It was a strength she had to harness.

Where did that come from?

She gazed up at the cross.

Really? Are you sure?

One thing she did know for sure. Her lungs were beginning to work again.

EIGHT

Detective Thom Keane scanned the SID crew. "Who's what?"

A woman held up her hand. "Prints."

Another woman said, "Serology."

"I'm Reynolds," said a man, pointing at the camera around his neck.

"Film or digital?"

"What's your choice?"

Thom liked the idea of film for a media case. No one could accuse the department of altering a digital image. "Film," he decided.

"You got it. I already shot the exterior, points of entry, generals, and compass points in digital. I'll switch to film for interiors and the bodies."

"Sounds great," said Thom.

"I'm everything else," said Spenser Hobart. "There's a nice wood floor inside. Like hair?"

"Love it. I want to know who's been here."

"I'll bust out the Swiffer."

"Great. Listen up gang, you know what to do. I want to be out of here by sunset."

Prints and Serology exchanged smirks as if to say, *like that's gonna happen.*

Thom read their expressions and said, "It's called efficiency."

He inspected the exterior of the Lawrence residence and made a notation on the fresh note pad: no sign of forced entry.

His cell vibrated with a message from George.

HEDZ UP POS TWIN 10YO XX

Thom's skin itched with irrational fear. How many twin-sets of 10-year-old girls could there be in Los Angeles? Hundreds? L.A. was a big-ass place. His girls were fine. His girls weren't in this house. They had no reason to be. But he couldn't help himself. He flicked his wrist. The family would be on their way to Mass at St. Joseph's. He stepped away and dialed his wife's cell.

"Hello," said Anne Keane with a clip in her voice.

"Hi, Honey. Everything okay this morning?"

"Yes." Cold.

"The kids … Pearse, Padraig, Liam …" he gulped. "Rose and Nora?"

"We're all fine." Anne was already impatient, thought Thom. One night without her husband certainly didn't make her heart grow fonder.

"Can I talk to Rose?"

"We're running late," sighed Anne. "I don't have time for this."

"Time for what? I just want to talk to one of my girls. Damnit, Anne, you're driving anyway. What's the big deal?"

Thom heard the distinct muffle of a phone being passed from one hand to another and then the sweetest voice. "Da?"

That was it. All he needed. A small reassurance that his girls were okay. "Hi, sweetie-pie. How's my red rose this morning?"

"*Daaaa*," she said. "I'm a yellow rose today."

"Grandma Nora said you had to save that yellow dress for your brother's birthday party."

"Ohhhh, I forgot." She giggled.

Forgot my ass, thought Thom.

"Where are you, Da? You didn't make pancakes this morning."

"I'm working, sweetie. Let me talk to Mummy."

More muffled passing. "Thom." said Anne. Then off to the side she yelled, "Watch cross traffic."

Then he heard less distinctly, "Ma, I got it."

Then he understood. Their eldest son, Pearse, was driving. Thom had taken Pearse to the DMV on his sixteenth birthday and he passed with a perfect score. That was a year ago and, still, Anne stomped the imaginary brake on the passenger side floorboard.

"Are you planning on taking the kids to the Manor?" said Thom. Magnolia Manor was Thom's childhood home. Every Sunday after Mass the Manor became the gathering place for brunch and family.

"Of course," said Anne. "The girls planned a one-year celebration for Bird."

"Girls" referred to Thom's mother, Nora, and Birdie's mother, Maggie. They'd been best friends since seventh grade. Married brothers.

"Ron's coming up early," continued Anne. "It's a surprise for Bird. Why do you ask?"

"I pulled a case. A city attorney named Lawrence and his family."

"That's too bad. I'll express your regrets. Anything else?"

"I love you."

"Okay. Bye then."

Click.

That was truly unsatisfactory. At least he knew where he stood. As always.

Thom slipped cloth booties over his shoes and put on a pair of latex gloves. On the way into the house he said to Cross, "Call the coroner's investigator. By the time he gets here, we'll be done."

Thom made another notation on his notepad: **paper-sized residue on front door—rectangle.** He touched an edge and detected tackiness. Something had been taped here. He peered at the deadlock, shone a light into the keyhole.

"Check this lock for graphite," said Thom to Spenser.

The front door opened directly into a great room. The walls were lined, floor to ceiling, with wood shelving filled with classic and contemporary literature. Upholstered chairs were arranged into several reading suites—the like found in libraries. No television, stereo, or radio, but there were plenty of boxed board games and card decks.

Across the great room was a breakfast bar that separated the kitchen and dining room. To the left a table shoved against the wall held two desktop computers. On the wall, two dry erase boards tracked chores, schoolwork, and rewards.

"This is our lucky day," said Thom.

"How's that?" said Spenser.

"Look at the Saturday chore list." Besides the usual dusting, toilets, and trash were three items that excited Thom: doors, floors, and walls. "With an interior this clean, it'll be easier to find what the killer left behind." *And less trace to process and sidetrack us.* "The floor is immaculate. Can you hydro-stat for shoe prints?"

Spenser squatted to get a sideway angle. "It's a possibility. I'll give it a try."

As Reynolds snapped photos Thom mapped the interior. Its tidiness and order were a stark contrast to the shambled exterior.

The kitchen was small, neat, and shiny. Several of the drawers and cabinets were locked, probably the ones containing knives or other lethal kitchen tools.

To the right of the great room was a full bath off a short hallway. Perpendicular to the bath was a wall partially covered with a woven blanket hung like a tapestry. It was attached to a rod with linen loops and puddled on the floor. Carpeted stairs branched off the right.

Thom pivoted. Looked at his notes. "A window should be here." He pulled the blanket aside.

"*No way,*" said Spenser. "A hidden door. With an electronic keypad."

"Photo and print. Then we'll pop it open," said Thom.

Thom took each stair slowly, hugging a wall decorated with framed photos of smiling girls of various ages and races. He tapped his knuckle against one and then another. Plexiglas. A safety house. Near the top was a formal graduation portrait of Jelena.

In the photo she wore little makeup. Didn't need to. Her beauty was natural. Clear, unflawed complexion, friendly green eyes, shiny blond hair. Her nose sloped downward and flared slightly at the end. Pink tinted lips were pressed closed to hide the braces she told him about. Jelena's lips resembled Anne's. Maybe that was why he liked kissing her.

He remembered her petite body in clothes that accentuated her small curves, the way she cocked her head to get a point across, the way her cool skin felt under his hands when she climbed on top of him and how quickly it warmed. He thought about her laugh in his ear as she teased him, the giggle when he sucked her nipples, the moans coming later. She made it obvious that she was smitten. He liked that.

Reynolds presence at Thom's elbow halted the adolescent reverie. "Man, you're slow. Most detectives go straight to the bodies."

"I don't," said Thom. He never did. He walked murder scenes as the killer might've—wanting to see what the killer saw. "This carpet is dark. Might conceal blood. Stay close to the wall."

"I've done this once or twice," said Reynolds. He whistled as the shutter snapped. "Isn't it strange there are only portraits of girls? A wall full of suspects."

The acidic scent of congealed blood in the kids' room prickled the nose. The sight of the Asian twins almost made Thom reel. There was no fury on the bodies, just deadly precision. They were spooned on the floor, covered in a princess comforter of blue and silver. Heads placed on a shared pillow. Their pale faces frozen in sisterly tranquility. One gunshot wound to each temple. Reddish-black goo like Halloween gel matted their hair. A rivulet of blood had spilled into the recess of a closed eye and pooled. The other twin died with her eyes open.

Thom squatted and placed the back of his hand near her plump cheek. "I wonder," he whispered, "did you hear the shot that killed your sister and open your eyes for a brief moment before your time came? Did you feel the bullet penetrate your skull? Would you have wanted to survive this world without your other half?" Thom thought of his own twin, Aiden. "I couldn't've." And Rose without Nora? Thom gritted his teeth. These little girls, both serene and violent, would stick with him. The kids always did.

Mindful that Reynolds was near, Thom stepped back and the hard-ass cop mask dropped across his face. He eyeballed the utilitarian room. It contained a glossy white bunk bed. White dressers with pink knobs were stenciled with their names. Amy and Amber. Two small upholstered chairs were shoved against the wall with a shared reading lamp. There was no toy box, no bulletin board stuck with shiny objects, no dolls, no teddy bears, not even a clock.

Thom said, "Two beds, two comforters, *one* pillow."

"And no fired casings," said Reynolds.

"Not expected in an execution."

Thom moved down the hall to the master bedroom.

On the bed Dominic lay on his back. There were two visible wounds: in the middle of the forehead and in the groin. The faded blue comforter looked as if it had been moved off him, but Thom couldn't inspect it carefully until the CI arrived.

Reynolds pointed at the groin and said, "That's personal."

"The head shot is personal," corrected Thom. "It indicates the killer knew his victim. The groin shot is business." Then why shoot the wife and kids? Personal or business or a little of both? His eye fell to a bloodied item discarded on the floor. The missing princess pillow. Used as a muffle. He pulled out his cell and sent a text to George.

TWINS DONE 1ST

Rachel lay curled up on her left side, bloodied temple peeking from the blanket that she held tight to her nose like a cocoon. She probably felt safe in a childlike way—never expecting to be murdered in her sleep.

Thom leaned over Lawrence, noted the disturbance in the glossy blood of the groin wound. "I'm sorry," he whispered, "but if this happened because you touched little girls, I hope you rot in hell."

Thom moved on to the bathroom and stared at two words scrawled on the master bath mirror.

Dead fish

Each letter had sharp edges. Nearly see-through and shimmery in the mirror's spotlighted reflection. A bloodied foam brush lay in the sink. The tool dipped into Dominic's blood to write the creepy words. Something dark caught Thom's eye. He leaned in to inspect what looked like a pubic hair stuck in the letter D.

Prints entered the bathroom. "What does it mean?"

Thom crossed his arms in study. "Pushover? Easy prey? Someone easily defeated or dominated?" Then he thought of Cross' description of Lawrence—'big fish'. He glared at the words. **Dead fish.** "Mostly it means the killer is a narcissist."

Prints knit her brows.

"He wants attention."

"Sick." Then as an afterthought she said, "The hidden room is ready."

"Excellent. As soon as George is done with the PR we'll crack it open and find us some dirty little secrets."

NINE

Mayo read the morning newspaper article about bad cops and quickly became engrossed in the story.

FORMER LAPD COMMANDER SUSPECTED OF RUNNING A RING OF ROBBERS

By Elizabeth Keane
Special to The Times
Part 1 of 2

Federal authorities believe a former LAPD commander organized a band of police officers into a network of thieves who engaged in armed robbery, extortion, and blackmail, according to law enforcement and people with knowledge of the investigation.

The gang, calling themselves the Blue Bandits, came to the attention of authorities when an associate, Gerard

Keane, Captain of Hollywood Division [the writer's father], dispatched—via a lawyer—affidavits, supporting documents, and depositions to the District Attorney's office. Also included was a ledger of misdemeanors going back twelve years.

Keane sent a duplicate set of the material to his daughter. The documents named many current and former LAPD officers as associates.

According to the DA's office there have been rumors for years regarding the Blue Bandits, but no viable evidence to support an investigation. The LAPD and the FBI have joined forces in a taskforce to investigate all claims made by Keane.

The alleged head of the gang and founding member was Ralph Soto, a retired commander of Central Bureau. The co-leader was West Bureau Deputy Chief, Theodore Rankin. They both died on February 7th.

In an excerpt from a letter that accompanied the documentation Keane sent to his daughter, he wrote, "It was well past time for the madness to end. I asked Soto and Rankin to join me in retiring from our life of crime. Disband the Blue Bandits. Disappear into oblivion. Rankin was willing. Soto was not. So I finished it. I shot and killed Soto with my service weapon. It was the only time it had ever been fired outside the range. After informing Rankin of the package I sent to the DA he took his own life . . . and I'll meet my end soon enough. This crime drama will end badly."

Keane's life ended shortly after mailing the letter. He led Indio police and the California Highway Patrol on a high-speed chase. According to a CHP spokesperson, when Keane finally stopped and exited the vehicle he fired a gun and was fatally shot in return fire. This is commonly referred to as suicide by cop.

Authorities close to the investigation wonder how a cop gang could go undetected for so long. The answer might lie at the beginning with Dr. Glen Soto, Ralph Soto's son.

According to a federal agent close to the investigation, Dr. Soto is cooperating with the investigation and has corroborated much of Keane's information.

Dr. Glen Soto was a successful psychiatrist who specialized in marital counseling. He ran his practice out of the Janko Medical Center, a drop-in, pay-as-you-go clinic for non-emergencies. He was a pioneer in unorthodox therapies. One of those utilized MDMA, a drug in the amphetamine family.

Its chemical composition releases massive levels of norepinephrine in the brain. Couples found the resulting feeling of empathy and sense of euphoria helpful as they talked through their issues.

Once MDMA made the transition from therapy drug to a popular, feel-good party drug of choice, the Federal Drug Administration reclassified it as a Schedule I drug. Even after it became illegal, Dr. Soto continued to use it and his practice flourished. Appointments were booked months in advance.

He found himself focusing less on patients as his dispensing profits grew. Fearing a supply problem, he funded a laboratory in Oregon to manufacture the drug.

In a statement to police, Dr. Soto said, "One day I realized I was nothing more than a drug dealer. But I continued because the money was so good."

Dr. Soto's worst fears were realized when the Oregon laboratory was raided by federal authorities. Only three days later, Soto's in-house pharmacy was robbed. In a brazen attack, three armed men stormed the facility in broad daylight and stole all of Janko's MDMA stores.

"That's when I called my dad," Soto stated to authorities. "I couldn't call nine-one-one and report a robbery. I'd be arrested. I did the next best thing. At first, all I wanted was my product back. Then I began to hatch a plan. Why not have the protection of the police on my side?"

According to Dr. Soto, his father was initially angry when he learned of his son's dealing, but with a little convincing he saw the earning potential.

Thus, a drug enterprise was born. One sanctioned and operated by a well-respected cop known as a hardliner...

————

Mayo shivered with exhilaration. Wait until Tuesday to get the rest of the story? Impossible. It was too good. Drug dealing. Robbery. Murder. By cops! How exciting. Mayo visualized how the Blue

Bandits interacted. The planning. The scheming. The late night rendezvous in dark places.

Mayo reread a part about Ralph Soto … *his seduction into a double life came on quick. Like a sudden fever … Soto became de facto president of Janko and in the first two years, he made eight years' worth of departmental salary.*

That kind of money is a great motivator, thought Mayo. Peanuts compared to what I'm gonna get. When this is done I'll take my own money and do whatever I want. Buy my own island like that rich guy, the one with the planes. Planes. Yes. I'll need one of those to get to my island. I'll need a boat, too. And a staff I can boss around.

The article went on about something called the Paige Street murder. It was very long and Mayo got distracted by another thought and made a phone call.

"Yeah?"

"Have you seen the morning paper?"

"Are you shitting me? Did you forget what I'm doing?"

"This reporter wrote an article about her dad. Ratted him out. Okay, he's dead. But still … her own father!"

"And this should interest me why?"

"I'm going to call her. Her email address is at the bottom of the article. That means she has an extension, too. I'll call information to get the number for the *Los Angeles Times.*"

"Don't be stupid! You're not calling the newspaper."

"Why not? This is the break we've been looking for. She can help us."

"We got our break when you killed the high-profile fish. Now the cops will get their shit together and figure it out."

"It's taking too long!"

"What got you wound up?"

"I like this murder thing. It was fun. I want more."

"There might be another chance. Be patient."

"You had more than me."

"I killed four. You killed four. We're even."

"When you put it like that..."

"We have to stay focused on the next phase. Are you ready?"

"I want my money."

"Be patient, my love. We're almost there. Remember how we worked it out? The killing was the easy part. We still have roles to play."

"I can't call the reporter and play with her?"

"No."

"Just one call?"

"NO. Listen to me, I'll be over soon and rub your feet the way you like."

"Will you ... you know ... lick me? I like that, too."

"It will be a reward for not calling the reporter."

"Okay, okay. I won't call."

"I have to go now. I'll see you soon."

It'll be a secret, thought Mayo, and I'll still get my reward. Mayo called 4-1-1.

TEN

THE LOCKED ROOM WAS not a torture chamber. Nor a den of child pornography. It was a home office. Beyond anticlimactic.

Thom had hoped for some big-ass clue pointing them in a solid direction. Instead he found a flat screen set on a mainstream news channel and a desktop computer with bookmarked cooking and craft websites. Two over-filled shelves of books were devoted to child rearing. Thom browsed the topics. Discipline, psychology, family health, drug abuse, sex education, spiritual philosophies. The books were bursting with Post-it page markers. It was apparent that Dominic and Rachel Lawrence took their roles as foster parents seriously.

A locked file drawer caught Thom's interest. He searched the office until he found the key inside a box of paper clips. The drawer was devoted to folders for every girl. They were in descending order. Amy and Amber's file up front. The Lawrence's didn't foster just any kids. They fostered at-risk kids. On the inside flap of each folder was a photo of the child and a ten set. Inside were psychological reports, compilations of troubled histories, observations made by child care professionals, logs of doctor's visits. Most importantly, detailed reportage written by Dominic or Rachel logging the daily care and schedule of the children. And the cost. Each file had an accounting of every penny spent.

Thom scanned the files for indications of troubled or mentally unstable kids. There were difficulties, but nothing out of the ordinary considering the demographic. He reached the end of the files before realizing that Jelena's wasn't there. He went through the files again thinking it had been misfiled.

Still no Jelena.

George stuck his head into the office, fresh from examining the rest of the house and eyeing the bodies. Thom noted the shell shock still on his face. It took a while to wipe away the image of death that seemed to etch itself onto the observer. Longtime homicide detectives seemed to wear it permanently, giving them a tough veneer. George had yet to grow his.

"A retreat from the mundane," said George.

"Not really," said Thom. "This is a work room." He handed George the twin's folder. "Each kid has one. A complete history. Amy and Amber were born in Cleveland, Ohio. Their parents came over from China on a tourist visa. Stayed long enough to give birth to the kids and knew enough English to ask for social security cards. A few weeks later they abandoned the babies at a fire station, their birth records and other documentation attached to their swaddling blankets. Then they returned to China and disappeared."

George shook his head in disgust.

"What does Lena's say?" he said.

"*Jelena's* file is missing."

"A big clue."

"Indeed. Could she have done it?"

"She made it clear she didn't like the twins. I've upgraded her to a person of interest. I inspected her car, then kicked her loose. It was squeaky clean. No murder implements. No visible evidence of you there."

"I'm pretty good at picking up my trash."

"You might be her alibi once TOD is established. Do you know what time you left her?"

Thom pinched his temples. "I've no idea. I don't even remember driving to Bird's. The good news is that she has an upgraded security system. The key log would've recorded when I arrived. We'll call her later. But I can't think about that now. Did you notice the decimated princess pillow? Five shots, close range. Foam everywhere. All that splatter."

"Serology lit up the hallway," said George. "Blood drops lead from the kids' room into the master. No doubt, they were killed first. Perhaps they were the target?"

"That'd mean the bloody mirror and Dominic's dick is window dressing. Maybe to throw us off. Too early to say. What we know for sure is that this homicide was committed by an organized killer."

"They're the hardest to catch."

"Usually. But this one wants attention. It's how we're going to get his sorry ass. Did you inspect the garages?"

"Yeah. The one on the far left is an enclosed one-car used for storage. Bicycles. Kid toys. Clothing boxed by size. The other two doors

51

open into an oversized two-car. A Toyota sedan had Dominic's swipe ID in the passenger seat. I bagged it. A minivan had the usual stuff you'd expect to find when one ferries kids around. Snacks, books, games, bottles of water, like that."

"Find a briefcase or a laptop?"

"No."

Thom held up the end of a cord with an adapter on the end. "Here's the power for a laptop. Maybe Dominic left it and the briefcase at the office for the weekend."

"Yeah, with Jelena's missing file."

"Like we ever get that lucky."

Crime scene tech, Spenser, stepped inside the office. "I have something to show you." He held up a succession of clear evidence envelopes with strands of hair. "Got these off the hardwood. Medium, straight, black—Amy and Amber. Long, auburn, wavy—Rachel. Short, ash—Dominic. Long, straight, blond—probably the PR's. Of course these are preliminary findings. I'll get exemplars after the CI arrives."

"I'm not feeling hopeful on finding evidence of our murder suspect," said George.

"This will cheer you up," said Spenser, grinning at him like a proud puppy. He held up a piece of foil that had vague etched lines in a random pattern. "A footprint."

"That the hydro-stat image?" said Thom. "Looks like crumpled paper."

"Close. It's fabric from cloth booties. Like the ones we're wearing."

"A clean executioner," said George.

"Yes, but he left us a tell. Here, in the middle, the pattern is denser. It indicates more weight. More pressure."

"Meaning?" said George.

"The killer wore shoes that were too big," said Thom.

"Right-o," said Spenser. "Your killer thought he was being clever."

ELEVEN

BIRDIE SHUT HERSELF INTO the Manor's time-out room. Outfitted with a porthole window, it allowed the offender to look down at the backyard pool to witness the fun being missed by bad behavior. The room was tiny—about the size of a public bathroom stall—and bare except for a box of tissues on the floor. As the kids grew, the time-out room morphed into a place to make out or talk on the phone without the threat of eavesdropping ears. Right now, it served as Birdie's retreat. A private place where she could snatch a moment to ease her anxiety.

A weepy gloom had settled over her. Drying out hadn't come easy. Every day a struggle. Yes, a year sober is a milestone worth acknowledgment. But the celebration downstairs where her family toasted her success with champagne was over the top.

Birdie couldn't fault them for needing an excuse to party. Life for the Keanes had become hard since Gerard's death. The pall of grief and disbelief hung heavy over the family. And it was going to get worse. Once today's installment of the newspaper article made its rounds there'd be unwanted attention—to what degree and end yet to be determined. Only one thing was certain. On Tuesday, her cousin, Arthur, would finally be exonerated from suspicion. Sixteen years past due. But even he wasn't happy. The cost to the family was too high and he was used to shouldering the responsibility.

Stress squeezed Birdie's neck. She had to figure out a way to tell Thom about his wife, Anne. But that could wait. Right now she focused on the news Anne had shared about a city attorney named Lawrence who had been murdered. She knew a Dominic Lawrence and wondered if he was Thom's victim. She hoped not. The Lawrence she knew was one of the good guys.

Years ago she was desperate to get help for a parentless kid named Huck who called the L.A. River home. Birdie wrote an article about him and people came forward wanting to provide a home. But it wasn't that easy. Huck felt comfortable on the streets. A bedroom of his own confined his sense of safety and he began acting out. Enter white-knight Lawrence. He had the knowledge to recognize Huck's special needs and the resources to get him the right kind of care.

Birdie sat on her hands. A year sober and they still shook from withdrawals. Cravings. Nerves. Right now they were shaking because she was on edge, a current-state normal caused by downtime, which gave her an opportunity to think. Not a good thing. Too much time allowed her to dwell on the one aspect of her life where she had no control: Matt Whelan—missing in the larger world.

In her struggle to find a solution to a very unwanted problem, she pursued what she could control: exercise, food, work, and research. The problem was that Birdie had an addictive personality. No debate. She knew she headed deeper into the rabbit hole of hyperactivity and dependency. She could not sit still. Reflect. Pray. Meditate. The constant busywork was like a narcotic. Obsessive. Bad for well-being. Bad for the soul. She desperately needed to find balance. She was a smart, young woman. So why had the simple parts of life become so hard?

Impatient as always, Birdie called Thom to ask about Lawrence.

"Hey," he answered, "I'm at a scene."

"Was it Dominic?"

"Yeah. I'm going to put you on hold. Change locations."

Birdie deflated with sadness.

Thom came back on speaker. "George is here. We can speak freely."

"Hi, George."

"Hi, Birdie. Congratulations on a year of sobriety."

"Thanks."

"Do you know something about Lawrence?" said Thom.

"I knew what kind of work he did. It'd give you a head start on background."

"Go," said Thom.

"He's a staff lawyer in the city attorney's civil division."

"He work cases?"

"The city office does prosecute misdemeanor crimes and defends the city against lawsuits, but Lawrence worked in the municipal counsel branch."

"What exactly is that?"

"Think of it as general counsel to city departments. Lawrence specifically worked with the city council and the housing authority."

"How do you know him?"

"Through his advocacy for at-risk kids. He and his wife were fostering kids for decades."

"We've seen files on the kids. Have you met any?"

"One. A Russian girl named Jelena. A clerk in the office. He introduced her as one of his girls. At the time, I was focused on getting assistance for a homeless boy, but later I profiled her and Dominic for a Column One feature. I'll retrieve it from archives and shoot you a copy."

"Thanks, but we'll do it from our end."

Birdie paused. Thom had never turned down help before. "What's going on?"

"It's complicated," said George.

"What were your impressions of her?" said Thom.

"I'm not sure if Dominic wanted to keep an eye on her or if he was extremely proud."

"Explain."

"First you have to understand that Dominic and his wife ran a kind of halfway house that served as a transition between the orphanage and a permanent foster family. Most kids stayed with them about a year while they learned to trust. Learn boundaries. Assimilate into family life. But Jelena was a hard case. Very angry. Kleptomaniac. She'd been with them for years."

"Do you think she was capable of killing?"

Ah, now she understood. The girl was a suspect. Birdie must be careful with her response. She didn't want to prejudice the process. "My impression of Dominic was that he had savvy instincts. If he thought one of his kids were capable of extreme violence, I'd wager that he'd get rid of them, hard case or not."

"Work-wise who'd want him dead?"

"No one I can think of since he doesn't deal directly with the criminally minded."

"Do you know why he fostered only girls?"

"Oh, boy. Well … he didn't impress me like a creep, if that's what you're thinking. I think you'll find the answer is a simple one. Like streamlining. Making things easy by staying with one gender. You know, you wouldn't have to change out decorating themes. Clothes could be handed down. Besides, girls are easier."

Thom laughed. "Trust me, girls are harder."

"That's because you have twins," said Birdie. "Rose and Nora were born a team. Two for one. There's built-in comfort and camaraderie which make them natural conspirators."

"You have a gift of putting things into perspective."

Birdie wished that were true in her own life. It was easier to aim an eye outward.

"Did Dominic suffer?" she said.

"No. He was executed in his sleep. So were his wife and twin girls."

"What kind of sicko would kill sleeping children?"

"The worst kind," said Thom.

"Hey, Birdie," interjected George, "Can you tell us when Thom got to your house this morning?"

"Sure, but I have to be in my office. Is it relevant to your investigation?"

"Unfortunately."

"In that case I'll print a hard copy and burn a disc."

"Thanks," said Thom. "And for the insights. But we've got to go now."

Birdie got a sense that she'd helped; this made her happy. And now time-out needed to end before her overprotective boyfriend, Ron, put out a BOLO.

TWELVE

Thom lit a cigarette and inhaled.

The sun reflected badly off the cloud deck and cast a slate glare over the Southland. May Gray. Marine layer. Onshore flow. Whatever Angelenos called it; a dip in the Western jet stream scooped up Pacific moisture and slammed it into the warm air of the mainland. It was so heavy today that Thom thought it was probably drizzling at the coast. The weather pattern was common for spring and early summer in Southern California. Yet, despite the haze, downtown lived up to its responsibility and rose like a sentinel from the colorless view.

Thom liked this weather; the low cloud cover kept the TV helos grounded and prevented them from filming his crime scene. He passed the cigarette to George.

It was silent up on the hill looking over the vast density of the city. No sound of humanity. No freeway. No birds or insects. Not even a breeze to rustle the eucalyptus.

Life on pause.

They passed the cigarette between them, soaking up the absolute quiet. They should've been talking about the case, comparing notes, evaluating the information Birdie had shared, but Thom was in his own head trying to avoid the cognitive bias that is a human predilection to see what it expects to see.

He worked the collection part of every crime scene internally. Inputted all the pieces and parts, then organized and sorted. It took several scenes together before George figured out how to work within the confines of Thom's strategic tic.

Crime scene tech, Spenser, joined them out on the crabgrass with his own cigarette in hand. "That is so swish," he said. "Two dudes sharing a cigarette like chicks."

Thom felt the silence-breaking intrusion at the base of his skull. "We also share chewing gum," he said with an irascible scowl.

"And bodily fluids," added George.

Spenser's jaw dropped.

"Jealous?" prodded Thom.

Confusion passed behind Spenser's eyes as they flicked from Thom to George and back again trying to get a read. Spenser was openly gay and it was no secret that he had a sweet spot for George. But no one knew for certain which way George swung. Thom saw the uncertainty in Spenser's eyes as they finally settled on George. Spenser allowed a small smile to eke out and murmured, "Maybe" before making a hasty retreat back to the house.

Thom grinned. "I do believe he hit on you."

"Only took him a year to work up the nerve," said George.

"We shouldn't tease the poor schmuck."

"Don't spoil my fun."

They chuckled as they walked toward the house to finish processing the home office. Thom dropped the cigarette butt into the coffee cup on the planter next to the folded newspaper. Someone had written the words Police Fags on the side.

———

Spenser ducked into the Lawrence office and said directly to Thom, "Press just landed."

"They'll have to get by with external shots and speculation."

"They already know that Dominic Lawrence and his family were murdered."

"There's no word from the detective in charge. They can contact Media Relations."

"Roger that," said Spenser as he left the room, his gaze avoiding George.

"What am I? Chopped liver all of a sudden?"

"He's probably embarrassed," said Thom. "The press will go nuts over shots of four body bags coming out. Especially the miniatures. See what you can do about setting up a screen."

Just then someone yelled, "Coroner's here."

Thom flicked his wrist toward George.

"Yay," said George. "Dinner with Birdie's buffed-out, former Marine, Deputy Detective boyfriend. Lucky you."

"Look at the bright side. Food gives me energy. Rest gives me stamina. Requirements for a thorough investigation."

"What does booze give you?"

"The ability to deal with it all."

THIRTEEN

THOM PASSED BIRDIE'S SECOND floor office. The drawn tapestry curtain meant one thing. Privacy please. As he rounded the corner into the kitchen, a black pug ran full out toward him, nails scratching the tile. She skidded to an abrupt stop and performed a doggie dance of excited circles.

"Hey, Louise," said Thom. "Nice to see you, too." He knelt to rub her head. "Come on, girl, give me a kiss." Louise licked his face.

Ron, dishtowel over his shoulder, greeted Thom with a hug—a quick chest bump and a slap on the back. "Thomas, my friend, I hope you're hungry."

"Starving. Been working all day on cold caffeine and nicotine."

"Dinner's tardy. I can offer an appetizer." Ron uncapped a bottle of Booker's bourbon and poured three fingers into a Waterford lowball, pressed it into Thom's palm.

Thom took a big pull. "Good shit, man, thanks."

"Anytime," said Ron. "Louise has a new trick. Interested?"

"Hell, yeah."

"LOUISE, roll over."

The dog lay on her back, feet in the air.

"LOUISE, play dead."

She opened her mouth and hung out her tongue.

Thom guffawed. Endorphins warmed his belly, cleared his head. He enjoyed the feeling.

Ron's satisfied grin was quickly erased. "Birdie wants to see you before dinner."

"Sounds serious."

"Sorry, man."

Yeah, Thom had a feeling. He was thankful for Birdie's help today, but he wasn't keen to discuss the Lawrence case. He wanted a good meal and a full night's sleep. As he noiselessly parted the tapestry and entered Birdie's office, he noted how the computer monitor held her intense interest. It lit her complexion with a bluish glow. When she became aware of Thom's presence she casually and discretely closed a book. A thin thing. Black leather with gilt edges like a fancy journal. Her hand nudged it into an open desk drawer. As she turned to greet Thom her right hand turned off the monitor and the left quietly closed the drawer. It was all so graceful and deliberate. And his first thought was, *what is she hiding*?

She leaned over the desk, kissed him in greeting, and sat back down.

Thom knew that despite the sleeveless cotton sundress, this conversation was going to be business, thus, the desk barrier. He determined to drag her off course.

"Look at you," said Thom, reaching over and pinching a bicep. "Ron is whipping you into great shape."

"In more ways than one."

"Really?" Thom took a seat across from her. "The sex must be good."

A flush moved across her cheeks. "He's got me on a healthier diet. Check out the fridge later."

"So the sex isn't good?"

She looked away—a fleeting moment before giving Thom a brave stare. "There's no sex. Not since the rape."

Thom shouldn't have teased her into revealing a confidence and his stomach clenched at the impropriety. It happened nearly four months ago to the day. Birdie had been kidnapped, bound, drugged, raped, and beat to shit for an entire week. She barely survived.

"You've been tight-lipped. Why now?" he said.

"It's human nature to confront tragedy and move on."

"I hear Father Frank in those words."

Frank was the family's priest, but most especially, Birdie's close friend.

Birdie picked up a pencil, tapped the eraser on the desk. "Yeah, Frank keeps telling me to embrace the experience. Declaration is the first step in a process to regain my power over the intimate terrorism. Like acknowledging I'm powerless over alcohol."

"As if you follow the program."

"You know me. Have to do it on my own terms. But this is me bearing witness. Hello, my name is Birdie Elizabeth Keane. I'm an alcoholic and a crime survivor." She snapped the pencil in half.

Thom glanced away. He couldn't bear to see the damaged woman behind the blue eyes. Birdie had spent her teens and twenties drinking her way through life and loving an unavailable man. She'd never dealt with emotional issues in a cerebral way before going sober. In many respects she was an emotional retard just learning how to deal with life.

"Keep this on the downlow for now," she said, flicking a pencil half off the desk. "I intend to bear my vulnerability on an individual basis. Also, I'd like your help in silencing the topic during family discussions."

"No one has ever spoken of it. That way it didn't happen."

"Our family is great at denial. We'll see how much they can drum up this week. Was there any blowback at work from the article?"

"There wouldn't be at a crime scene." Thom steered her away from work-related topics. "Ron must be a saint if he's sticking around."

"He's the best." She swept her eyes toward the window and the dark beyond. "Going sober was the hardest thing I've ever done. Surrendering to love has been the scariest. But I do love him."

"More than—"

"You know, Thom, we got sidetracked."

Thom respected that she didn't want to talk about Matt Whelan. The only man she ever pined for. The Whelan and Keane clans believed that one day Matt and Birdie would be joined in holy matrimony. That Camelot dream died when Matt overdosed. Another touchy subject no one talked about.

She slid a printout of the key log and a disc across the desk. He had forgotten all about that. No escape now.

"You came in at three-fourteen a.m. Want to talk about it?"

"No."

"Were you with a woman?"

Thom's non-answer was an affirmation.

"The reason I ask … well, there's something in particular we need to talk about."

"I don't want to discuss the Lawrence case." There. He said it outright.

"That's not …" Birdie slowly swiveled her chair. She opened her mouth as if to speak, then snapped it shut.

Thom knew then he was completely wrong. This was something else entirely and he couldn't escape the dread. Might as well get it over with.

"What?" said Thom. "Spit it out."

"When was the last time you saw your wife?"

"Yesterday."

"The last time you *really* saw her?"

"What do you mean?"

"I think you should follow my example and stop denying there's a problem. You screw around. Do you think Anne does as well?"

"Hell, no."

"Why not?"

Simple. There was no consortium in their marriage. Not by choice. Anne didn't desire sex and refused to perform for Thom's sake or for the marriage. It was legitimate grounds for annulment, but Thom'd never.

He hiked his shoulders.

"How many times has Anne asked you to leave?" Birdie said. "I bet you've lost count."

"You don't know the dynamic of my relationship."

"Continuing to separate and getting back together is a symptom of a broken marriage."

"All this time I thought you had a degree in journalism, not psychology."

"Ha-ha. Have you noticed that Anne's lost weight? Her clothes less conservative?"

"Her weight fluctuates."

"She's wearing a new shade of lipstick."

"Fashion in lip color changes."

"Today she wore a pair of pricey designer sandals that high-lighted a pedicure. Thom, I've never seen her toes on Sunday."

"Open-toed shoes are not a sin. Not even at the Tridentine Mass we attend."

Birdie sighed. "After Mass she and Karen were huddled closer than usual. I noticed that Anne kept fingering a new necklace. A silver chain with a small coin pearl that nestled in the hollow of her throat."

"So she bought a new necklace."

"Anne has turned into a butterfly."

"My wife is a butterfly every day."

"Thom, she was glowing."

"So?"

Birdie slapped her hands on the desk. "You are such a *guy* when it comes to the opposite sex. For Christsake, she's having an affair."

Thom froze like he'd just been hit by an iceberg. The world slowed. He saw Birdie's mouth move and form words he couldn't hear. They floated in whispers and slowly gathered together like molecules. Then they slammed into Thom's forehead with such a realizing force that his head snapped back.

"Not true!" tumbled out of his mouth in an eight-year-old whine.

"I love you, Thom. But you need to get your head out of your ass and take control of your personal life."

"Like you have?" Thom sniggered.

"At least I'm working on it."

"I appreciate your concern. Trust me, Anne is not having an affair." How could she? She hated sex.

Stalemate. Neither side would budge from their view. Thom hit the bourbon. Birdie played with silver balls of used chewing gum. Finally, Birdie pressed a button on the phone. A dial tone echoed.

"I get it. You're a detective. You need evidence." She held a finger to her lips and punched a number.

"Who you calling?" he whispered.

"Roger Wilcox. Shush."

Roger lived across the street from Birdie in the Tudor revival. His roses consistently won blue ribbons at the county fair. More importantly, his wife, Karen, had been Anne's best friend since they were in diapers.

"Hello," said a froggy voice.

"Hi, Roger, it's Birdie. Sorry for the speakerphone. You know me, multitasking as usual." Birdie flicked her fingertips across the computer keyboard. "I'm calling to see how you liked Buddakan last night."

"What?"

"I thought the food was atrocious. Totally didn't live up to the hype. How was your experience?"

"I didn't go there."

"Roger, I saw you and Karen."

"No. Karen and I were home all night. I'm fighting a cold."

"Oh, my mistake. Sorry for bothering you. Feel better soon."

"Don't worry none. See you later."

Birdie disconnected and said, "Who covers for you?"

"My best friend," said Thom, with a scratch in his voice.

"Like I said, Karen and Anne were huddling after Mass. At brunch I asked Anne what was going on. She told me they had a fabulous time at that new restaurant, Buddakan. She told me in detail what wine they drank and what food they ate."

Thom shrank in the chair, hit the booze. Unbelievability squeezed his brain. There had to be another explanation. Like a business dinner. Anne was co-owner of a very successful business. A working professional. She had luncheons and dinners with associates, men and women alike. But on a Saturday night? Date night? And why would she need to enlist Karen to confirm a cover story if she were conducting legitimate business? It made no sense.

"Thom," said Birdie. "I'd never hurt you with news like this if I weren't certain."

"I'll hire a private investigator. To prove she's not."

"Good idea. But Anne can smell a retired cop a mile away. If you want to be assured of privacy you can't use local guys. The family is too connected."

"What do you suggest?"

"Ask Ron. He'll have out-of-town resources."

"He knows your suspicions?"

"Why do you think he gave you such a large pour of his bourbon?" She leaned over the desk, waved her hand over Thom's glass and inhaled. Then coughed. "Yikes. One-twenty-five proof, bottled straight from the barrel, unfiltered." She waved again. "Oak with a hint of tobacco." She winked. "Just because I'm an alkie doesn't mean I can't enjoy distilled beverages."

"Be careful, cousin."

"I know. Alcohol is always seeking ways to seduce me. It's the lover I constantly yearn for." She shook it off. "Anyway, Ron will be discreet. Once you know what you're dealing with, you'll have the tools to get her back."

Thom was less certain.

He didn't want to admit that this had been coming for a long while.

FOURTEEN

Monday, May 14

THOM JERKED AWAKE, EARS ringing, body drenched. The image of delicate little girls spooned in death inserted themselves into Thom's dream—burned in like a television image with a bloody scroll across the bottom ... dead fish ... dead fish ... dead fish.

He dreamt that he was in the Work and Home Building. Set for implosion any second. Jelena was there, too. She danced naked with a princess pillow and a gun. Thom felt trapped. Knew that he'd be destroyed. And then the girls. Always the girls.

1:30 a.m. Thom stared at a ray of light that cast a thin opaline stripe on the wall. Still there thirty minutes later. Thom desperately needed to rest. A few hours would be enough to recharge the battery if he could just change the channel.

Thom threw off the sheet in defeat and got up. All the chandeliers in the hallway were fully lit. At the far end of the hall Louise lay curled atop a doggie bed in front of Birdie's closed bedroom door. A paw covered her eyes. Even animals need dark, he thought. He turned off the switches. The only remaining light came from the backlit Jesus in the Garden of Gethsemane.

He shuffled down the marble service stairs to the kitchen and opened the refrigerator. Birdie wasn't kidding when she told him to check it out. Black containers with pre-made meals were stacked three deep. He pulled one out and read the label. Monday breakfast. They were even stacked in order. Ron's version of helping her with a balanced diet or a way to control what she ate? Thom rooted around. Yogurt, cheese, grilled chicken, brown rice, apples, soup … there was plenty of non-designated food, but he wasn't in the mood for healthy. A stoner package from Taco Bell would taste good.

Thom exited the kitchen through the back door and went down another flight of stairs to the lanai. He grabbed an ashtray off the bar, lit a cigarette, and reclined on a couch.

He concentrated on the silence. The cool night air. The comfortable glow of a glass lamp. He closed his eyes and imagined the summer bloom of lotus flowers in Echo Park Lake. The image always came to him, like a much-touched photograph. Fan-shaped leaves floated atop the water and the delicate pink flowers reached toward the sun on top of thin green stems. It was his calm zone.

Heavy eyes fell shut. Mumbled voices, far away, inserted themselves into a smoky image of Anne on a dragon boat in the middle of the lake. They disturbed his peace. A yell broke through and Thom's eyes popped open. The voices hovered high above him. It took a few beats before Thom locked on. From Birdie's bedroom a night breeze carried an urgent argument.

"He's lost," said Ron.

"Exactly my point," said Birdie. "When something's lost, you look for it."

"You put us at risk."

"No one will know."

"I can't support this!"

"You don't have to. Furthermore, you can't stop me."

"Just watch."

The air shifted and Thom lost the words. After a drawn-out silence he heard Ron's iron lung become a menacing growl so low and deep it commanded attention. Thom had heard it after Birdie's kidnapping when Ron wanted to tear the city down, brick by brick, stucco wall by stucco wall. But that wasn't the Marine way. The smart way. So he channeled the rage, squeezed it back into his throat and held it there by the strong set of his jaw.

"It matters to me," said Birdie.

Growl.

"I need the closure."

Growl.

"He's not dead! Why can't you understand how this makes me feel?"

Growl, growl.

And then a slamming door.

Something sharp bit Thom's finger. "Shit," he hissed, flicking the cigarette butt into the ashtray. He jumped up and brushed ash from the couch fabric.

The burnt skin was nothing compared to the curiosity amped up by three words. *He's not dead.* There were two people Birdie loved who died recently. Matt Whelan and her father, Gerard. Both were unequivocally dead. The dead person must be a common acquaintance, which seemed unlikely since Ron and Birdie only met each other after Matt died in January. So what did Ron mean when he said she'd put them all at risk?

"Fall asleep with a cigarette in your hand?"

Thom twirled around. Ron stood there in tighty-whities, arms crossed over his chest, a sleepy, ever-faithful Louise at his heels. Thom wasn't easily intimated by men, but this guy was an impressive XY specimen. Straight and hard like a shotgun with attitude to match— safe and secure like a broke-open barrel or deadly reckon with a trigger squeeze.

"What are you doing up?" said Thom.

"Can't sleep."

"Must be contagious."

Thom sucked at the burn. Decided to conceal what he heard. "I came down because I couldn't sleep and then I actually fell asleep with a friggin' lit cigarette. What a bright shitty day."

"I have a cure. Come on."

Thom followed Ron and Louise to the gym that had once been a carriage house. He squinted when Ron flipped the switch that illuminated the warehouse-sized bulbs encased in bottomless bird cages. The gym was a masterpiece of old and new. Brick walls, hardwood floors, French doors, and the gleaming, modern exercise equipment offset by ornately framed mirrors.

Thom had seen Ron shirtless before. Seen the tattoos. A Saker falcon in flight covered the entirety of Ron's upper back. It was frighteningly realistic. On his right bicep a coiled serpent with gold and red scales had one green eye open, one closed. *Semper Fidelis* and *Semper Paratus,* curved around the serpent. In this light, the tattoos seemed to spark awake. Unlike Louise, who jumped into a basket of dirty towels. She rolled around in the damp filth, then curled up and covered her eyes.

Ron retrieved two sets of training gloves from a wicker basket next to the punching bag. He tossed a pair at Thom. "Not my thing," said Thom, tossing them back.

"Suit yourself. I'll punch and we'll talk."

While Ron warmed his muscles with basic calisthenics, Thom took a closer look at the new tat on Ron's chest. A blue bird over his heart.

"*Sialia Mexicana*," said Ron, "most commonly known as the Western Bluebird."

"I'm sure Bird appreciates the testament of your love."

"She doesn't doubt my feelings." Ron hit the bag. "With or without the art."

A large photograph of Matt was attached to the bag with clear packing tape.

"What the hell?" said Thom. "Bird wouldn't appreciate that."

"She's the one who put it there," Ron said with a sneer. He hit the face again and again.

"So it's okay for you to disrespect his memory like that?"

"Like what? Birdie comes down here and beats the shit out of him all the time."

"Why?"

"She's pissed that he died."

"It wasn't his fault."

"He was careless with his meds. How is that not his fault?"

Thom caught a twitch of hate on Ron's face while he jumped and swayed and punched.

"You know," said Ron, "Birdie has a powerful talent of observation. I'd trust what she says about your wife."

Abrupt change of topic, thought Thom. Even Ron didn't want to talk about Matt.

"I don't want to think about Anne in that way," said Thom.

"Who would? We dudes always get screwed. Even if we have all the right moves, do all the right stuff, sometimes it's still not enough. I sure as hell can't understand women." Ron punched left, right, right, left. He hit Matt's face so hard the hang chain shuddered. "Love is a bulky emotion. Relationships are easier without the entanglement."

"And far less satisfying."

Ron stopped short. He pointed a black-clad fist at Thom. "Good point." Then he turned his attention back to the bag.

Thom felt silly standing there watching Ron in his underwear working out an obvious frustration. Thom considered getting on the treadmill then remembered he was in pajama bottoms and a t-shirt. He decided it'd be too much work to put on the proper attire. Like shoes.

"What did you think of Anne?"

"Your wife is smokin' hot."

"Exactly what I need to hear. Bird said you have out-of-town resources if I want an investigator."

"One resource. The best. Private investigation is part-time stuff and he doesn't do domestics anymore, but he will with a referral from me."

"What's his name?"

"Noa. Big Hawaiian dude. A one-man combat force. Don't piss him off."

"A Marine buddy?"

"Yep. Saved his ass many a time."

"You trust him?"

Ron threw a faceful of mock disdain.

"How would I reach him? You know, for a consultation."

"He doesn't do consults. He's referral only. And he has strict rules. When you call, you'll get a recording that says, 'Just the facts.' You're going to tell him your full legal name and that you were referred by me. After that you'll leave the following information: the reason you want to hire him, Anne's full legal name and maiden name, birth date, driver's license number, social security number, home address, the type of car she drives and its plate number, and the places she frequents the most. And then you're going to give him the same information about yourself. And because you're a cop, you also give him your badge number."

Ron's breath remained slow and even despite the bag work and the detailed instructions.

"You'll feel violated by the time you're done," said Ron. "After he gets all the facts, he'll do a prelim to decide if he'll take your case. That will cost twenty-two hundred up front. He'll call you with payment details. Afterward, he'll call again and deliver his verdict and business terms. They are nonnegotiable."

"Sounds like you've been a customer."

Ron delivered one last round of explosive punches then stopped to regard Thom. "Yeah, I've used him before." He shut down further inquiries with a steely glare.

"It's drastic," Thom said. "And so freakin' invasive. Maybe I should just ask her."

Ron trapped a wrist strap in his teeth and pulled it free. Took off the gloves and flexed his fingers. "You think she'd tell you the truth?

Affairs are selfish." He threw the gloves into the basket. "Look, Thom, it's a bad business to consider hiring someone for spy work. But what if it's true? What if the lover is some nut case? You have five children. Is it worth the ten or twenty grand to protect your family?"

"Wait," Thom coughed. "Ten or twenty grand?"

"The best is the most expensive."

"I can't believe I'm actually considering this."

Ron shrugged. "Money can buy you peace of mind."

"Or destroy your world."

"He's fast and has special resources."

"What's his fulltime job?"

"He works for a government agency that requires God-like security clearance. Beyond that, I don't need to know."

"He's discreet?"

"Confidentiality is rule *numero uno*. I provide the referral. What you guys do beyond that is your business."

Thom thought about all the moral hazards that could be discovered during an investigation. Deep in the brain where denial resides he knew this wasn't just about Anne. What would this Noa guy find out about Thom himself? There was serious shit to consider. But Thom felt jagged, his pride spent long ago. He *had* to know. And this was a safe—albeit expensive—way of finding out.

Thom couldn't believe what he heard himself saying. "Okay. Give me his number."

FIFTEEN

A CURRENT OF DISCOMFORT pulsed through Birdie. She hated fighting with Ron. It always left her with agonizing self-doubt and twittering hands. She felt whittled afterward. Like the words carved a bit more flesh. She threw a cotton-covered pillow against the door he'd slammed a few moments ago.

Ron'd probably go downstairs and work off the stress with some crazy Marine-stud calisthenics. Maybe he'd punch the bag with Matt's face on it and get some satisfaction considering he was the only topic they ever fought about. It'd be hours before Ron would return to her bedroom. If at all. He might just spark out in the spare room across the hall. Last time they fought—about a month ago—he didn't return her calls for two days. At the time, she thought him immature.

Truth be told, she understood, couldn't blame him.

Birdie thought she had learned her lesson after the Big Kahuna fight a month ago. She flinched with the remembrance when—in the effort of good-girlfriend behavior, that open, get-it-all-out-there honesty—she told Ron that she was compiling data and running computer searches. Gathering intel in her quest to find Matt.

Ron's response was swift.

He got quiet.

Ron's quiet expelled out into the air in wavelengths of rage like a dangerous animal. Crouched, watchful, ready to pounce with deadly results.

Ron and Matt had been great friends once. The like of which gave Ron leave to willingly help his friend fake his own death. Not an illegal act of itself. It only became a felony when Ron—in his role as sheriff deputy—knowingly filed a false death-investigation report. Matt committed fraud when he started the process to obtain new identification documents. Birdie committed fraud when she collected Matt's estate and life insurance as his beneficiary. There were others equally guilty of punishable offenses. All subject to prison time. The consequences of a lone decision made by Matt were far reaching and damaging.

This was the crux of the issue. Birdie wanted to know why he was so selfish and put to risk those he professed to love the most. Matt was a man who organized every decision with exacting detail. So why did he leave her hanging with the multitude of unanswered questions? Did he know why Gerard got involved with Soto and his gang of blue brothers? She'd like the answer to that one. Since Soto excelled at extortion and blackmail, she wondered what he had on her father. Matt likely knew that answer, too. Mostly, she wanted to know why he left her breadcrumbs. He knew she'd do what she did. He knew that she knew he was alive and at-large in the world.

Birdie agreed with Ron in regards to the off-limit topic of Matt. He wanted to protect his ass. And Birdie's ass. And the other's, too. He thought that Birdie's search put them all in jeopardy of being found out. And he was right. Birdie knew this. So after discovering the truth about Matt back in February she should've just shut her mouth and never uttered Matt's name again. She should've gone about the business of finding him in secrecy. But she didn't. And now it hung over their heads. Always there. And what really tanned her hide is that she was certain Matt had been in contact with Frank *and* Ron.

"I feel left out," Birdie whispered to herself. "Why do you continually exclude me, Matt? Why am I not worthy of your surreptitious phone calls? I'm the one who needs the explanations, the closure."

To free himself from the threat of Matt, Ron had admitted that some secrets were destructive forces. That's why he confessed his role in Matt's death. Birdie reflected on this concept. Put her feet up on the headboard. Their relationship was young and unstable. What if Birdie had discovered the truth years from now when the relationship was entrenched? Built upon a lie? Ron took a risk by giving Birdie that information preemptively. His vanguard was the kind of maneuver military men were used to making. Ron put a lot on the line for her. In this instance the telling paid off.

She popped off the bed. She was doing the same thing. The whole purpose of trying to find Matt was to confront him. She wouldn't be able to conceal that visit from Ron. Nor should she. What might happen between Birdie and Matt affected Ron. She owed him the courtesy of truthfulness. And not just because she loved him. It'd be the right thing to do. Which was easier said than done in these days of compromised concerns.

Birdie flopped back on the bed in frustration.

Why had she been so careless and stupid?

That damned tablet.

George found it shortly after moving into Matt's Koreatown house. Matt had willed George first rights of sale knowing how much care he would take in maintaining the property. George snapped at the deal. Many of the furnishings included? Oh, yeah. The tablet had seemingly slid between the mattress and wood frame of a daybed. And though somewhat protected, covered in a thin layer of dust.

Long forgot? Or a plant?

It was an older model, off-brand tablet. Dead. Birdie bought a power cable and charged it up only to find the device password protected. She tried a number of passwords Matt might've used. After several failed attempts she cracked it open. Removed the back plate, the battery, and some components to get to the micro SD—a tiny memory card about the size of a thumbnail.

She attached it to an adapter and plugged it into her computer. Up popped the folders: application data, photos, movies, books, notes. She found the settings folder and edited some lines of code to make the device think it no longer had a password. Then she had access to the browsing history … a long list of seemingly random animal videos. So not Matt.

And this was where Birdie made her mistake. She left the tablet in plain sight. When Ron asked her about it she told the truth and a battle began.

It didn't help matters when Birdie told Ron that she didn't think Matt had been the tablet's owner. The photos were of people she never met. The movies weren't his favorites. The books she never heard of. The only thing "Matt like" in the device were maps. Lots of maps. State maps, county maps, city maps, weather maps, and even ocean maps of the Atlantic and Caribbean.

Well, nothing she could do about it now. The damage had been done. The words said, feelings hurt, not easily forgotten.

Birdie crawled into bed and pulled up the covers. As she drifted to sleep she was left with one last thought: she could see Ron's point of view in regard to the Matt issue. Why couldn't he see hers?

SIXTEEN

THOM WAVED HIS KEYCARD at the street entrance reader. The gates protecting the underground parking garage of the Police Administration Building were blast-proof roll-ups that went up and down lightning fast. Thom drove his vintage '75 Ford Mustang coupe—a gift from Anne—through the gate and parked it on the P1 level. The privilege to park here cost a monthly fee—worth the payroll deduction to keep his car safe and close. Somewhere below him he heard maintenance workers keeping the building alive and operational. The PAB never slept.

Thom stopped suddenly on his way to the elevator on the lobby level. He thought of Anne and what Birdie had said, "*For Christsake, she's having an affair.*" Eleven years ago Anne was through with Thom. Fell out of love, she said. Going to seek a divorce. Funny that. She insisted they display the happy façade to the world. Dinners out. Public events. Live in the fancy house. Send the boys to private school. Drive the newest cars.

Then one night of drunken intimacy resulted in pregnancy. The girls. Oops babies. Anne agreed to stay with Thom for appearances and gave him permission to discretely seek sex elsewhere—so long as she or the kids never knew and as long as it didn't affect their household. That was an age ago. Thom had had more than his fair share of women since. But he'd never had an affair by the classic definition. Never fell in love with another. And still, he desired his wife more than any woman.

Thom managed to skip through the last ten years, ignoring the fact that their life was a fraud. Inside his soul, where wishes dwelled, he hoped that one day Anne would forget their outlandish agreement and go back to happily-ever-after.

Instead, Thom got a beat down with one word. Affair.

What did that mean? Sex? Love? Either option devastated Thom's hope.

Birdie was right when she insisted he needed to know for certain and he already set that wheel a'rolling. If it be true? Then what? Murder her lover and rewind to what had been a threadbare relationship?

He knew, for certain, that she'd loved him once. They'd had an intense love affair. Marriage, children, and responsibility was the bucket of water that extinguished the flames. Perhaps it's *that* guy he needed to find. The one she fell in love with. The cocky young stud that fought for and won her attention.

Thom hitched his pants. Felt the strain on his waistband. Mindlessly, he headed for the stairwell. He'd never been up the stairs before.

———

Thom arrived on the fifth floor winded from vertical exertion. He stopped to take a breather. Good thing he didn't have to give chase anymore—all the runners would escape. Once his heart rate returned to normal, he rounded the corner and saw George in the glass-walled kitchenette making them coffee on the pod machine. Thom swiped his keycard and entered.

Once inside the building, the keycard was required for every door except the bathroom. The LAPD big brother/security geeks would know every move Thom made once he swiped the card with its special chip at the parking garage, or when he came through the front door and used it to get through the lobby turnstiles. They tracked all the employees, sworn or civil, and probably created performance reports with pie charts and graphs. Nothing was private. Except a piss. And, hell, they could probably guestimate when he'd taken one by how long it took before he swiped again.

George lifted his chin in greeting. "You okay? You look peaked."

"What does peaked mean exactly?" said Thom.

"Sick. You look sick."

"Just say you look sick. Why use a fancy word?"

"Because fancy guys use fancy words"—in Valley speak—"like, fer-sure, fer-sure, like totally."

Thom turned his back. "God, I hate morning people."

"The proper response would be, barf me out, or gag me with a spoon."

"Sometimes I really hate you."

George followed him out with a cup of coffee in each hand, briefcase strap slung across his torso. They walked the long corridor with the pumpkin-colored interior wall on their right. Out the left wall of glass, well-placed lights illuminated the bone structure of City Hall. She looked like a movie star awaiting her close-up.

The corridor ended at Robbery/Homicide's door.

Thom swiped his keycard and they entered the expansive squad bay. Long rows of high-tech lights hung from the acoustic ceiling on white cords. They snapped to life with the movement. Row after row after row of business gray cubicles sat empty.

The room was invisibly divided into three sections: homicide on the east, robbery on the west, special in the middle—they're the rowdy ones that wore street clothes.

"Freaky," muttered George. "I've never been the first one in before."

"Be here long enough and the novelty wears off."

"It's hot in here."

"Temperature's master controlled. The air won't kick on until daylight."

Thom dropped his briefcase on his desk chair and closed the vertical blinds. Their cubicles were located on the far east side of the squad. Their backs to the "100 building"—Caltrans District 7 HQ— with its four-story high numbers. Thom didn't like his back to the glass. Sniper-proof or not.

———

Thom and George assembled the Lawrence murder book containing what they had so far: various sign-in logs, law enforcement entry map, sketches of the home's layout, preliminary victim(s) background, Thom's entry notes, Field Interview cards, surveillance disc, signed consents, notes on SID's forensic evidence, the CI's body notes, checked evidence reports.

Reynolds had come in with the morning crowd to deliver the crime scene photos and CD. Thom was nearly done labeling the printed matter. He carefully slid them into acid-free sleeves and snapped them into the three-ring binder. George hunched over his computer, buds stuffed in his ears, fingers flying across the keyboard, finishing the transcription of the taped interview of Jelena Shkatova, person reporting, and now, person of interest. They had clerical for that, but that involved paperwork. George was faster.

Thom wrote a thank-you note to Reynolds for the speedy delivery of the photos. A hand delivery deserved card stock and it always made an impression. He'd be remembered—good future-favor status—just as Reynolds would with the fast processing. They both knew the game.

Thom rolled his chair over to George's cubicle and plucked a bud from his ear, tucked it into his own and listened. Jelena's voice—a raw mixture of nicotine and alcohol—gave him much pleasure Saturday night, but made him bristle on this Monday morning.

—*Were you drunk?*

—*No.*

—*Did this man … Thomas, take advantage of you?*

—*No. I ask him for sex. He say ok. We go to my car and have good sex.*

—*Not your apartment?*

—*I ask, but Thomas say no.*

—*Then what?*

—*Thomas leave at two-thirty. I go to apartment for sleep.*

—*Were your roommates home?*

—Not Claudia. Her door is open when I go home, but it is closed when I leave in morning. I share room with Dona. She is sleeping when I go home and sleeping when I leave.

—Can anyone verify your whereabouts from two-thirty until seven this morning?

—I not think so unless Dona wake up during night.

—I'll need to verify with Thomas. How can I reach him?

—I did not get his number. But bartender knows him so I can see him again.

—You had sex with a man you don't know?

—Is it necessary? I talk with him. I like him. He call me 'little Jelena.' I like having sex with him so I will see him again.

Thom removed the bud and flicked it away. He felt sick and disgusted. He nearly sprinted to the bathroom and ran cold water over his wrists. Relax, he told himself, don't hyperventilate. It's not that bad. How could you know she was connected to Lawrence? Who could've predicted that they'd be murdered hours later? The randomness was enormous.

Thing is, when it came to cold-blooded murder Thom didn't believe in random.

He shoved that thought deep down. The water was nice, but he needed a pick-me-up and didn't want to take the time to go outside for a cigarette.

When he returned George said, "Lena has been in the states since she was eight. That's fourteen years. Don't you think a child would've lost their native accent in that amount of time?"

"Eight, huh?" Thom searched through a messy drawer full of pens, Post-it notes, paper clips, and desk junk in search of nicotine gum. "I don't think it's that simple," he said. "She wasn't a native speaker when she moved here. She had to learn to speak English. Grammar, too. But I suppose it depends on the motivation. When Da and Uncle Gerard immigrated they worked hard at learning American English because they wanted to fit in. Maybe Jelena thought her speech pattern made her special. Or maybe she's a slow learner."

Thom finally found the gum and pushed a piece through the foil bubble.

"Something about it bothers me," said George.

"Roll with the gut."

SEVENTEEN

By now the squad had a quiet, library-like buzz as detectives worked their phones and computers. The air was on, too.

Lieutenant Lance Craig breezed in, stopped in front of Thom and George and frowned. After a few beats he said, "War room in ten," then went to his large desk in the corner and picked up the phone.

George whispered, "What the hell did we do?"

Thom shrugged.

Craig was two heads shorter than Thom—the type of short guy that would've worn a leather belt with a big-ass buckle in high school. The kind he could easily whip off and swing when he got jumped. Thom held no doubts that Craig's scrappy upbringing made him the prick he was rumored to be. Personally, Thom had no problems with Craig and seemingly he had no issues with Thom. They got along fine because Thom treated his supervisor with respect. That was the way in his father's house. Show disrespect and get punished. But Thom's relatively easy rapport with Craig was an anomaly in the squad. Craig had a chip on his shoulder that said don't-underestimate-my-shortness-because-I-can-kick-your-ass.

At the eight-minute mark, Craig nodded to Thom and George as he passed their cubbies. They gathered all the Lawrence materials and followed Craig to a war room. It was being used, so they ducked into an interview room for privacy. A glassless room about twelve-by-eight with a table bolted to the floor and three chairs. Small, cramped, and not designed for comfort.

George opened the murder book.

Craig flipped through the front pages and pointed at the disc in a plastic holder. "What's on this?"

"A neighbor's security surveillance with a partial street view," said George. "The resident lives three houses up on the other side of the street from the Lawrence's."

"Relevant?"

"Yes. At oh-four-fifty-seven an arc of light appeared on the right side of the frame. As if a car came up the hill and made a U-turn. The view is limited—doesn't get the vehicle, just the light—but it's a distinctive tell because the CI estimates TOD between oh-four-thirty and oh-six-hundred. It's possible our murder suspect drove up the hill, turned around, and parked on the opposite side of the street, pointing downhill."

"The potential parking area has been examined," added Thom. "That portion of the street is flanked by a hill of ivy. A perfect hiding place for a murder gun. It was exhaustively searched with metal detectors but yielded nothing of interest. No other vehicles came up or down the street until nearly oh-seven-hundred when the camera recorded another set of lights that didn't arc."

"Indicating that whoever drove the vehicle didn't make a U-turn," said Craig.

"Precisely. That squares with the PR's statement of an oh-seven-hundred arrival time. Also, her car was parked uphill when we arrived."

"Thoughts?"

"We don't have enough facts to shake out a theory," said Thom.

"Then why aren't you monkeys shaking trees?"

Thom patted the book. "We organized what we have so far so you can make an informed decision in regards to passing the Lawrence homicide to another team."

"This investigation is not headed toward round three. I made myself clear."

"Yes," said Thom. "But I had sex with their twenty-two-year-old foster daughter the night they were killed. She was the person who discovered the bodies and now she's a person of interest. I must iterate that I'm compromised. Even a rotten defense attorney will smear our case if I'm associated. It might already be too late."

"Did you know her relationship to Lawrence?" said Craig.

"We met at a bar. I had no knowledge of her family and limited personal background. But that doesn't diminish the severity of the matter. If she's involved with their murder we're screwed. If she's not involved we're still screwed. Four people were targeted and their murder was heinous. Justice won't prevail for our victims if at the backend the integrity of the investigation is questionable in any regard."

"You really had to stretch your mouth to get all that out," said Craig.

Thom snapped his mouth shut.

"I get the situation," said Craig. "You don't have to get all high-brow."

"Sorry, LT."

"Why is she a person of interest?"

"During the interview," said George, "she made it clear she didn't like the kids, nor was she sorry they were dead."

"They were killed first," added Thom.

"Did she have opportunity?"

"Maybe," said George. "According to her statement, she and Thom parted ways at oh-two-thirty and she went home. It's to be determined if one of her roommates can place her there."

"Motive?"

"Only whispers," said Thom, pointing at the binder. "There are a lot of angles. Lawrence was a city attorney and that fact alone smells like a hit. But a total blackout? It could be personal. And the message on the mirror is unclear right now."

Craig curled his fist around a coffee tumbler and took a long slug. "Step out, George."

George eyed his partner with a quick swipe of panic.

"It's okay, LT," said Thom, "Say what you need."

Craig ticked his head toward the door.

"Sure. Okay." George squeezed Thom's shoulder as he left the interview room.

Thom's sexual escapades finally bit him in the ass. He expected news of a discipline hearing, or forced counseling, but nothing prepared him for what Lance Craig said next.

"I'm in a fix here, Thom. What I'm about to tell you is off the record. If I get the slightest whiff that you've repeated what I'm about to say, I'll make it my mission to ruin you. Am I clear?"

Thom nodded and braced for the blow.

"Seymour and Morgan drew the case. They were the team on call. It was important to remove S&M before they got too involved. I took them off because I already knew you had been with the girl."

Fury lit Thom's face. He knew what would be next.

Craig ran his finger around the lip of the coffee tumbler to avoid eye contact. "You're the target of an integrity audit."

That he didn't expect. Thom fisted his hands and said nothing. Forced Craig to explain.

"It started when the feds were invited to assist with the Blue Bandits."

The Blue Bandit case was Gerard Keane's mess—Thom's uncle wasn't the mastermind, but he finished it in a big way. At the top were Ralph Soto, a retired commander of Central Bureau, Deputy Chief Theodore Rankin, and Gerard, a captain at Hollywood Station. Along with five other cops, they used the Janko Medical Center as a base of operations to conduct off-duty bad business: extortion, blackmail, high-end drug dealing. They revived the legend of a cop gang called the Blue Bandits to take credit for murders they didn't commit in order to induce fear on the street and keep their cop employees in line.

Due to Birdie's investigation into Matt Whelan's death, she discovered his undercover role and it all came crashing down to a horrific end. Rankin committed suicide, Gerard killed Soto, and the Highway Patrol killed Gerard. Janko's police staff were left to fend for themselves. In part two of Birdie's article coming out tomorrow, it will be revealed that Gerard was also the long-sought-after suspect in the Paige Street murder—a home-invasion burglary turned deadly. For sixteen years, his role remained unknown to the LAPD and the FBI. Instead, suspicion landed on Thom's brother, Arthur, who shouldered the scrutiny for his uncle. It was a shameful legacy to live with and all the Keanes in the department had to deal with the aftermath of suspicion and contempt.

Thom expected a formal 181 complaint: a status quo, run-of-the-mill, internal affairs complaint that went through the Professional Standards Bureau. An investigator would interview the target of the complaint, his co-workers, and anyone else of interest. Once the investigation started there was no way to hide the fact that it was taking place or who filed the complaint. Cops are big gossips. They liked to talk.

But an IA was an entirely different animal.

They were secret. Run by unknown officers out of unknown offices. The Police Protection League had tried for years to rid the department of the practice because there was no defense, no recourse. The verdicts on internal audits never saw the light of day unless charges were filed, leaving him no way to defend himself. If found guilty you were gone. Early retirement. Out on disability. Whatever.

If there had been a 181—so named for the form—Thom could fight off the beef, his reputation could be restored publicly to his peers. If word got out about an audit, the suspicion would solidify into fact—especially since Birdie brought the topic public in the newspaper article. It was going to be a long haul to save his marriage; and now, he'd have to stretch his limits to salvage his job.

"And my family?" said Thom in reference to those on the force.

"I can't speak to that," said Craig.

"Integrity audits usually involve money or drugs planted at a crime scene to catch dirty narco cops. As a homicide detective I rarely come into contact with either."

"That makes an IA a little difficult. You're not checking money or drugs into evidence so we can't determine if your hand's in the till. No, you've been under surveillance."

"To determine if I had a role in Gerard's business?"

"SOP and you know it."

"Why not ask, LT? No one has interviewed me since I testified for the Grand Jury."

"Would you admit guilty knowledge? Don't answer that. Look, there've been rumors about the Teflon coating of your family for a long time—and the close relationship with the Whelans. You're a bunch of slickers."

"I know. They call us the Irish Mob. So what? We're made to suffer for the sins of one?"

"Precisely," said Craig. "The department as well as the feds are pissed that Gerard went undetected for the Paige Street incident for so long. They don't forget shit like that."

"Who's surveilling me?" Thom hoped it'd be the FBI. They don't work in the same building. If it were the feds, his phones would be wired, a tracker on his car, and a crew of two following. That would equal six, twenty-four-hour monitors. A lot of man hours. What really burned Thom was that *they* probably had photographs of him and Jelena in the backseat of her Honda.

"It's so expensive I doubt the bill is being paid by L.A.," said Craig. "You were seen with the girl. Her plate was run, her identity established. Later, when she turned up again and discovered a crime scene it became my job to make the case yours to test your integrity."

"Damn you!"

"Okay, I'm damned. But that doesn't change the fact that you came clean about your intimate relations. You passed."

"You should've known better, LT. I'm the guy who thinks about the endgame."

"True. You're one of my best in that regard. I like you, Thom, this is the only reason we're having this confidential conversation."

"So now what?"

"You and George work the case."

"Seriously? After all this?"

"It's not my call." Craig pointed upward. The command staff offices were upstairs on the tenth floor. "Work it tight and right."

And keep looking over my shoulder, thought Thom.

When Thom stepped back into the squad bay, he detected a perceptual hush. Seymour and Morgan were standing together two rows over, their eyes on Thom. No one other than George and *they* knew about Jelena so something else must have happened.

George said, "We have another—" he quoted his fingers— "'*message* murder.'"

"A serial," said Thom.

"The victim is Jerry Deats of Santa Monica. The SMPD sent a law enforcement bulletin looking for similarities to their murder. I called the DIC. She sent me this." He gestured at the photo on his computer screen. **Dead fish** was scrawled on a bathroom mirror.

"Damnit!" said Thom.

"I told her we'd come by today to take a look."

Thom sped from the squad. Found Craig pacing the corridor, cell to his ear. Thom hung back while Craig finished.

"I just heard," Craig said a few minutes later. "We have a potential serial. The SMPD is willing to let us take the lead."

"This is a perfect opportunity to get out from under the train wreck. We should let them take it."

"We have the resources and manpower."

"Yes, but—"

"We're lead. That means *you*. Get to it."

When Thom returned to his desk, S&M were leaning on George's cubicle looking down at him.

Thom noted the impeccable press job of Seymour's white shirt. Morgan's muscular, squat frame was covered in black on black, with a bolo, and cowboy boots, as per usual. He reminded Thom of a frontier undertaker.

"Ever work a serial before?" said Morgan.

"No. You guys?" said Thom.

"Was on the Grim Sleeper taskforce," said Seymour.

"Your work just amped up exponentially," said Morgan. "Once it goes public the story will be chum in a shark-infested kiddie pool."

"Thanks for the visual," said George.

"Better you than us," added Seymour. "But really, if you need help, let us know."

Seymour passing out assistance? On the day after Birdie's article came out? Perhaps he felt bad about mucking up the investigation of her abduction and this was an attempt at penance.

"I mean it," said Seymour.

Whatever the motivation, the offer was a first and Thom wasn't going to let the opportunity expire. "How 'bout the computer rounds while George and I do the flat foot. And search the newspaper archives?"

"Done," said Seymour.

Morgan registered his unhappiness with a nostril flare and followed his partner back to their cubicles.

George leaned in. "Busy day ahead. We better fuel up." Besides the obvious food reference, fuel was code for 'share' as in 'need information now.'

"You got that right," whispered Thom. "*Huevos Rancheros* at El Tepeyac. We'll take two cars. We're gonna split up afterward. LT won't let us give it back."

"I work Lawrence. You work Deats. We meet in the middle."

"I wish it were that simple."

EIGHTEEN

El Tepeyac Café was on the east side of the Los Angeles River on Evergreen Avenue in patrol area 456 of Hollenbeck Division. In deference to the cops that populated its tables, many of its burritos bore the station's name. Hollenbeck *de Asada*, Hollenbeck *de Machaca*, or the most popular Hollenbeck—pork in chile sauce, rice, beans, and guacamole. Thom maneuvered his city car in the tiny lot and parked between a Lexus and a dingy pickup. El Tepeyac was popular with the high and low.

Thom pulled out his business cell. He liked this phone. It supported a full range of data capabilities. Photos, emails, reports. Information. Priceless for a homicide detective. Thom started carrying two cellphones a year ago. The department didn't reimburse work-related cell phone usage. Thom had tired of divvying up lengthy bills for the tax write-off—same as for his firearm, handcuffs, and other job-related hardware. With dedicated phones he no longer had extra work at tax time.

Thom realized he held the wrong phone. He replaced it with the personal cell and punched his parents' number.

Nora answered with sleep in her voice. "Thom, why are you calling so early?"

"Ah, Ma. Did I wake you?"

"No, I haven't had my coffee yet. You okay?"

"Fine. Sorry I missed brunch yesterday."

"Solving murder is important work. What's up?"

"I'm in the mood for coddle tonight." An authentic Irish casserole of onions, bacon, potatoes, and pork sausage.

Nora took a long, sad breath. "You want soda bread with that?"

"Ballymaloe would be better."

"Okay, son. I'll fix dinner. See you later."

"Thanks, Ma."

Thom had just told his mother to arrange an emergency family meeting at the Manor. Coddle = all hands on deck. Ballymaloe = wire sweep required. Paranoia or good measure? When Arthur was under suspicion for Paige Street, the FBI made no secret of their surveillance. They relished the intrusive nature of monitoring and the invasion of privacy forced upon the entire clan. The family established codes so they could meet and talk freely. No one liked the subterfuge, but they got used to it.

———

Thom leaned against the car and lit an after-meal cigarette. He took a deep pull, then handed it to George.

"I'll take a full one."

Thom wasn't surprised. George had been fidgety and unfocused throughout breakfast. "The IA is really upsetting you." He shook the pack.

George plucked one and fired it up with the tip of Thom's.

"The IA was to be expected," said George, blowing out smoke. "What bothers me more is the FBI surveillance."

"*Alleged.*"

"Whatever. Think I'm at risk?"

"You have something to hide?"

George looked away.

"I'm sure the feds don't care if the person you're sleeping with has a dick."

"What the hell?" groused George.

"Whoa. Gallows humor, man. Why are you so sensitive all of a sudden?"

"It's your crude delivery."

"It wasn't crude yesterday when we gave Spenser a hardon."

George got much worse from some guys in the squad. The most popular prank was a photo of two dudes having sex. George's head would be taped over one of them. Sometimes the top, sometimes the bottom. Occasionally, his face would be with a woman. The ac/dc hazing usually didn't bother him. He played it up like he did with Spenser. As the newest guy, it was George's role to be pizza boy until someone replaced him. So for now, he took it. What mattered was that people actually cared because no one knew for sure. Damn that stint in Vice.

"Hell, I know you're not a catcher," said Thom.

"What if I am?" All serious.

Thom loved George like family. He could care less. One way or the other or both. "Then you stop wearing pink, man."

George hit Thom in the arm. "Gotcha."

"Hell with you," said Thom.

They enjoyed the smoke in silence. After a few minutes Thom said, "Let's go over the game plan."

"Get a signature for Lawrence's office. Briefcase and laptop is priority." A warrant wasn't technically required, but they wouldn't give any future judge a reason to bounce a search in a high-profile homicide. Especially one involving a city attorney with a potential suspect tucked away in a file. Privacy rights and all.

"The judge that signs will probably appoint a Special Master to supervise us."

"Like we need a babysitter," said George.

"What then?"

"I'll interview the roommates. See if any of the girls can substantiate Lena's alibi."

"Don't call the person of interest by her nickname. Too personal and informal. Any misstep can be a disaster."

"I hate when you correct me."

"I've been doing this longer. Hit the bar, too. Hank's. On Grand. Track down the bartender. See what he has to say. What he remembers."

"What's his name?"

"Why should I know?"

"Hold on," said George. "Jelena told me you knew the bartender. She said she could contact you through him."

"I chatted him up. But I've never been to that bar before. Never met him before. I remember he was a young guy. Looked barely legal."

"Lie number one."

"Good enough reason to haul her ass in," said Thom. "Think she'll go anywhere?"

"Don't think so."

"Okay, let it sit for today. Bring her in tomorrow. We've got the cut at one. I expect you there."

Autopsies made George squeamish. They were hard business. The stench of disinfectant, the fluid on the floor, the medieval-like tools, and the general ickyness. As the lead detective, Thom's presence was non-negotiable. He let George off the hook when he could. But not this time. The high-profile situation made his presence necessary.

"George, keep in touch and be careful."

"As always." George flicked the butt and ground it into the pavement until it turned to dust.

NINETEEN

BIRDIE LEANED INTO THE file box on the floor and grabbed the last clipping. She glanced at the headline and tossed it back in. Around her in a semi-circle were three piles of yellowed newsprint: throw away, possibilities, put-back. She scooped up the put-back pile, dropped the articles in the box then shook it to settle them straight.

"Knock, knock," said Ron, entering the office. "I'm back."

Birdie hadn't seen him since their fight last night. He never did return to Birdie's bedroom. At least he left her a note by the coffee maker telling her he was going out on a run. He held a freshly blended green smoothie in one hand and a small china bowl in the other.

"Hey, babe," said Birdie, her tone bright and happy. "How was your run?"

"Long and tiring. I need a shower."

Louise looked up expectantly from her cushion. Ron poured a bit of green stuff into the bowl and set it down. Louise immediately stuck her short muzzle into it.

"Hmm," said Birdie. "Kale, cucumber, tomato. Just what a dog needs."

"Better than meal and byproducts. She knows what's good for her."

Birdie patted the floor.

"I ran twenty miles," protested Ron. "Surely your nose can pick up my stink."

She did smell the musk of exertion—lactic acid—the result of glucose conversion to feed the muscles for anaerobic activity. She also smelled the ocean carried in on the marine layer. Spongy grass. Wood shavings. Tar. Crushed rock. The makings of the earth that is the genetic scent of all men.

"I'm sorry about last night," she said. "I hate arguing with you." She scooted closer and leaned forward, lifting her chin in invitation.

"Me, too." Ron moved the rest of the way in.

Their mouths joined in forgiveness. Birdie ran her fingers across the fleece of his razored hair—always kept at a tidy quarter inch. They moved down his neck and across the hard muscles of his back. The soft down on Birdie's arms raised in suspense. Her nipples tingled. The erotic response took her by surprise—the first since the kidnapping. Just then she saw the promise of passion on the horizon. A future that did include intimacy. Of life slowly improving. Birdie watched Ron's hazel eyes light up in recognition. Felt his grin against her lips.

Their tongues caressed to a silent, sensual rhythm. Birdie tasted vague remnants of coffee and nicotine and … nothing else.

Her mouth broke away. "Kidding me? You ran twenty miles on an empty stomach? What about all the lectures about working out with the proper nutrition? And then you smoked a cigarette?"

Still in a hormonal daze, Ron said, "*Wha*? How do …? Really? *Really*? Are you purposely trying to kill me?"

Birdie's instant laugh filled the room with glee. The last time she laughed so purely was at her birthday party back in January. Before the deaths. Before the kidnapping. Before her dad was gunned down. And before being burdened with the truth. The laugh came from a true and honest place. Like happy fireworks in her belly. More healing than afternoon tea and conversation with Father Frank.

She rolled onto her back and guffawed. "I wish you could've seen your expression." She contorted her face into surprised interruption.

Ron laughed, too.

Of course, Louise wanted in on the action. She jumped up and barked. Ran in circles. Chased her curled tail. Knocked over the licked-clean china bowl.

A shrill beeping stopped Birdie cold.

Coming from the kitchen?

Ron sat up. Alert.

"Are you cooking something?" said Birdie.

"That's my phone. Crap." He hustled up off the floor and disappeared through the office curtain.

A deputy with the San Diego Sheriff's Department, Ron was the only detective in an area that covered nearly fourteen hundred square miles and a rural population of sixty-three hundred. His territory included the cities of Lake Henshaw, Warner Springs, and Borrego Springs. The last of which sat in Anza-Borrego Desert State Park— the largest state park in California and bigger than Delaware.

Being the lone detective meant 24/7 call. Interrupted days off weren't that uncommon. Ron worked Friday, Saturday, and Sunday when weekenders swelled the population. Monday and Tuesday were his "weekend days"—except this week because he drove up on Sunday for Birdie's one-year birthday celebration.

Continuing her project with the newspaper articles, Birdie gathered the throw-away pile and pushed it into the trash can. She picked up a few clippings from the possibility pile and quickly reviewed them for inspiration. She must be quick. Let intuition determine whether to drop it back in the box or set it aside for deeper consideration. Pieces of newsprint flew into the file box. Nothing striking an interest.

Ron returned. A grim expression on his face. He held out the phone. "It's for you."

Birdie knit her brows in confusion and uttered a meek hello into the phone.

"Bird, dear, it's Nora. Don't bother yelling at me. Ron already did. I hated to call his number, but you've not been answering any of your phone, and so, well … I needed to reach you to say I'm making coddle and ballymaloe tonight."

Birdie's eyes flicked to Ron who stared at her expectantly, arms crossed in his *I'm not happy* pose. "Okay. I'll be there," she said, punching off and handing the phone back to Ron. "Sorry about that. I've been avoiding the phones because of the article. Nora wants to have a special family dinner. Emphasis on family. Nothing personal."

"That's okay," said Ron. "I took Sunday off so I should get back to the job tomorrow morning anyway. I'll drop you off at the Manor on my way out of town. Thom can bring you home."

"Great. I'm glad you're not mad."

"But remind Nora that family dinner isn't worthy of activating an emergency."

Birdie held her tongue. Coddle and ballymaloe wasn't just any dinner. Only matters of extreme seriousness warranted a secret meeting of the entire family. Who called it? Aiden had lived on the East Coast for many years. Madi was at the *Festival de Cannes* with her movie star client. Nora was a housewife. That left those local and in law enforcement: Louis, Maggie, Thom, or Arthur.

"Why are you avoiding the phones?" said Ron.

"Major articles bring out the crazies."

"Your lines are unlisted."

"I still have the *Times* phone and email."

"What're you expecting?"

"Trash."

"Want me to sit with you while you listen?"

"No, thanks," said Birdie. "I'll be okay, but I should get to it today."

Birdie heard the soft puff of air pushed from Ron's nose. A tell of displeasure. And rightly so, she thought. Ron didn't drive ninety miles to watch her work. But he'd not say anything because he bore witness to her struggle when faced with the decision to write the article in the first place. And for that she loved him more.

She reassured him. "I'll take care of it while you're in the shower."

Ron seemed pleased with her response, evidenced by a smile. He sat on the floor, feet together and bent forward to stretch his back and hips.

"What's with the clippings?" he said.

"I enjoyed the process of writing again. Of finding my voice. I'm thinking about doing more. These are pieces of interest that I've saved over the years. Some have cycled and will have current relevance. Most don't."

"Don't you have enough work? What about the book coming out in the fall?"

"Finished except for line edits. Those won't take long."

"What about the new one?"

"Finished. I already had the bulk of it written anyway. With the documents Dad left me it practically wrapped itself. The topic is hot so my publisher may flip the two books and release *Darkness Bound* first."

"You said it wasn't done," said Ron, sweeping his fingers through the clippings.

"I said I wasn't happy with the ending. Not as in I have to re-write it, but in that there's no answer to why Dad did what he did."

"What happens if you find out?"

"It gets included in the reprint. Why the sudden interest in my work?"

"I'm always interested," he said with mock hurt.

Ron picked up a clipping at random—a photo of a scruffy man.

"Who's the homeless fat dude?" he said.

Birdie took the crispy piece of newsprint from his hands and her radar pinged. "This guy isn't homeless. He's Todd Moysychyn. One of the richest people in Los Angeles."

"This dude?"

"Don't let the appearance fool you. He's a large property owner. The foulest, scummiest bastard."

"Please, don't hold back. Tell me what you really think."

"Among other shady dealings, he's a slumlord who exploits the poor."

"WOOOOO," said Ron, wiggling his fingers. "Sounds scary."

"He's the worst caliber of human."

"There's an unbiased journalistic statement."

Birdie punched him. "What I write doesn't have to square with my personal opinion."

Ron held up his hands in defeat.

Birdie returned her attention to the image. The cutline had been removed. But that didn't matter. She knew who he was. The kind of dirty business he engaged in. He hadn't been in the news lately. How had he weathered the housing crisis? What had he been up to? She put the photo aside and raked up the rest of the possibility pile and dropped it into the box.

Inspiration found.

"You're wired to the world," said Ron. "I'm surprised you keep clippings. So old school."

"I'm an enigma."

Ron laughed. "There's no truer statement. Just when I think I've figured you out—"

"—I surprise you?"

"Yeah," Ron whispered. "You surprise me." He brushed his lips against hers. Wove his fingers through her hair.

"Time for that shower?" she said.

"A cold one."

Ron had been counseled. Birdie knew he'd wait for her to make the first move. He'd act on his desire only when asked.

She'd also been counseled. A failed attempt at intimacy could set back the progress a couple makes when dealing with the aftereffects of violent crime. She had the discipline to take it slow. Not push it until she was one hundred percent certain she could handle it.

Wet, naked, soaped? Not there yet.

TWENTY

THE SANTA MONICA DETECTIVE in Charge paced the parking lot. File tucked under her arm. Thom had barely unfolded himself from the Crown Vic's seat when she said, "My murder came first. I should take the lead, but the bully on the block called in"—she winked her fingers—"the resources card. I'm not happy."

"Clearly," said Thom, offering his hand. "Thom Keane. LAPD. Our resources are at your disposal."

"Your idea of sarcasm?" she sneered.

"My idea of service." He jiggled his outstretched hand.

They shook. The DIC held out a business card that read Anita Dhillon.

"Nice to meet you, Anita Dillon."

"Pronounced Ah-nee-TA HILL-on. Silent D."

Thom appreciated a lipstick swagger, but he disliked her psyching the position. It was unnecessary and unprofessional. The challenge reminded him why he hated working with other police departments. He let it go for now. He wasn't about to engage in a power skirmish with another homicide detective—especially on her home turf—nor would he reciprocate in an overt manner.

Beyond the alpha attitude, Anita was an attractive woman. Her dark hair had sweepy bangs that teased her brows. She wore a camel suit jacket that wrapped around her waist and closed with a leather buckle. So well-tailored no bulge revealed where she stowed her firearm. He should introduce her to George. Maybe they could shop together. Share designer resources.

Anita gave Thom the file containing a copy of all the investigative paper on the Jerry Deats homicide. Including photos. He slipped the file into his briefcase.

"Aren't you going to look at it?" she said.

"Later." He twirled the car key around his finger. "I'll follow you to the scene."

———

Jerry Deats lived and died in the B residence of a long skinny house crammed next to other long skinny houses in a densely populated impact zone a few blocks from the beach. His place was a studio apartment over a two-car garage with a Juliet balcony across the seaward side.

Thom approached the crime scene with his usual practicality. Curiosity at maximum. He surveyed the surrounding area slower than usual just to piss off Ah-nee-TA. He walked around the A residence. The ground floor windows were shuttered, but there were enough gaps in the slats to see that it was empty. He strolled up and down the alley checking for security cameras and motion lights. He met Anita's hateful glare when he finally stopped at the fence gate that opened to the side yard.

"No one had video of the alley," said Anita. "You'd know that if you'd read the file."

Thom wasn't about to tell her that he'd read the file after he saw the scene for himself. He didn't want a report to influence his investigative antennae. "These aren't Joe Schmo houses. You'd think someone would have a security camera considering that the garages face the alley. You know, thieves consider a garage the gateway into a home. Seventy percent of all burglaries are crimes of opportunity. You have robbery stats for the area?"

Anita answered with a false smile. All lips. No niceness. She opened the gate, sea-faded to ash gray, and Thom headed straight to the line of trash bins and opened the ones marked B.

"Those were empty," said Anita, pointing to the ones marked A. "We rummaged through the Bs. Most of his garbage is still up there." She pointed up at the apartment. "Junk mail, beer cans, empty cereal boxes. He favored Honey Nut Cheerios. Lots of milk jugs and fast food containers. The refrigerator is especially disgusting." She jerked her head up the stairs. Thom followed and observed a porch just large enough for a café table and one chair on top of a rag mat. The porch narrowed to form the deck. A rail of rusty wrought iron jiggled.

"There was an ashtray here on the table," said Anita. "Full of cigarette butts. All the same brand except for one oddball. We got a DNA profile, but no hits."

Thom wouldn't hold his breath. Their killer was smart. He wouldn't leave his identity behind. Then again, cigarette butts were an easy plant. An oddball would especially draw attention and would narrow the suspect field by establishing who might want to set up the DNA's owner.

Thom walked the length of the deck, gazing seaward. "Wonder how much extra rent he paid for that swipe of blue."

Anita determinedly ignored him.

"Who found the body?" said Thom.

"If you'd read the file, you'd know that the woman across the alley did. She saw the body through the window. You'd also know—"

Thom's palm shot up. "In due time." He removed his business cell and clicked a photo of the rectangular shaped rim of residue on the front door.

"What do you make of this?"

Anita touched the edge. "Sticky."

"Letter size. Like something taped here. There was a similar residue pattern on the Lawrence's front door. Same size, too."

"You going to tell me about your homicide?"

"As soon as we're done here."

Anita cut the seal and unlocked the door. She stood aside as she pushed it open. Over-scented air of garbage and decomp whooshed from the apartment. A swarm of flies followed. Thom coughed and turned his head as if he could actually evade the horribleness. His eyes watered. Death smells were always difficult—sometimes sticking in nose hairs for days.

Anita grinned at his discomfort and said, "This is a rental. It had been a bed-bath combo of the main house. Walled off and converted to a private apartment. Small, but well organized."

Whereas the Lawrence interior was spotless, this was its polar opposite. Anita wasn't kidding. Garbage everywhere. Another three months of accumulation and the place would spontaneously combust. Fingerprint powder and chemical residue left behind by the crime scene techs blended with the filth so well he had difficulty ascertaining which was which.

In the far left corner an elevated platform served as sleeping quarters on top and office below—the like of which could be found in a dorm room. A tiny kitchenette containing a half-sized refrigerator, an oven with two-burner stove, and a sink were roughed in on top of a linoleum strip against the alley wall. Electrical conduit drooped from the attic above.

"An outlaw apartment," said Thom. "Converted illegally. Not up to code. Unsafe. These types of units are created as an income source. How does the A owner fit into this drama? They aren't living downstairs, that's for sure."

"We're tracking that down," said Anita. "According to the guy next door, the main house is also a rental. He didn't know if the renters or the property owner added the apartment. It was already there when he moved in two years ago. We ran a title check. The address is owned by a holding company."

Thom stepped up the ladder rungs to inspect the mattress. The cotton cover still damp with decomposing bodily fluids. Thom imagined the soggy insides being devoured by writhing maggots. "Deats died here?"

Anita nodded. "Straight shot to the forehead."

Thom held up an arm in measurement. "There's about three feet of sleeping clearance. Our killer entered the apartment, waded through trash, went up this ladder, and practically laid down to get a straight-on shot. Do you find that as unreasonable as I do?"

"Maybe the killer was someone Deats knew. Someone he was sleeping with."

"There's not a lot of room for hanky-panky up here."

"It is still a valid possibility."

"There's no blood here."

"His head was on a pillow. It captured the blood."

"Something stinks," said Thom. "And I don't mean the mattress." He hopped down and entered the bathroom.

The words **Dead fish** scrawled on the bathroom mirror were the same as the Lawrence scene. Capital D. Lower case letters. The creep factor amped by the blood's oxidized blackness.

"Foam brush in the sink?"

"Affirmative," said Anita.

"What do you think the words mean?"

"We ran it through a slang dictionary and got a variety of the same theme. Someone who does nothing in bed. Turning a palm away when high-fiving. Bad kissing technique. A bad handshake. Like that. What did you come up with?"

"Off the top of my head I thought it might mean pushover, or easy prey, or someone defeated or dominated."

Anita nodded. "Taking into consideration the manner of death that makes more sense."

"I see it as a two-fold message," said Thom. "One, it makes a statement about either the killer or the victims or maybe both. Two, it draws the attention of law enforcement. I bet you a hundred bucks there are more victims with dead fish written in blood on their bathroom mirrors. And if the killer is smart, like I think he is, then the next one will be in the jurisdiction of a different PD or the Sheriff's department. He'll figure that it'll be harder to connect the dots. Except he made one vital mistake."

"What's that?"

"Those words are how we're gonna catch him. He can't hide behind jurisdictional red tape for long. You might not have wanted to work with anybody else, but you did release a law enforcement bulletin. You *do* want help because you're all about solving murder."

As Anita chewed on Thom's words he could almost see the smug alpha softening.

Thom removed latex gloves from his jacket pocket and snapped them on. He waded through the hoarded consumer waste in the mini office under the bed platform. "You take custody of his computer?"

"He didn't have one," said Anita.

"Everyone who has a home has one. Desktop. Laptop. Tablet. Trust me, he had something. We just have to find it."

"We tore this place apart."

Thom kneeled to look under the desk. He knocked down a stack of magazines and a wave of silverfish scurried in every direction. Thom jerked back in surprise and hit the underside. Something sharp nicked his head. "Damnit," he yelled.

"You okay in there?" said Anita, not sounding at all concerned.

"I got stuck." He turned his head. "A dangling staple. There are a row of them. Something was attached under here." Thom threw the magazines aside and found a black cord plugged into an outlet, stapled to the wall. Thom pulled and it came free. Snap, snap, snap. The cord's adapter was duct taped to the wall. He peeled back the tape and pulled again. Resistance. Thom jiggled the desk until the pinched cord came free. It had been cut. He crawled out of the paper and held up his find.

"The killer took his computer. What business was this guy in?"

"Deep background hasn't been concluded. One of the neighbors stated that he was unemployed. Always here. Day and night. Sitting. Smoking."

"Welfare or unemployment wouldn't provide enough to cover rent in this neighborhood. He had something."

Anita shrugged. "We haven't found it yet."

"What about family?"

"He has an estranged sister in Oregon. She thought he had died years ago and wasn't interested enough in her brother to take the time off her job to claim his body."

"What about business papers?"

"We didn't find any. No bills even."

Thom stood in the middle of the room and slowly turned. Eyes tracking. Something was here. A clue. A lead. There always was. Often, it's not what's present, but what's missing. Like the file on the Lawrence foster kid, Jelena Shkatova. A red flag. But how to determine what's what in a residence where the detective is a trespasser of sorts.

There was only one way to find out. Get dirty with it. Become one with the environment. Thom hung his jacket on a bathroom hook. Rolled up his shirt sleeves and went to work.

After nearly two hours of searching the closet and the living space he'd not found anything of interest. Anita hadn't helped either. She was outside making calls. She might as well have been filing her fingernails. Thom had found the cut cord within five minutes of entering. She knew her team hadn't been thorough enough. At least she could pretend to help.

The smell was suffocating. Hot. Claustrophobic. Thom wanted to be done. But he would not give up without something more. He opened the freezer. The ammonia from the refrigerator compartment leeched through the seal. *Damnit.* He really didn't want to go in there.

Thom recalled that California's natural disaster guru always did the media rounds after an earthquake or major fire. He talked about protecting possessions. What to do in an emergency. What to have in the survival kit. The freezer was a good place to store valuables he'd said. Thom pulled everything out. Opened the cardboard boxes. His search yielded nothing other than iced-through TV dinners and popsicles.

Thom held his breath and finally opened the refrigerator. Fuzzy round things oozed bacteria. On the top shelf sat a secondary reason for the stink. A warehouse-sized jar of mayonnaise. Big blue letters across the front: MAYO. Lid open. Long-handled scoop inside. Thom righted a stainless pot and began spooning the slimy-white contents into it.

Anita finally came back in. "What the hell?" she yelled.

Thom said nothing. He felt sickened. Continued to work the spoon around and around until he was certain nothing other than fat calories were in the jar. He'd vowed to never eat the stuff again. He finally gave in to the conclusion that he'd find nothing. That he was wrong. Wouldn't be the first time. But he didn't want to be wrong in front of Ah-nee-TA HILL-on.

His eyes swept the ceiling and landed on the mattress. The one Jerry Deats slept on. The one Jerry Deats died on. *No. Please, not in that thing.*

"Screw it," whispered Thom. Too late to save face. Might as well go for it.

Thom reached up with both hands and gripped the edge of the mattress. He lifted it over the ledge and slowly backed away, dragging. Heavy for such a thin thing. He pressed his lips in a tight, grossed-out grimace as the mattress came free and fell with a sluggish thump on the floor. He flipped it over, found no access cuts.

"You're out of your mind," said Anita. "Totally wacked."

"You're probably right," said Thom as he climbed the ladder once again. "But Jerry Deats is a homicide victim. He deserves my full attention and effort. I'll keep searching for discovery until I'm absolutely sure I completed the task."

This time Thom was rewarded. Stuck to the bottom of the pine platform was a Tyvek mailer covered on the top side in some kind of science experiment slime that he didn't want to think about. He opened the flap and happily found the papers inside to be dry. It only took a quick glance to know he found something important. His effort paid off. Thom held the envelope aloft in a celebratory gesture.

"*No way*," said Anita.

Thom jumped down and slapped the slimy envelope into Ah-nee-TA's stomach. Right on top of that beautiful camel jacket.

"Thom Keane. LAPD. At your service."

TWENTY-ONE

THOM RAN DOWN THE hall. The medical examiner, an efficient man named Rollie Clayborne—known simply as Clay—would give him an earful about how a scheduled time was a time to keep. Thom shook out a folded disposable gown required inside the exam room and put it on over his suit. The pale yellow cover made him feel like a lemon drop. Just about to push in, his cell rang. Lance Craig.

"LT," said Thom, breathless. "I'm late for the Lawrence postmortems. What's up?"

"The SMPD bulletin got two more hits," said Craig. "Two bodies in Culver City. One in Westchester. The big war room is scheduled for oh-eight-hundred for a meet and greet and information exchange. I'm leaving the option open for a taskforce. I've got S&M on their way out to liaise with Pacific. Before he left Seymour wanted me to tell you to check your email. Something about a computer search. See you in the morning. And Thom? You're quarterback. Bring coffee and donuts." The call disconnected.

Three more? Thom fell back, slowly slid down the wall. Felt the edge of panic. Eight murder victims targeted for a specific purpose. His job—no, his invocation—was to find out why and bring justice to victims and their families. Solving murder wasn't simple. The books and the movies turned it into entertainment. Made it seem easy. The reality was far more complicated with untold and uncountable consequences. This he knew from personal experience.

Quarterback. That meant taskforce lead—if it goes there—an investigator's career win. But Thom could not shake the dread. His involvement already compromised the case, especially if Jelena turned out to be a suspect. The what-ifs were storm clouds looming on the horizon and a swift wind waited in the distance ready to blow the darkness his way.

Thom stood and took a hit of stale, chemically disinfected air that filled the corridor. He was glad he'd already called a family meeting. He'd take all the guidance he could get.

Thom slipped into the room. Rachel's supine body was laid out on the exam table in front of Clay. He had just finished the Y incision to dissect the dead and was in the process of peeling back the skin to expose her internal organs.

Thom sidled next to George who stood against the far wall, arms crossed, head turned away from what some detectives called the canoe. George looked just as foolish in the yellow cover. Good company.

"You're late," said George. "Clay started promptly at one o'clock. And you're putrid."

"The Deats crime scene," said Thom. "It stank of garbage and decomp. The aroma infected everything, soaked into the carpet, the furniture. Walls damp with condensation."

"Enough," said George sharply. "I get the point."

"Anyway, didn't have time to change."

"Thom," said Clay, "glad of you to join us. You missed Mr. Lawrence's postmortem in its entirety and the external of his wife here."

"My apologies, Clay." For George's edification as well, Thom said, "We have a serial. Four scenes, three jurisdictions, eight bodies. Time critical and I'm the lead. We'll stay as long as we can."

George registered this new information and whistled the first few lines of the main theme song from a familiar Western movie. A distinctive, two-note melody.

"Hey," said Clay, "*The Good, the Bad, and the Ugly*. Clint Eastwood. Great film."

Apropos, thought Thom. It was about upsides, downsides, and the parts that could be better.

"Well, then," continued Clay, "how 'bout I have your attention for a short while so I can get you out of my exam room. First, Mr. Lawrence."

"Let me guess," said Thom. "Not a natural death."

"Correct. *Corpus delicti*. Massive damage to the brain incompatible with life. The direction of the bullet was front to back, slightly upward. Skull fragments in the wound track."

"Anything of the bullet salvageable?"

"Nothing of significant size for comparison."

"And the one in the groin?"

"A pelvic wound. Also front to back. Missed the penis. Both testes were in the scrotum and without trauma. Had a vasectomy at some point. A small-caliber round nicked the prostate and ureter, pierced the right kidney. That one was recovered and might prove useful. Were it not for the brain trauma this shot alone would've been survivable with immediate hospitalization. I did note marks on the abdomen strangely similar to resuscitative marks."

"Conclusion?" said Thom.

"Someone pushed."

To get more blood to write a message, thought Thom.

"I'll expedite the written reports," said Clay. "Meanwhile, the external examination of Mrs. Lawrence's body was unremarkable aside from the apparent gunshot wound to the head. Rigor mortis well-developed in the limbs and jaw. Livor mortis fixed and distributed. No foreign material in the mouth or upper airway. You may talk while I move onward to the internal. Please keep your voices hushed so the recorder doesn't pick them up. I'll give a verbal as I go."

"Thanks, doc," said Thom. Then to George, "I notice you're up against the wall. As far from the body as possible."

"Easier to talk," said George.

—*The high-pitched squeal of a rotating saw blade cut Rachel's rib bones.*

George flinched.

"*Right.* Did you find Dominic's briefcase?"

"On top of the credenza directly behind his desk, but I couldn't touch it. The Special Master won't be available until four. Meanwhile, I sealed the office."

"Was Jelena there?"

"She had been. According to Dominic's aide, a guy named Gordon, she pitched a fit when he denied her access to the office. Screaming in Russian. Beyond pissed. Face as red—"

—*Rachel's rib cage was removed with a wet, plunger-like sucking sound.*

"—as an apple. Gordon said that when Jelena finally understood she wouldn't get in, she went home claiming she was too 'emotional hardship' to work."

"Was she after the briefcase?"

"She didn't expressly say. And when pressed by Gordon she wouldn't say."

"Why did Gordon feel the need to prevent her from entering? She's his clerk."

"That's the thing. Gordon never liked Jelena. Never trusted her. He advised Dominic to fire her for her lackluster commitment and work ethic. His words. He also thinks she stole an ironwood bear that the governor had given Dominic. Some kind of California service award. When Gordon heard the news he immediately went straight to the office expressly to keep her out of it."

"Does he think her capable of murder?"

—The scale rattled with the weight of Rachel's heart. "Three hundred and eight grams," said Clay.

"He capitulated and eventually landed on a soft 'no.' Jelena has a roommate named Claudia Stepanova. Also Russian. No accent. She's a linguist. Speaks and writes several eastern European languages. Floats between divisions. She's been installed in Dominic's office for a couple of months."

"You're really bothered by the way Jelena speaks," said Thom.

"I am. Not sure why, but I'm going to find out. For now, Claudia confirmed she was with Jelena earlier in the evening on Saturday and left around midnight. Claudia was upset Jelena abandoned her for an old guy at the bar. That's why she remembers the time so specifically. That squares with what Jelena already told me."

"Old guy, huh?"

"Her words," said George. "According to Claudia, she met up with musician friends and hung out at their place. She didn't come home until near dawn. Jelena's bedroom door was closed so Claudia was unable to say if Jelena was home. There's a third roommate named Dona. She and Jelena share a room. Dona left for vacation on Sunday. I reached her via phone. According to Dona, Jelena's bed wasn't slept in Saturday night. It was still made up from the morning. However, Jelena reported that Dona was asleep when she arrived home and still asleep when she left Sunday for her foster parent's house."

—The scale rattled. "Right lung weighs 350 grams." Clay placed it on a slab. Picked up the other. "Left lung weighs 400 grams." He placed it next to the other then sliced the lung like a loaf of bread. "The visceral pleura are smooth and intact."

"A made bed could have several interpretations," said Thom. "The scenario can go either way. Nevertheless, when she returns from vacation bring her in for an official statement. We'll see if her story changes. Are there security cameras at the apartment building?"

"Exteriors and lobby door. I contacted the security company. They weren't cooperative. They insist on a warrant. If I get lucky with time I'll prepare the paperwork and get it signed by the night judge. We'll see. During the interview Jelena reported that she invited the old guy back to her apartment, but he declined. True?"

"Video and roommates."

"So the backseat of a Honda was better?"

"Apparently not. *They* have photos." Thom turned his back to the exam table. "I never felt the tingle that someone was watching."

"You were wasted."

Thom vigorously shook his head. "I'm an expert scoundrel."

"What are you thinking?" said George.

"Not sure. Go on, finish up. Who did Dominic have conflicts with?"

—*"What the—" Clay leaned over something that held his rapt attention.*

"According to several staffers, nobody. One of the lawyers called him a therapist. The one with the magic touch. He's the last person anyone would think of to die via homicide. Of course, they're lawyers. No issuance of guarantee."

Thom scratched his brow in frustration. "Who knew him best?"

—*Clay sliced into Rachel's reproductive organs.*

"The aide, Gordon. He's been Dominic's right-hand man for a decade. He has no clue why someone would want him dead."

"What was Dominic working on?"

"Gordon wouldn't say. He wanted to confer with the Special Master before telling me."

"Sounds serious. Stay on it. Meanwhile, maybe we'll get lucky with the office, the files, the briefcase. We also have to consider that Rachel or the twins were the primary target." Thom gestured toward the clock on the wall. "Don't be tardy. I'll stay here as long as I can. I'm not going back to the office today. I have the book, the Deats file. Seymour might have found something, too."

"Any connection between Deats and Lawrence?"

"Besides the manner of death? Maybe. I'll take a closer look this evening. There's a powwow at oh-eight-hundred in the big war room. I should have something to share by then."

—*Clay's silence cut the room.*

The background narrative, the ambient sounds of cutting tools and examination halted. Thom turned his attention toward Clay.

George continued, not sensing that the business of autopsy had ceased prematurely. "I'm gonna send you the audio of Jelena's interview," he said. "*How* someone says something is just as important as *what* they say. I want your feedback."

"You can do that?" said Thom, distracted by a bloody blob in Clay's hands.

"Yeah, Thom, it's called technology. You underutilize that expensive phone of yours. Have Birdie give you lessons."

"Ah, detectives?" said Clay.

George joined Thom in giving his full attention to the ME.

"Mrs. Lawrence was pregnant," said Clay. "Fourteen weeks by my estimation."

Confusion passed between the detectives.

"That's right," said Clay. "Mr. Lawrence was sterile."

TWENTY-TWO

BIRDIE LEANED INTO THE car and kissed Ron goodbye. Louise snarled from Ron's lap. She didn't like any amount of affection bestowed upon her daddy.

"To the back with you," said Ron. She jumped onto the backseat and immediately curled into a blanket for the ride.

"Text me when you get home?" said Birdie.

"I'm stopping in San Clemente to have a drink with Noa."

"You might not make it back to work tomorrow after all."

"It *will* be a late night."

"Text me anyway. I want to know you're home safe."

"You got it. Love you, babe."

"Love you, too."

Birdie watched the blue Audi shrink and disappear around the corner. A dull flush crept up her neck and her heart's bpm tugged inside her chest. She wouldn't see Ron again until Sunday night. Six days from now. She experienced the same mitosis as always: sorry they were separating, happy to resume the analytics.

She stood on the sidewalk a moment longer. Hesitating. Don't be a coward, she said to herself. Forward now. Do what Frank advised: find strength in every moment. You didn't want to read the emails. Didn't want to listen to the voicemails. And what happened? They weren't that bad. The world didn't stop spinning. Go on, find out what happened to whom and help the family seek a solution. You've done it before, you can do it again. She turned.

Magnolia Manor was a big square house. Its stark white paint reflected a bygone era of polite elegance. Magnolia Street was old and established. Large houses, deep lawns, plywood forts, and swimming pools nurtured multiple generations of the same families. It was Birdie's second home growing up and she held an emotional attachment to its unfussy furnishings nicked with time. She loped across the entry parquet. The same place Aunt Nora taught her and Madi how to jig. Pass the broad stairs and the wood banister smoothed with sliding butts. Birdie walked around the formal dining area and pushed open the swinging door to the kitchen.

Cooking smells of onions and sausage and yeasty bread overwhelmed the cigarette smoke. Nora usually had a strict no smoking rule inside her house. Family meetings were the exception and they always took place in the kitchen. One, it was the easiest room to shield from unfriendlies and two, smoke contaminates upholstery.

Birdie's eyes tracked the attendees. Louis, Nora, Maggie, and Arthur. They all had concern on their faces, but not stress. That left...

"Where's Thom?"

"Upstairs," said Louis. "I made him shower. He stank."

"He's also touching base with the kids," said Nora. "He'll be down shortly."

Maggie greeted Birdie with a kiss and hug. "How are you darling?"

"I'm okay, Mom. You?"

"Missing your dad."

"Me, too. Every day."

More hugs and kisses from Louis and Nora. Birdie eased toward Arthur. He was leaning against the counter, arms and ankles crossed. His image conjured aviator shades and black cowboy boots though he wore neither. Years on the streets of Los Angeles and a successful career as a mixed martial arts cruiserweight had shaped him into what Louis called a "toughie"—a word from his youth in Ireland. Yet, Arthur had a preternatural self-assurance and a reservoir of tremendous patience. Traits that served him well on and off the job.

Arthur pulled Birdie into him. A full-body hug tight with affection. He nuzzled her hair. "My little Bird," he whispered. Birdie felt his muscles relax. The cousins had always shared a mutual attachment going back to their childhood—the kind of love beyond a family devotion toward something more spiritual.

They stayed together for a few more beats before he released her and kissed the scar on her right cheek.

"How was your shift today?" said Birdie, taking a seat at the table.

"I scheduled vacation to coincide with the newspaper article. Taking an opportunity to get a shit load of handyman stuff done at the house."

"Smart."

"I wish I'd done that," said Louis. "Asswipe TV reporters were camped outside the station accosting everyone wearing a uniform. Phones were ringing all damn day. Publicly, there was a blue hedge shielding me from the mayhem. Privately, I got several turned backs and faces of indignation."

"I'm sorry," said Birdie.

"Not your fault," said Louis. "Gerard wrote his own story. If I hadn't seen the depos, not read Gerard's statement, I wouldn't have believed it myself. At least I'll be in meetings at the PAB for the next few days. My absence will ease the tension in the station."

"Trust me, Dad, it'll take less time to recover than it should," said Arthur. He sat next to Birdie and began filling water glasses.

"The second part comes out tomorrow," said Birdie. "It's Gerard heavy since he was the catalyst that took down Janko and the Blue Bandits. It's also about the operation that swept up the five remaining gang members. It'll clear up any leftover questions except why Gerard got involved and what happened to the Paige Street money."

"When did you start doing that?" said Maggie.

"Doing what?" said Birdie.

"Refer to your father as Gerard."

"He's 'Dad' except when I'm referencing the Blue Bandits." Birdie hiked her shoulders. "It's easier to separate the two halves of the man he was."

Maggie nodded with understanding and approval.

"People asked me how you can be uncompromised," said Louis.

"Understandable," said Birdie. She was used to defending her occupation and its seeming conflict with her cop family, yet she wished she didn't feel as if being ushered onstage to deliver a sudden speech. Her hands twittered, but she pressed on. "Next time, tell them I belong to the Society of Professional Journalists. Their ethics committee vetted the article for bias. So did the *Times*."

Arthur gave her a wink and a *so there* nod.

"I thought the article was a thoughtful, unsentimental analysis," said Maggie. "That's why I went to work. I stood up for it and for our family. Of course, I'm getting the same question over and over again. Did I know? A snort of indignation and 'of course not' goes a long way in shutting people up."

"Unless—" said Thom, making a dramatic entrance as if on cue. He wore his father's old-school police academy sweat suit, hair damp with the minimum amount of preening. "—you get the question, 'How could you not have known?'"

The kitchen went quiet in a group slap of submission. Silent except for the sound of tobacco ash falling.

The question had never been asked. And here came Thom, fresh from a shower and phone calls with his kids, late to the conversation, and he entered the kitchen and owned everybody—put everyone on notice—with a few words. The same attitude and skill used to sweet-talk women into bed.

Birdie bit her lower lip in anticipation. Now would be the time to get it out in the open. She wound up, eyes gazing avidly from one face to another wondering who was going to speak first. She guessed Louis. No, it'd be Thom. He's the one who brought it up. She stared at him, but he wouldn't catch her eye. The tick tick tick had an awkward lethalness that lasted too long. Realizing the ideal moment was about to slip away, she processed her thoughts, deciding how she'd encourage Thom to answer the question.

That's when Nora said, "Let's eat."

A big, silent sigh occurred and suddenly the kitchen was alive again. Another uncomfortable topic brushed aside by the Keane clan. Cigarettes were snubbed, ashtrays moved off the table, wine glasses refilled, bowls of coddle passed, a basket of warm bread set on the table, napkins placed on laps.

Louis said grace. "Bless us, Oh Lord, and these thy gifts, from which we are about to receive from thy bountiful hands. Bless this table and all who sit here. Please grant us strength and grace and make us humble in thine eyes. Through Christ our Lord, amen."

In unison: "Amen."

Even while she made the sign of the cross, Birdie's impatient frustration bubbled over. She'd answer the question clear and succinct. "I didn't know."

Maggie quickly added in a stand of solidarity, "Neither did I."

In brotherly synchronicity both Thom and Arthur looked up at each other, a silent discussion passing between them. Birdie tapped her fist against Arthur's thigh in a "go ahead" gesture.

Arthur pushed the chair back from the table with a loud scrape and got up.

Thom sat straight, a pained expression on his face.

"It's time," said Birdie, "that this family acknowledges that we're in the midst of undeniable traumas. Before we go forward, a confession is in order. We have to stop pretending that shit happens."

Thom got up. He and Arthur walked into the pantry.

Nora leaned into Maggie and they engaged in fierce whisperings.

That left Louis alone, staring into his wineglass, somewhat dumbstruck.

Birdie knew her dad's downfall and death was especially hard on Louis. They were twins borne from the same womb—as close as two beings could be. They immigrated to America together. Married best friends. They entered the police academy at the same time and had parallel careers. They even held the same rank—Louis was captain of Harbor Division down in San Pedro. They were identical in looks. Birdie saw her handsome father in Louis; the same silvery-white hair and intense blue eyes.

But the brothers were totally different in temperament and personality. Gerard had an outgoing, let's go enthusiasm; a gritty, in-your-face hubris. His softer side always reserved for his girls, Maggie and Birdie. Whereas, Louis had crisp borders hiding a sensible, soft humor, and an emotional sensitivity. Romantic, melodic, Irish pipes and a glass of wine could evoke tears.

Birdie wanted to give him some profound sense of courage and comfort, but she could not form the words. She grasped her uncle's hand instead. She shivered as if touching a ghost. His hand was shaped just like Gerard's.

She remembered the last time she held her father's hand. They had seen an action movie together. Shared a bag of popcorn. That was the night of the hard rain. The night a Belfast jobber broke into her house. The night a man died on her lawn.

Arthur and Thom emerged from the pantry. Four sets of eyes bore into them.

"I knew," said Arthur.

"I did, too," said Thom.

Louis burst into tears.

The truth will set you free, but first it makes you miserable.

TWENTY-THREE

THE TRANSITION FROM TEARS to frothy-mouth rage was exceedingly quick. Louis ricocheted the length of the kitchen screaming in Gaelic with the thick brogue of his youth. The same one he worked so hard to get rid of to assimilate into an American life. Birdie caught the few cuss words she knew—the ones her relatives taught her when she spent childhood summers in Ireland.

Birdie had never experienced this level of rage from her uncle. She'd seen him upset. Mad. He'd even taken a belt to her butt in punishment on a handful of occasions. But this was altogether scary. Birdie felt pained. What had she done? Why had she pushed for this truth to be revealed? She had already made a private deal with the district attorney that would protect her cousins. So, really, what had been gained? What Gerard did or why he did it mattered less than how the crime affected the family. She couldn't print, blog, post, or even whisper the truth. Neither could anyone in this kitchen. So who did the truth serve? Maybe the reason her family was so good at not discussing matters of import was because they served no useful purpose.

Drama that didn't end well and left nothing but hard emotions.

Birdie grabbed at a speck of denial. Maybe Louis hadn't yet processed his feelings for Gerard's steep downfall. To learn that his sons were fully aware and knew of the misdeeds must've been too much to bear. Of course, she speculated. There was no way to know because she had no idea what he was saying.

Maggie's shoulders were pinched, head bowed, trying to appear small. Nora's upset manifest in nervous energy. She busied her hands by laying a fire in the hearth. Thom and Arthur soldiered against the hutch. Arthur had once told her that when Louis was on a tear it was the safest place to be because he wouldn't risk throwing something at the boys and taking the chance of breaking the good crystal or china. For her part, Birdie felt rigid, glued to her chair in fascination, concern, and sincere regret for pushing the issue.

Louis stopped yelling and began muttering.

Good, she thought. *He's calming down.*

After a few more volleys Louis stopped and faced Thom and Arthur. His voice took on an even, authorial tone. "That's just stupid five different ways." His stock phrase of disappointment. Then he slapped the head of each of his sons. Grown men, taking punishment from their father as though still teenagers.

"What was I supposed to do?" said Arthur in a borderline whine. "I was the one under the federal microscope. I was the one the task-force kept attacking. Since I could handle the scrutiny, the invasion of privacy, why not take the heat for a man I loved like a second father?"

"It wasn't your burden to bear," said Louis. "Gerard should've manned up."

"Dad...he didn't know I knew. He asked me all the time. 'How are you holding up?' he'd say. He would've come clean if I showed any level of weakness, but I always told him I was good. I took my frustration out in the octagon. That was the truth for a long time."

"Arthur even got street cred out of the deal," said Thom.

"It's shameful," said Louis. "We came to America for opportunities. Not to game the system. Not to become criminals."

"Stop that," said Maggie.

Nora stepped behind Maggie and gently placed a hand on her shoulder. "You always say 'we' like you and Gerard were Siamese twins. Connected at the spine. Don't take on his responsibility."

"She's right," said Maggie. "Gerard charted his own path. Who knows what flaws flow inside a man?"

"Or a woman," whispered Louis, with a strange knowing in his eye.

Nora's mouth twitched.

Birdie perked up. "Wait. Arthur, how did you find out about Gerard?"

"I always had a bad vibe about Max McFarland. Remember him? He and Gerard went way back. You knew him, Dad."

"Yes," said Louis. "They were great friends."

"I had a sick intuition that stuck in my side," said Arthur.

"McFarland was Gerard's Paige Street alibi. As I recall, they were fishing at Lake Castaic," said Louis.

"They did that often," said Birdie. "The alibi was unshakable. Witnesses placed them at the boat landing. McFarland's wife confirmed that Gerard had been at the house that morning sorting gear and packing the boat with sandwiches and beer. She took a photo. It was date stamped."

"Exactly," said Arthur, finally moving away from the hutch. "And the date was verified by the images before and after. Every one of us in this room now knows that the date wasn't correct. But back then, we had no reason to doubt the proof."

"So tell us," urged Thom. "How did you come to learn of it? Tell us the story."

"And not the monosyllabic, cop version," said Maggie.

Thom sat at the table and caught Birdie's eye. He winked at her in a sly way as if to suggest they shared a secret. But Birdie already knew what he had done by encouraging Arthur to speak. He diffused the leftover tension in the room. A story would ease the family's transition into another difficult topic. Thom's topic. Which hadn't been broached yet. And besides, the Irish loved their tales, the more visual and movie-like the better.

Arthur began with a verbal fade in. "A casual observation that Matt made got me thinking about Max and Gerard's alibi. Matt and I used to get continuous calls for service to one particular address. About twelve times during a one-month period. A long-married elderly couple. They'd have extremely violent fights. One or the other was usually injured by a swinging walking stick or a plate being thrown. Thing is, we'd become jaded because their particular situation had become a mundane reality and we were sick and tired of the pair. They admitted to hating each other, but couldn't live without the other because of their advanced age. They had outlived their children, their families. They only had each other."

The family ate while they listened. Soft sounds of scrapping forks, buttering bread, and drinking became a background melody that didn't compete with Arthur's tale. They listened with a sympathetic ear that encouraged speaking.

"The old woman's continual complaint was that her husband was cheating with the hussy down the street. We never bought it. I mean, come on, the guy could barely walk. That day we rolled out to their house expecting the same ol' shit. Separating them, calming them down, acting like marriage therapists. Only this time, the husband's unconscious on the floor, bleeding from the head. The wife had hit him with a glass candy dish. Butterscotch nibs were scattered all over the house. She said she finally had proof of his cheating.

"Her proof was a flipbook of photographs she found in her husband's underwear drawer," continued Arthur. "They depicted the geriatric woman down the street. She's sitting on the edge of a bed, wearing a lacy nightgown, legs spread apart, old lady pussy in full view, sagging skin, and straggly white hair."

"Eeeewwww," said the collective at the table.

"They got worse," said Arthur. "I'm giving you the edited visuals. Anyway, the neighbor hussy took the photos herself by setting the camera on a tripod with a shutter cable release in her hand. She clicked a photo every few seconds and put them together in book form. The next few show a bald head covered in age spots between her legs. Then a wrinkled, saggy ass and then an old man on top of her. The last one shows the husband with a toothless grin, placid penis, and a thumbs-up. Sure shit, he had been cheating.

"Matt and I had a hard time not laughing. It was disgusting and extremely funny at the same time. Geriatric porn. Turns out that when the wife took her afternoon nap the husband would take his walker and shuffle down the alley to the hussy's house for a daily screw."

Birdie couldn't help giggling along with the rest of the family. Street cops always had the best stories.

"What happened to the couple?" said Nora.

"The wife had given her husband a fatal wound. He never regained consciousness and died. The DA was trying to figure out what to do with a ninety-something murderess when she died in her sleep a few days later."

"Maybe the hussy down the street drugged her in retribution," said Birdie.

"Or maybe she loved the scoundrel after all and died of a broken heart," added Thom.

"Or maybe she just died," said Arthur. "Anyway, Matt and I were talking about it a few weeks later when he casually mentioned something about that day I had forgotten. The photos the wife confiscated from her husband were all date stamped the day the old man died. Apparently, the neighbor lady had never set the camera's date correctly."

"It got you thinking about the fishing photos," said Birdie.

"Exactly. When a battery is removed for charging, the camera's settings have to be reset. What if the date were purposely reset on the McFarland camera for a particular event and then changed back? Easy enough to do. What if they had actually been fishing the day before? Turns out, they had. McFarland charged the launch fee and there was a receipt."

Birdie shook her finger. "I know where you're going with this. They *had* gone the day before. Witnesses put the two of them together at Lake Castaic all the time. Gerard and McFarland were regulars. Sometimes they'd go two days in a row. But when the cops come 'round months later asking questions the exact date is fuzzy because—"hey, they're here all the time"—they could've been here one day or the next or both."

"Precisely," continued Arthur. "Sanchez planned Paige Street in a hurry and Gerard would need to set up a quick alibi—no time for complication. I began to think that McFarland helped Gerard create one. He changed the camera's date."

"The dated receipts and photos were irrefutable proof that McFarland and Gerard were at Lake Castaic the day of Paige Street," said Birdie. "There were two complete sets from both days. But that wasn't unusual behavior for them. There was also McFarland's sworn statement."

"Max was never my favorite person," said Maggie, "but I doubt he'd help create an alibi for Gerard for a two-eleven."

"Agreed," said Arthur. "But what if he thought Gerard was engaged in some other way during Paige Street? Like an affair? Best friends cover for each other. I do for you, you do for me."

Thom dropped his fork and looked up at Birdie. She knew he thought of Karen Wilcox covering for Anne's affair.

"McFarland had a well-known reputation as a lady's man," said Arthur. "Gerard had probably been his cover story many times—the drinking buddy that never was. So when the time came to return the favor, McFarland was only too willing to arrange for his buddy to have an entire day with his amour." Arthur spread out his hands. Done.

"Gerard never had affairs," said Maggie.

"But McFarland wouldn't know for certain. Gerard could tell him anything and it'd be taken at face value. They were best friends."

"How did you prove it?" said Birdie.

"That's where I came in," said Thom, wiping his mouth. "Arthur told me what he thought our uncle had done. There was no way we could approach Max or his wife without raising suspicion. Sanchez was dead. And we sure as hell didn't want Gerard to know, just in case Arthur was wrong. So we waited and watched. One night we followed Gerard to a bar where he met up with Soto and some unknown guy. Soto stayed behind in the bar, but Gerard and Unknown took off in another vehicle. Unknown drove. We followed them to a flower warehouse. They put on masks and gloves and backpacks and went in packing shotguns. Just like at Paige Street. Not more than five minutes later they came out—just strolled, all casual—carrying a satchel between them. They got into a different car and drove away. Just then, the building began to burn."

"Wow," said Birdie, "I can't use any of this."

Maggie shot her daughter a warning that said, *not funny*.

"Turns out, the flower business was a front for drug smugglers," said Thom.

"I remember that one," said Louis. "The fire department found a cut lab. Word on the street was that the smugglers were looking for their stolen cash and put a bounty on the thieves who burned their product."

"That was the Blue Bandits MO," said Birdie. "They stole cash and destroyed product. So … since we're confessing … anyone know where the Paige Street money went? Or *any* of the drug or blackmail money? I mean, it's all coming out. Might as well fess up."

Silence at the table.

"Seriously? No one? Mom?"

"No," said Maggie. "We lived on our paychecks. There was never a slush fund."

"Gerard didn't give any clue in any of his depos or letters?" said Arthur.

"None," said Birdie. "What about a reason? Why did Gerard allow himself to get involved with Soto? What blackmail did he have that would compel Gerard to get involved in Paige Street?"

"We've already been over this," said Louis. "The answer is the same as before when you asked us about the article. That hasn't changed."

"I was hoping that someone had a change of heart and decided to share."

"There wasn't any blackmail," said Maggie. "I think it was the thrill. He became an administrator and rode a desk. He probably missed the adrenalin rush."

"He loved the badge," said Arthur. "He always talked to me and Matt about honoring it."

"Yet, he dishonored it," said Louis.

"True," said Maggie. "But, he never did anything illegal while on duty. He expressly stated that in his letters."

"It's irrelevant," said Thom. "Bottom line? He lost faith in himself and disparaged the job."

"Louis?" said Birdie. "Was there some reason two eighteen-year-old Irish boys decided to immigrate to the West Coast when there was family already established on the East Coast?"

"Yes," said Louis. "We met these two." He pointed at Nora and Maggie.

"You weren't running from the Emerald Isle to hide from something?"

Louis slapped his fist on the table. "I already said no. No means no."

"Alright!" Birdie put up her hands.

"Sometimes you just don't know when to stop. Spoiled only child."

Now all eyes trained on Birdie. "Okay! I said I'm sorry." She crossed her arms to keep her hands from shaking. "But there's something we can't forget." A quiet groan rose from the table. "Gerard participated. He made money. And yet, there's no evidence of his ill-got income? Where'd it go? If he gave it away, who got it? Also, there's a new department taskforce. A new FBI investigation. The Janko five are jockeying for deals. Not a single one of us in this kitchen is going to be spared the warrant swoop for our computers, our financial statements, and anything else the Feds deem relevant in their search for the money."

"She's right," said Thom. "It'll be worse this time around."

"Alejo feels cheated," added Arthur. "He'll want in on the action because he thinks the Irish Mob is dirty and he won't stop until he convicts someone. He may even make shit up or engage the Whelans to turn against us."

"Alejo couldn't manufacture evidence last time," said Thom. "He can't do it now. Who really needs to worry is the Soto family. He was the alpha."

"And Frank Senior wouldn't turn on us," said Louis. "We've had conversations about that very topic. Also … the families will soon be united by law."

"What are you saying?" said Nora, her eyes bright with excitement.

"Patrick asked for my permission to marry Madi." Patrick being the youngest of the Whelan boys, a police officer with the LAPD who worked at Hollywood Division.

Nora and Maggie screeched with excitement. The guys rolled their eyes. Birdie couldn't help but feel jealous. The Whelan and Keane clans had always thought it'd be she and Matt to join the families. That dream died along with Matt.

"Madi married?" snorted Birdie, the killjoy attitude seeping through.

"We can't say a word," said Nora. "We won't take away her moment when she makes the announcement."

"We all know how to keep a secret," said Thom.

"You just have to be told it's a secret," added Birdie.

Thom tapped his watch. "Let's move on. There are other items on the agenda. I'm in deep shit and a killer might escape justice because of me."

TWENTY-FOUR

ANTICIPATING A HEAVY NIGHT, Ron Hughes planned ahead and parked the Audi up the hill near the youth club. A brisk walk afterward would clear his head a bit before the thirty-five minute drive home. He wisely parked the car facing downhill. An easy glide and three right turns would put him on the southbound I-5. Simple maneuvers when impaired by liquor.

The coastal marine layer never burned off today. The ocean mist enshrouded the houses on the hill, pressed down on the baseball field. The wet, heavy air felt good on his skin as he walked to the bar.

He'd rather be home between cool sheets. French doors open, the Pacific air drifting into the bedroom, billowing the sheers. Birdie's warm body spooned with his. Ron wanted to see his friend, Noa, but the pending report put him on edge.

After the big fight with Birdie, it took two days to aggregate his emotions before he could think clearly and another half day of indecision before calling Noa. Planning wartime ops was easy in comparison. Then the long, agonizing wait. Nearly a month. And now he was about to know *exactly* what she'd been up to.

Mulligan's was a borderline dive bar in a place the locals called "the alley" in San Clemente—a funky, light-industrial area of surfboard shapers and consignment stores. Ron pushed through the door at the back to meet his buddy at a semi-quiet booth away from the baseball game on the big screens.

A native Hawaiian, Noa grew up on fresh fruits and the sea. At six-five he was two inches taller than Ron and had sinew that no sane man should challenge. It was he who convinced Ron into eating the whole foods way. It was he who continually gave Ron shit about the cigarettes he smoked. And it was Ron who Noa trusted more than any person alive.

"My brother! Great to see you," said Noa, clutching Ron in a battle hug. "It's been far too long. Jesus, I've missed you."

"Roger that," said Ron, pressing his forehead against his friend's. "It's hard to get together over a beer when you live in D.C."

"Yeah. I miss the beach. Hey, where's Louise? This place is dog friendly."

"She'd rather be on soft leather instead of hard floor."

"Don't blame her. Come on, sit. I've waited to order."

As they eased into the booth, Ron swept his eyes around the bar. Not many patrons on a Monday night—the Angels vs. Athletics not important enough to draw a crowd.

"How's life in Kalorama?"

"Oh, brother, what's not to like? Kick-ass estates, walls, and bored, rich women."

"Code for privacy. Still going for the marrieds?"

"Duh. The ones with the kids are the best 'cause they have stricter schedules. Play dates and off home."

"You're a dog."

"Never claimed to be otherwise."

The server arrived, hand poised over an order pad. "You need menus?"

"We don't eat bar shit," said Noa. "Bring a bottle of Peligroso Anejo. Two glasses."

She hesitated.

"It'd take a lot more than that to slam us on our asses," said Ron.

"We're tall, tough men," added Noa.

"Looks like you guys are outta Pendleton. Don't pull no jarhead bullshit."

"Don't worry, those days are behind us," said Ron.

"It's okay, darling," said Noa. "We're just frisky because we haven't seen each other for a while."

After she left Ron said, "How long you in town?"

"'Bout a week. Got some legit business, a little freelance, then I'll jet home."

Noa meant that literally. He co-owned a private business jet and traveled in and out of executive airport terminals.

"What brings you here? Now?" It was a rhetorical question. Ron already knew.

"Bad news deserves an offline briefing."

Ron punched the table. "Shit!"

"Sorry, my brother. That gal of yours is way too smart for her own good."

The manager arrived with a beautiful black bottle and two glasses. "Good evening, gentlemen." He uncorked the tequila and poured a finger in each glass.

"If his girlfriend were here," said Noa, "she'd take one whiff and tell us what flavors we'd taste. She'd tell us how it was distilled and aged and what proof. Then she'd take a moment to appreciate the glow."

"Ah," said the manager, "a connoisseur."

"An alcoholic with a refined nose," said Ron.

"Don't be pissy," said Noa.

"I see," said the manager. "In her absence I can tell you—"

"—sorry, man, not interested," said Noa.

"Okay…well, it's strong stuff. I'd feel better if you had some food with this."

"Bring us a big plate of nachos," said Ron.

"You got it. Enjoy." The manager left the bottle.

"Did you forget the rule?" said Noa. "Drinking and eating don't mix."

"I've no intention of eating. Just pacifying the guy." Ron raised his glass. "To love."

Noa raised his. "May it never find me."

They clinked and said together, "Semper Fi."

They drained their glasses.

"Damn," said Ron, shaking off the powerful hit. "Better watch your six. When you least expect it, one of those mamas is going to steal your heart and suddenly you'll find yourself a stepdad."

"A fate worse than death," said Noa as he refilled their glasses.

"Quality agave juice is designed for sipping. Enjoy the flavors."

"A polite way to say you're not gonna match me."

"Not at all. But before we get shitfaced we've got to do business."

"Alright," said Noa, reluctantly. "Here's my official report … that girl of yours is doing what I'd do. She's hacking her way through databases."

"She can do that?"

"And then some. She has legitimate subscriptions to the same databases that law enforcement uses. It appears she's had them for years. She probably hacked her way in to obtain pay-for-use. Call it pseudo legal. She also gained access to some government servers that even law enforcement can't use without paper."

The server placed two side plates and set-ups on the table.

"What's she looking for?" said Ron.

"You told me that Matt barely survived a shooting incident that was a hit."

"Right. He started planning his own death. Got a new identity and disappeared so the cop gang wouldn't come looking for him."

"Under what name?"

"He never said."

"Precisely. See, Birdie would need a name to find him. Then she'd need to match the name to his face. Without that basic information she used the next best thing. Application dates. That's what she used to frame her queries."

"Explain."

"What do you need to exist in America? A social security number and government-issued ID like a driver's license. Also, a passport would come in handy. She mined state and federal databases for new applications of those three items."

"To get those documents you'd need a birth certificate."

"He was a cop. He probably had knowledge of six ID rings in his policing area alone. Of those, he probably had personal contact with two. He could obtain a birth certificate with an official seal and everything. But here's a big *but*. The guy he dealt with would know. Matt's funeral was big news. He couldn't afford a loose end. But he could use a birth certificate he had easy access to. His sister's."

The server brought over a platter of nachos. Both men stared at it.

Noa said, "Beans fried in lard, tortilla chips from some factory, chunks of overcooked, hormone-fed chicken, a sprinkling of iceberg lettuce, and jalapeño peppers covered with processed milk artificially colored to resemble cheese. I'm not eating that shit."

Ron stuck his fork into it. "Do what skinny girls do … move it around the plate to make it look like you're eating. Where were we? Right. Matt didn't have a sister."

"You were at the Whelan family plot for his funeral. Didn't you see the piece of granite marking his sister's grave site?"

"I did. They named the child Mary Junior after her mother, but Birdie told me the child was stillborn."

"Because that's what the family reported. It's easy to explain a stillbirth because shit happens. Babies die in utero. But Mary Junior lived a day. That's a live birth. That's a birth certificate. And Matt was ten years old when Mary was born. He could pass for someone 10 years younger."

"She also has a death certificate."

"A different document."

"He can't pass as a female."

"No. But he can pass as a "Marty." Only the T is missing. On a keyboard, the R, T, and Y are next to each other. An easy misspell. Clerical error."

"You're telling me his new name is Marty?"

"Not necessarily, but Birdie's considered it. She investigated and discovered Mary's live birth. She's already cross-checked the list for that first name and found some. But she covered her bases and checked *everything* within her search parameters. Male and female. She's also seeking court records of name changes. Let's say he used Mary Junior's birth certificate. He might be able to claim that the first name was inadvertently spelled wrong, but he can't go around using the same last name. He'd petition a court for a change in surname. Birdie started with local counties—Los Angeles, Orange, Ventura, etcetera. It's only a matter of time before she acquires a long list of name-change requests. Then she could match the results with the data she's already acquired and come up with a shortlist of names that matches all three of her parameters. She'll investigate each name by obtaining a likeness." Noa held up three fingers. "Name, ID, face. She'll find him."

"How long?"

"Any day now. She might already have his new name, but not know which of the tens of thousands of names is his."

"She's seriously breaking the law."

"Yeah, well, algorithms don't have ethics."

"Thick-headed Irishwoman. He's the only thing we fight about."

"She's focused, no doubt. That kind of passion spills over to other parts of life." Noa winked.

"Once upon a time," said Ron and left it at that. He might've been willing to discuss the pre-Birdie sex life, but when you find the *one* all sharing ceases.

"She's a gorgeous nerdy girl. I see the appeal."

"What I'm hearing is that you're open to the idea of a proper relationship."

"Pshaw. I got into her life. Just 'preciating."

"Did her cousin call?"

"Who?"

"Honorable bastard."

"Corps values, man. Honor, courage, commitment."

"Ooo-rah."

They clicked glasses.

"Why is Birdie looking for Matt?" said Noa. "You never said."

"She wants a face-to-face accounting of his actions. Answers to outstanding questions."

"She loves him hard to go through this much work."

"I keep telling her that you can't pull one thread from a tapestry without destroying the whole thing. But she wants what she wants and nothing, not even me, can stop her."

"Poetic. You worried she might run off with him?"

"Oh, man … I've obsessed over that question. But to live underground? Logic says no way."

"Love isn't logical."

"No question. Their bond is strong. He's not around and yet he is. He invades our space. His power is illustrated by a narrative that didn't end with his death. I don't like it. Most times I feel like the second choice, man. The default."

Noa took a big pull of tequila, never removing his eyes from Ron. Studying. "Sorry, brother. I know you fell hard and fast."

"It hurts," whispered Ron.

The few patrons in the bar cheered when the Angels scored.

"Has she created a new identity?" said Ron.

"No. But now that you mention it … she queried both genders. I thought it was because some first names can be male or female, Blair, Pat, Dylan, Terry, Alex, like that. But, what if she suspects that Matt created a second set? One for her?"

"Son … of … a … bitch," said Ron. "That makes sense. During the death scene prep I cleared the house. He came in behind me and left breadcrumbs in the form of photos. He counted on the fact that she'd do what she does and figure out the truth. He also knew that Birdie would look for him because that's her nature."

"Even if she found him, and even if he has a new identity for her, that doesn't guarantee she'd actually join him."

"He might be able to persuade her."

"Then why not speak to her directly?"

"Because this way … because of the time and dedication required, she'd come to him of her own free will. That'd be important to him. He put the choice in her hands just like he did with the Paige Street evidence."

"We'll know eventually, won't we?"

"Will you know his new name and whereabouts when she knows?"

"We'll see. She's being extremely careful. She's spoofing her external IP and using proxy servers. She changes it up every so often."

"I've no idea what that means."

"She's making it appear as if she's elsewhere other than Hancock Park. That's why it took me so long to find her—she's slowing down detection. Keyword … slowing … not hiding. Even she knows that if someone's looking in the right places, they'll find her. She's not using her office computer so she probably has a burner laptop—something small and concealable that she can lock up. She'll wipe it clean and destroy it when she's done. Nevertheless, she keeps running security sweeps and my spyware is getting swept out. I have to continually re-insert it."

"You're big brother. Can't you put something in there that won't get kicked out?"

"Sure. I could even insert one that would self-destruct. But if it were ever discovered by some governmental agency … say the FBI … I get paid a shitload of money to do what I like doing. I'm not going to risk it."

"Why would the FBI–? Of course, they've been invited in by the LAPD to investigate the Blue Bandits. That would include Gerard's family. Most especially his daughter, the journalist with the mansion."

Noa nodded.

"She going to get caught?" said Ron.

"I don't see it. What she's doing isn't malicious so she's under the radar. Plus, she'll be done by the time the FBI serves the warrants."

"Should I warn her?"

"Absolutely not. First thing she'll ask is how you know. She's not stupid."

"If she'll be done by the time the FBI gets around then why are you worried about your spy program?"

"It's a rubber. I'm playing safe."

160

"As soon as she knows his name and gets his face, I need to know, too."

"Why?"

"Because I need it."

"Not good enough," said Noa.

"Matt wanted me to look after her. Build a future. That's what we discussed. He betrayed me when he left her clues to the real deal."

"You're full of shit."

"No, I'm not. Matt and I swore fealty to each other. He undermined me by leaving trace that he knew Birdie would follow. If he had simply died as planned, Birdie and I wouldn't be in this impossible situation."

"Don't screw with me, Hughes. I know you too well. Tell me straight. Are you going to go all Wild West and kill your so-called competition?"

"I'm thinking about it."

TWENTY-FIVE

"I'm tired," said Thom. "I still have a lot of work to do tonight and I have a meeting first thing in the morning. I'll give you the broad strokes. Let me finish before you hit me with questions or yell at me for my stupidity."

Once again, Thom had the Keane family's rapt attention.

"On Saturday night, I hooked up with a girl I met in a bar. We had sex in the backseat of her car. We liked each other, spent some time together, end of story."

Only it's not, thought Birdie.

"Sunday morning. George and I are dispatched to a multiple. A family. Two adults, two children. Funny that, we weren't on the call-out board. Once at the scene it immediately became apparent that we were going to play catch up. Division Command had originally dispatched Seymour and Morgan because they were the team on the board. They started investigating. Called out SID. My lieutenant, Lance Craig, came to the scene and discharged S&M and directed

162

DC to call us. Craig had already left by the time we arrived. Meanwhile, the field work had commenced. For one, a forensic tech did a field process on the person reporting. Her name is Jelena and she's the foster daughter of the dead couple—a city attorney named Dominic Lawrence and his wife. Uniforms had begun canvassing the area looking for weapons and interviewing neighbors. It's about here where I learn that Jelena was the woman I had sex with the night before."

There was a communal groan.

"I immediately phoned Craig," said Thom. "Didn't give it a second thought. I told him I was compromised because I had sex with her the night before. He didn't care. He said, and I quote, 'this case is not going to round three.' End quote. Since he refused to let me step out, what could I do? I couldn't have any contact with her at all, so we split forces. George interviewed the girl while I processed the house.

"The scene was extremely clean. Everyone executed in their sleep. The killer left behind a message on a bathroom mirror written in blood. I also determined that the kids were killed first. During the interview the PR told George she wasn't sad the kids were dead. She's since been upgraded to a person of interest."

Thom paused long enough to mop up casserole broth with a piece of bread and wash it down with the last of his wine. Nora took advantage of the brief lull to begin clearing the table and prepare dessert.

"Next morning," continued Thom, "George and I went to work early to prepare the murder book. Our plan was to pitch Craig in the hope that he'd reassign the case. We made our presentation and he asked a few questions. Everyone here knows that my encounter with the girl taints the process and it will follow me to trial. Craig knows this more than anyone. He's always quoting the manual about procedures and conflict of interest. But he's determined to keep us, meaning me, on it. Here's where it gets goofy."

"As if it's not already," said Louis.

"Right," said Thom. "Craig asked George to step out of the room. He threatened me with my job if I repeated what he was about to say."

Nora ceased dessert prep and returned her attention to Thom.

"He told me that he already knew I had been with the girl because I was under surveillance. He told me I was the subject of an integrity audit and by coming forward with my compromised position I had passed. He refused to say whether it was the department or the feds who were watching me, but he did say that the decision to keep me on the case came from upper command."

Louis began to speak, but Thom silenced him with a palm.

"Let me finish, Dad."

Louis nodded and jiggled his rounded palm in a "drink" gesture to Nora.

"While Craig is shitting on my career, George found a law enforcement bulletin from the Santa Monica PD. They had the same bloody message at a scene. So now we have a serial on our hands. Once again, I pleaded with Craig. Told him to let SMPD take the lead. It was the perfect opportunity to get out from under it. But he refused. And once again George and I separate forces. I went to Santa Monica to work on the Deats murder while George continued with the Lawrence murder."

Nora brought a tray with a decanter of brandy and glasses to the table. No one spoke as Arthur poured for Louis and then Thom. After a swirl, Thom continued.

"Deats' body was two weeks dead before it was found. After re-processing the scene I immediately went to the Lawrence autopsy. I'm just about to go in when Craig phoned me. There were two more hits on the SMPD bulletin." Thom held up eight fingers. "We now have eight bodies in three jurisdictions. Craig is assembling the detectives and made me lead. We're meeting at oh-eight-hundred. And that's what I know."

"No one can accuse the Keanes of living on the fringe. We are in the mucky shit all day, every day," said Birdie.

Arthur raised a glass of brandy. "Here, here."

"Something stinks," said Louis.

"Ya think?" said Thom, emphasizing the sarcasm.

"Watch it, boy," said Nora.

"Sorry, Ma."

"Don't take this the wrong way," said Louis, "but why is a pseudo taskforce being organized under Homicide instead of Special? Also, don't SIS detectives usually support taskforces?"

Thom spread his hands. "I don't know. The playbook seems to be continually rewritten based on some report or another."

"Did you tell George?" asked Arthur.

"Of course. He's my partner. It affects him, too. He wondered if he was also under surveillance. I didn't ask Craig specifically about George, but I asked about my family and Craig didn't say one way or the other."

"Have you been interviewed about the Blue Bandits?" said Maggie. "I mean, since we all were?"

Louis, Thom, Arthur, and Maggie were questioned by internal affairs and gave statements to the district attorney shortly after Gerard's funeral. At least the authorities had the courtesy of waiting until he was buried before they came knocking.

Birdie's only interview came from detectives—now members of the Blue Bandits taskforce. And she kept getting called back to the DA's office. No one knew it then, but Gerard had mailed her information that he had not copied for the DA: a journal of crimes going back nearly twelve years with a matching ledger. She used this information to negotiate with the DA. It helped that Assistant District Attorney, Daniel Eubanks, a friend and advocate, was on her side. At the same time, she was talking to her old bosses at the *Los Angeles Times* and got them on board with an exclusive. With a media powerhouse behind her, she leveraged the information and made a deal.

Complete immunity for every member of her family.

No admission of guilt. No criminal conspiracy. No aiding and abetting. No complicity. No obstruction. No accessory after the fact.

And none of them had any idea. Though they benefitted from the deal, she deemed it best they not know. They could go about their professional lives without prejudice or guilt for something they hadn't done anyway.

She realized now that the reason she pushed for their familial confession was to abate her own guilt because immunity implies wrongdoing. Thom and Arthur never participated in Gerard's activities, but neither did they confront him and try to persuade him to cease—as far as she knew. And even if they had, it was best they *never* share that information. Ever. Because that would exacerbate the original dilemma.

Now that everyone else knew that Thom and Arthur knew, they could better watch each other's back.

Only … one nasty thought niggled at Birdie. In an effort to protect her family had she inadvertently pushed the authorities to look for other ways to discredit or punish them for the crimes committed by someone they loved? Secret ways?

They all shook their heads "no" in response to Maggie's question.

"How did Craig know about the hookup?" said Arthur.

"The elusive *they* were watching me. He said the girl's plate was run, her identity established. After she popped up again as the person reporting a crime, Craig changed it up to test me."

"It doesn't make sense," said Louis. "A good supervisor knows his men. Who's stepping out, who drinks, who gambles. From what I know of Craig's reputation he's especially good. Even if he had a beef with you, Thom, he wouldn't jeopardize the case of a city attorney and then a serial. Upper command would never keep a compromised detective on a high-profile media case. No way. Also, you'd not be a solo target. As a dispatcher and Gerard's widow, Maggie would be first up. They'd be especially interested in her financials. I also doubt the FBI is already conducting surveillance."

"Let's suppose Craig were acting alone. What would his motive be?" said Arthur.

"Too difficult to know at this point," said Louis.

"We need to cut to the bone," said Birdie. "What's more important right now are the whys. Why would Craig tip you off? Why say something and put you on your guard? Also, if he were working alone, that is, not under a directive, he'd have a partner. To make surveillance effective it'd have to be twenty-four-seven. Otherwise, what's the point? Something important could go undetected. Who is that person or persons? I agree with Louis, even though the FBI has been invited to the party I don't think they're ready to serve."

"I also agree," said Arthur. "Is Craig close to Narciso Alejo?"

"You and Alejo," said Thom. "Get over it."

"I can't. I hate the dude."

Nora set a peach cobbler on the table. "It's too early in the season for stone fruits," she said. "This was made from last summer's canning."

Birdie took a whiff. "Sunshine, roasted oats, brown sugar, a touch of … hmm?"

"My secret ingredient," said Nora.

Maggie served Birdie first. She took a bite and detected a slight flavor not usually associated with cobblers. Birdie rolled it around in her mouth. "Anise?"

"You pip," said Nora.

"Can we get back to the discussion?" said Louis. "Look, son, you've done everything right. You've taken the issue to your commanding officer and got no result. You might have to go up the ladder. Meanwhile, call the defense league, get yourself a rep."

"Craig was specific that I not tell a soul," said Thom. "Besides this isn't an official misconduct complaint."

"Then make a record of your actions. What you learned, when you learned it, who you reported it to. Be as specific as possible. Note time and location. For example, after you learned of Santa Monica's bulletin did you notify Craig immediately?"

"Yes. He was in the hallway. On his cell. I had to wait a few minutes."

"Good detail. Add that to your notes. CYA." Cover your ass. "Keep the record updated. If you are being watched, your behaviors will be judged. Deviations noted. Don't remove any devices you find on your gear. That'd be a clear tip off. Don't vary your routine."

"There's no more routine," said Thom. "This case just exploded."

"What I meant were the women," said Louis. "How often do you do that? Is picking up women in bars normal for you?"

Thom's impatience with this aspect manifest in his jaw.

"It happens enough that he's earned a reputation as a player," said Arthur.

"So disappointing," said Nora. "My son, the adulterer."

"Yes, I'm a sleazeball," said Thom. "Let's move past it."

"Poor Anne," moaned Nora.

Thom jumped up from the table so fast the chair fell over. He knelt on the floor with upraised arms. "O my God! I am heartily sorry for having offended thee! And I detest my sins! Because of thy just punishments! But most of all because they offend thee! My God! Who are all-good and deserving of all my love! I firmly resolve! With the help of thy grace! To sin no more and to avoid the near occasion of sin! AMEN."

The Keane's were stunned. Not by the act of contrition, but by the sudden gear shift into angry mode.

"Happy, Ma?" said Thom. He punched through the kitchen door.

No one spoke. They just listened to the squeaky hinges as the door swung back and forth.

When it finally stilled Arthur said, "I was kidding about the player comment."

"Who are we to judge him?" said Maggie. "After all, my husband was a murderer."

Birdie shivered. There was a word the family had never uttered. Murderer. Gerard's downfall was referred to as "crimes." Birdie couldn't even write the word in the article. Instead, she quoted from his confession letter. She even tried to forget that he had killed a man while standing mere feet from her. At some point, the next break-through word would be rape. Birdie sat on her hands.

Nora sobbed. Louis took her into his arms.

"Thom's on the roof looking down," said Birdie. "Toes on the edge."

"I'll talk to him," said Arthur.

"I'll go," said Birdie.

———

Birdie opened the door to the timeout room and gently closed it behind her. Thom's profile was silhouetted by the poolhouse light. He blew cigarette smoke out the porthole window.

"I'm sick of Ma's condescension," said Thom. "Ah, *poor Anne*. She dotes on her daughter-in-law as if she walked on water."

"Has Anne pushed you away?" said Birdie.

Thom nodded.

"Her kicking you out ... it has nothing to do with women?"

"She could care less. If I'm getting it elsewhere I'm not bother-ing her for it."

"The affair? Is that what changed this time?"

"I don't know."

"So ... womanizing is a symptom, not a cause."

"Even Anne wouldn't expect me to be asexual forever."

"Why not just say so?"

"I'm devoted to my wife. I love her."

"How long are you going to love a woman who no longer loves you back?"

"Good question," said Thom.

Birdie gently rubbed his upper back. "Let's finish dessert and go home."

"Give me a few more minutes."

————

Nora hugged her son when he returned. "I'm sorry, Thom. My allegiance is with you."

"Ma ... I'm overly sensitive right now." He kissed his mother's cheek and retook his seat at the table. Thom cast his eyes at the untouched cobbler and pushed it away.

"The encounter with the woman ... is there a possibility it was a setup?" said Birdie.

"Maybe," said Thom. "George mentioned that in Jelena's interview she said the bartender knew me. But, I'd never been to that bar before. And I'm pretty certain that I didn't know him from another."

"When did you tell George about the IA?" said Louis.

"At breakfast before we split up."

"Is that normal for you?"

"Breakfast or telling him everything?"

"Both."

"Yeah, pretty much."

Louis rubbed his palms across the stubble on his face. What a rough night.

"The Paige Street protocols are back in place until we know the score," said Arthur. "I have your back, brother. Whatever you need."

"Me, too," said Birdie. "You can stay at my house as long as you need to."

"Thanks." Thom brought ashtrays to the table and the lighting commenced. "I'll clear." He stacked up dessert bowls.

"Bird, dear," said Maggie. "We never asked. How did it go for you after the article came out?"

"I got a few calls of sympathy for our family situation. Some colleagues congratulated me on my courage to bring the story public. Mostly, it was people saying shit because they thought they could do so anonymously. There was the usual smattering of crazies. One random person said something about pretty dead fish."

A loud crash made everyone jump. Their nerves already scrambled by Thom's sudden outburst. This time he dropped all the dishes.

TWENTY-SIX

"DRIVE FASTER," SAID THOM.

"No," said Birdie. "I have a suspended license. I can't risk getting pulled over."

"It's weird to be the passenger in my own car. I should be driving."

"You've been drinking."

"Not enough to impair my driving skills."

"Stop worrying. I promise I didn't delete the message. It'll be there when we get home."

"Is there a way to find out where the call came from?"

"No. It went to my extension at the paper."

"I might be able to get a hookup on the phone."

"Don't count on it. The *Times* and the LAPD are not good neighbors. Besides, I haven't had a physical phone in the building for years. Calls go to a voicemail service. Storage is on some switch."

"That might be better. Can you forward the calls?"

"I think so."

"Then I'll get a hookup on your phone."

"You'd have to get permission from the paper. And that would never happen. They'd consider any calls their property. And I'm not sure forwarding would capture the caller ID anyway."

"I'll still write an affidavit and try to get a warrant. Tell me again what the message said."

"Quit asking. I don't remember the specifics."

Thom's stressing gave Birdie a headache. She cracked the window for fresh air, smelled the perfume of the Pacific. Fish and seaweed. Firepit woodsmoke. It gave off a neorealism mystique. What secrets hid in the scented fog?

"Why do you think it's the killer?" said Birdie.

"He wants attention. It's why he wrote dead fish on the mirror. Reaching out to a journalist is a logical step for an attention-seeking psycho."

"But what's the connection? Your identity as the investigator hasn't been made public. Our family relationship can't be established."

"It has nothing to do with me. Your article made a splash Sunday morning. He probably got your name from that. Hey, when we get home I could use your help downloading an audio file George sent to my phone. I'd like to move it to my laptop. Also, some emails from Seymour."

"Easy enough. What else do you need?"

"Would you mind if I use the white board in your office for some meeting prep? I've got a couple of files to go through."

"No problem."

Birdie turned onto her street and caught a glimpse of a coyote walking on the sidewalk. The headlights caught the eyes and reflected back gold. She'd seen a few lately. She doubted this one came all the way to Hancock Park from the foothills. It was probably an urban coyote. Born and raised here. Living on house pets.

Birdie pulled into the driveway and braked abruptly. "There's a package on the porch."

Before Thom had a chance to say a word, she'd thrown the car into park and was out. She came back a moment later and flung the package at Thom. "It's for you." She pressed the remote for the massive gate. It slowly fanned inward.

"You're disappointed?" said Thom.

"I've been expecting something. No big deal."

Thom flicked on the dome light and examined the padded manila envelope. It was addressed to him c/o Birdie. A red post office stamp that read: KNOWN CUSTOMER was in the upper left corner where a return address should be. It had a Santa Ana postmark—a city in nearby Orange County. Inside, a cell phone and a sheet of printed instructions.

"It's from Noa. Ron's PI buddy. I'll call him first. Then we'll listen to the message."

Birdie was going to tease him about being all hot and bothered in regard to the message only to abandon work-related haste for emotional torment, but she saw Thom's misery in profile.

"Good," she said, trying to be upbeat. "You'll find out about Anne. One way or the other."

"One way or the other," echoed Thom.

Birdie drove down the driveway and swung the car around, lining it up for the garage. She hit a second remote and the garage door rolled upward.

"Take my stuff in?" Thom's briefcase, laptop, and case files were in the backseat.

"Sure. Noa's in town, you know. Ron's with him now."

"Discussing business?"

Birdie shrugged. "None that I'm aware of. They're best friends. Drinking buddies. Ron's gonna feel like shit tomorrow."

———

Thom stumbled in the moonless, foggy dark toward the rear of Birdie's property. Water dripped from the trees onto his head and shoulders. The fob light attached to his keyring didn't cut the darkness of late night, but it was enough to illuminate the paper. He should've grabbed the Mag-Tac in the garage. He wondered why he always took the hard road. His knee scraped against a viewing bench and he figured he had gone far enough. He sat down and followed the instructions:

1) Walk to back of garden. Check.
2) Turn on phone. Check.
3) Speed dial 2. Check.
4) At prompt, punch in password 2-6-6-3-5-3-2-6-3. Check.
5) Get instructions.

Thom listened to a salty voice: "Aloha, Thom. Noa here. Sorry for the pre-recorded message. During the prelim I discovered you have heavy eyes and ears so I resort to subterfuge.

"This is where we're at. I'm not sure I want to work with you. We're going to meet in person so I can get a read. Be on call for the next few days. I'm only going to say this once so pay attention. As our mutual friend, Ron, made you aware my terms are non-negotiable. If you fail to complete the monetary transactions by

176

two p.m. on Tuesday you will never hear from me again. No second chance.

"Call Anne on your personal cell and tell her you're going to wire twenty-grand from your joint BofA money market account to an escrow company. Make up a good lie for the transaction—something she won't question because it's being recorded for posterity and you don't want any more suspicion aimed at your back. The wire instructions are on the reverse side of the paper in your hand.

"We're planning for the future. If I decide you're not a maniac, I'll remove the money for my fee plus expenses. If I decide you are, it will be returned to you. What you won't get back are the twenty-two Benjamins you'll be giving me when we meet. Call it consideration. Tell Anne about this money as well.

"See you in a few. Aloha. P-S, the phone will self-destruct in ten seconds. Kidding. I've always wanted to say that. Keep this phone on your person. I'll use it to reach you."

Thom felt violated. Again. Leaving the required 'just the facts' stats had been hard enough when he made the preliminary call. Now it was for real. He covered his face with his hands. An indescribable bit of anxiety struck him. He knew what Noa would find. Felt it as serious as a heart attack.

Alone, on a wet bench, in the darkness, he began to sob. Hidden from sight and mind and feeling utterly sorry for himself, a muffled groan escaped his lips. What would he do when Noa came back with the proof? Could he win Anne back or would she slip through his fingers? He wasn't frightened of solitude or lovelessness. He had five children after all. He loved them completely. And they him despite the flaws the older ones thought they knew of him. There was a difference between being alone and being lonely. And he'd been lonely for a long time.

He laughed at himself—such a pathetic predicament. If he were at the bottom of the well, he had no place left to go but up. There was value here. Strangely, this thought gave him comfort. After a long while of reflection, he wiped his nose across the sleeve of his dad's sweatshirt and walked toward the light of the Bird House.

TWENTY-SEVEN

BIRDIE'S FINGERS CARESSED THE centuries-old grain of the altar and admired the rare burls that peppered its surface. The new acquirement was quite grandiose—in size, importance, and price—in a house void of purchased indulgence. But Birdie had to have it the moment it went to bid. She loved religious objects and this one spoke to her, sparked her imagination.

People and time moved on and it was forgot, abandoned and left to rot in the suffocating humidity of Louisiana. But this altar was borne of black walnut, an American wood prized for furniture. Straight, strong, and heavy; it resists rot and decay.

It survived, while the church that had once housed its magnificence had not.

Resourced from scavengers and lovingly restored, this solid, unmovable altar was repurposed and became a worktable in Birdie's office. She often wondered what glory or atrocities had occurred on its surface. Was that oxidized blood in the deeper grains? Or cleaning oil? What stories of worship could this wood tell if given the chance?

Perhaps it had been a pagan altar where young virgins or animals were sacrificed. One thing was certain: the inscription on the fascia was not Latin. She could have it translated, but the imaginings were far more interesting.

Birdie raised the shade covering the dry erase board. Made of metallic gray fabric, the screen served two purposes: one, to keep eyes off the work underneath; two, to prevent the massive whiteness from taunting her when she wasn't working. Either way, it was an aesthetic choice as well. Who'd want a wall-sized white board staring down at you?

She took a black marker and wrote a header across the top center: **The process to find the truth is methodical, precise, and provable. Intuition is not evidence.** Those words began every new investigation. The compass that prevented her from straying into second guesses or uncertainties. The provable being her path. At least that's how they all started, but sometimes, the absolute truth is not knowable—a recent lesson learned.

Laid out on the table were the Lawrence murder book and the Deats homicide file. She flipped open both and wrote five names and occupations on the board:

<u>Dominic</u>	<u>Rachel</u>	<u>Amy</u>	<u>Amber</u>	<u>Jerry</u>
city attorney	homemaker	student	student	unknown

"The hell you doing?" said Thom.

"Were the children homeschooled?" said Birdie.

"No. Give me that." He took the black marker from her hands.

"What school did they attend?"

"Don't know."

"Then how do you know they weren't homeschooled?"

Under Rachel's name Thom wrote: **pregnant**. Under Dominic's name he wrote: **sterile**. "Because she slept with someone else and the only time that could occur was while the girls were in school and Dominic at work."

"Ooooh, an intrigue. But your reasoning is flawed. Affairs can take place anywhere, anytime."

"Keep your paws off my work. I'm a damn good detective. I don't need your help."

"You're a *great* detective, Thom. But you're emotionally preoccupied and I'm a good investigator, too. I can keep an eye out for your blind spots."

"Not happening."

Birdie thought about sulking for a nanosecond. She didn't have time for Thom's stuff anyway; her secret project was nearly done. "Well, I found the message. Ready?"

"Go."

Birdie hit the play button on the phone: "*Sunday, eleven-thirty-five a.m. . . . Greetings, Elizabeth, I read your article on the Blue Bandits. Perhaps you should look at all the pretty dead fish.*"

Thom twirled his finger. Birdie hit repeat and they listened again.

"Jelena was still at the scene at that time," said Thom.

"Did she have possession of her cell phone?"

"I'll check George's notes for the timeline." He gestured at the work table where the Lawrence murder book and the Deats file lay open. "Doesn't matter anyway. It's not her voice."

"I don't think it's your killer."

"I think it might be. When was the last time you heard those two words put together?"

"Years ago when the massive fish die-off occurred in Redondo Beach."

"My point exactly," said Thom. "Millions of anchovies got caught in the harbor and suffocated. What does a biological event have to do with a serial killer? Probably nothing, but this killer…he wants attention. Wants *your* attention."

"A he? I think the caller is a she."

"Play it again."

Birdie pressed repeat.

"I'm not sure we can say one way or the other. The voice is gender neutral."

"Agreed," said Thom. "Got any new messages?"

"I haven't checked. But wasn't there some tech thing you needed help with?"

Thom handed her his cell phone. "Jelena's interview. George is bothered."

"A third opinion might be useful. I'll listen, too. Meanwhile, you can get started." She gestured at the board. "All yours."

On the far right side, a newsprint photo of a man was attached by a magnet.

"Who's that?" said Thom.

"Todd Moysychyn," said Birdie.

"Say again?"

"It's pronounced Mo-session. He's a big property owner in L.A."

"Why is his mug on the board?"

"He might be the subject of my next project. I'm curious how the housing crisis affected his business." She took the marker from

Thom and drew a vertical line, saving a little space for herself. "One last thing . . . that header is a phrase Matt used to say."

"Sounds like him. I'll do my thing while you prepare the audio. And don't forget to copy over the emails. Print, too, please."

———

Birdie and Thom read the last few lines of George's typed transcription as they listened to the end of the interview. When it concluded Birdie flipped over the paper.

"I'm impressed with George's transcription skills," she said, "but there's nothing in the interview to suggest she executed four people. Not liking the twins isn't a confession to murder. I'm not even sure it's worthy of upgrading her to a person of interest."

"There is one small inconsistency that bothers me," said Thom. "She reported to George that she heard Dominic's alarm clock. It's what prompted her to go upstairs. Yet, she told the first responder that she only touched door knobs and a magazine. A follow-up with Officer Cross is in order."

"Don't forget the bartender."

"George is handling that."

"What specifically bothers George about Jelena?"

"She speaks with a thick Russian accent even though she's been in America since she was eight years old. He thinks she should've lost it by now. She's twenty-two."

"Maybe she's attached to her accent as a way to get attention."

"It is what made me look at her. I heard an intriguing voice— struck up a conversation."

"Maybe she's a code switcher."

183

"A what?"

"Someone who can switch between languages and accents, speak with the proper syntax, pronunciation, cadence, vocabulary, and phonology of each. It's common with multilingual people. Matt was one. He could switch from Mandarin to Korean to Spanish without anyone knowing he wasn't a native speaker. George is one, too. Haven't you ever noticed how easy he goes from proper Anglo English to twangy Spanish? Even Louis did it this evening. You saw how quick he switched to Gaelic. I'd trust George on this one. Give him the freedom to figure it out."

"I'm going to, but like it says up there on the board, intuition is not evidence."

Thom's cell rang. "That's George's ringtone. Finally." He reached for it and wrenched his wrist when the adapter cord tethering the unit to the laptop didn't give way.

Birdie brushed her fingers against Thom's hand and unhooked the device. She laid it flat and answered on speaker.

"Were your ears burning?" said Birdie. "Thom and I were just talking about you."

"What about?" said George.

"Jelena," said Thom. "Bird listened to the interview and agrees that something is off with that girl."

"Well, I've got something more. Remember the aide, Gordon? How he wouldn't tell me what Dominic was working on until he conferred with the Special Master? After the search of his office—"

"—find Jelena's missing file?" said Thom.

"It wasn't in his briefcase or anywhere else in the office. But listen…"

184

The drop-off was so long that Birdie and Thom looked at each other and shrugged.

"George? You there, buddy?" said Thom.

"I'm here. Take me off speaker. No, wait. I'll call you back."

The call disconnected.

"That's weird," said Birdie. "George knows I can keep a confidence."

"I don't think it has anything to do with you," said Thom.

No sooner were the words out of his mouth, Birdie's office phone rang. The caller ID read Silva, George.

Birdie pressed speaker.

"George? What the hell?" said Thom.

"We have a colossal problem."

TWENTY-EIGHT

"Shit. What now?" said Thom.

"Am I on speaker?" said George.

"It's okay," said Thom. "Bird knows about the integrity audit. I expected to hear from you before now. What happened?"

"Jennet Fontaine is Special Master. Know that name?"

"Familiar…" said Thom.

"I know who she is," said Birdie. "She's from a public-service dynasty. Daughter of Councilman Rick Fontaine, granddaughter of an ex-mayor, and niece of a state senator. She teethed on the ankles of the power elite. She's an attorney who's considering a run for her father's seat when he terms out next year. A darling of the mayor whose political aspirations don't stop at city council."

"Her father and Dominic were extremely close," said George, "yet she froze everything until she's had an opportunity to go through it. According to the aide, Gordon … well, I'm getting ahead of myself. Fontaine let me look though Dominic's briefcase only after she inspected it first. Jelena's file wasn't there. She conducted a cursory search for it, but it didn't turn up anywhere in his office. We can't access the laptop until she's had an opportunity to take a peek. Bottom line, we'll get around to his stuff on Wednesday if we're lucky."

"As if," said Thom.

"Back to Gordon. Jennet's unhelpfulness rubbed him the wrong way and he had a change of heart about talking about Dominic's work. But he didn't want to talk at the office so he suggested Hank's."

"I don't like coincidence," said Thom. "That's where I met Jelena."

"Had he been there with her?" said Birdie.

"No, they didn't socialize," said George. "He's been going there for years, long before Jelena. So, good ol' Gordy orders a drink and gets all speed-mouth. He tells me that Dominic and Councilman Fontaine go way back to law school. We know Dominic was a staff attorney that gave legal advice to the council. Here's where it gets interesting … Fontaine is chair of the housing committee. He and Dominic have been working on housing reform for several years. A complete rewrite that doesn't overly favor tenants or property owners. Fontaine hopes to push through the new housing policy as his legacy because his is the deciding vote when it comes to housing issues.

"It's been a years-long backroom fight that has mostly stayed there. Other than raising relocation fees that landlords must pay to displaced tenants when apartments go condo, the policies haven't changed much because they're so complicated …"

Birdie's brow knit together in rapt concentration. The moment George mentioned housing her eyes shot to the photo on the white board and she paid close attention. Thom caught her eye and gave her a quick wiggle of the head indicating he was confused. She waved her fingers in a silent *I'll explain later.*

"... Since the housing crisis flooded the market with depressed prices and low interest rates, cash-flush developers and property owners started buying in bulk—condos, lofts, apartments, houses. People who can no longer afford their houses or can't get into the short sale market are in need of rentals. Because of high demand, rents are going up.

"According to Gordon, there's been some media interest lately that pits tenant's rights groups against property owners. It's gearing up to be a major issue in the election next year. So people are picking sides. Like I said, Fontaine wants a rewrite to be his legacy and, really, he has nothing to lose because he's leaving anyway. He's all-in and Dominic was at his side.

"Here's where it goes sideways—"

"Hold on, George," said Thom. "Let me catch my breath. You're telling me a lot and not telling me anything."

"Trust me, I was confused at first, too. But it makes sense after a while. Bear with me. You know that I locked down the office and posted a uniform at the door until the SM had a look. Well, Gordon wanted to make sure that Dominic's work for Fontaine was also secure, so he waited until the uniform took a piss break and went into the office. All the housing work had been deleted from Dominic's computer. Also, a Miss Kitty flash drive that Jelena had given Dominic was missing. It's where he kept all of the Fontaine backup files. Gordon expressly remembers seeing Dominic put it into his middle desk drawer on Friday afternoon before leaving for the weekend. So, sometime between then and Monday morning it was stolen and all the hard drive files deleted."

"Christ," said Thom, "did our case just get political?"

"Oh, there's more," said George. "Jennet is on the other side of the issue from her father. She has close ties to some major developers and capital investors. Remember the city's adaptive reuse ordinance that made it easier to turn old buildings to new uses? She was a student during those proceedings and saw the light, as it were. Saw that downtown and the surrounding area was going to explode with growth and that she could make big money. She borrowed from her father and bought her first piece of property. She turned and burned and made a small fortune, been a player ever since. You see, she's not going to be motivated to help us find the missing flash drive or figure out who wiped Dominic's computer. Also, if she wins her father's seat, she'll try to undo what he did."

"You got all that from Dominic's aide?" said Birdie.

"Like I said, he got chatty," said George.

"Is he credible?" said Thom.

"Everything he said is easy to confirm," said Birdie.

"The bottom line is that an insider with access to Dominic's office destroyed several years' worth of work. How does this tie into the other dead fish murders? We have to make a connection," said Thom.

"I'm aware," said George. "But we'll have a better idea after we get the case details on the other three homicides."

"What's next?"

"Gordon is scheduled to come in tomorrow to make an official statement. I'm bringing in Jelena, too. See if she gets flustered with the inconsistent statements."

"And the bartender?" said Thom.

"His name is Jason Kidd. That's K-I-double D. Folks call him Kidd. His father was the manager so Kidd grew up at the bar. Mopped floors, bused tables, washed dishes, took inventory, like that. When he turned twenty-one, he started working behind the bar. Very popular with the ladies. I got his address from the employee contact list and paid him a visit after Gordon and I were done. So, guess who's coming out of his place just as I'm parking? Our friend, Jelena. She and Kidd shared a kiss on the front porch. I let her pass because I didn't want to tip our hand."

"We don't have a hand yet," said Thom.

"I see different," said Birdie. She'd been listening quietly while playing with silver balls of wrapped up chewing gum. "You cannot ignore Jelena as the insider clerk slash foster child who knows the ins-and-outs of Dominic's life. She might not be your serial killer, but she has knowledge of something that may make the water effervescent."

"What?" said Thom and George together.

"Sorry, bad metaphor … she knows more than she's letting on. It's like a jigsaw puzzle. Once you find the edges, it's easier to fill in the middle."

"Tell me something I don't know," said Thom.

"Okay. How's this?" said Birdie. "The city attorney's office will have redundant systems to prevent hacking. Dominic's work may be lost on the front end, but the IT department will have data control on the back end. They probably have cloned computers that backup locally as well as online. The young IT guy that gets the printer up and running is the one to talk to. He can probably retrieve the data."

"Great idea," said Thom.

"I've got something too," said George. "Kidd lied to me. He said he's just a pourer, that he didn't know Jelena or the old dude—his words—previous to Saturday. However, he remembered both from that night. He held the party line and said that you and Jelena left the bar together at around one-thirty. He also remembered that you paid cash and tipped him well. His impression of you was that of a rich bastard. Of course, I didn't let on that I'd just seen him and Jelena suck face."

"Bring his ass in and make his statement official," said Thom. "See if it changes. We'll utilize the manpower of the maybe-taskforce to be our taxi service and conduct statement interviews on our timeline. The clock is ticking and we're fast approaching the forty-eight-hour mark. Also, arrange the visits so that Jelena and Kidd get a passing glimpse of each other. I want to see them squirm."

"What about Jennet Fontaine?" said George. "Gordon had valuable intell, but his action put us into a tight spot with her."

"Agreed. Use Gordon to get to the IT guy. Let's see what he can retrieve for us before she finds out. Hopefully, we keep our hands clean and outside of Fontaine's eyesight."

"We get caught and we're screwed."

"Didn't you know? We're already screwed."

————

The office was silently busy. Birdie sat at her computer, headphones covering her ears, fingers flying across the keyboard, documents spitting from the printer.

Meanwhile, Thom made investigative notations on the dry erase board. He heard her utter an expletive and turned to see a stricken look on her face.

"What?" he said.

"How many shots were fired at the Lawrence crime scene?"

"Five. Why?"

"*This* message was *definitely* left by your killer."

"Let's hear it." Thom sat in the chair and leaned forward on the desk.

Birdie unplugged the headphones and pressed play.

"Greetings, Elizabeth. Let me introduce myself. My name is Mayo. It took three minutes to kill four people with five shots. Good numbers, don't you think?"

"Holy shit," said Thom. "Why?"

"Like you said before, he wants attention."

Thom got up and paced. "Something is very wrong. There's more than attention-getting going on here."

Thom said something else, but Birdie zoned out. She unwrapped a piece of red Fruit Stripe gum and licked off the sugary dust from the foil wrapper. She folded the gum into thirds and stuck it into her mouth. Chewing gum was the multi-pack habit she acquired after she quit drinking. Lately, however, she noticed that she was down to a pack a day. Due to the improved diet and exercise? Time? A bit of all probably. But she chewed now because her heart raced.

"What's the origin of Mayo? Asian?"

Thom yawned. "It's short for mayonnaise. There was a big jar of the shit in Jerry Deats' refrigerator."

"You think the killer got a moniker from a jar of mayo?"

"How would I know? It just makes me remember that I spooned through it."

"Why on earth …?"

"I was desperate to find something. A clue. A lead."

"Seriously? You went through his food?"

"I even opened up his frozen dinners."

"Talk about driven."

"It paid off. I found an envelope that had eviction papers in it. The notice had been taped to the front door."

"Why is that significant?"

"Because Lawrence had the same type of residue on his door."

"So the Lawrence's were also being evicted?"

"Not sure on that. Let's get back to the message … same voice?"

"I think so. I created a new file so you can hear them side by side. Ready?"

They listened to the "pretty dead fish" message and then the "five shots" message.

"My ear isn't as refined as my nose," said Birdie, "but they sound the same to me."

"Yeah …"

Birdie saw Thom's fatigue in the way he stood, the heavy eyelids.

"What can I do? I want to be useful."

"Transcribe the call. The one about the fish, too. I'll take it to Craig in the morning before the meeting and see if there's any way to get the source of those calls."

Birdie didn't want to have the same conversation over again, but there was no way the *Times* would agree to give the LAPD access to their phones. She wondered if there was another way.

"I can run a parallel investigation."

"No way," said Thom, emphatically. "This case will be squeaky clean. Getting help from a journalist—especially the daughter of Gerard Keane—is not gonna fly with the powers that be. Justice won't be served if we break the rules on this one. It's already high risk and I'm not gonna lose my career."

"It's not like you'd become an outlaw cop. Just a resourceful one. I think Gordon's concern over missing files is legitimate and reason enough to dig deeper. Consider me a hunter-gatherer. I can get information without the department's procedural red tape. Look, Thom, the city is run by twelve departments. There's an entrenched bureaucracy that's especially hard for a cop to break through. My assistance will help, not hinder. We can wash whatever I get and it becomes yours. Like original discovery. You own it."

"Let me think about it."

"Alright," she said. "But if you agree, I don't think we should tell George. I totally trust him, but right now I think us Keanes need to stick a little closer than usual."

"Let's talk about it tomorrow. I need to catch some zees."

Birdie didn't tell him that it was already tomorrow. Nearing the forty-eight-hour mark where most of the valuable homicide work is done.

TWENTY-NINE

Tuesday, May 15

Birdie heard a ping. She jerked awake not realizing where she was. Then she remembered that after Thom went upstairs to catch some sleep, she did a bit of casework on his investigation. Last thing she remembered she had laid down on the couch to close her eyes for a minute. Now she paid for those few minutes … hours … with a stiff neck.

The ping was a text.

She picked up her cell on top of the altar. 4:04 a.m. *Are you kidding me?* He's just now getting home? Good thing she didn't doubt Ron's character. She visualized how it went: he and Noa talked and drank for hours, played a few games of pool, drinking past last call, all the way up to closing, and then talking some more at the car, not wanting to leave the best friend that you don't see often enough.

Ron's text read: **HOME**

Birdie texted back: **FINALLY. U OK?**

I HATE MYSELF

TOO MUCH LIQUOR. WHAT WAS IT?
TEQUILA
OUCH! ASPIRIN, LOTS OF H2O.
ROGER THAT
LOVE YOU.
LOVE YOU MORE. TALK LATER…

Birdie got up and stretched. She was tempted to wake Thom. He had the all-important meeting at eight. She'd let him get a bit more rest. With what she already discovered, he'd be amply prepared for the meeting. Make an impression.

———

Birdie knocked on the guest room door and opened it. Thom walked in from the bathroom toward the closet, his bottom half wrapped in a towel.

"Hey, I was coming in to wake you," she said.

"Beat you to it. Got coffee?"

"Nice and strong."

"Breakfast?"

"You eat breakfast?"

"I need the fuel today. It's Tuesday. Got the paper yet?"

"On the kitchen counter."

"Why are you grinning?"

"Because I found a connection between your two homicides."

THIRTY

LONG SOUGHT PAIGE STREET
SUSPECT IDENTIFIED

By Elizabeth Keane
Special to The Times
Part 2 of 2

On a smoggy, triple-digit day in July, two Los Angeles police officers, Hugh Jackson and Matt Whelan of Hollenbeck Division, had just finished lunch when the dispatcher radioed an armed robbery in progress. They were near the address and responded. Less than ten minutes later Whelan was on the ground with a bullet wound to the head, Jackson was dead, another man was dead, a man would die of his wounds the following day, and a woman was hospitalized. The only one who escaped injury was a suspect who got away...

———

Mayo read part two of the newspaper article, upset that the reporter hadn't gone public with the phone messages.

Why is she doing nothing?

The big fish was killed.

Why are the cops doing nothing?

Mayo was losing patience. It's been two days!!!!!

THIRTY-ONE

WHEN BIRDIE TOLD THOM she had taken care of the coffee and donuts for the meeting and handed him a pink bakery box, he assumed it was filled with donuts, bagels, or croissants. The fact that it was heavier than expected must've entered his mind and immediately exited because he never gave it a second thought. Only now as he opened the box did he curse himself for not realizing that she'd take the Ron Road to nutrition and press her new, whole foods agenda onto the unwitting Thom and the other detectives.

Inside were bran muffins, bananas, Fuji apples, and individual packets of mixed nuts, square packets of fruit cleaning wipes, and plastic knives. He picked up one of the muffins and peered at the tiny green bits poking through. He sniffed and smelled nothing other than sugar—a clever disguise to conceal the fibrous bowel-bulker. He was just about to toss the muffin into the trash when Anita Dhillon arrived.

Thom was momentarily taken aback by the detective. She wore a sleeveless tweed dress in shades of red that had frayed edges, seemingly on purpose. Or perhaps the distraction was the cut arms, shapely legs, and high-heeled pumps.

She didn't offer her hand.

"Thom."

"Anita."

She peered into the box. "Oh, thank God. Something good for a change. Your wife put this together for you?"

Thom didn't wear a wedding ring. Never had. As a cop he didn't like to reveal a familial vulnerability. Nor did he mention a wife when they met. Therefore, he was put off by her assumption that he couldn't put together meeting snacks without a woman's assistance—despite the truth.

Thom ignored the comment and said, "There's coffee, too." He pointed at the cardboard carafe from the corner bakery.

Anita claimed a seat by dropping a leather tote onto a chair and flung the jacket that had been over her arm onto the back. She picked up a muffin and bit into it. "Mmm ... zucchini ... delicious. Home-made or store bought?"

The door opened. George's arrival with a fist full of napkins made a response moot.

"Anita, this is my partner George Silva. George, this is Anita 'HILL-on.' Spelled with a silent D. She's the DIC with the Santa Monica PD."

George unceremoniously dropped the napkins and held out his hand. "Nice to meet you." He made no effort to conceal his appreciation of her attractiveness.

"And you as well," said Anita, shaking his hand.

"Chanel?"

"Good eye. Yours?"

"Custom."

"Ah, well done. You must share the name of your tailor. Does he do women?"

"*She* does, but she's not taking new clients right now. Sorry." George clocked Anita. "You don't need my source anyway. That dress fits great."

"Thank you."

"Where do you put your gun?"

Thom's ears perked up.

"Normally, at my back, but today, it's in my purse. That reminds me." She retrieved a piece of paper and handed it to Thom. "That's an estimate for the dry cleaning."

Thom fondly remembered how he slammed an envelope—slimy with decomp—onto Anita's jacket.

He smiled now when he said with all niceness, "Considering I was the one who waded through the detritus and successfully completed the task of finding a lead that you and your team missed, you know where you can put that estimate. Don't you sweetheart?"

Anita glared.

Thom ticked his head at George. "A minute?"

They stepped out into the hallway. "If you go out with that woman, I will hate you," said Thom.

George chuckled. "Yeah, I got the vibe. Don't worry, I won't go out with her. I'm just gonna nail her."

Thom's mouth dropped open.

George guffawed. "Dude, it's way too easy to goad you these days."

A group of men rounded the corner at the end of the hall.

"Game on," said George. He straightened Thom's tie and slapped him on the shoulder. "You look very fine today. Now, let's shake this thing out."

———

Thom Keane stood in front of the white board and addressed the people sitting around the conference table. "We're here to find an apex predator. One that executed eight people while they slept. By comparing our case details and pooling our collective experience and intellect, we will get the answer to the great, persistent question of why these people? We find the answer. We get our predator. He gets the needle. To begin, let's introduce ourselves." He pointed left.

"George Silva. LAPD. Robbery/Homicide Division."

To his left … "Anita *Hill-on*. Detective in Charge, Santa Monica PD."

"James Seymour. Detective three, LAPD."

"John Blabbershaw, by name not reputation." The table laughed. "Culver City PD. People call me Shaw."

"And people call me Diego. I'm with Pacific Division, LAPD."

A man who'd been typing into a laptop stood and said, "I'm Bennie Hy. I'm non-sworn clerical. Meeting notes, file share ops, I can help with—"

Lance Craig suddenly stood and gave Bennie a cease and desist look. "If this group grows into a taskforce, all members will have complete access to case files."

"Craig is our lieutenant at RHD," said Thom quickly to repair the awkwardness caused by the interruption. He gestured to the last man in the room. "Sir?"

A man of medium build who wore his pants low on the hips stood and said, "I'm Captain Carter of RHD. Hello and good morning. I'm due in a meeting, but I wanted to stop by to introduce myself and to say the department appreciates Culver City and Santa Monica's cooperation in finding a serial perpetrator and bringing that individual to justice. Every resource we have will be yours to utilize. I am confident that this group will get the task done. This gathering today is an illustration of the power of law enforcement bulletins. Thank you Detective Dhillon for your outreach. One last word ... silence. No one will speak to any print, broadcast, or online media regarding any aspect of the case. Nor will you make any post in any format. *All* inquiries will be forwarded to Media Relations here at the LAPD. At this time, there is no need to panic the populace regarding a serial killer. They have enough fodder to keep them busy for a while."

He caught Thom's eye when he said that last. Of course, he meant Birdie's article. Thom wondered if anyone else picked up on it. Or if anyone had read her work and connected their names.

Shaw raised his hand, "Sir, any plans for a press conference?"

"Not at this time," said Carter tersely. "Good luck to you all." He waved as he left the room.

Just like an administrator, thought Thom. Or a politician. Which is pretty much the same thing in a department where following the party line gets notice. Captain Carter wasn't well known. He came in a few months ago and organized a cheerleading meeting at the start of his tenure where he rallied the detectives with an actual cheer: *Hey, Hey, you get out of our way, today is the day we put you away!* After that he wasn't around much. When he was in the squad bay he closed himself into his office with its cherrywood desk and cabinets. But it sat dark and empty more often than not.

"Let's get started," said Thom. "I understand that the first dead fish murder took place in Westchester—a neighborhood patrolled by Pacific Station. Diego?"

Diego was a handsome man. On the short side and clearly gym fit. He wore a well-maintained mustache which he continually twisted at the ends—a quirk that already bothered Thom.

From his seat Diego held up copies of the case file. Bennie jumped up and passed them around. "Our victim is a thirty-five-year-old white male, Maxwell Williams. He lived on Boeing Avenue. He was an urban architect who worked out of his home. Cause of death was a single shot to the temple with a small caliber weapon. No casing was found at the scene. He was discovered in his bed and the coroner determined that the body had not been moved. We concluded that he was executed while he slept. The coroner placed TOD at around four to six in the morning of April first. There were no signs of forced entry. The victim was found by his boyfriend—a man named Joey—at around one p.m. that same day.

"According to neighbor statements and Joey himself..." twist ... "the pair had fought Saturday night. Joey had broken off their relationship and Maxwell hadn't taken it well. Joey stated he came back to the house to return Maxwell's house key. When he didn't answer the door, he used the key because he worried that Maxwell's despondency would lead to suicide. That is exactly what Joey thought when he found the body.

"The words dead fish were on the bathroom mirror. We thought it was a sick joke because there was a tank of exotic fish in the kitchen." Twist.

"We've extensively interviewed his associates and friends, but found no motive for murder. We eliminated Joey as a suspect almost immediately. He was in between apartments and living with his sister for a few weeks. She confirmed that he was at her house during the event. Joey calls me every Friday asking for updates. Not sure if he wants Maxwell's murder solved or if he's seeking absolution for the guilt he's laid on himself.

"We thought we had one good lead. Maxwell's house was a rental owned by Vermillion Management. They were quite excited to have it empty and couldn't even pretend to be sad for the deceased."

"I'd think a regular tenant would be an asset," said Anita.

"Except he wasn't a good tenant," said Diego, twisting yet again. "According to the documents provided by Vermillion, Maxwell was continually late on his rent and bounced checks. They were in the early process of eviction when he was killed."

Anita and Thom exchanged glances. Jerry Deats was also being evicted.

"We kept coming back to the entry method," said Diego. "All the windows and doors were shut and locked. No evidence of forced entry. We also examined the front door's dead bolt for microscopic signs of tampering. This lead us to the possibility that the killer had a house key. Maybe a past renter. At our request, Vermillion provided key records. When a new tenant moves into a property, the locks are rekeyed and the renter is given a number of keys based on their needs. Maxwell was given two. One of which he gave to Joey." Twist.

"Who does the rekeying?" said Thom.

"They have a locksmith on retainer that services all their properties. He voluntarily provided a record of his work for the house on

Boeing. His record matched Vermillion's. And that's where we're at. We're no closer to finding why Maxwell was killed or who did it."

"Any other questions?" said Thom.

"Was there a muffle used?" said George.

"A bed pillow," said Diego.

"And what was used to write the message on the mirror?" said George.

"A foam paint brush."

"What was the condition of the bullet?" said Anita.

"Pretty much unusable for comparison. Maybe an alloy comparison."

"Was there tape residue on the front door?" said Thom.

"None that we saw."

There were a few other questions that reiterated the information already given, so Thom gave the floor to homicide detective Shaw of Culver City PD. He did not have prepared copies so the others at the table took notes.

"We had two victims. A mother and her teenage son. Nitta and Nadeer Malik, forty-six and sixteen, respectively. The MO is the same as Diego's case. Single shots to the head. Decorative accent pillow used as muffler. The home is located on La Cienega. A townhouse. We determined that the residence was entered through a downstairs broken window and a patio chair. We found tracked glass shards on the carpeting. Mother and son were in the same bed—hers. There was no forensic evidence in the residence or on their person indicating sexual contact. Nadeer had his own bedroom so we concluded their co-habitation was a cultural thing."

"What was their ethnicity?" said George.

"Indian. Also, there were several books in the house on co-sleeping and attachment parenting so it seems to be an individual choice on her part. There is no father. He died in Afghanistan last year, not as a solider, but as a tourist. Dead fish was also written on the bathroom mirror, and a foam brush was in the sink; however, there were no fish tanks in the house."

"Was the house a rental?" said Thom.

"Owned by Ladder Capital. To my knowledge they were not trying to evict Nitta and Nadeer. The rent was paid on time and the checks were good. Regarding the weapon, the rounds were pretty much broken up inside the skull, which is common in small caliber rounds, the executioner's murder weapon of choice."

Shaw paused to drink some water and for a moment the only sound in the room was Bennie's frantic typing.

"When did the murder occur? And who found the bodies?" said Anita.

"April eighth—apparently, a week after the Westchester murder. The bodies were found that afternoon by a friend coming for tea. It was a standing date. When they didn't answer the door, the friend went through the gate to the back patio and discovered the broken window. She called nine-one-one."

"What I'm hearing so far," said Seymour "is that other than the manner of death and the message, there is no connection between the victims."

"None that we've yet found," said Anita.

Thom liked that she put one half of S&M in his place. It was early in the investigation; he shouldn't be ruling anything out. Too bad she couldn't be this agreeable all the time.

"That's right," said Thom. "Anita? You're up."

Anita stood to speak. "My case is highly unusual and at its end is an all-important statement."

THIRTY-TWO

THE CRIMINAL COURTS BUILDING was rededicated the Clara Shortridge Foltz Criminal Justice Center over a decade ago. The long and awkward name never stuck and it continued to be known as the Criminal Courts Building or CCB for short. Located on West Temple between Broadway and Spring Street, it was the location of the infamous O.J. Simpson murder trial.

During Birdie's staff reporter days she had spent a lot of time in the building covering court cases. So familiar, she knew which restrooms were less crowded and the bank of elevators used least, with the fewest floor stops, and therefore faster. But today she took the stairs. A year ago she wouldn't have dreamt about walking up seventeen floors. Sobriety, a healthy diet, and regular exercise had changed her life, and today the upward trek didn't daunt her.

She took the corridor toward ADA Daniel Eubanks' office. Once opening the outer door she walked into the inner sanctum of assistants, clerks, and other ADAs as if she owned the place. The press pass on the lanyard around her neck didn't match the ID badge of the employees around her, but a well-placed coffee cup concealed that fact.

As she approached Danny's office she noticed the dark spot, a shadow of a closed door. Danny always left it open when he was in. Any other time it was closed and locked—even when he jetted out for a quick trip to the men's room. Hell, she took a risk and lost. She hadn't made an appointment thinking surprise would work in her favor. She had almost reached his door and was about to turn around when it opened. The District Attorney exited with Danny in her wake.

Shit! She didn't want to be seen by the boss. Her past intimacies with Danny and subsequent friendship needed to stay quiet. Even a whisper would taint his standing and credibility with the DA.

She dropped her head and lead with her shoulder as they passed. She dared a peek at Danny's profile. His jaw set in displeasure, but not so mad, because he left the door ajar for her and she quickly slid inside.

Birdie glanced around the office. Bookcases were mostly hidden behind file boxes stacked every which way. A fire inspector's nightmare. There was so little elbow room that visitors had to sit in a folding chair that was shut closed when not in use. She'd never been alone in his office before and the temptation to snoop tugged at her sense of right and wrong. Had she not already known what he was working on she might let go and flip through the files laid open on his desk and look for a juicy tidbit. Instead, she respected his privacy and the trust he bestowed and sat on the still-warm folding chair and placed her hands in her lap.

A few minutes later Danny returned and promptly locked the door.

"You nearly gave me a heart attack," he admonished.

"I've been doing that a lot lately."

"Give me a hug." He pulled her up off the chair and firmly wrapped his arms around her. She sensed that he required the hug more than she did.

She enjoyed being enveloped in his embrace and fondly remembered what attracted her to him in the first place. He was her type: strong, handsome, rugged, and crazy smart.

"Danny, your heart is beating way too fast."

He let her go. "This is *not* the time to be seen in this office. Why didn't you call?"

"I didn't want a record of my visit. Did she notice me?"

"Too preoccupied."

"With the Blue Bandits?"

"And then some." He sat on the edge of the desk, which forced her to look up at him. She hated when he did that. She'd rather he sit behind the desk, at eye level. Although from this vantage she saw a thing she rarely saw. The pistol he wore on his ankle.

"The only time you spring a surprise visit on me is when you're unhappy about something. What's up?"

"Who's blowing the bugle?" she said.

"*What?*"

"Who's leading the charge against Thom?"

"What are you talking about?"

"When I got immunity for the family it was with the understanding that they didn't know Gerard was an outlaw. No one could come after them. So why is Thom being targeted?"

Danny shrugged and shook his head. "I've no idea what you're talking about," he said as he moved around the desk to sit. A body language expert might think the action a defense mechanism, but Birdie sensed his legitimate confusion.

"The immunity granted my family is a roadblock to prosecution for crimes they didn't even know about. But what if someone wants a Keane to pay for Gerard? Even when the charges would be proved unfounded, whoever was the target would have their reputation ruined and they'd lose their livelihood anyway."

"If that's happening, it's not coming from this office. The state cannot—"

"—the state … yes, you're right. The *state* cannot come after any Keane. Can the federal government?"

"Sure. But why would they? Prosecuting guilty knowledge is nearly impossible in the flush of times. Considering the budgetary state of the feds I doubt they'd waste their resources."

"That's what Louis thinks, too, but they were invited in by the LAPD."

"To run a parallel investigation of the Blue Bandits. There are five members of that gang awaiting trial as we speak. Our resources are busy with them. I can't speak on the record, but the feds wouldn't waste their time on Thom, or you, or any other Keane who *might* know something."

"You put the emphasis on might. Very lawyerly."

Danny smiled. He had a nice one. His brown skin contrasted with the white enamel and made his teeth shine all the brighter. Birdie felt a flutter in her chest. Another positive, physical reaction to a man. Very good progress.

"Why do you think someone is after Thom?"

"Well ... I'll tell you a secret."

Danny threw up his hands. "Whoa. No secrets."

"Based on what you've already said, this one doesn't compromise you."

Danny shook his finger at Birdie. "You know full well that I still find you deliciously enticing. You're such a vixen to take advantage."

"I'll tread carefully."

"Alright," he sighed. "Go on."

"Thom is the target of an integrity audit. He was told as such by his supervisor, Lieutenant Lance Craig. Thom was with a woman Saturday night who turned out to be the one who found the Lawrence crime scene."

"That's Thom's case?"

"Not initially. When Craig found out that Thom had been with the woman the night before—and, by the way, she was the Lawrence's foster child—he gave the case to Thom to test his integrity on the matter. Thom may have a reputation as being a screwup in his private life, but he takes his job overly serious. He passed the test, but Craig has refused to remove Thom from the case. And now it was discovered that the Lawrence murders are one in a serial."

"No, shit? And Craig still won't take him off?"

"Thom has practically begged. You know how it is with the department. They try to avoid all conflicts of interest."

"How did Craig know he'd been with the woman?"

"Thom's under surveillance. Eyes and ears. Thom was told the decision to keep him on the case came from upstairs."

"As in the command staff? Maybe even the chief?" Danny leaned back and tented his fingers in thought. "No. It's not the department."

"Are you privy to audits?"

"No, but I'm ninety-nine percent certain that upper command wouldn't be so stupid. And I just don't see the feds in on this."

"Who does that leave?"

"This Lance Craig for sure. Sounds like he's screwing with Thom. Why else would he tell the subject of an audit that he was being audited? Makes no sense. I'd question everything the guy says."

"Maybe he's not a poker player like you."

"Come on, Elizabeth, it's not in his best interest. He might have guilty knowledge and is simply putting Thom on his guard. Do they get along?"

"According to Thom they do."

"So he's being Thom's friend by giving him the four-one-one?"

"That's twisted and backward, but let's say it's crazy enough to be true. Who would that leave?"

"You know I don't like hypotheticals. But let's approach from another direction. Maybe it's not job related. Maybe it's personal. Maybe someone tattled to Craig about what Thom did the night before. Maybe Craig took it upon himself to test his detective. Thom passed, but Craig couldn't reassign it again. He makes up a cover story."

"Danny, you are not a maybe man. And you just said too many. And besides, Thom *does* have eyes and ears. The fact was independently confirmed."

"Fair enough. How's this? Who'd have the resources to conduct a personal vendetta?"

Birdie's skin prickled. "Ahhh, Danny. I knew there was a reason I came here today."

THIRTY-THREE

"On May two a woman looked out her bedroom window and saw a sight she'd never seen before."

Oh, Anita's a storyteller, thought Thom. Who would've known? He liked her at this moment. She had the attention of every man in the room—including his. And, oh, that red dress…

"The man who lived in the apartment directly across the alley from her had never once opened his curtains. On this morning he did. Only he didn't. Our killer did. The killer wanted his body found. We at the Santa Monica Police Department know this because Jerry Deats' body was in an advance stage of decomposition.

"Jerry Deats was a fifty-four-year-old white male. He lived alone and was—by all neighborly accounts—an odd man. He often spent hours on his porch smoking cigarettes. He was a loner. A hoarder. He didn't like conversation. Mostly, he shut himself into his garage apartment and did who knows what.

"His homicide was similar to all of yours: a single shot to the head with a small caliber weapon. The words dead fish were written in blood on the mirror and a foam brush was left behind. The coroner placed Deats' murder during a three-day window. April fifteen to eighteen. After listening to what's been said this morning, I now believe that Jerry was killed on Sunday the fifteenth. If this is so, our killer murdered someone in their sleep every Sunday for three weeks straight. Only Jerry's body was not found on the kill day like the others, hence the opening of the curtains.

"A decomp crime scene is the worst kind. Me and my team made the mistake of not looking closely enough through the garbage in his home. We had exhausted our leads and had no reason to believe his murder was one of many, but we put out the bulletin anyway in hopes that something familiar stuck with another jurisdiction.

"Detective Silva here was the first response we got. And only a few hours later Detective Keane came out and reexamined the scene. He discovered that the victim's laptop was missing, and he found an envelope that contained some papers that Deats took great pains to hide…"

Anticipation made the heartbeats of six men almost audible.

"Jerry Deats was also being evicted. Just like the Maxwell fellow. But he'd been paying the rent on time every month and he wasn't going to go quietly. In the envelope was a letter from an eviction lawyer. The language was abusive and bullying."

"Why was he being evicted?" said Diego of Pacific Station, with a twist of his mustache.

"It's unclear based on the one letter recovered. We suspect that the missing computer has the answers. What we do have is Jerry Deats' last words in an original handwritten letter dated five days before he died. It read: 'If they can't kick me out, they will kill me out.'"

A collective gasp filled the room.

"There was a singular cigarette butt left behind in Jerry Deats' ashtray that was different than the others," continued Anita. "Despite the moist ocean air it was in fair shape and the lab was able to construct a DNA profile. It didn't get any hits in the databases, but we have something for future comparison. Unfortunately, the bullet inside Jerry's skull was of no use—like the other Sunday homicides."

After a short round of questions Thom moved on.

"This brings us to the Lawrence homicide," said Thom. "Four people were also shot as they slept. Dominic, his wife Rachel, and their two foster children, Amy and Amber. The girls were only ten years old. The killer wrote dead fish in blood on the bathroom mirror. He also used a pillow as a muffle. And so, other than the broken window as point of entry, our subject's MO has been consistent, but he changed his signature. He shot Dominic in the pelvic region. We are considering the possibility that the killer meant to destroy the penis, but it missed the reproductive organs, tore through soft tissue and lodged in the kidney. We now have a bullet intact enough for comparison.

"We know that in the last two homicides the killer took something. A computer from Jerry Deats. There is a possibility the killer also took a file from Dominic's."

"Why do you say possibility?" said Seymour.

"It's missing from the home, but we're not sure why it's missing. Was it removed by the killer or by Dominic himself? Our adult victims in this case were foster care parents. They had detailed files on every one of their charges. The files were in a locked cabinet in a locked office that was hidden behind a tapestry. It is unknown if the unsub even knew this room existed. The missing file is that of previous foster child, Jelena Shkatova. She was the person who found the bodies, she is also a clerk in Dominic's office—who, by the way, is a city attorney. A Special Master has been assigned to assist us in searching Dominic's city office."

"More like hinder us," said George.

"In any event," continued Thom, "the file may not be significant, but until we find it, we won't know. There is another element of this case that is quite disturbing. The coroner determined that Rachel was fourteen weeks pregnant and that Dominic was sterile. We're awaiting DNA for a paternal profile. What, if any, significance the pregnancy had in the commission of these murders is unknown at this time. But that shot to the groin …? We'll know more this evening when the lab is finished."

"Going straight to the head of the line for lab work is a benefit of a high-profile victim," groused Shaw of Culver City.

"Indeed," added Lance Craig. "The press is hounding Media Relations for information on the Lawrence family. The chief is considering the scope and when or if to hold a press conference. Like Captain Carter said, we don't want any word of a serial to leak. We don't want a panic on our hands. Until we know what links all the victims and can give the population some reassurances that they won't be murdered in their sleep, we'll be keeping this dark."

"Late last night," said Thom, "I found a connection between the Deats and Lawrence homicides."

Craig threw Thom a look that bordered on incredulity. Thom didn't understand why but pressed forward with his presentation.

"Tacky residue was on both front doors," said Thom. "It was as though something had been taped there. We know Deats was being evicted and it is unclear at this time if Lawrence was as well. There was no evidence of such inside the home, and we've been unable to secure a look at Dominic's laptop."

"The SM wants to make sure we don't see privileged information," added George, "we're pretty certain that the laptop was for personal use, but until we get a look we won't know for sure."

"So what's the connection?" said Anita.

Thom was prepared to play it up. Like finding it was really hard work. In fact, Birdie had done it, but she told Thom how to make it appear as though he did.

"Deats was a renter. His landlord, the one trying to evict him, was Mobeck Finance Holdings. Lawrence was also a renter. His landlord was Great Western Group. We now know that all eight victims were renters, though I didn't know that last night. The note Jerry Deats wrote really bothered me: *If they don't kick me out, they'll kill me out.* On the surface, we have two seemingly unrelated companies: Mobeck and Western. They each have different companies managing the properties. However, after searching databases for articles of incorporation, tax rolls, and such we now know that both companies are owned by L.A. National Housing Trust. Whether this is coincidence or a matter of import is yet to be determined."

"Fine work, detective," said Craig, in a dismissive manner. "There are also other details that need to be established. What was our perpetrator doing during the four weeks between the Deats and Lawrence murders? And is the killer planning to murder again this Sunday? The way I see it, gentlemen ... and ma'am ... is that we have four days to get the SOB. Now, let's talk about assignments."

THIRTY-FOUR

BIRDIE CHANGED CLOTHES IN the backseat of her Taurus. No dress and high heels needed where she was headed. She shimmied into jeans and laced the steel-toed Wolverines, pulled on a white tank top, buttoned a tattered denim shirt. She pulled back her long hair and quickly braided it, securing the end with a #16 rubber band. She swiped a makeup remover sheet gently across her eyes, removing most of the eye shadow and mascara, but not all of it. Then she took off the blush and added a bit of translucent powder. She wrapped white medical tape around the joint that connected the intermediate and distal phalanges of her right and left hands then dirtied the tape by rubbing the cleansing cloth across its bright whiteness. She flexed her fingers, used tweezers to pull out a few threads of the tape—the small details of the blue collar costume.

She opened the trunk and removed a hardhat covered in stickers denoting the reserve, rig, and other affiliations of the oil drilling business. She had once lived on an offshore oil platform to get an insider's view of the business and write a feature about drilling off the California coast. She may be left of center in her politics, but she was all for ocean drilling and against fracking and those positions were proudly stated on the skull cover—with the required equipment: a pair of safety glasses perched on top and a pair of earplugs dangling from a yellow cord down the back. She shoved her phone into a fake leather holder that was at least ten years old and attached it to her waist, stuffed a pair of work gloves into the back pocket. Lastly, she picked up the battered Grainger aluminum storage clipboard and made sure the steno book was fresh, the pencils sharp, and the digital recorder had fresh batteries. She tossed in her press credentials for good measure.

Finally, good to go.

She started footing west. She could've taken the Metro to get a bit closer, but walking would work up the necessary sweat to make it appear like she'd been working all morning. Every now and then she'd walk across a dirt patch and made an extra effort to kick up dust. In one empty lot an abandoned bag of redi-mix lay nearly hidden in yardstick-high mustard. She kicked it open and ran through the billowing white powder. By the time she arrived at the construction site she felt like the cartoon character Pig-Pen, complete with the requisite dust billowing around her.

Once upon a time, in the alcoholic version of her life, Birdie was filled with cocksure bravada. She could sweet-talk her way into (and out of) nearly any situation. Not so much today. Sobriety had knocked the stuffing out of the what-the-hell adventurer. Take right now, for instance. She had to get into character. A persona. In a city of wannabe actors, where people ran lines at the corner coffee shop, it wasn't that hard to visualize what she needed to become. But her hands shook so hard she almost asked some random dude for a cigarette. And that was another vice she determinedly avoided. Besides, he looked at her like some junkie so she stuck two pieces of Juicy Fruit in her mouth and started smacking.

If caught, the worst thing that could happen was that she'd be escorted off the premises by some Taser wielding, overzealous security guard. Or they could call the cops. That would've been a good thing six months ago. All she had to do was figure out which station patrolled the area she was in and drop one of many names: her father, uncle, cousin, or any number of Whelan boys. She probably knew at least one cop in every division. Still did, but she was pretty certain that she had become an eight-point buck in the laser sights of the LAPD first liners.

Birdie frowned and popped gum at the security guard patrolling the chain-link gate and gave a disgruntled wave as if she were late as hell and *had* to work another day at this shithole. Once in, she hid behind a stack of rebar and mapped the terrain. She'd been told that the man she wanted to see would be here today.

But where?

She considered the construction offices. A series of singlewide trailers with umbilical electrical. But if he were "inspecting" as she'd been told, he wouldn't be holed up in an office. No, he'd be at the site of the newest construction. Considering high-rises are built from the ground up, she figured he'd be "up there." She looked at the towering height, and got instant vertigo just by squinting skyward.

Birdie decided on a course of action when a line of beat-up food trucks rumbled past the gate and parked in a semicircle. These weren't the kind of trucks L.A. foodies followed with zeal from one location to another. The ones that sold twelve dollar hamburgers. These were the barely legal ones that spewed grease into the air. A horn blew and a sudden swarm of men poured out of the tower. Birdie stood her ground and inspected every person, looking for the one she wanted. The man she had once interviewed would never miss a meal. This seemed the perfect opportunity for an impromptu, totally unplanned meeting.

The rebar provided the perfect spot for reconnaissance. From where she stood, she had a great eyeline at the lift cages. They went up and down transporting more men to ground level and she had a great view of their faces. They peeled off gloves and jackets and lined up at the trucks. She waited patiently and continued to search the men, but the one she sought had not materialized.

Finally, a gaggle of suits wearing hardhats exited the cage. She swallowed the anticipation and tried on a fake smile then promptly wiped it from her face. She was a worker bee. They didn't smile. She casually strolled their way to catch the conversation. They were all talking at once; like at a dinner table when all the diners knew one another and were telling tales and finishing each other's sentences and laughing. She could barely keep up. Geez. She rolled her neck. To think what she had put herself through just to get here. She determined not to be so wasteful with her time from now on. She had better things to do than to *accidentally* run into a man who—in all likelihood—wouldn't give her the time of day anyway.

That's when she heard one of the suits ask where *he* was.

Another one thumbed behind his head and said, "Doing lunch up there."

The suits cleared off into the construction trailer and slammed the door. Birdie headed for the lift. She'd never been in one before and was surprised by four things: first, the cage door slid much easier than anticipated. She threw her weight into the closing and it slammed shut with a metal on metal shudder that shook and clanked and caught the attention of a few men. Second, it actually had a panel with floor numbers. She pressed the dirty one, the one that had been pressed the most. Third, it was fast. As it lurched upward so went Birdie's stomach. Fourth, it had a grated bottom. She looked down at her boots and beyond to see the ground shrinking from view and quickly turned her view inward, away from the surrounding high-rises and the bottom far, far below.

The lift passed floor after floor. The innards of modern buildings became a blur of concrete, ducting, electrical conduit, plumbing, insulation, and lots of plastic scrim. She'd catch glimpses of pallets of glass, drywall, tile. And just when she thought she could no longer hold down her breakfast it stopped.

She crossed herself. "*Glória Patri, et Fílio, et Spirítui Sancto.*"

Birdie's knees went weak and she stumbled off the lift and fell onto the cold concrete. The wind, jetting in from the Pacific, blew chalky dust and debris into some kind of net, whipped her braid. She hadn't prepared for the wind and now realized why the crew coming down all wore jackets. *Great planning, Birdie. Almost thought of everything.* She crawled away from the edge until she was in the middle of the floor and had the courage to stand. *Be still my heart.*

A man sat on top of a stack of moving blankets sipping something steamy from a thermos. At his feet sat a hard hat and a metal lunch pail. He turned to look in her direction, seemed to recognize her, but said nothing. Birdie wasn't sure he was the man she sought. She remembered an obese eccentric, always shoeless, who wore cargo shorts and a Hawaiian shirt so short his belly stuck out. His hair, typically long and greasy, was always pulled back in a thin, straggly ponytail, and he wore a beard that grew in tufts around his chin.

The man before her was much, much thinner, wore a pinstripe suit, and had a clean-shaven head and face.

"Mr. Moysychyn?" she said.

"Who wants to know?"

"My name is Elizabeth Keane. We've met before."

"I remember you. You're that print reporter that said I was a slumlord."

"No, I reported what someone else said about you. The thing about journalism is that I don't get to express personal opinions."

"That the way of it?"

"Yes, sir. Do you mind if I sit? Have a chat?"

"Since you have the balls to sneak onto a secured job site to accost me, I suppose I can give ya a few minutes."

She gingerly moved toward him until she was at his side and sat down on an adjacent blanket, crossed her legs and looked up at him. She wanted him to perceive her as the weak one. She wanted him comfortable in his power and arrogance.

"There's no wind here."

"It's called the eye. There's always some sweet spot where it's calm. Like the inside of a hurricane. That's why the blankets. I like to sit, be comfortable, and eat lunch while admiring the view." He regarded her. Up and down. "I don't remember the scar."

"Car accident."

"Why do you want to see me?"

"Excuse me, sir, I just have to confirm. You are Todd Moysychyn. Yes?"

He harrumphed. "You haven't seen me since I've lost weight. Nearly two hundred pounds. I have a wife now, too. She picks out the clothes."

"Congratulations. You must be proud to have accomplished such a feat."

"Don't stroke my dick."

"Now that's something the old you would say. Can't the new you just say thank you?"

He laughed. "You're alright Elizabeth. My wife's a new fan, you know. Read your article on Sunday. Today's, too. Went out and bought your books. Goes on and on about you. You should come to dinner. I'd get laid every night for a week straight if I brought you home."

"I'd do dinner if you agree to an interview."

Birdie retrieved the tools of her trade and turned on the recorder, placed the press credentials around her neck.

"What now? Didn't you get your fill last go round?"

"I want to talk to you about the housing meltdown. See how your business weathered the storm, so to speak."

"There's a worthwhile topic. I did better than most. The majority of my portfolio was in rentals, not retail. When the crash occurred, people stopped buying consumer goods. Store owners couldn't pay rent. Shops closed up and retail space emptied. But people still needed to live somewhere so I still got my rents."

"You said, *was*, past tense. Are you still in the rental market?"

"Oh, yes, it's very lucrative, especially now. Housing prices fell so far that those of us with cash scooped up the bargains. It's trending our way. Inventories are declining and rents are going up. I'm buying and holding for short-term profit and long-term appreciation. I'm doing extremely well. I'm also branching out some."

"This building for example? A hotel? Right?"

"Mixed use. Retail, offices, apartments."

"Luxury apartments?"

"Mid-price. The economy hasn't recovered enough to fill the luxury inventory still out there. I'm not making that mistake. I want my tower filled to capacity. When it's done I'll have the top two floors with wraparound observation decks. An indoor pool. You should see the engineering required for that sucker. My wife is looking forward to living here. She wants out of the Biscuit."

The Biscuit Building was a five-story bakery located on the edge of downtown's industrial area and a stone's throw from the north side of the I-10—commonly known as the Santa Monica Freeway. It got its name because biscuits were made there about ninety years ago. After the plant closed it sat empty for decades. Whenever Birdie drove past, she always wondered about that building with its beautiful brick façade and yellow glass windows. She often wondered what it looked like inside. She'd have dinner with them just to tour it.

"You live there?" said Birdie.

"Me and the missus."

"I heard the place got converted into lofts."

"Never got that project off the ground."

Todd screwed the cap back on his thermos and placed it into the metal lunch pail. He removed a sandwich wrapped in aluminum foil.

"So … dinner? An extended interview?"

"Tonight at six. My place. The missus will be mighty happy."

"Great. Since I'm here may I broach another newsworthy topic?"

"Make it quick. I don't want my colleagues catching you here." He bit into a bologna and cheese sandwich.

"Have you heard that Dominic Lawrence and his family were murdered?"

"Couldn't avoid that news."

"In a house you own."

"Yeah. The Nobel house, up in the Hills."

"Any thoughts?"

He talked while chewing. "I didn't like the SOB. But I'll miss Rach."

"Have the police talked to you?"

"Why would they? I was his landlord, not a golf buddy."

"But you were trying to evict him." This was a bluff that paid off when …

He threw his sandwich down. His neck reddened and the vein in his forehead pulsed. "You know how much that house is worth on the open market?" he said. "But I can't compete with my own damn house! Back in '79 that house got arbitrarily swept up into rent control shortly after Dominic started renting it. Some coincidence right? Then the greedy bastard used a frickin' loophole, applied for, and got a section eight voucher. You know how much he pays in rent? Eight-hundred dollars! For a house in the hills with an epic view. I can sell that sucker, as is, for three-point-five mil. Easy. But no, I can't because the schmuck has used his political influence to keep me from doing so 'cause he don't want to lose his view. It's a great frickin' house! Once, it looked real good, too. He used loophole after loophole to stay where he was and never spend more than eight in rent. Rent for that place should be thirty-three a month. At the low end. Maybe four. SHIT. I made my mistake way back in the eighties and nineties when my real estate holdings were growing. The Nobel house fell through the cracks and I forgot to raise the rent by four-percent annually as allowed by the stabilization law. He took advantage of my forgetfulness. So yeah, I was trying to get him out, and you know what that sucker did? He stopped maintaining the place and let it go to shit and blamed it on me. Man ... I sure was stupid in the beginning. But I'm a lot smarter and wiser now. Most times, renters just pack up and go when they're getting evicted. But sometimes you come across a guy like that Dominic prick that twists the law of ownership around so that he has more rights than I do." He picked up his sandwich, blew on it and continued eating.

Birdie was momentarily stunned by the rant. She glanced down at the silver recorder and hoped it had picked it all up because she was too flummoxed to take notes. She was still processing all he said when the sound of mastication stopped.

"Sorry 'bout that," he said.

"You may have lost weight, but not your ... enthusiasm."

"I own that house. He gets a free pass to pay rent on a house that is undervalued as a rental property? At his income level? That's what makes me angry. He can afford to pay higher rent. Section eight is for low-income families. I swear, how people game the system. And he ... a city lawyer ... gamed it the most. It's disgusting. I'm just looking after my property. Bought and paid for by me and he thinks he can prevent me from making a profit on something I legally own? Damn squatter."

Birdie kept her mouth shut, tried to still her shaking hands. She didn't want to provoke anymore of his ire, especially since she was on the thirtieth floor of a tower with no walls and a swift wind.

"I should apologize," she said. "I had no idea of the circumstance behind his residency. I was just wondering how you felt about the murders."

"Good riddance to him. But Rach? She was a classy lady."

"Had you met the twins?"

"Those foster kids? Naw. That house was a revolving door of them. That's one of the things he used in his section eight application. You know he got paid for having those kids? He was paying shit rent and had a great salary. What the hell did he do with his money?"

What indeed? thought Birdie.

"Well, Mr. Moysychyn, thank you for allowing me to sneak up on you." She gathered her things. "Are we still on for dinner tonight? Also some follow-up questions?"

"Sure," he said distracted. "My wife will be very happy."

"What's her name?"

"Iris. Like the flower."

"Ask Iris if she'd be okay if I brought a date. See, my cousin is currently estranged from his wife ..."

"Sure. Bring him along. She won't mind."

"What can I bring?"

"Nothing. She'd be offended."

"Tonight then." As Birdie stood he pulled out his cell to notify her "new fan" of the dinner plans.

"Hey," he called back, "you got any diet restrictions?"

"I'm not a fan of fish," she called back.

"Yeah, I don't much like dead fish either."

THIRTY-FIVE

THOM PULLED TWO PAPER towels from the dispenser and dried his hands. A toilet flushed and Bennie Hy, the clerk, emerged.

"Guess we're almost done," said Bennie, washing his hands.

"About time," said Thom, glancing at his watch. He made a quick calculation, still on track to make Noa's wire deadline. "So, hey, how quick can the meeting notes be ready? And Culver City's file copy?"

"I can send you the raw transcription immediately. If you want the edited version, I'll need the day."

Thom handed Bennie a business card. "My email's on there. Send what you have now. Too bad Shaw didn't bring copies."

"Yeah, slows the process. Don't know what format he'll provide. But as soon as I get it, you'll get it."

"It's nice to know someone in this building is efficient."

"Thanks, detective. We don't get much recognition. See you in there."

Thom's personal cell pinged. "Yeah, see you in there."

A text from Birdie: **STARVING. MEET 4 LUNCH?**
He texted back: **HAVE ERRAND. COME WITH. EAT ON RUN**
WHERE? WHEN?
PAB. NOW. CALL WHEN ARRIVE

Thom grinned as he tucked the phone away. Starving = urgent. Birdie's news was important, and hopefully, valuable.

He felt energized as he exited the bathroom. There were hot leads, new information, cooperation, efficiency. This case might get solved, another life saved. Another thirty minutes of meeting, tops, and he could sprint.

Thom opened the war room door. Bennie caught his eye and held up his thumb. Email sent. Thom gestured *okay* in return. Anita and Diego were at the pink box eating. Anita gazed at Thom with an unexplainable expression. Shaw was texting or checking email on his phone. Craig and Seymour were whispering in the corner. George ticked his head toward the door. Thom backed up and they walked down the hall.

"What did she do now?" said Thom.

"Who she?" said George.

"Anita. Did you see her face?"

"It wasn't ... Craig—"

Craig and Seymour came through the door.

"LT?" said Thom. "What's up?"

"It has come to my attention that your participation will jeopardize our case. We think it best ..."

Thom's brain whirled. He's being thrown off? Had someone, somehow, found out about Birdie's eyes on the case?

"... very disappointing," Craig droned. "I think you'll agree the investigation will be better served with Seymour and Silva as lead."

Seymour said, "Morgan had a family emergency and George is already up to speed since the begin—"

"—as of this moment you're no longer working the case," said Craig. "We need to have a few private words. Gentlemen?"

George reluctantly pivoted toward the door. "I'll call you later."

"We'll need the murder book," said Seymour, somewhat smugly.

As soon as the door shut, Thom said, "What the hell, LT? I told you *immediately* about Jelena. I begged off, but you wouldn't listen. And now that the case has legs and is gathering speed you're pulling me? And reassigning my partner?"

"Trust me," said Craig. "I'm not happy either. But we got an official complaint." He held up his hands in defense. "A one-eighty-one was filed. Complaint of Employee Misconduct. The IA investigator will want to talk to you immediately. Call the League. Get a rep."

"You kidding me?" said Thom with a hitch in his voice. "You file on me?"

"Hell, no," said Craig. "I don't want this attention. I don't know who filed. I don't know what the problem is. Hell, it might've been filed a week ago for all I know."

Only Internal Affairs—operating under the umbrella of the Professional Standards Bureau—located in the Bradbury Building on Broadway would know who filed. Anyone can file a complaint for any reason. A disgruntled citizen, a fellow officer, a supervisor, *anybody* has the right to file. The department even made it easy. PDF forms, complete with instructions, were available on the LAPD's website.

When Craig initially told him about the integrity audit he actually would've preferred a 181. They could be approached head-on. Now, Thom wanted it to go away.

Be careful what you wish for.

"Is this aligned with the IA?"

"You can't know about that," warned Craig. "I told you as a favor."

Thom felt like he rode the break toward an inescapable fate. About to crash on a reef. Sharp. Deadly. A serious sense of menace vibrated in his body. *Who the hell is screwing with me? And Why?*

"I've got a good package," said Thom. "If this dings me in any way, you're going down with me. Everything will be on the table."

"Don't be stupid, Thom. That's a hollow threat. We both know I have no control over that situation."

"Do we?" Thom mad-dogged his supervisor.

———

Thom gathered a few things from his desk, stuffed them into his briefcase. Most of the important shit lay on that creepy altar Birdie had in her office. He had heard rumors that the tech geeks could block access to email so he forwarded Bennie's file to a personal email account — just in case. He quickly wrote out a note of thanks to Bennie, looked up his mail stop and dropped it in outgoing near the shared printer. As he turned to return to his desk something hit him in the back of the head. He pivoted to find his friend, Scott in Robbery Special, laughing. A five-gallon container of peanuts sat nearby in an empty cubicle. Thom saw the peanut on the floor. He picked it up and chucked it back. He wasn't even close to hitting Scott.

"Guess you're not on the softball team," said Scott.

"Never was much of an athlete," said Thom.

"You okay there?"

"Yeah. Okay."

"You need anything …?"

"Thanks, Scott. I'm good."

At least one guy in the squad had his back. Two if he counted George.

———

Thom threw his briefcase into the trunk of the Mustang. He walked up the stairs, through the lobby, and out the front doors of the PAB aiming toward the smoker's pole. He lit a cigarette and breathed deep. Damnit, damnit, damnit. Why did it seem that practically overnight his life had gone to shit?

A body hugged his. He pushed back, not immediately recognizing Birdie. Patches of white dust were on his suit.

"What the heck?" said Thom. He clocked her construction-girl outfit. "What would Madi say about all that dirt?" He brushed his suit jacket.

"I snuck into a construction site to see Moysychyn. Please, please, please tell me you left out the part about him being owner of L.A. National Housing Trust at your meeting."

"As you asked," confirmed Thom. "Not that it matters anymore. I have news."

"So do I," she said.

"Come on then, let's walk. I have to hit the bank. There's one on Broadway."

"I have money for lunch."

"It's not that, I have to send a wire. That's how Noa is getting paid."

"How much?"

"Twenty grand."

"Geeze, that's a helluva lot of money. I hope he's worth it."

"Tell me about it. So, news … you first."

"I saw Danny this morning. He gave me fresh insight on the great matter."

"Bird, family meetings are secret."

"You have no idea how much I trust him. Besides, I didn't tell him everything. I just thought he'd know who was behind the surveillance. He said it's not coming from his office."

They stopped at the corner and Thom hit the pedestrian button.

"Hence, not the department," said Thom.

"Correct. He agrees with us that it's not the FBI either. He has a theory that we didn't consider …"

"Beat added for emphasis? Come on, hit me."

"He thinks—well, I supposed it to be a private citizen—that it's someone with the motivation and means for a high-priced investigator. He used the word vendetta, but I think it's something else entirely."

They started across the sidewalk on the walk signal.

"This person gave your supervisor the means to hurt you," she said.

"And who would this person be?"

Birdie didn't answer.

"Yes?"

"You're going to think me crazy."

"I already think that. Now spill."

237

"Anne."

Thom guffawed. "That's ridiculous."

"It makes perfect sense when you think about it. Look, Thom, she's having an affair. We're not talking about a one-night stand, a fling. It's a *relationship*."

Thom held up his hand. "Stop. You really don't know the dynamic."

"California is a no fault, community property state. With the right divorce attorney you could petition, and probably be granted, spousal support. She's being proactive by gathering proof of your adultery. To head you off at the pass."

"Wow. You really are crazy." He snuffed the cigarette on the smudgy edge of a concrete trashcan, adding his ash to the blackened rim. "First off, Anne would be horrified of the potential scandal. Scared of the impact it'd have on her business, on the kids. Second, we're Catholics. WE don't get divorced. Third, she and I have an understanding. An agreement."

"What kind?"

"The kind that has allowed me to do what I've been doing all these years."

Birdie stopped suddenly. "She gave you permission?"

Thom turned. "When she was pregnant with the girls. We've been roommates since Liam was a child. The twins were conceived during a drunken, one-night-stand."

Birdie frowned. "Well, that theory is blown."

Thom put his arm around her. "Ah, cheer up. You're the queen of theories. You'll come up with an equally outrageous one before long."

———

Birdie and Thom approached the teller: Anna, according to her nameplate. "I need to send a wire and make a withdrawal."

"Yes, sir, swipe your bankcard please."

"Why do I need to do that?"

"So that I may process your transaction."

"It also allows her to see your accounts," said Birdie, winking at Anna. "She'll confirm that you're the account owner, check pending transactions and balances."

"So she'll know how much money I have," said Thom.

"She could care less," said Birdie.

"To make sure you have enough for the transactions, sir," said Anna. "What is the amount?"

"Twenty thousand for the wire, twenty-two hundred cash."

"Yes," said Anna, looking at her computer screen. "Are you familiar with the wire process?"

"No."

"Let me get a form." She stepped away to a back office. A few moments later she came back with a piece of paper and slid it under the thick Plexiglas barrier. "Please fill out the wire instructions. I'll also need your driver's license."

Thom pulled the license from his wallet and passed it under. "I'm going to make a copy. I'll be right back, Mr. Keane."

"Why does she need my license?" complained Thom. "I already swiped my card."

"Are you really complaining about digging out your ID?" said Birdie. "They're not trying to hassle you by asking for a second form of identification. They're confirming who you claim to be. Cards and pins can be stolen. The bank is looking after your assets. It's for your protection."

"What do you know about it anyway?"

"You know how much work it was to close out Matt's estate? Especially me not being a relative? All the people ... all the banks. Each one with different procedures and guidelines and processes, each one with strict federal regulations and compliance. Which gets audited, by the way. Come on, a little inconvenience is worth our piece of mind."

Anna returned and passed Thom's license back. She also had a copy of the signature card he and Anne both signed when they opened the joint account.

"Triple checking," said Birdie, smiling.

Thom looked down at the instruction sheet. There were boxes to check, account numbers to fill in, routing numbers, beneficiary account numbers, addresses, banking information. "Holy cow," he said, "I had no idea."

"Just think what would happen if twenty thousand dollars came from the wrong account, or was sent to the wrong account. They have to be extra careful," said Birdie. "After Anna does her part, it'll go to a supervisor for review, then it will get processed and go to the bank's wire department. The whole process takes, on average, thirty minutes. Providing Anna has no other customers to service, because she's the one who enters the initial data. Don't piss her off."

"You're really liking this, aren't you?" said Thom.

"Oh, yeah."

And sure enough, nearly thirty minutes later they were walking out of the bank.

He had just paid Noa. No backing out. No return.

Throughout the financial transaction Birdie had fun at his expense. Teased him. Normally, he'd be resentful. Mad even. But in his heart he knew she meant well. A bit of light-hearted distraction from the emotional process. To move him past the horror of paying a stranger to gather God-only-knows-what dirt on the love of his life. His wife. The mother of his five children.

What masochistic tendencies allowed him to sell what was left of his pride for twenty thousand dollars for something he intrinsically knew would lead to pain, heartache, loss? Last night he thought he had reached the bottom of the well. Not so, as it turned out. There was a false bottom. More levels of hell remained.

Birdie slipped her arm around his. "I really am hungry. And I think we need a boost. Let's walk to the cathedral and light some candles. Take prayer in the sanctuary. Give ourselves over to His grace for a moment of reflection. Stroll in the garden. Appreciate the gift of light through the alabaster and the stained glass and the spiritual nature of the building." She leaned in, blue eyes gazing upon blue eyes. "Then when our souls are nourished, we'll grab a bite at the café. You tell me your news, I'll tell you the rest of mine, and then … we make a plan of attack."

Thom reluctantly smiled and nodded as though the side trip was the most obvious next step in a day not nearly half over and already filled to capacity with the morbid for an average fellow. How did she read people so effectively and give them what they needed?

As they walked toward Our Lady of the Angels on Temple Street, Thom realized he could not reciprocate. He didn't know how to interpret her deep emotional contours. Didn't know how to reach the dark places that dwelled inside her. Didn't know what she *needed*. Was this because she always seemed so self-sufficient? Self-contained? No, he didn't think so. As kids, he remembered a different Birdie. Open. Accessible. Carefree. So what changed? Was it the usual teenage angst? Were her burdens so great they lead to a life of alcoholism? At what age did she become so efficient at concealment?

How could he know? He was too wrapped up in his own life to give notice. Really, did it come down to something as simple as missed observation?

These thoughts made him sad.

One thing he knew for sure. His drama came from external sources. Birdie's came from internal sources. Still, there had to be some tell.

Thom determined to be more mindful in the future. After all, he was a detective. He already had the skill in some measure. Used it well on the job. It wouldn't take much effort to hone his gift and utilize it for his personal life.

If he had, he might have seen Anne's affair before the bomb dropped.

THIRTY-SIX

"Hello, my love, guess who's coming to dinner tonight?"

"Who?"

"Elizabeth Keane. That reporter I told you about."

"What? Are you crazy?"

"Why do you always say that?"

"Okay ... sorry ... this might actually be good for us. Do you remember what you have to do? The role you are playing?"

"Yes. I will be an actor."

"Be very careful. I remember her from before. She's ..."

"What is she?"

"Crafty."

THIRTY-SEVEN

BIRDIE WIPED HER MOUTH with a paper napkin and pushed the salad away. Whereas Thom had already finished a sandwich, a bag of potato chips, and downed a large soda.

"That's it?" he said, suppressing a burp. "You've not even eaten half."

"I'm full."

"How can that be possible? You didn't eat the breadstick and only dipped your fork into the dressing."

"I'm full," Birdie repeated.

"I know you eat more than this. Your boyfriend makes sure of that."

Birdie leaned back in the chair and crossed her arms. "What do you mean?"

"Ron brings you all that food. Stocks your refrigerator. Controls what you eat."

"Whoa. Remember who you're talking to. Do you think I'd let a man control what I eat?"

"Sunday morning the fridge is empty. Ron rolls into town and suddenly it's full of foods ready to heat and eat. He's got you exercising. He completely changed your diet."

Birdie shook her head. "No, no, no. That's on me, dude. Okay, at first it wasn't. Back when I came home from the hospital I didn't like his interference. But really, he forced me to exercise for rehab purposes and practically force fed me to put weight on, the right way, with a healthy diet. The regime made me feel better so *I* took it to the next level."

"What next level? You don't cook. Never have. So he's doing it for you."

"Ron has a job. Responsibilities. You think he has free time to cook and prepare a week's worth of food for me? I buy it from a nutritionist. He's just transportation."

"You *pay* someone to cook?"

"Why is that so shocking? Like you said, I don't cook. So I hire a service to do it for me. The place I use is in Carlsbad, just south of Ron's house. He picks it up for me when he comes to town, when I go to his house I bring it back."

"I didn't realize that you're pushing this agenda on yourself," said Thom. "All this time I thought you had a controlling boyfriend."

"Well, he is … by nature. He's also extremely disciplined, not prone to weakness."

"Because of his military training."

"He was a Marine for twenty years. You can't just hang up the uniform and forget the training. Hell, he'd still be there if he hadn't reached the zenith, the top rank for an enlisted man. But I won't tolerate that kind of bullshit in my private life so he has to temper his … oh, how do I put it?"

"Jealousy?"

"Why that word?" said Birdie.

"I saw how he beat the bag with Matt's face on it. He was angry."

"He hits hard."

"It was right after you guys argued about someone not dead," he said.

Birdie was taken aback. He heard their argument? She'd have to be mindful that another person lived in her home. The freedom days of complete privacy were gone.

"You misheard," she said.

"No, I didn't. I heard it clear as a bell. You said, 'He's not dead. Don't you know how that makes me feel?' So, who were you talking about?"

Birdie remembered clear as a bell, too. Her exact words to Ron were, 'Why can't you understand how this makes me feel?' She sought his compassion on the topic of Matt Whelan. She still did. And she'd have to have it soon.

"I don't want to talk about it."

Thom gave her a sideways look. "Alright. Let's move on then. Why have you been pacing our conversation? Avoiding the rest of your news?"

"I sensed you needed a bit more time to deal with the Anne angst."

Thom dropped his head. "Fair enough, but the day is passing and there's a lot I still need to do."

"The meeting. Did the case get hot?"

"Yes, but not in the way you're thinking. I'm off."

"Off the case? That's good isn't it? That's what you wanted."

"I did, but Craig pulled me off because a complaint of misconduct has been filed."

"Wasn't he the one that said the decision to keep you on came from upstairs? That blows his story. If *they* could keep you on for an IA, *they* can keep you on for a complaint. I mean, aren't they commonplace?"

"For street cops with constant contact with the public. But not in my position."

"What is the complaint about? Who made it?"

"Dunno. I'll be able to tell by the line of questioning once the assigned internal affairs hack interviews me."

"Is it procedure to take someone off an active case before a proper investigation?"

"Depends. In a high-profile case like mine, I might pull me off, too. Craig thinks my involvement would be a distraction."

"What do you do now?"

"Right now we jet." Thom bussed their table, filled his soda cup with water. As they walked back toward the PAB he said, "I'm invested in this case. The way we see it, the killer will strike again on Sunday."

"Why Sunday?"

"Because all his kills took place on Sunday. One every week for three weeks then there was a four-week break before the Lawrence murders. We believe he'll strike again on Sunday. That gives us four plus days. I've been thinking about your plan of helping me. You know, launder the information? Make it like original discovery?"

"You want help after all?"

"I do. Craig is going to assign me menial duty. Desk shit. But I can still help ... I mean, we can help, but not if I'm at my desk. When we get back I'm going straight to HR and put in for personal time. I have loads saved up. I need you to go back to the Bird House and copy all the files. Can you do that for me?"

"Easy."

"Seymour or George or maybe both won't wait for me to deliver the files. They'll come to me. So copy and put the pages back exact. George and I assembled the book together. He'll know if it's different. Can you scan and color copy photographs and burn discs?"

"All that. What happens if they arrive before I'm done?"

"Stall. Say you won't give them anything without my approval. Make them wait. Under no circumstance let them see the dry erase board. How are you with forgery?"

"Like documents or signatures?"

"The board needs to be re-worked anyway now that I've got additional notes. It has to appear like I've done the writing."

"I can identify your writing, but for something like that, I'll need exemplars. You have something of significant length that is handwritten?"

"My original case notes and drawings. They're on white sheet paper in the murder book."

"Okay. I have my assignment. Now yours. You need to be back at my house no later than five. We have a dinner date."

THIRTY-EIGHT

BIRDIE OPENED THE JUDAS hole on her front door. George stood on the stoop.

"Hello, George," she said.

"Hi, Birdie. Thom here?"

She opened the door. "Come on in."

George stepped into the small entry and clocked Birdie's denim pant suit.

"You look nice," said George. "Very seventies with the flare legs." He twirled her around. "Flat front, zipper in the back, very slenderizing." He tugged at the sleeve. "The miracle of Lycra. Going out?"

"I have a dinner interview tonight. Thom's my date."

"Is he here?" he repeated.

"I expect him soon. Come on up."

"By chance you have coffee?"

"You know me, there's always fresh brew in my house."

"I do know you," he said with a hint of lascivious.

"You flirting?"

George bit his lower lip. "Is it off limits?"

"You know better."

George followed Birdie up the curving mahogany stairway; past the collection of crucifixes, the niches with religious artifacts. At the second-floor landing he rubbed the head of the marble statue of St. Joseph. They continued past the office with the closed tapestry entrance and the sound of machinery.

"What's going on in there?" said George.

"Printing some documents."

They continued to the kitchen. Birdie pulled out a bar stool. "Sit."

"Where's Thom?"

"Don't know." Birdie opened a glass cabinet door and pulled out a small porcelain cup and saucer. "We had lunch together and separated afterward."

"He tell you what happened?"

Birdie poured the coffee and added one cube of sugar. She swirled it gently with a spoon and set it down in front of George.

"Yes. It sucks."

"Damn straight. Thom's my partner. We have a rhythm. Then we're suddenly yanked apart and I have to work with that asshole Seymour. I don't like it."

"Where's Seymour now?"

"Getting food. We never had time for lunch and we're between interviews. I'm here to pick up the murder book and the Deats file."

"Thom will want to know what's going on with the case."

"I know. I'll call him later."

George blew on the coffee. "I need the files."

"You'll have to wait for Thom."

"Don't play with me. You're copying the files right now."

"How can I? I'm in the kitchen with you. Speaking of which …" She opened the refrigerator and pulled out a black container with a sticker on the lid. She gave it to George. "I'm eating out tonight. This will be better than anything Seymour picks up."

George read the label. "Tuesday dinner. Roast turkey with fresh cranberry salsa, baby red potatoes, haricot verts with thyme, warm baby greens and spinach wilt. Remove lid, remove greens, microwave two minutes. Add greens and cook thirty seconds. Sounds delicious. You need the container back?"

"No, but don't throw it away. It's reusable."

George drained the coffee in one large gulp.

Always the same, thought Birdie.

"Thank you for the coffee. The dinner. Now give me the book."

Birdie crossed her arms. "Wait for Thom."

George pirouetted. Headed out of the kitchen and tuned left toward the office.

"George," said Birdie following him. "You best respect my space."

"Birdie, I'm trying to catch a serial killer. I don't have the time." He thrust aside the tapestry and strode into her office uninvited.

"You just crossed a line, George Silva."

George stopped dead in his tracks and pointed at the altar. "That new?"

Birdie stepped around him and picked up the investigative material. She thrust it at him. "Get out."

"Sorry, Birdie … just one more thing." He removed a few papers from the printer's catch and flipped them over. He knit his brows in confusion.

"Not what you expected? Now get out before I really get mad."

251

"Birdie...I thought...shit, I'm sorry. Real sorry. Tell Thom I'll see him later."

A few moments later Thom emerged from the supply closet holding the file copies and an empty binder. "That was close. Poor George, he'll be apologizing for a week. We shouldn't have fun at his expense. He's going to hate working with Seymour."

"Too bad you couldn't have seen the look on his face. You get the last of it?"

"Everything. Ask about the interviews?"

"Didn't have time. He did say they were 'between.'"

"Sounds right." Thom emptied his arms on the altar. "Come on, we need to prepare for dinner. Bring the gun from the desk."

————

Birdie and Thom stood in front of the gated weapons locker in the garage.

"You're being paranoid," said Birdie, punching in the passcode.

"Who's paranoid? You've got more shit in this thing than me, Da, Aiden, and Arthur put together. And we're on the job. Besides, don't you remember the last time you met a fan?"

"He was a stalker." She opened the gate.

"Precisely. And that's how you got the permit. And now a serial killer may have just invited you to dinner."

"You're taking the dead fish comment too seriously. In the context of the conversation it was an appropriate thing to say."

Thom rolled his eyes. "And you're not taking it seriously enough. You said he gave an exercised performance on that job site. Said he hated Dominic."

"I said 'enthusiasm' and I don't recall the word hate."

"You know how I feel about coincidence. Let's plan for the worst, expect the best." He hefted the Sig from Birdie's desk. "Have anything smaller? You might get separated from your purse." Thom vigorously shook his head. "Scratch that. You're not taking a purse."

Birdie pointed. Thom pulled open the top drawer. A selection of antique fist pistols and palm-squeezers lay on deep red velvet. "I inherited those from Matt."

"Ever shoot 'em?"

"Too afraid they'll blow up in my hand."

"Smart."

"Here, let me." Birdie moved in and opened the second, deeper drawer. She pulled out a lockbox and slammed it on the counter, dialed in the combo, and opened it up.

"Now that's what I'm talking about," said Thom. "You sure like your Sigs."

"It's not legal in California."

"I won't tell if you won't," said Thom, winking.

Birdie picked up the black pistol and palmed it. "Less than nineteen ounces fully loaded. Seven rounds. Double-action trigger with a ten-pound pull. Three-eighty. Fixed barrel blowback."

"Shorter than the nine-mil. Will stop a man up close, shit for distance. Got a holster?"

In the end, Birdie carried the pistol on her ankle, her smartphone in its holder attached to her waistband at the small of her back, and a six-inch slim knife on the left side of her rib cage. Car key tucked into her bra. That left her hands free for nothing more than a steno pad and pen which could be easily abandoned.

253

Thom wore his usual BUG in an ankle holster, Birdie's Sig P239 in the rig under his left arm, a switchblade in the front pocket of his jeans, and his personal cell also at his back.

The plan was to walk in heavily armed, but not appear so.

Keep the hosts at ease.

After all, it was just dinner and an interview.

Oh, and they removed the license plates from Birdie's car.

THIRTY-NINE

BIRDIE PULLED OVER TO the curb.

"Are you sure?" said Thom, looking around suspiciously.

They were in front of a five-story brick building that appeared abandoned. A row of shuttered warehouses were on the north side of the street, the 10 freeway behind the building on the south and, east and west, a succession of condemned buildings, empty lots, rental garages, and lots of trash, weeds, and broken bottles.

"I've always known this as the Biscuit Building," said Birdie, confused. "But I've only seen it from the freeway above."

She looked past Thom at the dark building. It sat almost in the middle of a massive asphalt lot with faded reminders of white lines and broken tire bumpers.

"The weeds are doing well," she said. "I must get the name of their gardener."

Thom chuckled. "This isn't a home. It's the backlot of a horror film."

"The chain-link fencing surrounding the joint a dead give-away?"

"Maybe the house is full of zombies."

"Or the ghosts of long-dead bakers."

The forced humor didn't rid Birdie of the dread. Her antennae were vibrating. Matt once told her to never be afraid to offend, especially if you feel the prick of danger. "Better to get the hell away and, if need be, apologize later. Don't ever risk safety for politeness." Those words came to her now.

"There's no lighting other than ambient from the freeway. No sign that people live here. And I'm getting bad vibes. I think we should bounce."

"I don't have the power of authority," said Thom.

"You're a licensed law enforcement professional with the state of California, which means you're a cop twenty-four-seven."

"In regard to this case, this instance, all I can hope to accomplish is a survey."

"He owns two properties where people were murdered in the same manner. What does that tell you?"

"That he owns two properties. Owning houses or not liking someone isn't just cause. But I've been invited into his home. If I see something, I take action. These golden opportunities are rare."

———

Todd toggled the camera. He could only see the passenger. A man.

"It looks like they're deciding what to do," he said.

"Turn on lights!" said Iris.

"No. I want to see if she remains motivated."

———

The fingers on Birdie's right hand twittered.

"Okay," said Thom reluctantly. "We can go."

Birdie eased off the brake and pulled forward to the corner.

"Is that a frontage road?" said Thom. "Let's just see where it goes."

Birdie turned right. The pavement smoothed out, felt maintained under the tires. She followed the single lane street to a turnabout in the shadow of the freeway. She was about to make a U-turn when a dimly lit sign caught her attention. DELIVERIES. Next to the sign was a modern security panel.

"I'll check it out," said Thom. He swiveled out of the car, left the door open.

———

"Damn, no plate," said Todd.

"Zoom in car," said Iris. "What see?"

"Nothing. Just hands on a steering wheel drumming to music. Basic car. Nothing on the dash, nothing on the seat."

———

Thom pressed a button marked "assistance."

The gate electronically unlocked and slowly rolled open. A row of driveway lights clicked on, illuminating the way forward.

"Your choice," said Thom.

Todd Moysychyn had once yelled at her so ferociously that spittle wet his chin.

But that was nothing compared to this: a dark and formidable building where they were the away team. At a disadvantage.

Her stomach flipped. Did she really think Todd was a methodical killer? Was this visit really necessary? One truth to the journalism profession is that great stories often come at great risk—that's how she earned the Pulitzer—why else did she go up thirty floors on a tower with a swift wind and no walls? Besides, she had a cop at her side and they were heavily armed.

"Let's go in," she decided.

"That's my Bird. So … leave the car outside the gate and walk in?"

"If we have to leave this haunted manse in a hurry I doubt you could scale that fence. Besides, this car is built Ford tough. With enough speed it'll bust down the fence."

Thom laughed and got back in. "Okay, Miss Spokeswoman, been drinking from Anne's Kool-Aid container?"

"I need a story."

"I need a survey."

"Forward then."

Birdie followed the runway-like lights to the end. At the southeast corner were five loading docks too low for modern trucks. Too high for regular automobiles. On two, metal ramps were retrofitted to allow vehicular access to the warehouse. Birdie made a three-point turn and parked the Taurus near the perimeter fence facing the exit.

A mercury-vapor light cast a yellowish glow over a doublewide door. Moysychyn sat on the stoop smoking.

"And there's our host," said Birdie, removing the press credentials from the visor. She unhooked the pass from the lanyard and clipped it to her waistband.

"Help me get one of those butts."

"Roger that." She grabbed her steno pad and stabbed a pen into the wire.

"I hope he doesn't mind that your date is a cop," said Thom.

———

Iris moved the toggle and zoomed in on the woman, scanned her up and down. Wondered how she got that strange scar on her face. Hard to tell what kind of build lay under that suit. She moved well. Confident. Had a strength about her. She moved the camera to the man's face. Nice looking except for the gray hair. Definitely related to the woman. So far her story held.

———

They walked toward the light.

"You made it." Moysychyn pumped Birdie's hand.

Thom swooped his hand out and filched the still-smoldering butt, pinched it out.

"Hello, Mr. Moysychyn," said Birdie.

"Call me Todd, please."

"This is my cousin, Thom."

"Nice to meet you. Welcome." He gestured inward, closed and locked the door with a retractable key attached to his belt.

Birdie took a deep, silent breath of worry.

"Thank you for letting me tag along," said Thom. "I hate coming empty-handed, but Elizabeth assured me that your wife—Iris, I believe—would be offended if we brought anything."

"And that is correct," said Todd. "Iris likes to be the complete hostess. Elizabeth, I am impressed you found the right way in. We failed to get each other's phone numbers and I forgot to give you directions."

"Perseverance," said Birdie.

The threesome walked through a reception office: Formica countertop, sliding window, empty clipboards on the wall, then through another door into a modified garage. Two cars were parked side-by-side in the warehouse: matching Mercedes CLS coupes; one white, one black.

Beyond the dome of light a massive sense of space. No shadows. Just dark space.

Todd jumped into a pristine white E-Z-GO golf cart. "Get in. We live on the top floor."

Birdie and Thom exchanged quick glances. "We don't mind walking," said Birdie.

"I do," said Todd, starting the battery-powered cart.

Thom took the backward facing seat and Birdie sat in front. Todd maneuvered the cart around some barrels and took a sharp left turn and up a wide ramp with a metal railing. The ramp circled the building, spiraling ever upward like an amusement roller coaster about to pitch off the edge. A reflective yellow number marked each floor. Multi-colored carnival lights were strung up on metal brackets attached to the brick. They weren't bright enough to pierce the dark interior, and the decades-old smell of yeast and mold gave Birdie no context.

As the ramp wound around and the big "4" came into view she saw several crookneck lamps that illuminated workbenches, key-cutting machines, metal filing cabinets, and several desks. Todd braked abruptly. The cart stopped with a jolt. He mumbled an expletive and jumped out, opened a metal panel on the wall and started flipping circuits. The lamps went dark one by one. Just as he flipped the last one Birdie's eye caught something moving in the middle of the room. She swore it was a shark.

FORTY

TODD PARKED THE WHITE cart next to its black mate.

Thom disembarked and squeezed Birdie's arm in reassurance. "Did you catch all that?" he whispered.

She nodded and took his hand to still hers.

Straight ahead, a massive set of doors. Ten feet high at least. Hand carved and accented with gold leaf, it depicted the twelve animal zodiacs of the Chinese New Year cycle in a writhing, orgy-like relief.

"That's a spectacular door. What's its origin?" said Birdie, her voice shaky.

"Iris had it commissioned. Made it look ancient."

"She's Chinese?"

"My mail-order bride. She was only seventeen—" he held a finger to his lips—"but had a lifetime of experience, if you get my meaning. Who else would have me in my previous state except someone anxious to live in the United States? Don't let her size fool you. She's the boss around here."

He pulled a retractable key attached to his belt and unlocked the door. A smaller door within the larger one opened inward.

A woman wearing yellow silk capris, black flats, and a tunic-length red cheongsam with a dragon design stood in an entry created by rolling screens and potted ficus. She had jet black hair tied back in a loose chignon and secured with a jade comb.

"Iris," said Todd, "may I present Elizabeth Keane of the Republic of California and her cousin, Thom."

The woman bowed. Neither Thom nor Birdie knew the protocol, but in a familial synchronicity they tilted their heads. The woman didn't reach out to shake hands so the cousins kept their arms at their sides.

"You are Irish, yes?" said Iris.

"Yes," said the cousins.

"Good. I make Irish stew."

Thom and Birdie exchanged peptic glances. They were extremely spoiled when it came to stew. No one made it like their paternal Grandma, Birdie. Nora's came close because she understood that good stew took hours to prepare. Stews are patient, simmered over time. A Chinese woman telling the cousins they were about to eat a favored traditional dish didn't thrill them.

Birdie smiled and said, "How lovely."

"I'm looking forward to it," said Thom.

Iris waved her hand forward. "Husband, show them, show them. I finish."

The loft took up much of the entire fifth floor. The furnishings and accessories were label heavy as if the designer showrooms were emptied of gaudy swag and thrown into a massive space without regard to a theme. Money sure couldn't buy class.

"A designer crib is not what one would expect of you," said Birdie. "As I recall, you were quite the slob."

"When Iris came into my life five years ago I lived in my workshop. I had a desk, telephone, a TV, a recliner, and a mattress. She whipped everything into shape. Including me. Those timbers up there are original. She hired an engineer to do the lights. All the screens are movable so we can rearrange rooms, open or close as needed. The wood floor is original, refinished of course. Iris is very good at spending my money. We have a few solid walls. The bedrooms and bathrooms for instance. Guest bath." He pointed in a vague, right-hand direction.

"When we were out on the street we couldn't see a mote of light," said Birdie. "Did you have these lights off?"

"The windows are covered in black acrylic."

"I don't understand," said Thom. "There are huge cantilevered windows with yellow panes of glass on every floor, including this one."

"You like those windows? I sure do. They're original of course. Damaged by vandals and time. The acrylic on the inside blocks the light. See, no one knows we live here. We'd like to keep it that way." He nodded at Birdie's press badge. "We don't live here legally. This area is still zoned for industrial. Also, the building isn't earthquake safe. Hasn't been retrofitted. I'd appreciate it if you kept that from your interview."

"As long as it's not relevant to my queries," said Birdie.

"When the big one hits, you're screwed," said Thom, quickly.

"What if there's a fire?" added Birdie. "Have an escape route?"

"Two reasons Iris is anxious to move. Plus, she's a little freaked out by the floors below. She likes light and clean spaces. Not dark and dusty."

And yet the light was artificial. Nothing natural, thought Birdie. Not even skylights as is common in industrial spaces.

Todd gave Birdie and Thom a meandering tour. The art elements were diverse: prehistoric fossil reproductions, ceramic vases, woven baskets, koi fish carvings in wood, stone, and glass. Birdie studied a triptych of square abstracts with highly unusual patinas. It appeared as though reflective flecks were mixed with a wash that highlighted sections of the paintings. It had an odd, fishy scent, as well.

"I did those," said Todd.

"Very interesting," said Birdie. "What is that unusual wash?"

"Ground-up fish. I keep exotics. When they die, I puree them and add a gel medium. It's my tribute to such beautiful jewels."

A riot of exclamation points bounced in her brain. She backed up a step in slow motion and would've keeled were it not for Thom suddenly at her side to prop her up. He led her to a nearby table.

"Look at this." His voice sounded liquid and distant. "It reminds me of Matt."

A miniature Dharma Wheel made of plastic was displayed under a bell jar. There appeared to be writing on the spokes. Just as Birdie leaned closer to read it, she perceived a subtle movement of air and heard, "Like it?"

Birdie jumped.

A sudden shift of tone and mood occurred when Iris suddenly appeared behind her, quiet and surefooted like a bobcat.

"So sorry," said Iris.

"You're a Buddhist?" said Birdie.

Iris pointed at the Wheel. "You know this?"

"Each spoke represents the right view, right thought, right behavior, right speech, right effort, right livelihood, right mindfulness, right meditation. I've never seen one so small."

"That is one of the few possessions Iris came to America with," said Todd, sidling next to his wife. "They were tokens. Toys. Given to children to keep in their pockets."

Iris gave her husband a harsh stare.

Birdie wondered why such a sweet thing should evoke Iris' response.

"Dinner, if you please," said Iris, tight lipped.

———

Birdie peered into her bowl of steaming stew, felt bile move into her throat. She didn't trust the meat. Was it beef or lamb? It looked like bloody stool floating in brown broth surrounded by carrots and potatoes. Sweat formed on her forehead. She felt her irregular heartbeat in her neck. She pushed back from the table. "Excuse me." She pointed toward the area Todd had indicated the bathroom was located.

Thom got up as well. "Need help?"

In her mind she said, "Actually, my pants zipper gets stuck," as she pointed at her back. What came out was gibberish and she didn't understand why everyone stared at her with alarm.

"I will help," said Iris.

"That's okay," said Thom, protectively. "We're family."

He placed a firm hand across Birdie's back and led her toward the bathroom. They walked behind a cinder block wall and found themselves in a long, narrow passageway painted bible black. A flickering overhead light cast strange patterns on the surface. Shiny bits on the walls caught the light like rhinestones.

"Guess this place is larger than it appears," Thom whispered.

Birdie felt unsteady. Disoriented. The passageway shrunk, closed around her.

Thom held her tighter. "You're shaking," he said into her ear. He was about to open the first door they came across when a tap on the shoulder stopped him.

Iris.

Birdie nearly screamed.

Iris gestured. "Bathroom this way," she said.

They followed her to the passageway's terminus. Near the entrance of the hall was a green lighted frosted glass door.

"Thank you," said Thom. "We walked right past it."

He pulled Birdie into the bathroom and shut the door. The glass tint changed to red.

"That's cool," said Thom. "Must be LEDs."

"Lock ... lock door," said Birdie.

"There isn't one. It's the light. Green for unoccupied, red for in use."

"Shit," moaned Birdie, sitting on the toilet lid. She gasped for air—her breathing fast and strained.

Thom knelt. "Take it easy, Bird. Calm down. Deep breaths ... inhale ... one-two-three ... exhale ... one-two-three ... nice and slow ... that's it." He hugged her, rubbed her back. "It's okay." He rocked her until she her breathing returned to normal.

"I think you were on the verge of a panic attack," he said.

Birdie tried to laugh. "Verge?"

"What's got you so jumpy?"

"Todd paints with ground-up fish and the meat in my bowl looked like shit."

"It was sausage with red peppers."

"Huh?"

"Iris didn't remove the casing. I thought it looked weird at first, too."

"This place is totally messed up. Something lurks in the shadows. That hall? It reminded me of the pump house, but instead of crude I smelled fish."

"Oh, Bird." He smoothed the hair from her face. "I'm sorry."

"It was my mission to talk to this guy. Hell, I went to an extreme. When he invited me to dinner I snatched the opportunity. I thought … shit, I don't know … I thought …"

"The murder weapon would be lying on a coffee table?"

Birdie managed a weak smile.

"I heard what he said about the paintings. I'm getting good intell. I agree, something is wacky, but I don't think we're in harm's way. If you really believe it and can't handle staying, I'll take you home."

"Nothing will happen to us?"

"Do you think I'd let anything happen to you?" He kissed her forehead. "Except we might not like the stew."

"I'm not eating it. I'm claiming a sudden stomachache and will ask for crackers."

"Deal. Let's get back."

"I need to pee."

"Make it quick," said Thom, turning his back.

Birdie got off the toilet and lifted the lid.

She covered her mouth and muffled a scream.

A dead goldfish floated in the bowl.

"That's it!" hissed Birdie.

"Hold on," urged Thom. "It's the common way to dispose of goldfish."

"You heard what Todd said. He grinds them up. Get it out."

Thom took a photo of it with his phone then gingerly put his fingers into the toilet water and picked up the fish by its tail. He laid it on the edge of the sink and poked it. "It's solid. Do fish go into rigor?"

Birdie picked it up and held it close to her cheek. Then she held it to Thom's.

"It's frozen," said Thom.

"Which means it was just put in there."

"By Iris. Right before she retrieved us from the hall."

"She's messing with us."

"Then we mess back." Thom wrapped the tiny fish in toilet paper and put it into the breast pocket of his bomber jacket.

———

After the gawdawful dinner Birdie and Todd moved from the dining area to a well-lit vignette near one of the blacked-out windows to conduct the interview. Thom began clearing the table.

"No, no thank you," said Iris. "I do. You are guest."

"Let me help," he said, carrying several glasses to the kitchen. "I don't mind washing dishes. I'm an expert at loading dishwashers, too. I can overload one without breakage."

"Yes, yes, very nice. No help."

"Alright. I'll keep you company then."

Iris scurried back to the table.

Thom leaned against the refrigerator and looked around. Wood, stainless, stone. A typical kitchen. When Iris didn't immediately return, he pushed off the fridge and accidently knocked a photo and magnet off the door. He picked it up. A fat Todd in a suit and his new bride in a traditional wedding outfit posed in front of the seal of Los Angeles. He was about to put it back when, inexplicably and, without forethought, he slipped it into his trouser pocket.

He peeked into the dining room. Iris wasn't there. She stood behind a table lamp spying on Birdie and Todd who were seemingly engrossed in conversation.

Throughout dinner Thom noted that Iris couldn't take her eyes off his cousin. Yet when Birdie caught her eye, Iris would look away.

Dinner was beyond weird. Todd was upset that Birdie felt bad and kept asking if she were okay. Iris was put out that Birdie was sick and begged off the stew in favor of rice crackers and chewing gum. Todd was antagonistic toward Iris. Iris hateful toward Todd. A match made on a computer and not working in real life? And Thom sat back and observed.

He examined the fridge photos. He found a better one of the pair, a close-up, and made an exchange. There was one of Iris as a young girl. She wore a uniform and posed with some classmates in front of a school. He plucked it from its magnet and peered at the faces, but couldn't see them clearly. It seemed his up-close vision was hit and miss these days. He saw Jelena's tiny face on a driver's license quite clearly and days later couldn't focus on a photo. He made a mental note to make an appointment with an optometrist. He might be ready for glasses. He was about to put the photo back on the fridge when he heard Iris in the dining room. He palmed it just as Iris returned to the kitchen with silverware and napkins.

"May I please have some coffee?" said Thom.

"No coffee. Tea only."

"Perfect. Thank you."

Thom didn't want coffee or tea. He wanted an opportunity to talk to Iris alone.

Divide and conquer.

When Iris turned to plug in an electric kettle he dropped the photo into his pocket for a total of three items, none of them legal seizures, all unusable.

"Was Todd teasing when he said you were a mail-order bride?"

Iris giggled. "We meet on computer. I want to come to America."

"How long have you been married?"

"Five years."

"Are you happy?"

"Most happy. Husband happy, also."

If this evening was any clue, that was a complete lie.

"Living here must be a challenge. Groceries and home goods coming up via a cart ride, trash going down the same way."

"We have shoot."

Thom wondered what she meant. How does one shoot trash? Ah …

"You mean C-H-U-T-E?"

"Yes, the same."

Shoot. Chute. Two words with different definitions and spellings yet pronounced the same. He thought this odd. How could a non-native speaker know this so easily? His spine stiffened, each hair on the back of his neck bristled one by one with a vague familiarity.

FORTY-ONE

Todd sat on the front stoop and lit a cigarette as the cousins waved one last farewell.

"Feeling better?" said Thom.

"Now that we're leaving," said Birdie. She reached into her bra and removed the car key, handed it to Thom. "You're driving. I have to make some note corrections before I forget. My shorthand is rusty."

"I want to talk to the kids," Thom whined. "The girls have an eight o'clock bedtime. It's nearly that now. And I need a smoke."

"Can't it wait until we get home?" She pointed up at the freeway. "Rush hour is over, traffic will be light."

"I'll sacrifice the smoke, but not the kids. Set me up on wireless?"

"As soon as we clear the gate and get off that frontage road. I'll feel safer on a city street. The place gives me the creeps."

"The building or the occupants?"

"Both."

Thom followed the driveway lights and the security gate slowly closed behind them.

"I'm glad we're outta there," said Birdie.

"Me, too. But I wish I could see Todd's face when he finds the dead goldfish on the cart's seat."

"I can't believe you did that."

"Messing back."

"Go down the block and pull over. You'll have to use my cell. It's linked to the car's wireless. No privacy though. Calls go through the stereo speakers."

"Surround sound."

"It'll be like the kids are in the car."

Thom pulled over in front of a dark storefront with shutters and bars and switched on the dome light. Birdie attached her cell to the port and turned on the system. The face of the phone glowed. "Call Thom home," she said.

"Dialing Thom home," said an electronic voice.

"Cool. You have the best toys."

After a few rings a boy answered, "Keane residence."

"Liam, my man."

"Da! Where have you been?"

"I'm on a big case, son. I miss you so much. How was school?"

Birdie tried to dial down the volume of the voices echoing in the car and turned her attention to her notes. She used Gregg shorthand—something she learned from a nun during a month's worth of after-school detention. It'd been over a year since she used it and found herself out of practice and struggling to keep up during the second Moysychyn interview.

Gregg used elliptical figures and lines for sound—not the actual spelling of a spoken word. It was a handy skill for stenography and reporting purposes. And only a few old-time reporters used it anymore—no one of her generation that she was aware of. The method of note taking gave her an advantage at press conferences and interviews. Since no one could read it, there was also a level of built-in security.

She sped read the stenography and added notations or corrections. She'd been at this for at least ten minutes before she noticed that the cacophony of voices had risen, like each of the kids had picked up an extension and were talking at once, wanting Thom's attention. Then she realized he wasn't driving either.

She nudged him. He frowned and nudged her back in a *don't bother me* gesture.

"Okay, boys and girls, cousin Bird needs her phone now. Rose and Nora, kiss-kiss, Dada loves-loves you. Now get to bed. Liam and Padraig, lights out at nine, love you, too."

Pearce said, "Say goodnight to Da and hang up."

Four voices said goodnight-love-you-bye-bye all at once and hung up their phones until only Pearce was on the line.

"What's up big guy?" said Thom.

"Are you and Ma getting divorced?"

"What? Why would you say that?"

"Because you're not living here anymore."

Birdie's heart ached for what Thom must be feeling after hearing those words from his eldest child.

"Who said that?"

"Da, I'm not stupid. Even on the hard cases you come home every day and we haven't seen you since Saturday."

"I'm sorry I haven't seen you in a few days, big guy, but it's a big leap from a few days gone to divorce."

Birdie mouthed, *we can go over.*

"You want me to come over now?"

"It's okay, Da. I know you're busy. It's just that Ma has all those meetings lately and I'm tired of babysitting the brats." Meaning the twins.

"Ma isn't there?"

"Naw. But she's paying me twenty bucks an hour and leaves money for pizza."

Thom knit his brows. Birdie returned a perplexed expression.

"At least you're saving money for a car."

"Uncle Jerome"—Anne's brother—"offered me one for free if I get straight As this semester."

"Well, Pearce, we'll have to talk about that one later."

"Me and my big mouth. I knew you'd say that."

"You know me too well. Now, go check on the munchkins, tuck them in tight, and earn your twenty bucks. Don't forget, lights-out for you at ten."

"Promise me first you're not getting a divorce. It'd totally suck."

"Don't worry P-man. Me and Ma are solid. I love you, son."

"Love you, too. Goodnight Da."

Thom disconnected the call. He got out of the car and screamed into the night air. Punched the roof.

"That better not have left a dent," yelled Birdie.

"Damnit," said Thom, jumping back into the car. "What the hell?"

"Kids are smart. They know when something's wrong and the big-D is a kid's worst nightmare."

Thom knocked his head against the steering wheel.

"I suppose this means you have to have that smoke now," said Birdie. "Go ahead."

Thom got back out and lit up. Sat on the hood of the car. Birdie watched his back shudder and couldn't ignore his anguish. She closed the steno pad and went to sit next to him. She placed her arm around his waist and put her head on his shoulder.

Even after the cigarette was smoked gone, they still sat this way and listened to the dull roar of the freeway. After many minutes, Thom said, "Thanks."

She let go.

"So? How'd you like your new fan?" said Thom.

"She's not a fan. A fan would ask me to sign the books. And the article was never mentioned."

"Think Todd's the fan? Made it up to get you into the house?"

"Don't know. Iris couldn't keep her eyes off me."

"I noticed. Maybe she has a crush."

"Hum. Did you take your survey?"

"And then some. I got two photos and a fag. What'd you get?"

"Todd hired Block Levin to evict Jerry Deats."

"He the one who wrote the bully letter?"

"Yes. He's an eviction lawyer. Landlords love him. Tenants hate him. He plays hardball. Todd told me he gave Levin leeway to get aggressive to those who refused to move. According to Moysychyn the average landlord isn't rich, especially since rent controls passed back in '80. He expanded on what he said earlier today and said that many owners are losing their shirts because they're forced to float rent-controlled tenants. Some owners can't even pay their mortgages. They hire Levin to get them out in order to get tenants who can pay market rates. Todd was very clear that he doesn't feel sorry for evicting tenants. If they break even the smallest contract detail, he can get them out. Meanwhile, he's selling off his rent-controlled houses and those that need repairs and investing in big projects like the high-rise."

"He selling at a loss?"

"Hell, no. He's savvy, changing the business model. Diversifying."

"Yes, but Deats felt threatened. He wrote that letter about getting killed out."

"I know, but I couldn't say that. Todd was very open. He spoke freely, without hesitation or righteousness."

"Nevertheless, he can't illegally evict."

"According to him he's not. But that doesn't prevent tenants from fighting back. Most of what he said can be verified. It's a lot of searching, but I'm good at that. And databases are always open."

"Sounds like *you're* the fan."

Birdie shrugged. "I'm impressed by his transformation. He's mellowed. Introspective. I mean, he's a freak, no doubt. Who paints with fish blood? But he didn't act like a man trying to conceal homicidal mania."

"What about cursing when he turned off the lights when we got to the fourth floor? He didn't like us seeing his stuff. You saw the key machines."

"I know it's odd, and I didn't feel comfortable. Didn't feel safe. But he said something peculiar ... I quote, 'I'm very good at making money and Iris is good at spending it. It's my big dilemma.' And something else, when I talked to him up on the tower I mentioned his ownership of Dominic's house. He never asked how I knew. He even called it the Nobel house. So, why has a man who'd gone to great lengths to hide his ownership within multiple corporations suddenly be so transparent?"

"Love? Religion?"

"Don't know, but he had a lot to say about Rachel. Choked up, actually."

"Oh?"

"He really admired her. He called her Rach."

"Sounds intimate."

"Yes, it does." Contemplative.

"Let's get home. You know George will call and update me on the day's developments. We should be ready in the office when he does."

"Good idea."

"Got any hooch at the house or should I stop at a liquor store?"

"Ron left the Booker's for you."

"My man."

Thom started the engine just as a pair of fast-approaching head-lights zoomed toward them. A dark four-door coupe passed.

Neither Birdie nor Thom needed to say a word. He threw the car into drive and hit the accelerator.

"That was a CLS," said Birdie.

"I know. Did you catch the plate?"

"Too fast."

"Catch the ones in Moysychyn's garage?"

"The angle was wrong."

"Where'd you put my work cell?"

"Way ahead of you." Birdie opened the center console and pulled out Thom's second phone. She turned it on. "Faster."

"No shit!"

The CLS slowed, made a sharp left, a sharp right, then sped on. The speedometer on Birdie's Taurus hit 60 with a street speed limit of 45 and still the CLS was a quarter mile ahead.

"Shit," said Thom. "That car can move."

"What number?"

"Star five. But not yet. We need the plate. The interchange is coming up. Shit, shit, shit. Which way you gonna go?"

"Traffic up ahead. Whoa. Left on Union, left on Union. He's bypassing the interchange."

"I'm on it."

The light turned yellow. Thom accelerated and drifted through the intersection on the red. A horn honked.

"Shouldn't we have the hazards flashing," said Birdie. "This is unsafe."

"We don't need the extra attention. Okay, red light at Venice. He's got to stop."

But the CLS didn't stop. It slowed, then blew through the red. Thom also slowed, glanced east and west, then blew the light as well. Birdie white-knuckled the door handle.

"What?" said Thom, "gonna jump out?"

"He'll have to stop at Pico. There are way too many cars."

Thom passed a little four banger as they approached Pico, but the light was green. The CLS accelerated, passed three cars, and changed lanes. Thom followed suit.

"Next major is Olympic," said Birdie.

Cars in the first position at the intersection forced the CLS to stop at the red. This gave Thom an opportunity to catch up with one car between them.

"That may not even be Moysychyn," said Birdie. "The CLS is common in L.A."

"I know, but what if it is? I'm not missing the opportunity."

As soon as the light turned green, Thom squeezed the Taurus between two cars and passed the one in front of him, then pulled behind the coupe.

"Got it," said Birdie, writing down the plate. "Star five?" She palmed Thom's phone and he called it in, giving his name, rank, badge number, division, and the license plate.

"Next major is Wilshire and then I think Union dead ends at Sixth," said Birdie. "He might be headed downtown."

"We'll know soon enough."

The response came back. The Mercedes CLS was owned by Todd Moysychyn. No wants no warrants.

Birdie stowed the phone while Thom stayed directly behind the coupe and rode its bumper.

"Don't you think we're a bit obvious?" said Birdie.

"Should I care?"

They stayed the course past Wilshire and took a right on 6th.

"It splits under the one-ten and turns into a one-way," said Birdie.

Thom slowed and put a little distance between them. At Flower and 6th, the coupe pulled right. A woman ran to the car and jumped in.

"Holy shit," yelled Thom. "That was Jelena! Did you see that?"

"You sure it was her?"

"Yes, she lives in the Pegasus."

"What now?"

"We follow."

They stayed on 6th, past Grand, past Pershing Square on the left, and took a left on Broadway—the first street with two-way traffic—then a left on 5th, another one-way.

"He's gonna double back to the freeway," said Thom. "Which way? North or south?"

They made a red light stop at Grand.

"Both use the right lane," said Birdie. "Can you see who's driving?"

"It must be Todd. Jelena lived with the Lawrence's for years. Their paths probably crossed. Todd was on familiar terms with Rachel so it follows he'd know Jelena as well. And remember, she marks wealthy men."

"So they conspired to kill her foster parents? Her boss?"

The light turned and the coupe moved right. Thom moved right.

The coupe accelerated, bypassed the northbound onramp. Took the south. It sped and took the ramp faster than Thom.

"Stay with them," said Birdie. "There are three options coming up, stay the course, take the ten east or westbound."

But it was already too late. Once the CLS hit the straightaway of the freeway it was gone. Speed, agility, red taillights. Thom punched the steering wheel.

They rode in silence as the adrenalin burned off and Thom took the I-10 west toward the Bird House.

"At least we have something to work with," she said. "Remember what Lawrence's aide, Gordon, told George? That Lawrence worked with councilman Fontaine on housing issues. Jelena could've easily spied for Todd. She said in the interview that living with the Lawrence's was hard. They were tough on her and she seemed resentful that the twins got away with shit. She also had opportunity to destroy the computer files and steal the flash drive."

"Yeah, she just got upgraded from person of interest to suspect."

FORTY-TWO

BIRDIE MOVED HER EYES from the computer monitor and looked up at Thom. "Will you please stop pacing?"

"George should've called by now. Jelena, Kidd, and Gordon all gave official statements today. We need that information." He pointed at the board where they'd been whittling out the pieces and parts of the four crime scenes. He flipped his wrist. "It's nearly midnight."

Yeah, thought Birdie, *almost a new day.*

"He probably thinks you're sleeping."

"Bullshit. He'd know I'd be up."

"Call him."

"I did. My calls went straight to voicemail."

"You're out on personal. Maybe he's taking that seriously."

"All George knows is that I'm off the case. He doesn't know anything about the personal time. Craig can be a jerk, but he doesn't talk about employee matters."

"How would Craig know?"

"Personnel forwards leave requests to supervisors for approval."

She threw a piece of gum at him. "Chewing helps." He ignored it and it fell to the floor.

"He's probably sleeping then," said Birdie. "He loves his beauty sleep."

Thom snapped his fingers. "That's right. He's probably getting laid. He and Anita, the Santa Monica detective, made a connection."

"There you go," said Birdie. "He'll call in the morning. Now relax. Go to bed. Sleep."

"Too keyed up."

"Go downstairs and sweat it out."

Thom spread his hands as if to say, *what? me, work out?*

"I need a smoke." He made for the door.

Birdie felt wired as well. These days she didn't have the capability to slow down. She filled hour upon hour with exercise, her search. The busywork having become a narcotic; a replacement for booze. She slept four hours on a good night. Averaged three. She was once an eight-hour gal. The hyperactivity took a physical toll. Her blood-shot eyes were in a constant state of fatigue. Headaches, muscle aches, stress in the neck, jaw pain from gum chewing. The only time she relaxed was when she was with Ron.

Ron. He never called her today.

She left Thom a note: bath, bed, see you in morning.

Upstairs, she ran a hot bath, added sweet pea-scented skin softening oil and started the jets. She placed the phone on a hand towel, undressed and slipped into the blissful water and took a deep breath. She called Ron's house phone.

After a few rings he answered with a sleepy voice. "Hey, baby."

"I woke you."

"That's okay."

"How'd your day go?"

"I'm too old to get wasted like that. I don't know how Noa does it."

"He's bigger."

"And younger by a few years."

"There you go." Birdie moved her right foot directly in front of the jet. It tickled.

"I'm sorry I didn't call. I spent the day on the couch in a semi-coma, TV binge."

"Ron Hughes being lazy? I don't believe it."

"Sounds like you're taking it easy, too. Is that the tub I hear?"

"Yeah, I'm trying to relax. Had a busy day helping Thom with his case."

"What happened to wanting to write about the scruffy guy in the newspaper?"

"Turns out, he's connected to Thom's case and I interviewed him this evening."

Ron chuckled. "No one can accuse you of wasting time."

"Do you want to go back to sleep?"

"I'd choose you over sleep any day. What's on your mind?"

"I'm wondering how long you're going to stick around."

Ron sniggered. "Seriously? You doubt me?"

"I've been thinking about Thom and Anne. The core of their problem is lack of intimacy."

"Is that what you're worried about? Because we aren't having sex, I'm going to fall out of love with you or screw some barrack babe?"

"It can happen. You have physical needs."

"One day, we'll be together again and we'll satisfy each other's needs. Meanwhile, I have a hand and an active imagination. It's not like you to feel insecure. What's going on?"

"I like the way you say we. Like, it's not my problem, it's our problem."

"Babe? Answer the question."

"I don't know what's wrong."

That wasn't true. She did feel insecure of the relationship and worried that it wouldn't survive the confrontation with Matt. Birdie felt tears welling. She loved Matt completely and he left her. She loved Ron completely and was afraid he'd leave, too.

"I'm not going to quit you."

"Even distance and a phone signal can't stop you from knowing what I need to hear."

"It's true."

"What if I quit you?"

Silence.

Finally Ron said, "What's worse, to have loved and lost, or not to have loved at all?"

"Cliché, but okay."

"I can't afford to worry about that. You hold my heart in your hands and there are but two choices. You'll nurture it or you'll squash it."

"You give me too much power."

"You think?" said Ron. "I have no other view. I'm an over-eager puppy around you and you're the jaded mother hound that puts me in my place."

"Do I really? That's so sad."

"You laid out the rules of our relationship that first day I spent with you. Nothing has changed since then."

"A lot has changed."

"Not really, no. The essence is the same. You have an agenda I don't agree with, but my opinion be damned."

"Please … let's not go there."

"Alright. But be honest with yourself and admit one thing. You're feeling mopey because you're torn about the decision you'll have to make one day. Because he is the only thing that stands between us and you know I'm not going to share. I won't do a threesome."

"Ron …"

"Don't say anything, Birdie. I'm not asking for an answer. Just be honest with yourself. Someday you're going to take a trip. You'll either come back or you won't. Then I'll truly know where I stand."

"You know I love you."

"I don't doubt it. Birdie Keane is not the kind of woman to say a thing she doesn't believe. But you'll have to decide who you love more."

"It's not fair."

"What the fu—? Never mind. This conversation took a wrong turn."

"Don't hold back."

"Look, baby, I'm glad you called, but let's hang up now. We both need some good sleep. I know you're afraid to take the meds, but cut one of the sleeping pills in half. Just to take the edge off. Put your head on the pillow and rest easy for a change. Okay?"

"Okay. Goodnight, Ron."

"Goodnight, Birdie. Sleep tight."

As soon as the call disconnected, she burst into tears. Suddenly, Thom's case lost all importance. She did have work to do. All the colliding thoughts and theories and schemes no longer mattered. She needed to focus her energies on herself.

Tomorrow.

Right now, she'd stay in the tub until the water turned cold.

Then she'd take Ron's advice and swallow half of a pill.

She'd go to sleep and dream about making love with Ron.

And then tomorrow everything would be different.

Tomorrow.

FORTY-THREE

Wednesday, May 16

Thom knocked on Birdie's bedroom door.

"Come in." She sat up, stretched, checked the clock. Six-fifteen.

Thom entered the room with a cup of coffee and placed it on her nightstand. Gave her a good morning peck on the lips, sat on the edge of the bed. He was dressed in jeans and, despite being out on personal, still wore his firearm and handcuffs. Habits die hard.

"Coffee. Such service. Thanks."

"Sleep good?"

"Great. I took half a pill. You?"

"Naw. I got a couple hours on the couch. I worked on the case most of the night."

"Any development?"

"George called. He's on his way. Bringing breakfast burritos. Want to sit in?"

"*Yeah.*"

What happened to taking care of Birdie? It's tomorrow.

———

"He said, 'It's going to be nice working with a two again,'" said George. "It was practically the first thing he said to me."

"What an ass," said Thom.

"I don't get it," said Birdie.

"It was a slight," said Thom. "Seymour is a D-three, I'm a D-three. George is a *new* D-three."

"It was his way of putting me in my place as if I were a rookie," added George.

"Rookies don't work in RHD," said Birdie.

"Thank you. Someone who appreciates my worth."

Breakfast over and yet the three of them were still at the breakfast table in the glassed kitchen nook. Birdie stared out the leaded glass windows at the malaise that is Southern California's annual May Gray. This year's season has been especially heavy. Angelenos haven't seen the sun in over a week because the onshore flow was so strong. The sunless depression began to wear on her.

"This room is cold," said Birdie. "Let's move to the living room and light a fire. I'm sick of this weather."

"I'm with you," said George. "I'll bring the coffee service."

Thom and Birdie went ahead to the living room.

"He's so agreeable this morning," said Birdie.

"Like I said, he got laid," whispered Thom.

"You going to ask him about her?" said Birdie.

"Hell, no. He's very private about stuff like that. He'll joke occasionally, but he never tells. He's never even admitted to having sex with you and you guys dated … what?"

"Six months."

"Point made."

Birdie opened the flue and used the gas lighter to start the blaze. Ron had laid the fire the week before last. He always had one ready. In Ron's Oceanside Craftsman he had a two-sided fireplace made of river rock in the middle of the great room. There was always a fire at the ready. This past winter they enjoyed them often. Fires were nice, but she was looking forward to sunshine and summer heat. That would be August through October, once they got past the May Gray and then the June Gloom. She curled up in the chair.

George carried in the coffee service and placed the tray on the coffee table. He poured for Birdie first, then Thom, then himself.

"Labs came back," said George. "The pubic hair in the blood belonged to Dominic. The bullet lodged in his kidney was a twenty-two. Dominic was not the father of Rachel's baby."

Thom spread his fingers. "What's the punch line? We didn't need labs to tell us that."

"Okay, how's this?" said George, "The owner of the cigarette butt left at the Deats crime scene was a paternal match for Rachael's baby."

Thom and Birdie exchanged glances of possibility. Todd Moysychyn?

Thom gave George a small envelope. "I collected that last night."

George looked inside. "A cigarette butt."

"I witnessed the smoker discard it. He was on his own private property and would have a legitimate expectation of privacy considering I had to go through a locked gate to get in. It was still smoldering when I picked it up."

"You get permission?"

292

"Of course not. I'm on leave. I was a private citizen when I picked it up off the ground. He didn't know I was a cop. In fact, I was never asked what I did for a living."

"Oh, yeah," said Birdie. "We never had the *what do you do for a living* conversation."

"You were there?" said George.

"Yes. I told you Thom and I were going out. He was my date."

"Who does this belong to?"

"I can't tell you that," said Thom.

"Do you think he's our killer?"

"Hard to tell. Birdie?"

"Fifty-fifty."

George leaned away from Thom as though he had cooties. "This was illegally obtained. How am I going to get this in without a case number? Even if it was determined to be a match, it'd taint the prosecution."

"You keep forgetting that the case is already tainted. Craig saw to that when he wouldn't release me after I told him I was compromised. Now it's a serial. He's the screw-up here." Thom pointed at the envelope. "Find a work around and submit it. See what shakes out."

George nodded and slipped it into his portfolio. "Speaking of which …" He handed Thom a CD.

"What's this?"

"That's Craig telling you about the IA."

Thom's brows raised in confusion.

"Remember showing Craig the murder book?" said George. "The war room was being used so we ducked into an interview room? When Craig asked me to leave I thought … well, I went to the monitor room and recorded it."

"You've had this for two days and said nothing?" The carotid artery pulsed in Thom's neck. His face turned red.

"It was my moral dilemma. I wanted to protect you, but I didn't want you to know I invaded your privacy."

Thom jumped up and aimed straight for George's face. George held up his hands in defense, but Thom shoved them away and planted a big kiss on George lips. "I love you, partner. This is going to save my ass!"

"George is blushing," said Birdie.

"This gives me the leverage I need," said Thom. "Thank you."

"Alright," said George. "Might as well take these as well." He gave Thom three more CDs. "Interviews. I've been forbidden from telling you about them. But there must be a reason there's a duplicating tower in the monitor room, yes?"

"Did Jelena and Kidd get a glimpse of each other beforehand?"

"Unfortunately not. The choreography wasn't timed right."

"Give me the abbreviated version. Did their stories change?"

"Dominic's aide, Gordon, gave a statement that matched exactly what he had previously stated. Jelena's changed slightly. She now remembers turning off the alarm clock. Said she misspoke when she initially told Officer Cross about what she touched."

"Remind me," said Birdie, "who is Cross?"

"Cross ran the log. As first responder he asked her what she touched when she arrived at the scene. She admitted to touching the doorknob when she unlocked the front door, a magazine in the great room, and the doorknob to the master bedroom.

"When I interviewed her she said the reason she went upstairs is because she heard the alarm clock beeping, but she didn't mention to Cross that she turned it off. Yesterday, she admitted to turning it off."

"Which means," said Thom. "She got a close-up look at the bodies."

"Other than that detail, it was exactly the same. When asked why she didn't tell Officer Cross about turning off the clock she said she must've been in shock. She didn't even back off from her dislike of the twins."

"And the bartender, Kidd?" said Thom.

"His story changed. He told us he *did know* Jelena. She's a regular at Hank's. That's where they initially met. They hook up occasionally at his place. He also admitted to seeing her the night I visited. He said that one of the perks of being a young bartender is lots of women. He gets laid consistently. Oftentimes on the premises. His story got interesting. Seems Jelena is always looking for a mark. An older, rich man. She's money hungry. Looking for a sugar daddy like the one her friend has."

"What friend?" said Thom.

"Some Asian chick she went to school with. Kidd said he only saw her once, but that Jelena talks about her all the time."

"And I walk in and she marks me," said Thom.

"Yes. According to Kidd, she watched you and eventually moved your way."

"How did Jelena respond to Kidd's representation?"

"Her interview was first."

"Now everyone knows about me," said Thom.

"No," said George. "She only knows you as an older gentleman named Thomas. Remember, she never got your last name. She'd never met you before."

"How does Kidd feel about Jelena marking men?" said Thom.

"He could care less. He gets his rocks off," said George.

"May I ask a personal question?" said Birdie to Thom. "How did you explain the gun when you were with her?"

"I never wear one when I go out," said Thom. "I keep it locked in the car."

"Smart," said George. "If anyone were to ever figure out you were a cop, they couldn't claim malfeasance or coercion."

Thom clicked his teeth. "Exactly."

"I need another reminder," said Birdie. "Who asked who?"

"She asked me," said Thom.

"And she reiterated that yesterday," said George. "I played this up in the interview. At some point Thom's identity will come out and we'll have two independent statements that she targeted you. Hers and Kidd's."

"Not a setup after all," said Thom. "Anything else?"

"That's it. So much for me being forbidden from talking to you about it."

Thom said to Birdie, "Since we're exchanging gifts should we give George ours?"

"Yes," she said. "I'll get it." Birdie went to the office and came back with yet another CD. "These are phone messages left on my extension at the newspaper. I believe they belong to the serial killer."

"What? Why didn't you call the police?"

"I thought they were crank calls. They were out of context until I happened upon Thom's case file, you know, the one you collected from me last night? You know me, an unattended file, an active imagination … and well … you are the police. Now I have to tell the paper."

"This might've just busted open the case."

Birdie grimaced. "Not sure about that, but hey, go to town. Take it to the bosses. Have them work it out."

Thom felt Noa's phone vibrating in his pocket. "Excuse me," he said. He went to the bathroom and answered. "Hello?"

"Aloha, Thom. This is Noa. Did I wake you?"

"I've been up awhile. So … it's you."

"Live in Memorex. Seems you passed the point of no return yesterday when you fulfilled my terms. I want to meet you in person before we take the next step. Tonight. Seven p.m. Chinatown. Have paper and pencil? You'll need to take down directions."

"I'm not in a place I can write."

"Okay. Hang up. I'll call back and leave a message. Still have that password?"

"Yes."

"Terrific. See you tonight. And Thom? Don't forget the Benjamins and come with an appetite. Aloha." The call disconnected.

"What if I wasn't available tonight?" whispered Thom.

He returned just in time to see George off. They hugged. "Good luck with Dominic's office today," said Thom. "Don't forget the IT guy."

"Will, do. Take care."

"Walk me down?" said George to Birdie.

She escorted him downstairs. When they got to the bottom of the stairs he kissed her on the cheek. "I'm sorry again for last night."

"The George Silva I know wouldn't have crossed that line."

"Guess I was impatient."

They said goodbye and Birdie rejoined Thom upstairs in the office. He had a phone to his ear and was scribbling notes. After he disconnected he said, "Noa. We're meeting tonight."

"He got his money and isn't wasting time. That's good, I think, gives you less time to back out."

"I couldn't even if I wanted to. He's going to judge me. Make sure I'm not crazy. If he chooses not to take my case I get the money back. But if *I* change my mind, he keeps it. Listen, I want to be at home when the kids get back from school today. They need a daddy fix just as much as I need a kid fix. I have to be out of here by two-thirty. Help me keep the schedule?"

"Of course. When are you going to tell George about Jelena getting into Moysychyn's car?"

"Not sure. Maybe she marked her previous landlord as well."

"Who's making theories now? Maybe she killed for him, too."

FORTY-FOUR

"THANK GOODNESS FOR BENNIE Hy," said Thom, checking emails on his laptop. "He's the clerk. Sent me the CCPD case file. He either sent it as a courtesy, or he doesn't know I'm off the case. Shit! I have to go to the Bradbury Building at ten."

"Internal affairs found you, huh?" said Birdie.

"It just says I have an appointment in office two-fifteen at ten. Well, that won't work. I have a life and need more notice. Besides, I haven't been officially notified of a complaint. I haven't seen any documentation and I want written notification, with my required action made clear in black and white."

"Isn't that what they just did?"

"No. They didn't say why I needed to come. This one can be put off." He furiously typed a response.

"Is there an attachment?"

"None."

Birdie looked past Thom's head at his work on the dry erase board. It seemed squished. Not like her method of arrows, equal signs, and question marks. But, hey, everyone worked differently.

WESTCHESTER
Det: Diego, Pacific Div.
TOD: Sun, Apr 1; 4–6 am
Vic: Maxwell Williams
Occ: urban architect
POE: front door?
PR: ex-boyfriend Joey
Landlord: Vermillion Mgt.
Eviction? Yes
FU: Locksmith

CULVER CITY
Det: John Blabbershaw, CCPD
TOD: Sun, Apr 8; ?
Vic: Nitta & Nadeer Malik
Occ: unemployed, student
POE: broken window
PR: "tea lady" Jill Moran
Landlord: Ladder Capital
Eviction? No
FU: ?

SANTA MONICA
Det: Anita Dhillon, SMPD
TOD: Sun, Apr 15–18?
Vic: Jerry Deats
Occ: ?
POE: front door?
PR: neighbor
Landlord: Mobeck Finance Holdings
Eviction? Yes
FU: Locksmith

HOLLYWOOD
Det: Thom and George, RHD
TOD: Sun, May 13; 4–6 am
Vic: Dominic Lawrence, Rachel, Amber, Amy
Occ: attorney, homemaker, students
POE: front door?
PR: Jelena Shkatova
Landlord: Great Western Group
Eviction: Yes
FU: Locksmith

CONNECTION
Mobeck Finance Holdings, Great Western Group = L.A. National Housing Trust
L.A. National Housing Trust = Todd Moysychyn

WHY FOUR WEEKS REST?
Why Sunday?

"P-O-E is point of entry, and F-U is follow-up?" said Birdie.

"Correct," said Thom, leaning over his computer.

"Did the same medical examiner do the Westchester and Hollywood autopsies? They both have the same time of death, but the others don't."

"Because of Deats' state of decomposition it was too difficult to pinpoint the exact day—that's why the three-day window—let alone the hour. We're all convinced that he was killed on the fifteenth, making a case for the Sunday pattern. I can't speak for Culver City, will have to get the autopsy report."

"Culver City is the oddball," said Birdie. "It's the only one with forced entry. All the others have a proposed front door entry."

"Maybe the killer forgot his key. Had to break in."

"What did you say?"

"It was a joke," said Thom.

"What if it's not?"

Thom looked up. Gave Birdie his full attention.

"Last night when Todd locked the downstairs door he used a key attached to his belt. When we were up on five and he unlocked the beautiful carved door, I think he used the same key. A master key. He had key-making equipment in his workshop."

Birdie rolled her chair to a bookshelf and removed a reference book: *Locksmithing Basics*, and tossed it to Thom.

He caught it and said, "Why do you have this?"

"Garage sale. Two bucks. I've had it since I was a kid. When Dad put me on house arrest, I'd pretend I was a prisoner in a jail cell. I played with that book to plan my great escape. I knew it'd come in handy someday. See what it says about master keys."

Thom fingered through the index. "Here's a chapter titled *masterkeying*. There are several systems depending on the level of security required. For example, there are master keys, change keys, grand master keys, great-grand master keys." He read silently, moving his lips ever so slightly. "Any of these could work in our circumstance. Let's say there are a number of houses. Each one with a different key. Yet there could be a master, a grand master, and a great-grand master."

"Let me get this straight," said Birdie. "The renter could have a key, the management company a different key, and the property owner another different key, and all three would work the same lock?"

"That's what I'm seeing in this book regarding pin tumbler locks. It's all about the locations of pins within the chamber slash chambers and something complicated about shear lines."

"Let's simplify. Vermillion Management has a locksmith on call. He provided changeout records to Detective Diego for the Westchester house."

"This is so logical," said Thom. "The renter has peace of mind regarding the security of the home, management has legal access for inspections and work orders and the owner has access to his property. All legal. The locksmith isn't doing anything wrong."

"Except back to Culver City—"

"—you're getting ahead of yourself. We still haven't established a connection—"

"—we have the bloody message and manner of death. They're connected. We haven't established *ownership* like we have with Santa Monica and Hollywood. We need to find where the buck stops, who has access."

"Can you do that for me? You've already done it and know the steps. I'm really curious if Moysychyn can be tied to Vermillion Management and Ladder Capital. Also, there must be some database of licensed locksmiths, like for contractors. See if he's on it."

Birdie threaded her fingers and pushed forward, palms out, cracking her knuckles.

"Ready," she said.

"You're going to get arthritis doing that," said Thom.

"I did it for effect. Lighten up."

"I can't. We're gonna catch a killer before Seymour and Silva."

———

Two hours later Birdie did the honors of writing a new notation on the board:

Vermillion Management, Ladder Capital, Mobeck Finance Holdings, Great Western Group = L.A. National Housing Trust = Todd Moysychyn = locksmith (32 years)

"What's wrong," said Thom. "Why aren't you happy?"

"Just because he owned all four properties and had access doesn't mean he killed those people." She rolled her shoulders, shook out her arms. "Something else is bothering me. Remember the message from the killer? Here, let's hear it again." She went back to the computer.

"*Greetings, Elizabeth. Let me introduce myself. My name is Mayo. It took three minutes to kill four people with five shots. Good numbers, don't you think?*"

"Now look at your board. There are *three* murder scenes, *four* weeks of no activity."

"I don't know," said Thom. "I think you're stretching. Where's the five?"

"There were *five* shots at the *fourth* scene."

"I think it's the killer giving us a specific about the scene. To prove he is who he is."

"Why do you think there were four weeks between murders?"

"I've no idea. Usually, a break occurs when the perpetrator is busy or out of commission. But we need a viable suspect before we can determine the timeline."

"And why Sunday?"

"Early morning Sunday," corrected Thom. "Wee hours of the morning."

Birdie rolled her neck. "Come on, we need to loosen up. We're going downstairs for some exercise."

———

Thom walked a steady pace of three-point-five miles per hour on the treadmill. Birdie turned the spin bike facing the treadmill so they could talk.

"You know what bugs me?" said Birdie. "Why these people?"

"I don't think it has anything to do with the people. I think it's the houses the killer wants empty. He killed them out just like Deats predicted."

"That assumes that Moysychyn is the killer. Let's explore that scenario."

"You told me he had a lot to say about the Hollywood Hills house. The Nobel house he called it. About how it was worth a boatload of money as is. I've seen it. It's a decrepit piece of shit. The only thing worthwhile is the view. Whoever buys it will tear it down and build another. Guaranteed. And also, Moysychyn told you it was rent stabilized and Dominic also had a special wavier. So, if he could get the deadbeats out, he could rent or sell at market value. Did he say he was losing money on the house?"

"No. Just that he couldn't capitalize on the market. What's special about the Santa Monica house?" huffed Birdie, as she pedaled faster.

"Well, the apartment Deats lived in was an illegal conversion."

"Why would Moysychyn want him out?"

"Deats was a hoarder. He lived in a fire hazard. That'd be legal grounds for eviction."

"Maybe he didn't have any other place to go."

"That's a good one," said Thom. "Anita couldn't find employment history on the guy. He lived off social security. If he were also in a rent stabilized situation he'd want to stay at the beach in a cheap apartment he could afford. Who wouldn't?"

"The downstairs, or A residence, was empty, right? Did they get evicted?"

"Don't know. Remind me to check with Anita."

Birdie jumped off the bike. She fished through a wicker basket and found a dry erase marker. She wrote on the closest gilt mirror:

Anita → "A" people evicted? Confirm Deats financial situation.

Then she got back on the bike.

"What's special about Westchester?"

"Don't know," said Thom. "Culver City either. Road trip?"

Again, Birdie got off the bike and wrote: **Westchester/CC houses**. When she got back on she said, "There's this great program that Google has. We can see the house, the street, even the overhead. We don't have to leave the comfort of Hancock Park, spend money on gas. Also, there are lots of real estate web sites that provide specifics like square footage and floor plans."

"Smartaleck. I thought you were old school."

"I'm both. I utilize whatever tool is best for whatever I'm doing."

"Speaking of tool," said Thom. "The killer was certainly efficient and displayed deadly accuracy. One shot each without the benefit of sight."

"What do you mean sight?"

"A pillow was used as a muffle in every murder. It was between the gun and the head."

"Why do you think that's hard?" said Birdie.

———

Birdie and Thom huddled in the middle of the garden in some shrubs. A light drizzle fell on their heads. Though the marine layer provided cover, and Birdie had an acre of property he was still concerned that a neighbor might hear the noise.

Birdie had another of Matt's guns: A beautiful Smith & Wesson J frame with an exposed hammer and wood grip. Eight rounds of .22 LR—cheap and reliable ammo. A perfect gun for personal protection.

Or turning brain matter into soup.

They had an argument about the type of pillow to be used. Down or foam? Thom was unsure what type was used at the other homicides. They eventually settled on foam because that's the kind the killer used at the Lawrence house. It was the cheap kind of pillow available at discount stores. Birdie had only one so they had to make it count. She slipped a floral cotton cover over it to simulate, as near as possible, the actual pillow used.

Birdie marked a cantaloupe with a black circle. "Temple," she said. "We get one shot each just like the killer. You first."

Thom took the gun in his right hand and held the pillow in his left. At only 11 ounces the gun still shook in his hands.

"Don't shoot your left hand off," said Birdie.

"Shut up."

Thom had a problem holding the pillow steady. It flopped. So he pressed it against the fruit. It was a standard-size bed pillow so it completely concealed the head-shaped fruit. He pressed his palm against the pillow to feel the fruit underneath. His legs began to quiver from the squat.

"You can't wake up your victim," said Birdie.

He bit his lip in concentration, made his best guess as to where that black mark was. He squeezed the trigger. POP. It was louder than either of them expected.

They ducked in reflex.

Birdie giggled. "That was fun. Let's see what you hit."

Thom lifted the pillow. The bullet scraped the right side of the cantaloupe clean off. He missed the mark by two inches.

"Okay, smarty-pants, your turn," said Thom.

Birdie took the gun in her right hand, the pillow in her left, just as Thom had done. She backed ten paces away, turned, and came back fast. She dropped the pillow over the cantaloupe, pressed the barrel against it and squeezed the trigger. POP. Even though they expected the sound, they still ducked.

Thom removed the pillow. She hadn't even hit the cantaloupe.

"How in the hell did I miss it completely?" she said.

"See? Not so easy."

They collected the trash and walked toward the house.

"We're both familiar with a variety of weapons," said Birdie. "We're both great shots."

"On the range. But in a real-life scenario? How many times have you had to squat or bend over your target? In a life or death gun battle, I doubt either of us would do well."

"That's disappointing."

"Well, our little exercise just brought to light a new option."

"What?"

"A professional killer."

"A professional isn't going to leave a message to draw attention to himself."

"Unless he was setting someone up."

"Like a landlord who uses an aggressive eviction lawyer. 'If they can't kick me out, they'll kill me out.'"

"Like an oddball cigarette butt left at a crime scene to be discovered two weeks later."

"The killer, or someone, came back to open Deats' curtains. Why not deposit a fresh butt then? Make sure the forensic material is intact."

"Here's a big but. Who'd have motive to hire the professional? The one who'd benefit is Moysychyn. Why hire a killer and set yourself up?"

"Someone else hired the killer."

"Iris?" they said together.

"A money-hungry, mail-order bride."

FORTY-FIVE

"ANITA," SAID THOM. "I'VE got you on speaker while I type."

Birdie tapped her fingers across the keyboard, looking up the Westchester address on the Internet.

"Just a quick question about the A residence in Santa Monica."

"I heard you were off the case," she said.

"Who said that?"

"Seymour."

"He's a kidder. Has a bad sense of humor. Naw, I'm following the money. It doesn't take two. About that A residence ... your team determined it was owned by Mobeck Finance Holdings. Did you ever find out who had rented it?"

"Yeah, under threat of subpoena Mobeck granted us access to the house file and we contacted the last occupants. A middle-aged couple. Been in the house nearly twenty years. Raised a son there."

"They were the ones who altered the bedroom into an apartment?"

"They said no. They said it was there when they moved in. As was Deats. They didn't benefit from what little income it generated."

"Was the house rent controlled?"

"The couple paid just under nine-hundred a month. Deats paid two-fifty."

"No wonder he didn't want to move. Where else could he live for that rent? Were the people in the A residence evicted?"

"Yes. They received a letter from an attorney that gave a long list of reasons why. They got so scared they packed up and left within a month. Deats obviously decided to stay on and fight."

"Until the end."

"Right."

"Hey, thanks for your support in the meeting yesterday morning."

"I give credit where credit is due. I don't like what you did to my jacket, but considering my stinkin' attitude I can't blame you."

"Thanks. Oh! One last thing. About that oddball cigarette butt … was it soggy when you collected it?"

"Strangely, no. Nor was it fresh. It was somewhere in between."

"Thanks, Anita. See you around."

Thom punched off. "Next up?"

"The Westchester house on Boeing Avenue," said Birdie. "Built in '48. Still in original condition. Look at the floor plan. It's tiny, just nine-hundred-eighty square feet, single-car garage, has a picture window with a city view and unobstructed downtown from the backyard. Look here at the neighborhood." Birdie maneuvered the mouse to zoom out. "The only one on the street not remodeled. Most current sale of a comparable model puts it over six-hundred-thousand."

Thom coughed. "For less than a thousand square feet? Wasn't there something going on with Westchester? Something in the news?"

"Yeah," said Birdie. "They've teamed with Playa Del Rey to fight the LAX master plan. They think moving the northern runway two-hundred-sixty feet and upgrading the terminals would generate more air traffic, thus, more noise and air pollution."

"Let's play landlord. What's the value here?"

"If it were my property, I'd add a second story, remodel, upgrade. There's plenty of lot to do so. Then I'd sell it before the airport agency gets a re-do."

"You did say he was selling some stock, diversifying. So far, we're three for four in motivation to get people out. Culver City?"

"Located on La Cienega," said Birdie. "This one is an oddity. It's a townhouse set back from the street. It's actually above the boulevard. Across the street is a field of pump jacks. Not sure what the story is here. It's going to involve more research."

"The message is the only thing that ties it to the others."

"And the tenants were not in the process of being evicted."

Thom flipped his wrist. "I'm going to take off now. See about gathering a few more clothes before the kids get home. I don't want them seeing me moving things."

"I'll see what I can dig up on Iris. Chances are that isn't her birth name. Easy enough to look up marriage licenses. If I get lucky I might find her current immigration status. Where'd you put the photos you stole from the refrigerator?"

"They're on the altar."

"Okay, I've got plenty to do. Go. Say hello to the kids, give them hugs and kisses from their cousin Bird."

———

Thom was mid-raid on the cookie jar when Anne entered the kitchen.

"Thom? You should've called."

He whirled around. Chocolate chip cookie in his mouth. Glass of milk at the ready. He swallowed and took a gulp to wash it down. A little too fast, he choked and coughed up the cookie into the sink. Drank some more milk and wiped his mouth on his sleeve. What a way to receive the woman he hadn't seen in three days.

He noticed the butterfly before him. The teenage freckles across her nose were long gone, but the blue eyes were just as vibrant as the first time he ever saw them. Her lips, luscious with an understated nude tint and a bit shiny made them all the more desirable. Gone was the red lipstick that had been her trademark for years. Hair, a few shades lighter and cut into a stylish bob tucked behind her ears. Feet, slipped into a pair of jeweled sandals that buckled across the vamp. She wore slender slacks that stopped at her ankles and a gauzy blouse with embroidery. Simple, clean, and free of the stiff, constructed business dark she usually wore.

She took his breath away.

If she'd only give him a smile he could die a happy man right now.

"I'm worried about Pearse," said Thom.

"Me, too," she said. Agreeable. A good sign. "He thinks we're getting a divorce."

"I told him we're solid and that the only reason I haven't been home is because I'm on a big case."

"You shouldn't have lied. He's old enough to know the truth."

"Which is?"

"That we're not. We haven't been good in over a decade. How much longer are we going to pretend that our relationship is working for either of us?"

Thom felt the blood drain from his face. He backed up, went into the sun room. Anne had the lights and heaters going, simulating summer. A book lay face down on the chaise, a glass of white wine sat on the cocktail table. It felt as cozy as the brief fire at Birdie's house this morning. He sat on the adjacent chaise.

"You didn't go to work today?"

"I've been backing off hours."

"But still have evening meetings?"

"Yes." She jutted her chin in a defensive manner.

"Shall I pick up the kids from school?"

"Pepper is getting them today."

Pepper was the UCLA undergrad Anne employed occasionally on a part-time basis. She ran errands like picking up/dropping off dry cleaning, grocery shopping, driving the kids to soccer practice, piano lessons.

"What does she know?"

"About us? Nothing. It's none of her business."

"Who do you confide in?"

"Karen is my only confidant."

Of course, Karen Wilcox. The best friend who covered for Anne's dinner out. Anne picked up the glass and took a petite sip.

"May I have one of those?"

She nodded and went to the kitchen to pour him a glass. He watched her walk away. A slight sway of the hips. Thom always appreciated this backward view of his wife, no matter the wardrobe.

She returned and handed him the glass.

"Thank you," he said and took a man-sized gulp.

"Thom … I've consulted a divorce attorney."

The words were a stab to the heart yet he held steadfast in her presence. She had always been strong and he determined to be the same.

"Do you understand the ramifications of that decision? You've always insisted we maintain a pretense."

"Life is too short to be unhappy."

"Are you seeing someone else?"

"Of course not. We're still married. Honestly … I've been thinking a lot about it lately."

"Have anyone in mind?"

"No."

"I don't think we should get divorced."

"We're not going anywhere as a couple and neither of us is getting younger."

"You seem to be."

"I've lost some weight, that's all."

"You know what Bird said to me on Sunday? She said you had turned into a butterfly. I told her you were a butterfly every day. God, Anne, I love you just as much today as the day I met you. But I feel like I'm always playing catch up, still chasing the girl in the white sundress. It's like you're just outside my reach. How could we have disintegrated into this mess? It wasn't like this in the beginning. What happened?"

Thom reached out to her. She turned her head. She had already left him.

"Life happened, Thom. Kids, responsibility, the business, it all took a toll."

"You didn't mention my job."

"I signed up for that. Against my father's wishes. I knew full well what it'd be like married to a cop. I don't blame you for any of this. Nor do I blame myself. We let it happen, Thom. Together. We're both to blame in equal measure. I have no illusions about how tough a divorce would be on the kids. If we work together it's doable."

"If we couldn't work together to make our marriage work, why do you think we'll succeed at divorce?"

FORTY-SIX

BIRDIE LIKED PHOTOS ON her work board. Next to the original scruffy Todd she put the photo of the happy couple on their wedding day. She squinted at the school photo taken in front of a building. The only clear face was Iris'. It was as if the other girls turned their heads at the same time to look at something off camera, slightly blurring their profiles. Pretty useless. She added a photo from the newspaper article Birdie wrote about Dominic and his foster-child-clerk that Seymour had called up from archives and sent to Thom. In it, Jelena sat in a chair and gazed up at Dominic with an expression of adoration.

She flipped through the photos she printed for Thom. Her eye kept going back to the photo of the bloody message. Dead fish. She added it to the others on the board.

She got to work on the marriage license. Good thing Todd had an unusual last name. As is true with most public records the query must be framed exactly. It's not like a search engine on a navigation bar where similar criteria pop up. The city doesn't make it that easy.

Birdie utilized a hand-drawn grid on graph paper. Each box represented a date. She checked boxes as dates came back negative. An easy, old-school way of keeping track. Unfortunately, each query had to be typed in one by one. All those Ys. It was tedious and strained the eyes. She put on her glasses, turned on the TV, popped a fresh piece of gum, and settled in for the long haul.

An hour later, she finally found what she was looking for. Todd Moysychyn and Li Sū were wed at city hall five years ago February 14. Valentine's Day. How sweet.

So where did Miss Li Sū come from?

Birdie started with a basic LexisNexis search. Available to anyone who paid for subscriptions, it offered one of the largest databases of legal and public records in the world. Birdie thought that a name as unusual as Li Sū should pop on the immigration grid. She found thread after thread but never a complete picture. She kept running foul in crap searches and dead ends. Her frustration level rose with each key stroke.

Data searching wasn't uncommon of late. But this wasn't her project. It was Thom's. And while he was home playing with his kids she was doing his work.

"Screw it," she said aloud.

She called Ron's cell. She usually didn't call when he was on the job, except when important—which this was not—but she wanted the diversion.

"Well, lucky me," he answered. "Two days in a row."

"Did I catch you at a bad time?"

"I'm good. What's happening?"

"I'm doing some research for Thom's case and it's proving to be frustrating."

"How so?"

"My subject is a mail-order bride."

"Are you sure?"

"What do you mean? Of course, I'm sure."

"The multiple Thom caught on Sunday, right?"

"Yeah," she said, unsure where this was going.

"When investigating homicides assume everyone is lying."

"So, she's not a mail-order bride?"

"I don't know, babe."

"I don't understand what you're saying."

"What specifically are you looking for?"

"Her immigration status."

"Why?"

"Um ... I'm looking for background. She's a person of interest."

"How old is she?"

"Twenty-two-ish. She hooked up with her husband when she was seventeen."

"Did you check the 'looking for love' websites?"

"I went straight to the government agencies."

"Simplify your search. Think back to when you were that age. What did you like to do?"

"Party."

"Exactly. Go to the social networking sites. Check out the websites of the hot clubs. Look at their online photo albums. That will complete a profile better than her immigration status."

"Why didn't I think of that?" groaned Birdie.

"Because you've been going at breakneck speed for too long. You make life difficult for yourself. All it takes is a deep breath. When was the last time you binged on TV or read a book for pleasure or dug up weeds in the garden? The only time you relax is when you're with me. Or Frank."

"Because neither of you will tolerate anything different."

"Expect that of yourself. Stop avoiding self-examination."

"Heal thyself. That's the drum you keep beating."

"I'm your boyfriend—it's a job requirement."

FORTY-SEVEN

THOM TWISTED AROUND, UTTERLY lost, looking for a familiar sign. *Great cop work*, Thom thought. Chinatown wasn't that tricky if one kept to the main streets, the storefronts, the gold shops, the restaurants with the hanging lanterns and pictures of menu items. But Noa's directions took him between stalls of cheap tchotchkes, down narrow walkways covered in slimy filth, and past stinking dumpsters. He was seeking unmarked concrete stairs that lead to a basement. He had just given up hope and began to think he'd been taken for a ride when he caught the smell of something resembling barbeque. He followed his nose and found the industrial vents that led him to the location. The descent was slick and steep, and something algae-like grew on the wall. Above the door at the bottom was a wood sign carved with one simple word. *Aloha*.

Thom entered a restaurant kitchen, quite large and immaculately shiny and clean—a complete dichotomy from the drippy exterior. A large, rectangular table with twelve chairs took up a significant portion of the right side. On the table, an explosion of colorful foods. Exotic orchids and other delicate flowers filled vases and decorated the table.

"Poo-poos," said a salty voice behind him.

"Excuse me?" said Thom, whirling around to face a tall, brown man.

"P-U-P-U-S," said the man. "Hawaiian for appetizers."

The man standing before Thom was straight and secure, shaped by the Marine Corps and obvious to the world. Unknowable deadly skills hid behind golden, tender-hearted eyes and Thom liked him immediately. Instinct said this man would have his back.

The man reached out. "Noa at your service."

They shook. "Nice to meet you. I was expecting—"

"—a fat man?"

"When Ron said big Hawaiian—"

"—a common stereotype. I don't take that stuff personally." He gestured to the sink. "We eat with our fingers tonight."

Thom shrugged off his jacket and hung it on the back of a chair. He rolled up his sleeves and pumped the soap dispenser. The water went on automatically and he washed his hands. He had never worn a wedding ring. Never wanted a bad guy exploiting his connection to a wife or family. What irony. Noa stood next to him and also washed. Thom noticed his long fingers. Almost delicate. Thom finished and looked around for a paper towel when a tiny Chinese man with bad teeth handed him a white tea towel.

"That's Jin," said Noa, also receiving a drying towel. "My friend. The best chef this side of the Pacific. I want him to work for me, but he refuses."

Jin smiled and bowed. Then he held out his hand for the tea towels.

Noa sat and gestured at a chair for Thom.

"You weren't kidding when you said come hungry."

Noa waved his hand over the table. "This is all authentic Island food. Some of these you'd find at a luau." His fingers pointed at various bowls and plates. "This is char siu—spareribs. Long rice. Huli-Huli sauce—made with Island brown sugar cane and fresh ginger. Delicious." Noa winked. "It's okay to double dip. This fish is dorado, most commonly known as mahi mahi. In Hawaiian, it means very strong. And they are! Man, what a workout to pull one in. It is the most beautiful fish in the world. It is steamed in taro leaves. This one here is pulled Kalua pig, coconut lime shrimp, fresh pineapple, mango, caramelized Maui onion dip with baked taro chips. All fresh and tasty and made by Jin."

Jin bowed again.

"And over here," said Noa, pouring a glass for Thom, "is the best water ever. Taste it."

Thom took a sip. "Yes, very good. Is it spring water?"

Noa laughed. "It's L.A. tap. Isn't it great? Angelenos are missing out. Bottled and filtered? Waste of money." Thom didn't know if he were serious or joking.

"Dig in."

Everything on the table was unfamiliar. Thom followed Noa's lead and picked up a sparerib. Tried a bit of everything. They engaged in small talk that centered on life in Los Angeles: the weather, traffic, cars, surfing (which Thom had never done), beaches, taco trucks. Noa eyed Thom. Watched, weighed, examined. At first it made Thom uncomfortable. As the minutes passed Thom began to relax and ignored the intense study.

"This is the only way to eat," said Noa, putting a piece of fish into his mouth. "The whole foods way. I taught Ron the benefits of this diet."

"Did you also teach him to cook?"

"Ah, no. The pupil passed the mentor. Do you cook?"

"No. Anne does."

"A traditional family, then?"

"Yes."

"Except not so traditional, is it Thom?" Noa leaned back on his chair and patted his flat belly. He sighed with contentment. "I'm going to rest my stomach."

Jin placed two warm towels and two water bowls on the table.

Thom cleaned his hands. "What do you mean by, 'not so traditional'?"

Noa's smile was genuine. "When I take on a domestic I become a therapist. A very expensive one. It's in your best interest to speak the truth and be frank because we don't have time for bullshit. There is no judgment. Everything we discuss is privileged. Our business is our business. Just you and me. I've lived in the wide world and I'm smart. I'm observant. And if you listen to my advice you'll get what you want."

"And Jin?" said Thom.

"Ah, yes. Jin. He's like the monkey—sees no evil, hears no evil, speaks no evil."

Jin smiled and bowed.

"And...?"

"Anne Carmichael of Carmichael Ford. The biggest dealership west of the Mississippi. A dynasty started by her father, inherited by Anne and her brother, Jerome. The gated estate, private school, cars, bills, maintenance, all paid for by Anne. Trust funds, broker-age accounts … a lot of money. You write the checks, but she provides the funds to do so."

"So? I married a rich woman. Money doesn't matter to us in the way you suppose. I've loved her since the day I met her. I still love her. She loves me, too."

"Really? Is that why you think she's having an affair? Are you protecting your feelings or your lifestyle?"

"Screw you!"

Noa laughed. "Yeah." He reached across the table and slapped Thom's arm. "Pissed off?"

"What are you playing at?"

"Why do you want this woman?"

Thom swallowed the emotion swelling up.

Noa spread his hands. "Hey, man, I have to know where your head's at."

"I fell in love with the freckles across her nose, the gold in her hair that catches the sunlight. Her lips."

"Hey, that's just biology. That happens to me every day. What happens in your heart, Thom? What does she bring to the table?"

"I don't understand the question."

"Is she a good wife?"

"She used to be."

"What happened?"

"Children."

"You and Anne are no longer an engaged couple?"

"No."

"Does she know you cat around?"

"How could you know that?"

Noa leaned back in the chair. "I know where you spend your money."

"I pay cash when I go out."

Noa nodded. "Sure. And where do you get it? From the ATM, man. Like clockwork."

"Is this about me or Anne?"

"Both of you. A marriage takes two."

Thom didn't know where Noa was going with the questions, and he began to seriously feel uncomfortable.

"Did she even question the wire?"

Of course she hadn't. Thom didn't have to make up a lie. "She doesn't care about the money."

"Everyone cares about money, Thom. Especially Anne. She's been spending a lot of it lately."

"So? She works hard. She's up with the kids, gets them to school, goes to work, picks up the kids from school, helps them with homework, makes dinner. She's entitled to spend money."

"The bulk of your salary goes into a retirement fund. You live off her."

Thom's anger flared. "So what? I'd love her if she were poor. I wear off-the-rack suits, nothing fancy. Our children are not raised in a privileged household. We have old-fashioned values. Anne cooks dinner every night, the kids clean the kitchen, they do chores and yard work, everyone has a job. Sunday is family day. We attend Mass and spend time with our relatives. We're hands-on parents."

"But not a couple."

"Not anymore."

"Do you understand what would happen if she forced you out? Where could you live on a homicide detective's salary that's even close to what the kids are used to? Your cousin's house? It may not matter to you and Anne, but trust me, the kids know their economic status affects peer relationships. All rich kids know this because they learn it from other rich kids. If you and Anne separated they'd stay with the money. They know who provides. Which brings us to the issue at hand. A potential affair. What if it's true? What are you going to do?"

"I seriously have no idea."

"Do you want to stay married?"

"I want the kind of relationship we used to have. I want to sleep in our marriage bed. Mostly, I want her to look at me with love and respect. A smile would be nice, too."

"But that doesn't prevent you from catting around."

"Apparently not."

"I can see that by looking at your financials. I know where she spends money. I know where you spend money. There's no intersection. You co-parent, but live parallel lives. When was the last time you went on a date?"

"We went to an automotive industry dinner dance."

Noa leaned forward. "That's not a date, Thom. And I bet you didn't even dance."

No, they hadn't. Anne spent much of her time talking to colleagues and Ford representatives. He drank at the bar.

Noa said, "Okay, I've rested enough. Time to eat more. Thom?"

Thom picked at the pulled pork. Dipped it into the Huli-Huli sauce and rolled it in rice.

"You eat left handed," said Noa. "Yet, you're right-handed. I can tell by the cross-draw holster worn under your left arm. You're very comfortable with that weapon. You sat down and didn't even adjust it. It's a part of you. As are those handcuffs you tuck into the back waistband of your pants. Have you ever shot someone?"

"I get it," said Thom, wiping his fingers on the now-cold towel. "You think I'm going to kill the man who's screwing my wife."

"Are you?"

"If you're as good as Ron proclaimed then you'd know I've never shot anybody. I spend a lot of time on the range."

"Yet you keep your gun hand free. Ron's a lefty. Draws left. Next time you see him, watch how he holds things. Always with his right hand. Never his left. His gun hand is ready and always available. It's a warrior thing, you know. I still do it even though I no longer carry a firearm. You don't draw your weapon, and yet you're a warrior, too."

"I'm a cop. It's habit. Don't read into it."

"That's the thing, Thom, I have to consider it. If we are to do business I have to know that you won't go mental. I'm going to give you one free thing right now."

He paused for emphasis. "Anne is having an affair."

Thom jumped up and spun toward a prep table stacked with metal bowls. One second he intended to reach over and knock them off, the next second he found himself face down on the red tile floor and confused about how he got there. Then he felt Noa's hand on the back of his neck and his mouth near Thom's ear.

"You really want Jin to wash all those bowls?"

Noa lifted Thom to his feet and pushed him onto the chair.

Thom sat, stunned by the speed in which Noa moved and paralyzed by the hard word.

Affair.

He already knew. Why had the confirmation taken him by surprise? A disembodied voice said, "Well, that's an inconvenient truth." He almost laughed when he realized the words were his own. "She already left me. I've left her. Where do we go from here? I don't know why this happened to us."

A tornado of dark swirled around him. He felt outside himself, looked down at the wretch he'd become. Just yesterday he prayed to God; asked for illumination, a light, an answer. As he sat here in an underground kitchen, aware of Noa's eyes trained on the geography of his face, he felt God's response. A glimmer of light cut through the darkness. A wisp of warmth.

"How did this *situation* happen?" said Thom. "Why did Anne and Thom allow a good relationship to go bad?" He reached out, grasped at air. "I don't remember. It was so long ago."

A voice said, "They did it to each other."

He waved a finger at Noa. "Yes. Like he said, we are living parallel lives."

"We're both to blame in equal measure." Yes. Like she said.

"Yes! Both. Of. Us. Are. Guilty!" He stood, waved his arms as if swimming. This time the red tile came up to him.

———

Noa slapped Thom's face. "Okay, there, man? Have a drink."

Thom sipped a sharp liquid. Felt the warmth down his throat, behind the eyes.

"Jesuschristalmighty," said Thom. He awoke, as if from a dream. "I'm a mess. No wonder she went looking for someone else."

"Just sit, man."

Jin placed two small bowls on the table. A scoop of ice cream in each.

Noa picked up a wooden spoon and took a bite. "Mmmm, homemade lemon and lavender. Thanks, Jin."

Thom took a bite as well. Found the sour and the sweet a bit too much. He chuckled. "Ah, I get it. Take the sweet with the sour." He took another bite. "Okay, Mr. Expensive Therapist, what do I do now?"

"That's up to you," said Noa. "What do you want?"

"I want everything."

"Everything? Video, photos, emails, text messages? How much of everything?"

"I want every bit of everything."

"Why?"

"My cousin, Bird, thinks Anne is having me watched. That she's responsible for the eyes and ears. She told me Anne was planning divorce before Anne told me herself. Bird thinks she's scheming to avoid spousal support. I could care less about that. But I have to think about the kids. They're old enough to choose. Sure, they'd visit me, but where would they sleep? I'll fight like with like."

"Sounds like this Bird is a smart woman. What if the man is someone you know?"

"Ah, damnit. Really? What exactly are you asking because I have no idea what I'm capable of, but I tell you this, I haven't devoted my life to doing good so I can be bad."

"I already know that Anne is having an affair just by examining her financials. That was the easy part. I'll give you proof, but not a complete history. I'll provide plenty of evidence to conduct private negotiations. You can't use it in a court of law. If you attempt to do so, there will be consequences."

Thom rested his forehead on the table. Tired. Spent. "I just need to know for sure. That's all I ask. I asked her outright and she lied to me."

"You bring the twenty-two Benjamins?"

Thom pulled the bank envelope from the breast pocket of his jacket and placed it on the table.

Noa picked it up and handed it to Jin who discreetly tucked it into a pocket under his smock.

"Thank you. Always the best."

Jin bowed then removed his smock, put on a duster, picked up a backpack, and departed.

Noa nodded with satisfaction and pressed a button on the wall.

Two assistants entered the kitchen through a side door and immediately began clearing the table.

"So what now?" said Thom.

"Keep the phone a few more days. I'll be in touch."

"Guess I'm not a maniac after all."

"Just a man trying to find his way through the dark."

———

Thom found Birdie in front of the dry erase board bouncing with excitement. She turned toward him with complete joy.

"It's been an awesome day. You won't believe what I've learned about Iris. We've turned a corner in this case."

Thom didn't hear. His eyes focused on a manila envelope lying on the altar.

"Oh, yeah, a messenger delivered that for you. A cute old man about this big." She held out her hand breast high.

"When?"

"About ten minutes ago."

"Sonofabitch," said Thom. "Noa already had it."

"Wait. Is that what I think it is?"

"Yeah."

"Already? You just saw him."

Thom picked up the envelope. Tossed it hand to hand. Weighed the decision.

"Open it," encouraged Birdie.

He tossed it to her. "You open it."

Birdie ripped it open, laid the contents on the altar.

A stack of documents, a photo sleeve, and three discs labeled **Anne, Thom,** and **misc.**

The label on the photo sleeve read: caution.

The label on Anne's disc read: **enter at your own risk.**

———

Thom knelt at the prie-dieu at the eastern corner of Birdie's living room. Birdie hung back while he finished praying. When he was done Birdie gave him a hug for good luck. He wavered and fell onto the couch.

"Anne's disc is ready. Just touch the play button," she said.

"The documents?"

"Culled from different sources. A financial history of Anne's expenditures. Clothing, shoes, jewelry—both men and women's. The earliest transactions out of the norm appeared in October of last year. In December she opened a private account at a small bank. She also has a dedicated credit card. Right now the bank account has a balance of just over three-hundred thousand, but nearly four times that much has moved through it. The biggest purchase was a house. A three-bedroom place in Brentwood. Gated of course. A private love nest.

"There are a number of bills paid through the account: two cell phones on a shared family plan, maintenance fees for the house, the credit card, of course. The biggest expense besides the house has gone to an investigator. It confirms that Anne paid for the eyes and ears on you. I assume the disc labeled Thom is proof of your malfeasance, but I didn't look at it. Nor did I look at the miscellaneous disc."

"The photos?"

"Didn't look."

Thom stood and took a deep, weary breath.

"I'm going upstairs," said Birdie. "Give you some space."

"No. Don't. Watch with me? I can't do this alone."

Birdie held out her hand. They threaded fingers and went into the office.

FORTY-EIGHT

Birdie had set up a second monitor next to the one on her desk.

"A spare. The video is split screen. I thought it'd be easier to view this way," she explained.

On the left monitor were establishing shots of Anne's Ford Five Hundred. The camera zoomed onto the license plate.

"Impressive," said Birdie.

It moved upward and got a straight-on view of the driver. Anne appeared to be singing, her fingers tapping out a rhythm on the steering wheel. At this very moment Birdie lost all respect for the woman.

Thom fisted his hands, his face set to a stony glare.

Anne waited until the gate closed behind her before proceeding down the driveway and turning out onto the street. The follow car pulled behind her.

"An active camera," said Birdie.

"As opposed to?"

"One that's static, stationary. The operator has control of the view."

On the right monitor, a GPS street map. Anne's car appeared as a blue dot. The follow car as a green dot.

"A tracker," said Birdie.

"Is that the date and time?" said Thom pointing at the lower left corner of the real view. "Holy shit. This was taken yesterday." Thom's mouth fell open. He slapped his head. Spun around the office. "I can't do this."

Birdie pressed pause and waited. She had no idea what agonies he felt. She only could guess based on her own struggles to recover from recent tragedies—every day an effort.

Thom paced the room muttering. Anne was the light of his life. The woman he loved. The one who slowly slipped through his fingers like sand. His life was about to change in unexplainable and tragic ways. His future uncertain.

Thom said, "Bird . . . I can't watch."

"Okay." She turned off the monitors. "It's redundant, anyway. Her love affair is confirmed, that's sufficient."

"That's not what I meant. I need to know who. I want you to watch and tell me. Please be the eyes I can't be."

"How would I know who the guy is?" she said in a borderline whine.

"His identity is in there somewhere." He pointed at the package.

"Thom . . ." she pleaded. She really didn't want to.

"Please, Bird. I'm going to wait in my room." He held out his arms. She went to him and he pulled her into a tight hug, buried his face in her hair. His body shuddered with grief.

"I don't think I can live without her," he whispered.

"You're already living without her," said Birdie, gently. "You'll get through this. I survived Matt. You'll survive Anne. We Keanes come from rugged stock. We get knocked down, we get back up."

Thom kissed her forehead. "Thank you for being my family, my friend. I love you."

"I love you, too, Thom."

"I'll wait for you upstairs. I'm sorry."

He let go and departed.

Birdie sat back down in front of the monitors; popped a fresh piece of Doublemint into her mouth and turned them back on. Her finger hovered over the play button. Afraid for Thom. Anne had forced her husband into three rotten choices: to be celibate, asexual, or seek sex elsewhere. Instead of working on the marriage with the father of her children, she took the selfish road to pleasure—Thom and the kids be damned.

With a deep breath of sorrow she pressed play and restarted the video.

Her eyes tracked between the images as the car drove streets familiar to Birdie. Anne headed toward Brentwood. The love nest.

This was a two-camera follow. The one shooting Anne's car appeared to originate from the top of the car. A second camera had to be mounted on the ceiling and aimed at the dash, the GPS monitor screen in the center of the field. Every now and then she'd see a gloved hand move an analog stick and the view from the top of the car would change. No wonder this friend of Ron's was so expensive—he had cool toys.

The green dot passed the blue dot. The hand toggled the analog stick and the camera swept 180-degrees and now shot Anne from the front. Birdie couldn't help being impressed by the technology.

Anne continued the singing, driving casual, no cares in the world. Seeing her this happy was hard to watch and Birdie understood why Thom couldn't do it.

A green light, like that from a laser, flashed briefly from the follow—now ahead—car. The signal was returned from some bushes. The images on the monitor went blank. A banner scrolled *holding... holding... holding...*

The hand-off had occurred.

A greenish image flicked up on the left monitor. Night vision. Though it wasn't completely dark, the day waned and the light diminished. Whoever operated it had a steady hand. It moved quickly up the street and slid into the gate just as it closed and up the driveway that curved left. A garage door rolled upward. The camera operator was no more than sixty feet away, possibly shooting from the ground. It zoomed onto a second vehicle already in the garage. Got a close up of the license plate...

Birdie covered her mouth and suppressed a scream.

She knew the car. And its bastard owner.

Birdie paused the video and pushed back from the desk.

Oh, this couldn't get worse. She got up and paced, just as Thom had done. Shook out her hands. What to do? This betrayal would be a soul-searing injury to Thom. His reaction to the man's identity would be swift and potentially deadly. There'd be no way she'd be able to stop him.

She picked up the phone and dialed Arthur. "Hey," he answered, all sleepy. "It's late."

"I have an emergency situation. I need you to come to the Bird House immediately."

"What's going on?" all serious and wide awake. She could hear him moving around quickly, prepping to depart.

"I'm going to need help with Thom. I won't be able to handle him alone."

"What happened?"

"I'll explain when you get here. Pick up Father Frank on the way. I'll call and give him a heads-up. The new code for the front door is 9-9-3-8. Let yourself in."

"Roger that. I'm on my way."

Birdie dialed Frank's number. At this hour, the volunteer would be gone and she'd get the message machine. She crossed her fingers that he'd at least screen the call and pick up. It rang and rang until she finally got the generic greeting for St. Joseph Catholic Church. She sat impatiently through the Mass times, hours of confession, ways to make a donation, and directions to the church before she finally got to the point she could press "1" to leave a message.

"Frank, this is Birdie, I have an emergency—"

"—Bird?" said Frank, picking up the phone. "Are you alright?"

"It's Thom. He's going to need our help. Arthur's on the way. He's going to swing by and pick you up."

"Oh my. What's wrong?"

"I don't want to say on the phone. But he's going through a crisis and he'll need all of us just to get through this night."

"Okay. I'll be ready."

With her support team on the way Birdie debated whether to continue the video. After all, it really was redundant now. What more did they need? The paperwork alone laid out the specifics. She knew the identity of the man. Did she need the visual?

It was like being stuck in traffic that had slowed due to a crash on the other side of the freeway. Drivers paused just long enough to get a quick view of the destruction, but long enough to snake the traffic behind. It was human nature to watch the wreck.

In the end Birdie couldn't help herself. She pressed play.

… Anne lifted the trunk lid and removed a grocery bag. She walked to the door and pressed a button. The garage door slowly rolled down. Birdie half expected the cameraman to run and slide under. Instead, he placed three fingers in front of the lens and counted them down. The image flickered and a quad screen lit up. Four video views.

Noa had already wired the house. So totally illegal.

Anne put the bag on the kitchen counter. "Hello, darling," she called out.

With audio, too.

There was no way Thom could ever see this. She dialed down the volume just in case he decided to come back into the office. Looking at it was hard enough; she didn't need to hear it as well.

The man approached Anne with a limpid look on his face. He embraced her from behind, wrapped his arms around her waist and nibbled her ear. His hands moved down her body and came back up under a loose blouse and cupped her breasts. She raised her arms and he pulled it off. She attempted to turn, but he pushed her against the counter. He hooked a finger under her chin and turned her face toward him. They kissed slowly, deeply. He moved his hands to her throat, kissed the back of her neck, down her back and released her bra with his teeth.

"Tricky," snickered Birdie.

He held her there with one hand while the other shimmied down the skirt and she stepped out of it.

"Elastic. Sure, make it easy for him."

He pulled her panties down, but couldn't pull them off because they hung up on her shoes. Anne managed to kick them off and then she was utterly naked. He undid his pants, pulled them down to his knees and thrust his erect penis inside her.

"No condom? Sleezeball."

Anne held on the counter as he urgently screwed her from behind. Her mouth opened, her back arched, and too soon it was over, both of them shaking in orgasm.

Birdie fast-forwarded through the video, pausing every now and then. They did it multiple times, utilizing a bedroom, the shower, the living room couch. Three hours later, spent and hungry, they turned their attention to the groceries and she finally turned it off.

Birdie felt as though she were a dove that had just flown into a window and fell to the ground, too stunned to fly away, even as the neighborhood cat stalked. It was many minutes before she could even move.

The betrayal wasn't just Thom's. Her emotions traveled an entire road starting at gloom and ending in anger.

Birdie gathered all the material. The documents, the photo sleeve, all three discs and shoved it back into the envelope and put it in the safe. She spit out the gum, wrapped it in its foil wrapper and rolled it into a ball. She unwrapped two pieces of fresh gum and began chewing hard as she walked angry circles around the altar.

There was no way she'd go upstairs and tell Thom the awful news until after Arthur and Frank arrived. They'd advise her on how to proceed. Thom might be furious with Birdie for breaking a confidence, but he'd need all the help and support she could get for him.

As she continued circling she actually considered a scheme to conceal the man's identity. But she knew Thom. He'd torture it out of her. Then she determined that she'd give him one of her anxiety pills. Take the edge off before hearing the news. It might also calm him enough to make him forget about committing murder.

A loud pop came from upstairs.

A distinctive sound. A gunshot. No mistake.

Instinctively, she threw herself on the floor and started crawling to the desk to get her hands on the loaded Sig when she realized what the gunshot meant.

Oh, no-no-no-no-no-no-no-no-no-no-no-no!

He didn't.

He wouldn't.

Birdie pushed up off the floor and sprinted out of the office, ran down the hall and hit the service stairs, taking them three at a time. She pushed open the guest room door.

On the bed, laid out with care: Thom's Class A uniform, his service weapon, and badge.

Oh, God, please no.

She ran into the bathroom and came to an abrupt halt.

Her eyes focused on one thing: Thom's leg dangling over the edge of the bathtub.

FORTY-NINE

THOM'S UNDERWEAR-CLAD BODY LAY in an awkward position inside the small tub. His head, wrapped in a bath towel, rested on the back edge as if he were taking a soak. His right index finger was hooked around the trigger of the Smith & Wesson they had shot earlier in the day.

Birdie was seriously stressed.

The primitive parts of the brain had triggered the reflex to duck when she first heard the gunshot—the chain reaction of brain-body impulses already engaged. The adrenal glands located on top of her kidneys had squirted the stress hormones adrenaline and cortisol. These fight-or-flight hormones caused her pupils to dilate and her heart to pump at an exercise rate of one-hundred-sixty beats per minute. Her blood pressure jumped to dangerous, heart-attack levels and she began to sweat. Her body, already in panic mode, gave her the strength to move faster than the norm.

Once her higher brain acknowledged the situation, she could choose which way to deal with the stress of seeing her cousin in full-on suicide mode in her bathtub.

Birdie dropped to her knees and screamed. A common stress release method.

Then she yelled. "Goddamn you, Thomas Alfred Keane. You know what happened this year. You thought it'd be okay to scramble your brain in my bathtub? Make me find your lifeless body? I hate you right now."

Thom wept as he tore off the towel. "I'm so sorry. I couldn't do it. I couldn't do it."

"But you considered it and shot a bullet into my wall."

Disgusted and thoroughly pissed off, she pushed up off the floor and stumbled into the bedroom. Her hands shook so hard she felt the quake in her shoulder blades.

Thom entered the room, the gun still in his hand, and attempted to hug her in apology. Two things happened at once: Birdie spun around and snatched the gun from his hand, she aimed at a spot high on the wall and squeezed the trigger; Arthur ran into the room and tackled her. They fell to the ground and Arthur's body weight forced the breath from her lungs when they hit the floor.

Arthur disarmed her and rolled away. Birdie gasped for air. Thom crouched, confused by Birdie's frustrated shot at the ceiling and his brother's sudden appearance.

In his calm, priestly way, Father Frank said, "Who were we called out to control?"

———

The foursome sat in the library: the three men with crystal snifters of Birdie's ex-favorite liqueur, B&B, she with a cup of steaming hot tea with lemon held directly under her nose to prevent her from smelling the decadent and tempting aroma of the Benedictine and brandy.

Birdie had no need to betray Thom's confidence to Arthur and Frank. He told them all after an impromptu prayer circle to thank God for giving him the common sense not to end his own life.

Arthur said, "I cannot believe you've allowed that woman to emasculate you."

Thom shrugged in resignation, all pride gone. "How can I explain how much I've always loved her? From the first moment I saw her sunny smile and freckles."

"We cannot always know the path that God has laid out for us," added Frank, "but there are five reasons Anne and Thom came together and their names are Pearce, Padraig, Liam, Rose, and Nora. And it is those innocents for whom we must focus our energies."

"It's apparent that Thom and Anne will never repair the damage her affair has caused," said Birdie.

"That's not true," said Frank. "Thom doesn't yet have enough emotional distance from this situation. We cannot speak for Anne."

"Oh, yes, we can," said Birdie. "I saw her"—she winked two fingers—"emotion planted on another man." She felt Thom's gaze aimed at her. She avoided his eye because he had not yet asked who and she didn't want to go there.

Then again, this would be the perfect time for him to know. He had the willing support of his priest and brother nearby. She flipped her eyes in his direction to gauge his state. He still had his eyes glued to hers. She knit her brows in question. He shook his head no.

Well, okay, that decided it for Thom.

But it did not satisfy Birdie's need for confrontation.

FIFTY

Thursday, May 17

THERE ARE THREE WAYS of doing things:

The right way.

The wrong way.

And Birdie Keane's way.

Four-fifteen a.m. Birdie turned off the headlights, killed the engine, and coasted until the car came to a halt against the curb. Nothing stirred in the neighborhood. She understood why the dead fish murderer picked this hour. It was an ideal time of morning. Night owls were asleep; the morning people not yet up. If there were an awakening noise, say a scream or a gunshot, who among them would be able to transition from REM to cognition? The noise would be interpreted as something from a dream.

She relished the moonless dark and the gauzy fog concealing her presence. The only light source flickered from an unreliable lamppost at the corner. She didn't need it anyway. She knew the landscape of this street. The target house. She approached in stealth, knew each step from this moment forward having already worked out the plan.

Birdie stopped at a familiar copper gate and unlocked the dead-bolt. It opened silently. She slipped inside the courtyard and inhaled the scents of spring: honeysuckle, pink jasmine, and green bam-boo—the smells of renewal and hopefulness. She refused to take a moment to reflect on the correct course of action because her value system of right and wrong and common sense would force her to turn around and abandon this crazy, and potentially deadly, quest.

She crouched near the porch and picked through the shiny black rocks until she found the one she sought: a ceramic rock that con-cealed an emergency key. Then she sat back against the wall and waited for the sound of water running through the pipes. When the water heater in the closet near the front porch fired up, she knew the home's owner was in the shower.

The moment had arrived.

She unlocked the front door and stepped inside.

She knew the floor plan. The layout of the furniture. Knew where the master bath was located. She walked down the short hall hung with photos of family and friends. She opened the bedroom door. The bed had already been made, the pillows fluffed.

The bathroom door was ajar, yet its occupant could not see her. The shower door was made of clear glass etched with a design of lotus flowers. The moment she stepped inside the bathroom she'd be seen.

Birdie whispered an ecclesiastical prayer: *Miserére mei, Deus, secúndum misericórdiam tuam; et secúndum multitúdinem miseratiónum tuárum dele iniquitátem meam. Amplius lava me ab iniquitáte mea et a peccáto meo munda me.* Have mercy on me, God, in your kindness. In your compassion blot out my offense. O wash me more and more from my guilt and cleanse me more from sin.

A prayer such as this would usually be said after the offense. Birdie said it upfront to get ahead of the game. She counted to three and pushed open the door.

The man's hands were in his hair, in full lather mode. He eyes widened in disbelief and his head shook slightly as though seeing a mirage. Birdie didn't waste time with pleasantries. She pulled open the glass door and slammed her taped knuckles into George Silva's face; felt the cartilage in his nose break, saw the shampoo and blood sluice down his face.

He screamed something unintelligible.

"That's for cheating on me," yelled Birdie.

She punched the left side of his chest. Right near his heart.

"That's for betraying your partner."

George slumped to the shower floor, legs askew.

Birdie wound up for a kick.

"No, no, no," he cried. "It's not wha ya think."

Birdie stepped back.

"I saw you screwing Anne with my own eyes. Your partner's wife! I can forgive you for the trespass against me, but not for Thom's."

She spit on her past lover, past friend. Thom's past partner.

"Did you really think that Anne would divorce him and you'd take his place at the family dinner table and become his children's stepdad? You don't mess with the Keane clan and come out okay. Bastard! You're out, George. Banished. You resign the department or transfer to another division. You don't attend Mass at St. Joseph or

Bonaventura. You don't come to the Manor. Thom never sees your face again. And don't forget, the Whelan clan is our ally."

———

Thom, Arthur, and Frank were still talking quietly in the library. Birdie tiptoed back to the kitchen. One of them had made a fresh pot of coffee. Birdie poured herself a cup and took a long steamy inhale to wash the stink of George from her nose. Her fingers were beginning to swell.

Arthur entered the kitchen and went straight to the freezer and pulled out a plastic bag of popcorn kernels and threw them on the counter. He picked up Birdie's hand and kissed her bruised knuckles.

"The devil is in Bird's right hand."

She tried to pull her hand away, but Arthur's grip was strong. He covered her hand with the frozen popcorn.

"Where'd you hit him?"

"Who?" said Birdie. She had claimed sleepiness and went upstairs to her room before sneaking away to George's. She thought her get-away clean.

"You think you're clever," said Arthur. "You take the role of family protector a little too far. Hope he doesn't charge you with b-and-e and assault."

"Who?" she repeated.

"George, of course."

"What?" She attempted to move back, but Arthur's grip was stronger than hers. "How did you know?"

"Thom found his nuts. Had to know who the scumbag was."

"I put that stuff in the safe."

"But failed to lock it."

"Kidding me? How stupid am I? Did he look at the video or find his name in the file?"

"The file. I doubt he'll ever watch Anne doin' George. That shit is messed up."

"How is he?"

"We've been through the alphabet soup of emotions. He's especially mad at himself for considering... you know."

Birdie finally managed to free her hand from Arthur's and sat at the bar. He followed her and put the popcorn back on her hand.

"Once we knew it was George we knew where you snuck off to."

"I banished him."

Arthur laughed at the absurdity. "Oh, really, tough girl? How do you plan on enforcing banishment?"

Birdie snorted out a giggle. "I won't need to. I reminded him of our ties to the Whelan's. I told you don't mess with the Keane clan and come out okay."

"That much is true. What'd you do to him?"

"Took him by surprise, naked and vulnerable in the shower."

"Had to. He's taller and heavier than you."

"I wanted him to know we could get to him."

"Where'd you hit him?"

Birdie touched the bridge of Arthur's nose. "One shot. Broke his nose."

"Very nice. Broke all those tiny blood vessels in the orbital region and got the nose in one shot. That pretty face of his will be messed up for weeks."

"I punched him in the heart as well."

"Well, it's protected by a breast plate. All you managed was a metaphor."

"That was my intent."

Arthur nodded with approval. "Don't know if I'd be so reserved."

"It's over."

"For you maybe. But not for Thom."

FIFTY-ONE

BIRDIE DREAMT SHE WAS in a cinderblock cage. The walls were painted crude-oil black mixed with fish scales, making the walls shine. She pushed at the walls, trying to find a weakness, a way out. The walls closed in around her. She screamed for Matt to save her. Then she was in an old stone abbey, gun in hand. A Franciscan monk in leather sandals moved along the far wall. The hood of his robe obscured his face. A pair of lovebirds in a simple cage fashioned from twigs hung from a rope under an archway. As the monk turned his head to gaze up at the birds the sunlight caught his face. The man had bright shamrock green eyes. Matt's eyes. The gun went off and scared the birds. The female flew into the twig bars of the cage, damaging her beak. The male kept tweeting, *birdbirdbird-birdbirdbird*.

"Bird," said Arthur, shaking her legs, "wake up. You're screwing up your sleep patterns."

Birdie pulled the covers from her head and opened an eye. The room was pitch dark and her heart lurched.

Arthur opened the blackout shades. Light flooded her bedroom. A pair of cooing doves that were sitting on the window ledge flew away.

"Come on, I know it's hard. If you sleep too long you won't sleep tonight." He pulled the covers off her.

"Alright, I'm awake." She sat against the headboard, and pulled the covers back up, looked at the clock. 12:04 p.m. "What day is it?"

"It's still Thursday."

"I don't understand. Last thing I remember is talking to you in the kitchen."

"Then you came up here for a nap."

"Who closed the shades?"

Thom stuck his head into the doorway. At least Birdie thought it was Thom. His hair was gone. Well, mostly gone. "Good, you're up. Anne's on her way."

"What the hell happened to your hair?"

"Arthur shaved it. Like it?"

"What's going on?"

She heard Frank's soothing voice in the hallway. "Thom, would you like to serve coffee, tea, or wine?"

Thom turned and disappeared. She heard him say, "Do I need to serve that bitch anything?"

She didn't hear Frank's admonishment.

Birdie looked to Arthur for clarification.

"George called Anne to tell her that they were found out. She called Thom to explain. Frank intervened and agreed to mediate a face-to-face meeting. Anne's expected any moment."

Birdie moved the covers aside and threw her legs over the edge of the bed. She was groggy; bearings lost. She stretched her stiff fingers.

Her stomach growled. When had she last eaten? How long had she been wearing these clothes? When was her last shower? She lifted her arm and took a whiff. Then she remembered a recent bath. What day was that? One day morphed into another and she had lost track.

"You don't stink," said Arthur. "But your hair looks like shit. Put some powder in it."

"I need exercise."

"You exercise too much. Take a few days off."

She threw him a hostile look. "When did you become task-master?"

"Since I discovered you and Thom are a mess." Birdie opened her mouth to protest, but Arthur stopped her. "Remember, you asked me here."

"True enough. Why'd you shave Thom's hair?"

"Us guys were talking about how the gray doesn't do him any favors. Frank suggested dyeing it."

"Thom couldn't go back to the job with dyed hair. Cops are the worst bullies."

"That was Thom's main concern. We decided that if he wore a crew cut like I do that it'd give him a younger look. More hip. We sent Madi a photo and she loved it. Said when she comes back home she'll take him shopping for a new wardrobe."

"It's a drastic change. He doesn't need more drama right now."

The doorbell rang.

"Speaking of drama … she's heeeeeere," said Arthur.

———

Frank gently escorted Arthur and Birdie from the library. "Only the principals need be present," he said.

Thom read Arthur and Birdie's concerned faces and gave them a smile of reassurance. *I'll be okay.* As the doors clicked closed, he felt a moment of insecurity about the course of action he determined to take with Anne. Frank had advised him against it. Said the hurt was too fresh, that it was too soon. But Thom had been living an emotionally incorrect life. Anne had moved on, he needed to as well.

Frank held out his hands, "Let us pray."

Thom and Anne each grasped one of Frank's. When she reached for Thom's free hand he noted his refusal by sticking it into his pocket.

Father Frank lowered his head, "Our Lord and God, we firmly believe that you are here, that you see us, that you hear us. We adore you with profound reverence and ask your pardon for our sins. Please bless us now as we enter a time of mediation, of discussion, and we ask that this time be fruitful. Please grant us the courage and strength to forget the trespass we assume for ourselves and let us come to good resolutions. We put ourselves at your mercy and humbly ask for the grace to forgive. Please shine your everlasting light of grace upon us for we are mere sinners and need your guidance. Come, O Holy Spirit, fill our hearts with your fire and love. Send forth your spirit so that we—your humble servants Thomas, Anne, and Francis—may be worthy of you. We ask this in your name. *In nomine Patris, et Filii, et Spiritus Sancti. Amen.*"

Frank's prayer filled Thom's heart with endless respect for a man he knew, but not really knew. Like most parishioners, he sought guidance from a man who stood behind the altar, the pulpit. But being a pastor was more than delivering an inspiring message. Frank had inserted himself into their meeting as if to state we will trill and mine for solutions together. As an equal partner of the discussion to be, he placed upon himself a subtle authority that would no doubt steer the couple to an understanding of mistakes, to forgiveness and, eventually, the solidarity and strengthening of a marriage. Frank's psychological play was low-key, but with an undertow of intensity at the seriousness of that which would be soon embarked upon.

Thom no longer felt like he was above the treeline in a barren land of aloneness. His will to thrive came bubbling up from the deep well inside his soul. He shook his free hand as if unshackling the hurt. Anne was not the villain, but he would not go back to a life that had run dry. He was thirsty again. And he owed it all to Frank's brilliance.

Though this wasn't what Frank likely had in mind.

Thom whispered to Anne, "I'm sorry for the rebuke." He reached out and gave her hand a quick squeeze. For the first time in a long while she blessed him with a smile. And he knew then that the dusty memories of what their life had been would not shape his future.

Frank motioned Thom and Anne to sit together on the couch. Frank chose a seat off to the side where a friend might sit. He gestured at the tea set, but Thom and Anne declined with a polite wave. He pointed to the wine decanter and both shook their heads. That didn't prevent Frank from pouring himself a glass and placing a small bowl of nuts on the coffee table.

"If it makes you feel any better," said Anne, "George is just sick. He loves you."

"He should've thought about that in the beginning," said Thom. He stood. There was no way he'd be able to sit through this. "What if we were in a life-or-death situation? We don't ride a black-and-white, but we have a responsibility to and for each other. Partners protect each other. Instead of throwing himself in front of a bullet would he think, *naw I'll let Thom take this one so I can take his place with Anne.*"

"It wasn't like that," said Anne. "He always spoke of you with great respect."

"Yet he disrespected me by sleeping with my wife!" He began to pace.

"Thom," warned Frank. "There will be no yelling here today."

"Would it make you feel better if I told you that we were surprised by the seduction that an affair promised?"

Thom snorted with derision.

"I can't say anything in our defense," said Anne. "What we did was wrong. We knew it. That's what made it more thrilling."

"Yeah, and you'd still be doing it if you hadn't been caught."

Anne wrung her hands. "We were selfish. You may not believe this, but I'm truly sorry that we hurt you."

"You're a piece of work. You're sorry for me, but not the screwing around, the house, the gifts. And what really chaps my hide is that you're trying to destroy my career. My marriage is gone, take my career, too."

"I didn't do it," said Anne. "The private investigator emailed your lieutenant the photo of you and that girl in the car."

"That girl has turned into a suspect in a homicide. Do you understand what that means? Your actions not only screwed me, but they've screwed this case! There may not be justice for the victims."

"Temper," reminded Frank.

"Why did you have to hire someone, Anne? You're the one who set the parameters in our marriage. You knew what I was doing."

"I did it on advice. The attorney said because of my financial situation that I had to have some asset protection. Testing your integrity seemed the easiest—"

"—wait, wait, wait. Are you telling me that the PI emailed the photo and suggested to my supervisor that I be tested in this manner? That means he had prior knowledge of the homicide."

Anne vigorously shook her head. "No. That's not true. He'd been sending one photo a week. This one's importance was coincidence, I swear."

"How long has this been going on?"

"Two months."

No wonder George was worried, thought Thom.

"So George knew."

"Absolutely not. I never spoke about it."

Thom thought about this. George had been worried about the surveillance because he didn't know Anne was behind it and he was worried *they*, the FBI or LAPD, would snare him and Anne in the process. So he really didn't know.

"And what about the report of misconduct? Did the PI do that as well?"

Anne's eyes widened. "Thom, I swear on the life of our children that I didn't know about that until after the fact. He filed the report two weeks ago. He assured me that most reports lack corroborated evidence. He said this one had no merit because the girls were off-duty stuff, that it wouldn't damage your career. He filed the report and forwarded the photos to establish a pattern. Just in case we'd need it for divorce negotiations."

Bird sure was right on that score, thought Thom.

"Did it ever occur to you to wave off your bloodhound? You know what the family faces with Gerard's Blue Bandit bullshit swirling around us. Are you that dense?"

Anne's eyes welled. "Apparently I am. I followed bad advice. I'm sorry."

Thom stopped pacing long enough to take a pull from Frank's wineglass. He picked up a pad of paper and a pen off the desk and dropped both into her lap. "Write down the PI's name and number."

"Thom—"

"Do it."

Anne bent over the paper.

"Thom," said Frank, "revenge is a dangerous thing."

"It's not revenge, Frank. I wonder what game he's playing. A woman with a fat checkbook and a questionable, ex-cop PI doesn't make a good relationship."

"How do you know if he's an ex-cop?" said Anne.

"Because of what you said. What else has he got his fingers into?"

Anne shook her head. "I don't know. We—the attorney and I—hired him to find proof of your adultery."

"Glass Houses, Anne. What about yours?"

Anne's tears overflowed and fell down her cheeks.

"Anne," said Frank. "Do you love Thom?"

"I don't know."

"Be honest, Anne," said Thom. "We haven't had sex since the twins were conceived and just yesterday you told me you didn't love me and you wanted a divorce."

He poured himself a glass of wine and fantasized about throwing it at her.

"Is that true?" said Frank to Anne.

"I've been considering it for a long time," she admitted. "Long before George. I've been dead. It was nice to feel alive again. To be wanted."

"What?" Thom said with indignation. "I've always wanted you. I've never stopped loving you. Not even now. Know what? I'm going to save us a lot of time. Deed me the Brentwood house, furnishings included. I'll move out of the house for a trial separation. If you can convince the bishop to annul our marriage then I'll consider a civil divorce. Meanwhile, I don't want to be a pathetic weekend dad and uproot the kids every week or even every-other. They deserve stability. I suggest you convert the pool house into a guest cottage. You can stay there when it's my turn with the kids. I'll stay in the guest room when I'm in the main house. We will *always* be respectful of the other in front of the kids and our families. No trash mouth. We have the same parenting values, but should there be an issue on that score we'll work it out privately and always present a united front for the kid's sake."

"Anything else?" said Anne.

Before Frank could get in a word, Thom concluded, "I want ten grand a month."

"Done," said Anne.

———

The guys had finished what was left of Birdie's in-case-of-emergency stash. Arthur called up Rod's liquor and placed an order for replacement booze. And a few extra bottles for Thom. And two six packs of beer. And potato chips. Then he ordered pizza.

"What do you think they're discussing?" said Arthur in reference to Anne insisting she drive Frank back to the rectory.

"The same stuff we discussed," said Thom. "She's getting her share of Frank's ear."

"Poor Frank," said Birdie. "He's got to be exhausted."

"We're all exhausted," said Thom. "What were they thinking? How could this ever have ended well?"

"Maybe they thought the affair would burn out and they'd go their separate ways. No one the wiser," said Birdie.

"Why aren't you madder?" said Thom.

Birdie shook her head. "Past experience has told me I'm a hard girl to get along with. Besides, your situation is the higher offense."

"What I don't understand is that after you guys broke up he whined constantly about missing you. He obsessed about how Matt's death freed you from the emotional barrier and that there was real potential for a new-and-improved relationship. Then Ron came along and that threw him into a tizzy. And yet, all that time he was banging my wife."

"Wife is the key word," said Arthur. "Like you said, there was no way it'd end well. She was an aside, a wealthy woman who treated him lavishly, but there was no future there. With Bird the potential existed."

"Wonder where he'll go," said Birdie.

"What do you mean?" said Thom.

"Birdie banished him," said Arthur. "Told him to leave RHD and never show his face to you again."

"That's sweet," said Thom. "But I can take care of myself. George and I will have a face to face."

"Or a fist to fist," said Arthur.

FIFTY-TWO

Friday, May 18

YESTERDAY, ARTHUR WAS WISE to have wakened Birdie when he did. After a full seven hours of sleep she awoke with the energy for a workout. After a cold shower and breakfast she was ready to tackle Thom's case again.

If the pattern were correct, the killer would strike again in two days.

Birdie was surprised to see Thom already in the office. He sat at the altar typing away on his laptop. If the altar was going to be used as a table, she'd need to buy taller chairs. Thom looked like a little person behind the mass.

"Please tell me you got some sleep last night," she said.

He looked up from the computer. His eyes were swollen, but the rest of his face seemed relaxed, rested. He wore the haircut well. Who knew such a handsome man hid underneath a mop of gray hair?

"Six hours. You?"

"Seven."

"Right on. Hey … thank you for calling Arthur and Frank. I don't know how I would have gotten through the last thirty-some hours without you all. Frank said the healing has just begun, but I—"

"—don't make my mistake and ignore the personal. Don't put undue pressure on yourself. Don't allow the job to distract you from Thom time. You have major challenges ahead."

"I know. Frank kept saying something similar. And I've been seriously thinking about it, reflecting on the investigation. There's a team in place. I'm officially off. My skills aren't needed this go-round. Why should I continue? But here's what I was going to say before … I'm a detective. I started this thing five days ago. I care about the victims. They deserve my attention. Normally, I'd push on and everything in my life would suffer. This case is especially stressful because the killer might strike again on Sunday."

Thom shook his head. "I feel like I've fallen into a nest of snakes. They're writhing around me and I don't know when one of them is going to strike. I can't do it, Bird, I almost committed suicide. How bad does it have to get before I back away and save my sanity?"

"What are you saying?"

"I've been doing a lot of research this morning. I have a new plan that involves Anita. We need her help. She's agreed to come over."

"She's coming here?"

"Uh-oh."

"You should've asked. This isn't just my office where I do *my* work, it's my home."

"Shit, Bird. I have kinda taken over." He spread his hands in apology. "I can cancel."

Birdie hadn't considered the ramifications of space sharing with Thom before she agreed he could use the board. Her mission-in-progress required the utmost privacy and Thom already heard the argument she had with Ron about the not-dead person. She couldn't risk his accidentally coming across her intell. She had to be mindful about where she left her materials, the laptop. Failing to lock the safe? Huge mistake. But he lived here now—even if temporarily—and his stay would be of unknown duration. Still... she felt uncomfortable with the prospect of a cop she didn't know in her office.

"Is it essential she come here?" said Birdie.

"Tick-tock. She'll be here in a few hours. We don't have much time."

"Alright. But later on we'll need to set some boundaries. You wouldn't've invited her to your house, so why mine?"

"Now I feel like a schmuck."

"That's not my intent. Yes means yes. Let's move on, okay?"

A phone in Thom's pocket buzzed. He reached in and pulled out the burner.

"Noa." He aimed for the deck and scooped up his smokes along the way.

———

"Aloha, Thom, how are you doing?" said Noa.

Thom held the phone between his ear and shoulder and lit a cigarette. "You calling to make sure I didn't kill the bastard?"

"I called to see how you're feeling... considering the participants."

"I didn't watch the video. The warning label scared me."

"What did you look at?"

"None of it. My cousin gave me the broad strokes of the financials and watched the video as my representative. Later on, my brother went through the documents and told me George was Anne's lover."

Noa exhaled. "It'd be easier if it were a stranger."

Thom took a lengthy drag, flicked the ash over the deck's edge. "My cousin accosted him. Broke his nose. Banished him."

"A centuries-old concept."

"In this case effective. I suspect George will take it seriously."

"You'll have to face him eventually."

"Later. When I'm not so broken."

"How much of the Anne video did your cousin watch? All the way to the end?"

"I don't know."

"Have her look at it if she didn't. It'll take the edge off. Do you need anything?"

"Actually, yes. Anne hired an attorney and, in turn, a private investigator. He's an ex-cop. If I give you a name can you give me the four-one-one? I'll pay for it."

"You already did. The disc marked Thom has all that information. Mostly emails between the attorney and the scumbag PI. There's bonus material of interest. Of course, photos of you and your gals."

"We're way off grid, aren't we?"

"Only good for private negotiations. The Thom disc is the only remaining copy. The prick's computer caught a wicked virus."

"Nice. Anne said she didn't know what they were doing until after the fact."

"That's not entirely true. She had a suspicion. Read the email threads and make up your own mind."

"Ron said you were the best."

"You got your money's worth, man. So … we're done now. The names Noa and Jin no longer exist in your vocabulary. You never go back to the kitchen. As soon as we hang up, this phone will no longer work, the number disconnected."

"I'm not sure what to say. Thanks sounds masochistic."

"Aloha, then."

"Aloha."

Thom finished his cigarette. He liked Noa and felt sorry that their pseudo relationship was over. He'd be a guy you'd always want at your side.

Birdie hung up the phone as he re-entered the office.

"Voicemails," she said. "No new message from our killer."

"Did you watch all the video of Anne and George?"

"No. Why?"

"Noa said there was something at the end. Watch it for me?"

Thom moved his laptop to the couch and played at nonchalance as Birdie loaded the disc. She turned the monitor away from his eye-line and put on headphones. He watched her as she fast-forwarded through the video. Thom could only guess how she felt watching a man she used to be intimate with doing who-knew-what to his wife. To her credit, Birdie kept her face neutral and Thom was certain she did this for his behalf. The pressing of buttons stopped and she leaned forward, watching with rapt attention. Then it was done.

Birdie took off the headphones. "Do you want to see for yourself?"

"Just tell me."

"After the sex they hit the groceries. This is where I originally stopped. George does most of the talking. He said they had to break up. That he couldn't live the duplicity any longer. It was stressing him out. He told Anne he loved you and owed you for being his advocate and vouching for him—whatever that means. That he hated himself for the betrayal. He shed tears."

Thom braced his cheeks, held back the tears.

"At first Anne got angry, but George continued and said that you're under surveillance and it's a strong possibility that they'll get caught. That they should end it now before anybody finds out and gets hurt. There's some back-and-forth with tears and undecipherable conversation. It's unclear to me if they actually broke up or if George just made the attempt."

"That's it?"

"Pretty much. After George left Anne straightened the place and that's where the video ended. Noa wanted you to see that George loved you."

Thom wiped his nose with his shirt sleeve.

With a hitch in his voice he said, "They don't deserve a love song. Nothing will ever be as it was." He exhaled. Slapped his thighs and stood up. "And maybe that's not a bad thing," he said bravely. "Thank you. Give me a few minutes? When I get back we'll prep for our meeting with Anita. We'll have to sell it . . ."

FIFTY-THREE

Birdie opened the Judas hole, spied an attractive woman on her porch.

"Anita?"

"Hi," said Anita, squinting through the bars. "You must be Thom's cousin. Elizabeth?"

Birdie opened the door. "Come in."

"I knew there was a woman involved."

"With what?"

"The zucchini bran muffins and apples. A guy wouldn't do that."

"Mine would."

"Have an extra? In my world I don't meet many men like that."

Birdie chuckled. "You single?"

"A chronic condition." She flicked her eyes and casually said, "Is Thom married?"

"Newly separated. He's real fragile right now."

"Children?"

"Five."

"Ah, a Catholic boy."

"You say it like he has the plague."

"Not at all. Just an observation."

"You interested?"

"Curious. Mostly."

The way Anita said "mostly" as an aside gave Birdie no doubt that she was interested in Thom, which if true, would discount his assessment that their working relationship was tense and antagonistic. Then again, people often disguise interest behind a veil of disinterest. *This should be interesting.*

Birdie ticked her head toward the stairs. "We're up here."

As they walked up the mahogany staircase Birdie felt Anita's sizing eyes behind her. Judging—or maybe admiring—the artifacts in the turret, the stained glass dome, the living room. They turned into the office.

"Anita," said Thom. "Thanks for coming."

Anita stopped short. "Whoa. Like the haircut. It makes your eyes pop." She reached out to shake his hand.

"Coffee?" offered Birdie.

"No thanks. I'd like to get started. The investigation is imploding and Craig is freaking out about the way Seymour is ramrodding the team."

Thom gestured at a chair for Anita. Birdie sat in an adjacent chair while Thom leaned against Birdie's desk.

"Why don't you get us up to speed," said Thom.

"Us?" said Anita. "What qualifies your cousin to sit in on police business?"

"I come from a family of cops," said Thom. "Elizabeth grew up in the police business. She's an investigative journalist. See that medallion up there?" He pointed to the wall. "That's a Pulitzer—the top prize for journalists. She started out as a crimebeat reporter, writes true crime, and is extremely successful in her career. She's very intuitive and has great insights into the criminal mind. But mostly, she's smart."

Anita shook her finger in recognition. "You wrote the article in the paper that has everyone in an uproar."

"And that," said Thom.

"All we ask," said Birdie, "is an open mind. You share with us, we share with you. As investigators our jobs are similar. We may approach the task differently based upon the rules of our professions, but we have the same goal in mind. To get a killer off the street."

"What do you have to lose?" said Thom. "I promise that whatever you tell us stays confidential. Elizabeth isn't here as a reporter. She's here as … my researcher."

"Okay," said Anita. "Like you said, Thom, I'm all about solving murder. Let's see what we can do together."

"George updated me on Wednesday. Two days ago. I'm aware of the DNA match and the content of the statements made by Jelena Shkatova, Dominic's aide Gordon, and Kidd, the bartender. What else can you tell me?"

"George gave me a cigarette butt on Wednesday. He was cagey and wouldn't tell me how it was collected, or who he thought it belonged to. He asked me to attach it the Deats' case, which I did—despite my misgivings—because it was the same brand we found at the scene. The lab liaison called this morning. It's a match to the other cigarette butt *and* Rachel's baby, but it's not a match to anyone in the database. So now we have a suspect. But George has suddenly dropped out of sight. He's not returning my calls or emails. In our meeting this morning, Lieutenant Craig said that George called in sick yesterday, said something about a flu. George forwarded his notes from the search of Lawrence's office. Apparently, it took most of the day. This morning, Craig elevated Seymour to lead investigator and he's a pompous SOB. Worse than you, Thom, no offense."

"None taken. What happened with the search of Dominic's office?"

"Let's clear something up first," said Anita. "You claimed to be on the case. Craig told us this morning you were on leave and George called in with the blue flu. What the hell?"

Thom sighed. "Okay, it's like this. On Tuesday, the morning of the meet and greet, Craig got word that a complaint of misconduct had been filed on me." Thom waved his hand. "It's bogus, of course, and I know where it came from and why, so it will get cleared. But Craig didn't know that on Tuesday so he cut me from the case as a precaution. I didn't want to ride a desk so I took leave and started freelancing from here. As for George, I haven't seen or spoken to him since Wednesday morning."

"What have you been working on? What do you have?"

"Why don't you tell us about the search of Dominic's office first," said Birdie. "That way we can present our findings in a linear fashion."

"Fair enough. Just know, I wasn't there." She pulled a slim file from her tote. "Here's George's narrative." She handed it to Thom, who promptly put it down. "It basically says that the file on Jelena's foster care was not found in Dominic's office. He did get to inspect Dominic's personal laptop. Seems Mr. Lawrence was in an eviction battle with his landlord."

Birdie and Thom exchanged slight nods.

"According to the IT department, on Saturday, May twelve, Dominic accessed his computer. All the files regarding his housing work with Councilman Fontaine were deleted. On Wednesday, the sixteenth, the IT department was able to restore the files. Copies of which were sent to the district attorney for safekeeping and, against the wishes of the Special Master, George was also given discs. He checked them into evidence. A missing flash drive was not recovered. George surmised that Dominic did not delete his own files and that someone else did."

"Jelena," said Thom and Birdie together.

"What was happening yesterday?" said Thom.

"Seymour and Diego were working on connecting the victims. Trying to answer the question 'why these people.'"

Birdie rolled her eyes at Thom. What a waste of time.

"You and Shaw?" said Thom.

"Shaw's been a no-show since Tuesday. Apparently, he's working on some other case. Remember when Diego gave his presentation and he mentioned the possibility that the killer had a key? Perhaps a past tenant? And that he examined the locksmith's files? Well, I've been running with that. I've interviewed the locksmith for Mobeck Finance Holdings. We're working on affidavits for Ladder Capital and Great Western Group because they've been less than forthcoming."

Birdie smiled at Thom. Anita was on the right track. Getting her here was a good move on his part. He saw the endgame and knew he'd need an insider to push forward. George would've been that person. With that possibility gone, Anita was the default. But Birdie was now certain that Anita was perfect for the job. Even if or when Thom's one-night stand with Jelena was made public, the trial might still be a winner.

Thom winked at Birdie. They were on the same page.

"Anything about the killer calling a reporter?" said Thom.

"Craig mentioned it this morning. He didn't give specifics beyond saying that a local reporter got two phone calls she believes to be from the killer and that the department was in contact with the *Los Angeles Times* about setting up a wire. He said it seemed promising."

"That was me," offered Birdie. "We know the killer wanted attention because of the bloody message, and I believe Sunday's article brought out the killer's impatience and she wanted more attention by calling someone she considered connected."

"She?" said Anita. "You think the killer is a she?"

"We do," said Thom.

"Who?"

"Before we go there. Have you studied the files? Listened to or read the interviews, the statements?"

"I've studied it all," said Anita.

"Good. Then allow us to show you what we see," said Birdie.

Thom's pep talk came back to her now. "We'll have to sell it. We must seduce Anita into seeing the case as we see it. You're taking the lead because she won't compete with another female. Play up your background as a female in a man's world. Anita will respond to that. Give her something she can sink her teeth into. Finesse her."

Seduce and *finesse*. Fighting words.

FIFTY-FOUR

BIRDIE POPPED A PIECE of gum. "There's this man I know," she began as she chewed, "a distinguished FBI agent. We used to have discussions about the differences between the FBI and modern police departments like the LAPD. He said PDs rely too much on forensics, eyewitness accounts, and circumstantial evidence."

"Key elements to a successful prosecution," said Anita, shrugging.

"Agreed. But the key word here is *evidence*. How many times does a crime go unpunished because of the lack of evidence? Or wrongfully obtained evidence? What's missing is profiling. He wasn't referring to thick psychological files about complex psycho killers. He was talking about everyday people profiles. He said that detectives often forget the reasons why people murder. He'd always remind me of the three Ws. What, why, who."

"Leaving out when and where."

"Precisely. Think back to law enforcement one-oh-one. What are the common reasons people murder?"

"Profit, revenge, jealousy, to conceal a crime, to avoid embarrassment, rage, and there's always homicidal mania—just for the hell of it."

"My friend's favorite was profit. Follow the money. He used to say that when it came to the everyday, run-of-the-mill criminal mind—not like sexual sadists—that the basics always apply. Base impulses, justification, circumventing, recklessness, flawed behavior. I don't know about you, Anita, but every day my emotions are ruled by one of these basics. But what keeps me normal, what keeps me veering too far from the acceptable norm are consequences. These basics can be ordinary flaws or they can lead to murder."

Birdie handed Anita the crispy newspaper clipping of the scruffy slumlord.

Anita furrowed her brows in confusion.

"For me, it started on Monday when I went looking for a new story to tackle. My boyfriend and I were in this office when I came across this old clipping. The man's name is Todd Moysychyn. He's a very successful property owner, big portfolio. I've interviewed him in the past and I was curious how his interests fared in the housing crisis. I thought an updated story would be relevant and newsworthy. Little did I know then that this guy would be the key, literally, to the homicide Thom caught the day before.

"What Thom and I did was apply these basic one-oh-one rules to this case. We broke it down to the essential elements. The simpler the better. It's all about the money. You'll see."

Thom raised the shade covering the dry erase board. Sections of it were covered with taped-up newsprint.

"These are the current, as is, market values for the four houses where the homicides occurred," said Birdie.

Westchester: $600+ K   **Culver City: $969 K**
Santa Monica: $1.2 M   **Hollywood: $3.5 M**

"Moysychyn owned all four houses."

Westchester: Vermillion Management
Culver City: Ladder Capital
Santa Monica: Mobeck Finance Holdings
Hollywood: Great Western Group

Vermillion, Ladder, Mobeck, Great Western = L.A.
Housing Trust = Todd Moysychyn.

Anita's mouth formed an O.

"Elizabeth has mad computer skills," said Thom.

"Todd wasn't making enough money on these properties. They were worth more on the open market, but first he had to get rid of the tenants. I interviewed him twice on Tuesday. The first time was at a job site where he talked freely about his dislike for Dominic. He was unapologetic about wanting to make money on property he right-fully owned and Dominic stood in the way. At some point he men-tioned his wife was a fan of mine. He invited me to dinner and said it was okay if I brought my newly separated and lonely cousin."

Thom rolled his eyes and shook his head, not appreciating Bird-ie's representation.

"I had already been removed from the case," said Thom. "I couldn't go into his house as a cop. All I could accomplish is a survey and be there as Elizabeth's backup. That's where I collected the ciga-rette butt George gave you," said Thom.

"This Todd guy killed Deats? He's Rachel's baby daddy?" said Anita.

"He's the father, but we don't think he killed Deats or any of the others," said Birdie.

"Like we're meant to believe," added Thom.

Birdie picked it up. "The dynamic between Todd and his wife, Iris, was odd. He told us she was a mail-order bride come over from China to marry a rich American and that she was very good at spending his money. Believable. Here's where it takes a turn … I wasn't feeling well and Thom escorted me to the bathroom. We took the wrong passage and ended up in a dark hallway. Iris came and directed us in the right direction."

"There was a dead goldfish in the toilet," said Thom.

"Not just dead," inserted Birdie. "Frozen. Still cold to the touch." We believe Iris put it there as she walked past the bathroom to get us. She had opportunity."

"Todd likes to paint," said Thom. "He's a freak. He keeps fish and when they die he grinds them up and uses the … whatever you'd call it in his paintings."

"He told me he didn't like dead fish," said Birdie. "The utilization of recycling dead fish is his way of respecting them."

"That's sick," said Anita.

"Agreed," said Thom.

"And this is where Iris piqued our interest," said Birdie. "She is the only one who had the opportunity to put the frozen fish in the toilet. It was like a calling card."

"Also, Iris was fascinated with Elizabeth. Couldn't take her eyes off her—"

"—yet when I caught hers, she averted them. After dinner while Todd and I were talking, Thom filched two photos from their refrigerator." Birdie removed one sheet of the newspaper from the dry erase board. "This one was taken the day they were married at city hall. Her legal name is Li Sū. This is her as a schoolgirl."

Anita peered at the photos. "Okay. Where are we going?"

"It's coming," said Thom. "Without the big picture, it won't make sense. We're almost there. I promise."

Birdie continued. "When we left the Moysychyn's, we stopped on the side of the road to make some unrelated phone calls. A car that looked identical to one we saw in Todd's garage passed us at a high rate of speed."

"We gave chase," said Thom. "I called in the plate and it came back Todd."

"Who was driving?" said Anita.

"We don't know," said Birdie. "The windows are tinted. But we followed it downtown and saw Jelena Shkatova get into the vehicle."

Birdie waited a beat for the name to register with Anita. When it did, her eyes widened.

"Jelena could know Todd several ways: one, as her foster parent's landlord. Two, as Rachel's special friend. Three, through her job as a clerk in Dominic's office. As you know from George's report, he worked with a city councilman on housing-related topics. We considered that Jelena could've been spying on Todd's behalf. Also, remember the statement made by Kidd where he reported that Jelena was always on the make for a rich man like her Asian friend. Maybe she marked Todd."

Again Birdie waited for Anita to catch up. Make the connection.

"Jelena is the killer?"

"Her whereabouts during the TOD window are unsubstantiated," said Thom.

"For the Lawrence murders," added Birdie. "We haven't veered into the other three. Back to Moysychyn's wife . . . the morning after the dinner we began researching Iris."

Birdie handed a lighted magnifier to Anita. "Look at this childhood photo more closely."

Anita moved the glass back and forth, concentrated. "The faces of the girls are blurred."

"Look at the building behind the girls. See the partial of the school seal?"

"Yeah. It looks like . . . hum, a compass?"

Thom pulled up a website on his laptop. "This is Compass—an orphanage for troubled girls. See this thing that looks like a ship's wheel? It's a Dharma Wheel. It was the official symbol of the school a hundred years ago. Before political correctness, before the symbol changed to a compass. It's the place Jelena lived before she became Dominic and Rachel's foster daughter. She mentioned it when George interviewed her." He paused for emphasis. "It's also the place Li Sū, aka Iris, lived."

"Jelena and Iris were childhood chums," said Birdie. "Iris did not come to America as a seventeen-year-old mail-order bride. She was already here. We believe she scammed Todd."

"This is all very fantastical," said Anita

"Actually, it's simple. Iris and Jelena met as girls. They're still friends."

"How do you know that?"

"Social networking," said Birdie. "Todd told me Iris was a fan, so I friended her."

"Which opened up her life to you," said Anita.

"And her friend's lives. Jelena is prominent in Iris' posts. They're club girls just like I used to be. They have phones, they take photos, videos. This was posted by one of their friends."

Thom clicked the mouse and the video began.

The two girls, dressed in short skirts and high heels, were standing near the red velvet rope of a club and Iris conducted a mock interview with Jelena.

Iris: *"Greetings, America. I'm here tonight at Club Go-Go in Hollywood with supermodel Lena. Lena, you look fabulous."*

Lena: *"Thank you, Iris. I'm so excited to be here tonight to make my singing debut."*

Thom stopped the video.

Anita cocked her head. "I listened to Jelena's interviews. She spoke with a Russian accent. It's not detectable here."

"That accent really bothered George from the beginning," said Thom. "He thought a girl in the states since age eight would've lost it after fourteen years."

"She sounds like a native. And the other one?"

"We only met Iris the one time," said Birdie. "She had a definite lilt. Clipped her words. Kept it simple, soft. Her voice doesn't sound anything like what you're hearing on this video."

"She said something peculiar." Thom told Anita how Iris knew "shoot" from "chute." "It's too English specific. She didn't come to America five years ago."

"And then there's this," said Birdie.

Thom minimized the video and opened an audio file. "This one came in on Sunday at eleven-thirty-five. Jelena was still at the Lawrence scene." He hit play:

"Greetings, Elizabeth, I read your article on the Blue Bandits. Perhaps you should look at all the pretty dead fish."

"This came later."

"Greetings, Elizabeth. Let me introduce myself. My name is Mayo. It took three minutes to kill four people with five shots. Good numbers, don't you think?"

Thom went back to the video. "Close your eyes and tell me what you hear." He restarted the video from the beginning.

Iris: *"Greetings, America. I'm here tonight at Club Go-Go in Hollywood with supermodel Lena. Lena, you look fabulous."*

"I'm no expert," said Thom, stopping the video. "But that is the same gender-neutral voice."

Anita harrumphed. "A mishmash." She walked across the office, pulled open the French doors, and stepped out onto the deck.

Thom huddled with Birdie. "She doesn't see it."

"Can't blame her. It's hard to communicate what we've seen— what we experienced—without sounding like crazy people. Yes, we think Iris, and possibly Jelena, are involved—it's a good working theory because the message has but one purpose. It's a calling card and points attention to Todd's predilection. Would a killer really be that obvious? There are four crime scenes and eight victims. All we can offer is a direction."

"Like a compass," said Anita behind them. "Let me show you something."

She removed another file from her tote and pulled out four 8x10 blowups of the bloody messages. She removed four magnets from the board and stuck up the first one. Across the bottom: **Westchester 4/1**. She put another next to it: **Culver City 4/8**. Then: **Santa Monica 4/15**. And lastly: **Hollywood: 5/13**.

Lined up, side by side, the difference between all four messages was very clear. They were all written the same way. Capital D. Lower case letters. But the first three were written by the same hand. The last one was different in the way the letters were stroked.

Anita pointed at the clipping from the article Birdie had written about Jelena and Dominic. "See how she's looking at him?"

"With adoration," said Birdie.

"Love," said Anita. "See, I like simple, too. Know what I thought when I saw this photo after reading Thom's case notes? That Jelena was in love with Dominic and when she found out Rachel was pregnant...well, she registered her displeasure by getting rid of the new family and attempted to blow his dick off."

Thom chuckled.

"You two aren't the only ones who see things differently. Show me again. Only this time, give me more detail."

———

Birdie and Anita stood on her front walkway.

"Thank you," said Birdie. "For coming over and helping Thom. He needs someone on his side right now."

"I'm very impressed by him," said Anita. "He has a lot of courage. I'm not sure I'd be able to do it."

"Do what?" said Birdie.

"Throw the ball to another detective for the touchdown. The work you guys did … the way you approached it … a game changer. Don't worry. I'll see it done to the end."

Birdie took a step back. "I don't understand."

But she did. In her heart she knew.

"Didn't Thom tell you?" said Anita. "He's no longer freelancing. He's using that leave for its intended purpose."

They shook hands and Birdie watched all their hard work and research disappear down the street.

"I'll be damned," whispered Birdie. *He's the smart one.*

Back upstairs, Thom erased black marker from the dry erase board.

"What about tick tock?" said Birdie. "Sunday?"

"I haven't forgotten. There's one last thing I need you to do."

FIFTY-FIVE

BIRDIE TURNED ON THE 11:00 p.m. news and perched on the edge of the couch next to Thom. A graphic in big red letters read: **Developing News**.

"*Good evening. You saw it here on our six o'clock broadcast. There is so much to this fast-developing story... in late-breaking news, law enforcement officials have confirmed that the recent murders of city attorney, Dominic Lawrence, and his family might be related to the homicides of four other people in the Southland. Authorities issued the brief statement late this evening, but would not confirm rumors of a serial killer on the loose. A source close to the investigation did say homicide detectives are working around the clock and have identified more than one person of interest in the murders. While the unnamed source offered no details of the murders, the source did clarify the department is certain the victims were expressly targeted and the general population is not in danger. We'll be monitoring the situation and update you as information becomes available.*"

"There's frenzied activity going on in the PAB tonight," said Thom, clicking off the TV. "People on high alert. A department under pressure. Affidavits are being written. Search warrants will be served. Evidence will be discovered and an official taskforce will be in place to sift through it all. The arrest of the killer or killers is eminent. No need to kill again and risk detection." He placed his hands behind his head and leaned back. "Not a bad day's work."

"Wonder how the reporter found out?"

"Most likely an anonymous tip from a trusted source to a colleague."

"Hum. At least the press has something new to focus on instead of our family."

"A nice side effect."

"Indeed."

FIFTY-SIX

Saturday, May 19

Birdie sprinted the last few yards to the lip of the ridge. She threw up her arms and danced a jig, then sat on a rock to catch her breath. She sucked on the water tube, washed the grit from her throat.

She cupped her mouth and yelled down the trail. "Come on slowpoke."

A red-tailed hawk drifting overhead amused her attention while she waited.

Thom slowly came into view, panting, bent over, hands on his knees.

"Oh, Jesus, save me."

He gave Birdie a weak high-five, then slumped to the ground with a thud and billowing dirt.

"You call this fun?" He wiped his face and neck with a bandana.

"The best kind. When I'm back here in the hills, or in the desert, or in a forest, I'm forced to push back all the melodrama and concentrate on my footing, the environment. I reflect on how small and imperfect I am. It's like church without the congregation to compete with. He hears my voice above the din. I haven't done much meditation lately and I needed this."

Thom nudged his cousin in a gesture of understanding and support. "I suppose I needed it, too."

"So many people consider this landscape as nothing more than scrubby brush, but the chaparral is so vibrant. Highly flammable, of course. But after a fire? The terrain bounces back, regrows quickly. The black sage, sugar bush, manzanita, sumac, yucca, the buckwheat. It all comes back stronger than ever."

"Like us Keanes."

"Hm-mm."

"I can't believe I made it to the top intact."

"Hey, Thom? I hate to break it to you, but we're not done yet. We're only halfway. We still have to hike down."

"*Yeah*, downhill."

"Hard on the knees. Trust me, we still have a journey."

"Oh, cheer up. See that?" He pointed seaward. "The marine layer is retreating. I think May Gray is finally over and we're gonna have some sun."

"I hope so. I really hope so."

FIFTY-SEVEN

Sunday, May 20

As if in premonition Ron's eyes popped open. Breath labored. Did he wake from a bad dream? If so, he didn't remember. He reached out to touch Birdie's hip, felt the warmth of her skin beneath the sheet. Her slight movement palliative. The dying embers from the bedroom fireplace cast a warm glow on her cheek. She lay stretched out on her side, fingers and toes curling around the mattress edge as if holding on. The pillow between her legs a psychological stop sign.

Still, each week brought a new improvement.

Gone were the flannel pajamas with the scissored cuffs (because she didn't like anything touching the ligature scars). Nearly gone were the fights with the covers and the moaning.

Yet, she still required light. The fire a compromise. Ron threw off the sheet and got up to lay another log. He didn't want her to awaken in the dark, disoriented.

Father Frank had told him that Birdie needed the light because it represented the peace and warmth of heaven. When she rediscovered that in herself she'd flip the switch of her own accord. Until then ...

The cell on the dresser lit with an incoming call. Ron scooped it up before it began to vibrate and palmed it against his stomach. He checked the caller ID as he ran downstairs then continued to the garage where he slumped to the floor.

"Hello, Noa," he answered.

"My brother." No happiness behind the words.

Ron waited as his friend took a breath before delivering the bad news.

"She has his name and location."

Ron dropped the phone and covered his face, fingers pressing into his eyes. He wished he could place a capstone on his feelings. Hold back the revival of uncertainty.

His three favorite things were right here: the Pacific Ocean, his Craftsman house, and Birdie. The ocean was his sustenance. The place where he drew upon earth's energy to supply him with the strength, will, and discipline to become a better man. The right man. The house was his sanctuary. The place he relied on for shelter, safety, and serenity. Birdie was everything else. The thrumming heartbeat of his life. The nails that held the parts together. The promise.

And he was always fearful of losing that last.

"I know you're still there, brother," said Noa's voice from the floor.

Ron picked up the phone and wiped his eyes.

"When?"

"Yesterday."

"Forget to call me?"

390

"I worry. What are you going to do?"

"I've been thinking about warfighting."

"Which aspect? The philosophy, the doctrines?"

"Everything."

"So … in the progression of conflict you've moved past observation and are currently in orientation?"

"Yes. I'm making an estimate of the situation."

"Next up, decision."

"Then action."

"Let me remind you of something … the function of war is to impose our will on our enemy. That requires violence or the threat of. He's not yours."

"Oh, yes he is. He's the friction that has become a constant in my life."

"Brother, I'm your second. As such, I've already gone over every scenario since I last saw you. They all have one outcome. Loss. Listen to me, your feelings for Birdie are not a weakness. Your emotions are inflamed by a love that has eluded you for forty-four years and you're still trying to come to grips with a simple word for a complicated device that's screwed up mankind."

"Screwed up is right."

"If the great poet laureates can't figure out the pulse that resonates in all humankind, how can a simple man profess to know anything about the great mystery of love?"

"This from a man who gets involved with married women to avoid it."

Noa cleared his throat. "Enough philosophy. What of diplomacy?"

"An understanding with Birdie is fruitless. That battle was already fought and lost."

"What about with him? Could you negotiate a deal with him?"

"That depends on who gets to him first."

"Keep in mind that in every campaign there is no division between offense and defense. They are necessary components of the other. Remember what Sun Tzu wrote in *The Art of War*, 'He will win who knows when to fight and when not to fight.'"

"He also said, 'The general who wins a battle makes many calculations in his temple before the battle is fought.' I told you, I'm in orientation. I haven't made a decision."

Noa blew out a frustrated breath. "You've had enough death in your life. I don't want you to kill him."

"I understand."

"So tell me you won't."

"I wish I could."

THE END

ACKNOWLEDGMENTS

I thank Robert Bub and Scott Smith of the LAPD who continue to be sources of inspiration and on whom I rely for the procedural matters and the inside view. Thanks to Ron Bowers who takes the time to answer my legal questions. I am solely responsible for alterations of fact in service to the story.

To my disbanded drinking group with the writing problem: Linda Cessna, Anna Kennedy, Kurt Kitasaki, Doug Lyle, Rob Northrop, and Theresa Schwegel, I miss you all and the valuable lessons you've taught me over the years.

To my new writing group: Sandy Battista, Craig Strickland, Laurie Thomas, Donna Todd, Anne Van, and Barbara Varma, thank you for your professional critique, laughter, and friendship.

I remain indebted to my literary agent, Kimberley Cameron, who is always accessible and supportive of the writer's dream and vision.

To the staff at Llewellyn/Midnight Ink: thank you for your support and expertise, especially Terri Bischoff who will always have a special spot in my heart and Connie Hill for making the task of editing so easy and enjoyable.

Thanks to Todd Moysychyn who loaned his name to a man he most certainly is not.

A special thank you is reserved for my ever-faithful and reliable family, Scott, Brenna, David, my parents and, first fans, Pat and Margie. You all have my love and admiration forever and ever.

© Tanni Tronsen

ABOUT THE AUTHOR

Terri Nolan is a novelist and freelance crime reporter. She lives in Southern California. Visit her at www.terrinolan.com.

www.MIDNIGHTINKBOOKS.COM

From the gritty streets of New York City to sacred tombs in the Middle East, it's always midnight somewhere. Join us online at any hour for fresh new voices in mystery fiction.

At midnightinkbooks.com you'll also find our author blog, new and upcoming books, events, book club questions, excerpts, mystery resources, and more.

MIDNIGHT INK ORDERING INFORMATION

Order Online:
- Visit our website www.midnightinkbooks.com, select your books, and order them on our secure server.

Order by Phone:
- Call toll-free within the U.S. and Canada at 1-888-NITE-INK (1-888-648-3465)
- We accept VISA, MasterCard, and American Express

Order by Mail:
Send the full price of your order (MN residents add 6.875% sales tax) in U.S. funds, plus postage & handling to:

> Midnight Ink
> 2143 Wooddale Drive
> Woodbury, MN 55125-2989

Postage & Handling:

Standard (U.S. & Canada). If your order is:
> $25.00 and under, add $4.00
> $25.01 and over, FREE STANDARD SHIPPING

AK, HI, PR: $16.00 for one book plus $2.00 for each additional book.

International Orders (airmail only):
> $16.00 for one book plus $3.00 for each additional book

Orders are processed within 12 business days. Please allow for normal shipping time. Postage and handling rates subject to change.